Mewassin:
The Good Land

Fifth in a Series of

Historical Novels

Lillian Ross

Member of:
Writers Guild of Alberta
Canadian Independent Book Publishers
Fellowship

Ross, Lillian, 1931
Mewassin, The Good Land

Note for Librarians: A cataloguing record for this book is available from Library
and Archives Canada at www.collectionscanada.ca/amicus/index-e.html

ISBN: 1-4251-0091-0

Printed in Victoria, BC, Canada.

Order online at:
trafford.com/06-1848

10 9 8 7 6 5 4 3 2 1

Dedication and Acknowledgement

This book is dedicated to the memory of John Lenny who immigrated to Canada from The Orkney Islands in Scotland during the Highland Clearances along with hundreds of other Scots.

It is also dedicated to Adolphe Perrault who found his way to Canada by very unusual means. It is dedicated to their families who survived the hardships of the early years in the West.

I acknowledge the following people who helped me in compiling much of the information necessary for the story:
>Connie Ross – Archivist on the Perraults, and the Berards
>Debbie Robb – Archivist on the Gladus, and Lennys
>Charlene Dorey – Archivist on the Lennys

I also thank historian, Charles Goulet, for his input and guidance on the French usage and information about the Grey Nuns of St. Albert among other historical references and corrections.

Thank you to Isabella and Eric Brown for their guidance in the use of the Gaelic dialect.

Finally, I especially thank Iris Tuftin for her patient editing of the lengthy manuscript.

History books for research on Father Lacombe and Louis Riel who figure prominently in the story, as well as many others, and incidents at the time that John Lenny and Adolphe Perrault lived in the Northwest are listed:
>1AB in the 20thCentury-United Western Communications
>Mavericks Aritha Van Herk Penguin/Viking Publishers
>Alberta Golden Jubillee Anthology McClelland and Stewart
>Lac Ste. Anne Sakahigan   E.O Drouin, OMI
>The Strange Empire of Louis Riel - Joseph K. Howard
>   James Lewis and Samuel Publishers
>Riel, A life of Revolution - Maggie Siggins –
>   Harper Collins Publishers

Printed and Published by

Mewassin: The Good Land   First Printing   June ? 2006

Also available by the same author:

A Trilogy of Canadian Historical Novels

The Gentle Gamblers	December, 1998
The Tender Years	October, 1999
A Full House	December, 2000

And

Cougars Crossing	March, 2003

Edited by: Iris Tuftin,   English Teacher and Author

Cover Design: Pat Kiehlbauch,
Frogbelly Printing and Promotions,
Drayton Valley, Alberta

Photo: Josie Davidson

Maps: Alberta in the Twentieth Century
United Western Communications

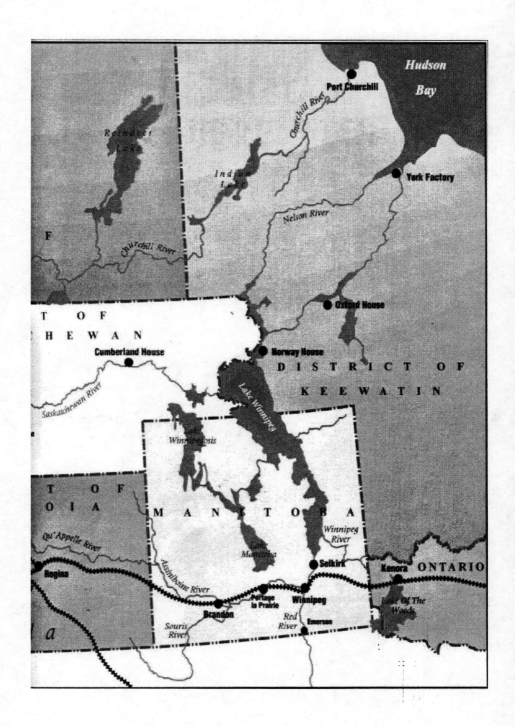

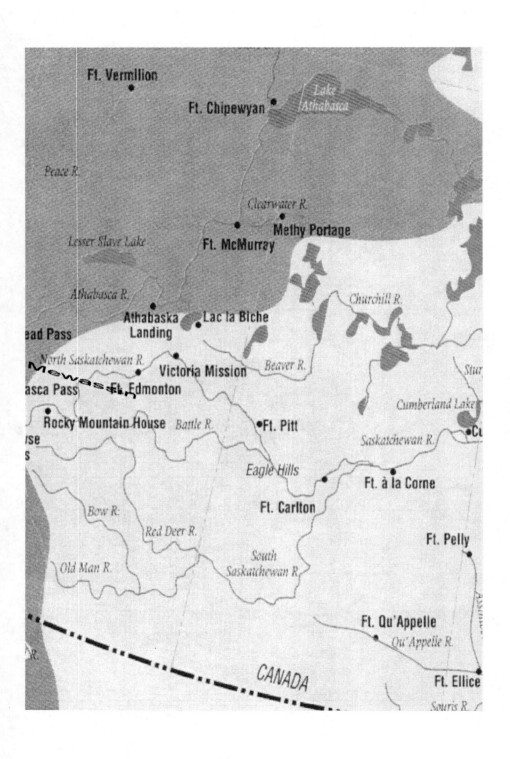

Introduction

This is the fifth book in a series of Canadian historical novels. Although the book includes many real characters there are also many fictional characters to help tell the story. The author has tried to stay true to the historical time frame that the main characters lived in.

Two men, one from the Orkney Islands in Scotland, and one from France are drawn to Canada to find their places in the new land. One becomes involved with the fur trade and the other with the missionaries who pledge themselves to saving the natives of the West from unscrupulous fur traders as well as saving the native souls.

The natives' 'Dreamer' religion often conflicted with the Eastern beliefs but there were many similarities as well.

Earth, the mystic Mother to the natives of the West, suffered the indignities that the white man in all innocence brought with his settlements. Ownership of property was a foreign concept to them and brought about the inevitable culture clash. The wanderers of the wilderness, a tall, straight and enduring race of people soon discover that change and acceptance are certain.

Reviewer's Comments

Lillian Ross chooses a time of critical juncture in western Canadian history.

John Lenny, with his fellow Scots of the Hudson's Bay Company ply their boats upriver from the Hudson Bay in a quest of the ever dwindling fur supply. John decides to stay and try for a new life and for the love of a beautiful, gifted Métis woman.

Adolphe, a young man of great compassion comes to the new world from his native France. He meets and falls in love with a Métis woman forcing him to choose between her and the priesthood.

Ross does an excellent portrayal of the Métis people in their struggle to cope with a rapidly changing world. She also manages to give us a glimpse of two towering figures from Western Canadian history, Louis Riel and Father Lacombe.

Eric Brown, Magnolia Press
Author of Ginny and Anna

Contents

From The Story

"... they only want Orkney Islanders, they said, because we can stand the northern winters; we're tough, hard-working and eager..."

"... whah air ye doon here?" he demanded, his breath exploding in relief. "Doon here," she mimicked, unaware of what the words meant.

The frightening sensation of weightlessness as the crane swung his barrel out into the air, back and forth like a pendulum.

"... Louis Riel! I've heard of him – some kind of revolutionary who's trying to stir up trouble."

"... I am not a priest but Brother Adolphe. Can we not still be friends?"
"Oui," she apologized, "I swallow my bad words."

At the sight of Sean's boyish face below his toque fringed with yellow-gold hair Alex saw an angel come for him.

"Plunging with the weight of the water was like being tied to a stone."

1

Water Highway

John Lenny sat around the campfire with the rest of the voyageurs of the fur trading York boats, listening in fascination as Campbell took them back to his first adventures into the Canadian wilderness.

"It was on the Churchill River; up from Fort Churchill on the Hudson's Bay that I started with the fur trade," Campbell said to the young men as the firelight played across their fresh young faces. "The river, they all told me, is not meant for the faint-hearted. It's a maze of rocks connected by raging white water and treacherous rapids. Veteran fur traders often said that they had to portage their canoes around so many rapids that they may as well hae walked the whole distance to the Athabasca in the West. It's nae a man's land up there - only fit for otters, birds and fish. Even in the winter on snowshoes it's a tough jairney, they used to say. But the Athabasca is the best fur producing area in the whole of Ruperts land."

Campbell's rich Scottish brogue was no problem for his listeners for they were all Scots. As Campbell painted the picture for them, they could see and feel every rock, every outcropping, and every watercourse.

"Lining the Churchill are great banks of pink granite, hard gray rock, and a black rock they called basalt – there since the airth was formed billions of yairs ago. There, ye find the most beautiful sights a man has ever seen, ye ken. But the fight to get there, and the danger in the struggle, is ye're payment for the view."

That adventuresome Scottish lad of seventeen, Donald Campbell, had not tasted fear before his confrontation with the Churchill River. Now in his late forties, he had lived his stories and they would prepare his young listeners for their journey into the wilderness and instill in them the fear of God, he hoped.

After portaging around the treacherous falls, Campbell went on to tell them, the voyagers of the fur trade slid the canoes into the water, well back from the top of the thundering drop-off. However, one canoe got away and drifted towards the top of the falls. Without thinking twice, Campbell, a strong swimmer, impulsively plunged into the water to haul it back to shore. Loaded with precious provisions, he knew the loss of the canoe would be devastating.

The current was unbelievably strong and though he fought with all of his strength, it dragged him closer to the top of the falls. However, he was still unafraid. Not knowing how treacherous the river might be, he even thought it might be a thrill to ride over the falls.

Plunging with the weight of the water was like being tied to a stone. And when he finally hit the first basin, it took all of his strength just to fight to the surface. While trying to hold his breath long enough, he fought his way to the surface but he kept getting sucked underwater repeatedly. Hammered against the rocks until they nearly knocked him unconscious, the pain told him that he was getting ribs broken.

The boiling turbulence tossed him around like a rag doll, and he could do nothing to protect himself. After passing out for a couple of seconds when his head banged against a rock, his limp body experienced another long dive over a high rocky shoot, plunging into a deep pool at the bottom where he revived. The undertow then seized him and sucked him under until he felt himself dragged along the rock ledge at the bottom. His lungs were nearly bursting for want of air when he gathered his feet under him and kicked for the surface.

Only time to catch a breath, he struggled to fight the eddy that spun him around in a circle. Before being sucked down into the spin, in desperation he grabbed a tree branch that had come over the falls with him.

Sucked underwater again, he held his breath and tried to swim with all of the strength he had left, away from the pull of the undertow. After struggling through two more undertows, he feared he would not get enough breath to last another drag underwater. He had begun to lose the battle and the will to keep breathing.

I'm going to die, he thought. *I'm never going to get out of this. I'll keep going around and around until the undertow finally takes me down to hell with it.*

Suddenly realizing that he was still clinging to that branch, he kicked away from the bottom, even as he felt the undertow pulling his legs like quicksand and tangled seaweed. He stuck out the branch, and it brushed along the rock wall of the cauldron. It was not much but it was hope. The next time that he spun around that eddy he stayed under longer. Pushing away, the undertow did not seem so strong this time. When he popped up to the top he stuck out the branch a little further this time, a little more desperately. This time it caught in a crack in the rock, just long enough for him to break free, push the tree branch from him, and dig his fingers around outcroppings along the wall.

The wall was slippery, but he inched along and away from the undertow. Throwing himself up onto a rock just above the cauldron, he hung there too exhausted to move any more, waiting for the crew to catch up and rescue him.

"When they climbed doon and made their way over tae me," Campbell said as the audience around the campfire sucked in their breath, "they thought I was dead. Bloody, scratched, black and blue, but I was alive!"

Looking around at the rapt faces, Campbell told them, "We are all at the mairrcy o' the wilderness, b'ys! Make nae mistake; the river is a force that ye never ever take for granted!"

After hearing Campbell's story around the campfire the night before, John wondered why he had always been so anxious to travel west in the big Hudson Bay Company York boats. From the time that he was ten years old and had first heard about the fur traders who travelled the three-thousand-mile ribbon of rivers and portages across the face of this great new land, he had been building fantasies in his head of travelling with them. Now, here he was, bending his twenty-year old back to the paddles. And older, more experienced voyageurs told stories around the campfire that made one wonder what one was doing here.

Every day he was roused from sleep before the sun came up, in his skimpy bedroll under a little tent crowded next to his fellow travellers. After his trip behind the nearest bush to attend to his toilet needs, he knelt by the river to splash cold water on his face before attacking his breakfast of salt pork, cold hard biscuits, and hot black coffee. It was the usual routine. If the morning was not too cool and if he felt the need, he waded into the river for a bath, washing clothes and all. The clothes would dry on his back in the heat of the sun and the pull of the paddling that heated his muscles.

John Lenny had always heard about the romance of the West, the stories of the boatmen, the strong, rollicking, smoking, hard drinking workhorses of the fur trade, who paddled, bled, and died on the rivers and trails of the Northwest. People still sang their songs. Those fur traders who followed on the heels of the explorers and mapmakers carried their one-hundred-and-eighty pound loads of furs and supplies on their backs and transported their long and light canoe on their backs as they portaged across land from river to river. Theirs was a monumental task of opening up the West and bringing the rich furs of beaver, fox, muskrat, and marten from the Indians to the buyers in the East – a rich trade.

Then the Hudson Bay Company revolutionized the fur trade by developing the big and clumsy York boats, named after York Factory on the Hudson's Bay. They were not as easy to manipulate or carry over the portages, and they were slower, but they carried five times as much as a canoe – more men, more furs and supplies and they now dominated the fur trade.

In the beginning, John's muscles ached and burned so that he felt he would not be able to pull the paddle back one more time. Then if he slacked off, the guide would hurl insults at him and demand to know if he thought he was only along for the ride.

This morning as he looked out across the river valley at the trail of smoke from their campfire which hung like fog in the sultry air above the river, he noticed the change in himself. No longer was he the callow youth with the white, slim shoulders, flushed face, and slack muscles. He had hardened. Now the white and sunburned skin turned to a tough, light copper-brown from paddling with his shirt tied around his waist. His face, after much sunburning, changed from the red-cheeked, sweat-streaked boyish innocence to tanned manhood under the red sweatband wrapped around his forehead.

"All right Lenny," Murdock, the guide shouted at him from the boat pulled partly up on shore, "I'm puttin' ye on the front rudder t'day. Wai'll be tackin' the rapids west ae here this marnin' so I'm countin' on ye to get us around the rocks." Murdock Chisholm had been in Canada many years before John and his family came, but he still had his Scottish brogue. The reason he was chosen to head this crew was *because* he was Scottish. The whole crew was of Scottish descent.

Donald Campbell made his way down the bank to the York boat along side John. He was one of the old-timers on the voyage west. He had plied the waters of the northern river passage to the west for sixteen years, and John wondered every day how Campbell could have hung in there this long, especially after hearing his camp tales. But Donald was lean; every ounce of flesh was muscled. Wiry and raw boned, he looked fifty but was likely not far into his forties.

He usually took the job of steersman, but today John had the dubious honour. "Why is it that Murdock calls ye by ye're first name while all the rest of us get singled out by our last names?" Donald asked as he put his shoulder against the high wooden front of the craft to push it into the water.

"That *is* my last name; my name is John Lenny." John grinned. He was always a serious sort – never smiled nor talked that much. That came from his father who was a stern, no-nonsense Scot. Andrew Lenny knew nothing but working hard all of his life for very little reward. He was stern with his children, showed very little passion or emotion, but his family never doubted that he cared deeply for them. And even though his life had always been hard, he always clung tenaciously to his home, his land, and the Church of Scotland until the church betrayed his family and fellow Orkney Islanders.

The family had boated across the firth to Kirkwall on the main island of the Orkney Islands to attend service, which often lasted three to four hours and not a peep or a squirm was allowed from Andrew's brood during its entirety.

Donald Campbell was pleased to see the occasional smile from John. He knew what these lads had gone through to get here. "We're awa'! I'll be right up behind ye on the front right paddle – will nae be switchin' to the left side until after lunch, so just holler if ye're in doot."

"So ye really went o'er the falls like ye said last night in ye're story," John asked as he held the boat steady while the river tugged on it.

"Och aye lad," Campbell nodded seriously. "Ye must understand, though, that was on the mighty and mean Churchill River. We're followin' the Nelson and the Saskatchewan. There air verra few falls or rapids and nothin' as high as on the Churchill. This route is a picnic compared to that northern route. That's why they made these York boats because there wasna portaging necessary. We never could hae carried the loads we do and packed a canoe as well, on the routes they took to avoid the falls. Och, ye b'ys have it a lot aisier than the airly voyageurs that travelled the southern rroute – from Lake Superior to Fort Garry especially." Even though they had all learned English when they got to York Factory, the Gaelic brogue stood out more in the older voyagers.

John was silent as the crew climbed in and took their places at the paddles. He would not say that theirs was such an easy trip.

"Looks like it maught rain on us t'day," Campbell shouted from the rear of the cumbersome boat as the paddlers brought it around, pushing away from the sandy bank with their paddles. The paddlers nodded without comment. Rain would be a relief from the summer heat that beat down on them for the past week. The pull against the current as they made their way upstream was hard enough without the hot sun sweltering them hour after hour.

Only occasionally now, did they slip into Gaelic while on the journey with only their fellow Scots. After seven years of being urged by the English Hudson Bay personnel to learn the language they spoke it most of the time.

Two York boats set out from York Factory and they stayed fairly close together, usually stopping at nights to sup together and bed down. Murdock Chisholm was overseer of both boats but Campbell, his steersman, was his right hand man and second lieutenant. He was a fur voyager/trader as long as Campbell and was older, but he was the strong silent type. Nothing fazed Chisholm, but he put up with nothing from his young crew. As long as they did their jobs he had no reason to speak sharply to them.

Next to John was McTavish. They all knew him only as McTavish. He was huge, all muscle and big boned but with a voice that was almost timid and boyish that belied his appearance.

The only paddler that John knew well was Alistair Ronaldson. He had known Alistair since they were ten years old. They came over on the same sailing ship from Scotland.

To Campbell's shout, "Haive ho, m'lads! Let's awa'!" the paddlers dug in the paddles, and the York boat shot out into main stream. John worked the rudder until he became used to it in his hand, and it moved the boat according to his bidding. This was not an easy or a lazy job, he soon discovered. When you are paddling, the job became automatic. Your eyes on the man ahead of you, you leaned forward as you lifted the paddle, dug in and pulled back in time with the other men. They became like a well-oiled machine. No thought was required, just brace your feet, lean forward, dig and pull, over and over thousands of times a day. Someone else looked out for where you were going.

Now that he was the steersman, it was his responsibility to do just that, especially when they got into the rapids, and there were many on this Nelson River on the way upstream from York Factory on the Hudson's Bay. This rocky, muskeg, and bog area of Ruperts Land had many rocky outcroppings as part of the Canadian Shield, some of them too steep to navigate by boat and had to be portaged.

So John had to be on the lookout constantly for rocks in midstream and to steer around them and between them. As well, he had to follow directly behind the boat in front of him lest he get their boat into a strong current that pulled them into the rocks. It would be better once they got on the other side of Lake Winnipeg, past Grande Rapids and Cumberland House and heading up the easier, more navigable North Saskatchewan River.

When John could relax on the rudder he enjoyed looking around the countryside. The deer that came down to the shore for a drink, the moose that waded out into the shallows, the birds that swooped and dived overhead and the soft gurgling, trickling music of the water fascinated him. The dark line of the northern shore growing larger and clearer ahead to his right, and the wind as he faced the eastern flush of the sun just coming up, all made their voyage an adventure into the secrets of the wilderness.

2

Sailing Ships to the New World

In a way the countryside reminded John of the Scottish moors where he explored when he was a small boy. There was very little forest in the Orkney Islands anymore, however. The freedom out here, though, was invigorating and lent him an untiring vitality.

Alistair, who had the best voice of the party of men, started up a song that echoed back from the Scottish Highlands and rang out in the memories of all the Scottish born on board. Alistair knew all the words, all of the many verses. He sang them around the campfire in the dying light of day when they sat around after their meal sipping coffee from their tin cups. And he sang them again on the York boat lending strength to the arms of the paddlers.

His rich tenor voicing the verses Alistair sang, and the men listened and joined in on the choruses, singing the parts they remembered. Even the boat ahead of them could hear the singing, and the men dipped their paddles into the river quietly as the song drifted across to them:

> *Cruel was the snow that sweeps Glencoe*
> *And covers the grave O'Donnell*
> *Cruel was the foe that raped Glencoe*
> *And murdered the House of MacDonald*
>
> *They came in the night when the men were asleep*
> *The vandals walked in through snow soft and deep*
> *The conquering forces among helpless sheep*
> *They slaughtered the House of MacDonald*

Some died in their beds at the hands of the foe
Some fled in the dark and were lost in the snow
Some said to accusers Who struck the first blow?
But gone was the House of MacDonald

It was such a sad song, and it never failed to bring a tear to the eye of the tough but sentimental river men of the north. To John, it was a reminder of the cruelty that his dear land came through in the past – through hundreds of years of its existence.

First, it was the tribal wars going back to their Celtic roots, the clan wars of the song Alistair sang, then the British oppression, and the Highland Clearances. This was the time when the gentry, with no pity, sought to clear the land of rental crofters to make way for business – pasture for sheep. If the crofters refused to leave they burned their cottages and drove them out. Summons and writs of removal were evidence that the poor could go nowhere for justice.

In the wake of the evictions large emigrations took place to Canada. Wave upon wave of homeless was shipped to the new land. Riots took place to no avail for the evictions were relentlessly carried out.

Then upon the heels of the 'Clearances' came the cholera epidemic, and then the famine following the potato blight in Ireland as well as Scotland. That was about the time of John's birth. Even in the remote Orkneys they were not immune to the food riots. John's father told him of the time when John was three years old in 1846, when in September a fine white dust fell on the Orkneys like a shroud. Terrible storms broke along the Caithness coast long before winter, destroying boats and nets leaving hundreds of men, Andrew included, without employment.

A sickening warmth and stillness was in the air. As young as he was, John remembered his father, a mountain of a man, on his knees broken and in tears as his last hope for salvation lay in shambles.

Andrew watched his potato plants wither and blacken, turning to slime as though struck by frost. Fierce droughts sucked dry the streams and lochans and men swore that they saw salmon swimming in red dust. Following the drought, great storms came that flooded all low ground where his family lived and rotted the feet of the sheep.

Sheep had already destroyed the black cattle economy and John's father, Andrew, turned to wild game in the hills, what little was left. He planted what seed he saved of oats and barley, moving to higher land and out of the flooded lowland. But adding insult upon injury the 'lairds' restricted the shooting of game all across Scotland. With stubborn determination and in desperation Andrew Lenny struggled to support his family and refused all suggestions that they join the many people who gathered together what was left to catch a ship for Canada.

Many times, unaware of the despair in his father's heart, John roamed and hunted the hills and moors of the Orkney Islands with his father and older brother who later left for a better life in the city of Glasgow. He watched as his mother wept when his older sister also left home to live a life in the city of Inverness. He never saw either of them again. Before John was born they lost one boy to the cholera epidemic and then his younger sister wasted and died during the famine.

When his mother lost another child to an unknown malady when John was eight and his younger sister was six, Andrew shook his fist at the God who had forsaken him and decided to leave for Pomona to join the movement to petition the government for aid.

It was on the main island of Pomona in the town of Kirkwall that he met a man who was forming The Orkney Islands Emigration Society in 1852. In the crowded church where he always came for worship he listened heartsick and torn as angry men shouted and waved fists in the air. And as the church co-operated with the gentry and the lairds, his father turned his back on it as well.

"The land was taken from us when we were not a penny in debt," one lowland farmer complained.

"My new house was burned down over my head, and I burned my hands rescuing my dear wee children," another cried to the minister who would do nothing to help stop the injustice they suffered.

Andrew, for one, refused to give up his land. *Forsake all I worked for all of these years and move away to satisfy the rich lairds and the king who care nary a whit for me?* He stalked out.

But the next year, when he tried to find a way to replace his lost fishing boat by trading half of his land, he heard of the Skye evictions. It was not long until they spread to the Orkney Islands. It was then that John's father gave up. The Land and Emigration Commissioners appeared in Kirkwall offering free passage and assistance on the ships sailing to America. Hat in hand, Andrew went to them, tired of fighting, tired of losing his children, and tired of the struggle just to survive.

"You are a smart man," the emigration man told him. "Other people on the mainland who turned down this opportunity are sorry now."

"Why is that?" Andrew raised a bushy eyebrow.

"Because they were offered the opportunity for *free* passage on the boat to the New World. It was a one-time offer and now, since they decided belatedly to go, they have to pay for the journey," the man smiled as though he held a delicious secret that he was letting Andrew in on.

Andrew shrugged his bent shoulders tiredly. He knew that if they did not get rid of him one way they would get rid of him another. They were doing him no favour. The lairds were simply paying to get rid of the crofters and the *free passage* on the sailing ships was simply the lairds way to just that.

Andrew signed up for the next ship that came to the Orkneys. They loaded the pitifully few possessions that they could carry on board and waved good-bye to a home they would never see again. John watched from the deck of the sailing ship, a spirit of adventure growing inside of him, as the rocky island of Hoy disappeared on the horizon. His father, on the other hand, was saddened beyond imagining. He always thought of Hoy as being his island. It did not belong to the rich and greedy lairds who never visited.

Dawn began to bleach the darkness out of the eastern sky as the boat with John at the helm rode the choppy water of the Nelson River on its way to the big waters of the largest lake in Ruperts Land, Lake Winnipeg. The waters were wider now since they passed the stretch of rapids downriver. John looked forward to meeting up with two more York boats at La Grande Portage Village where the river flowed from Cedar Lake into the river that carried it to the lake. Here they would spend the night and leave in the morning with the other two boats that would come north up the Big Lake from Fort Garry. But now, aside from the waves on the choppy waters of the little lakes along this stretch, it was easy paddling.

The men were hitting their stride as well, for with Alistair's lead they started the familiar old Scottish song:

Hil-ya-ho boys, let her go boys
Now altogether
Hil-ya-ho boys, let her go boys
Sailing homeward to Mingulay

When the wind is wild with shouting
And the waves are forever higher
Anxious eyes turn forever seaward
To see us home boys to Mingulay

Then the voices would boom out on the chorus, and the men paddled with power and enthusiasm. A highlander, John had often heard his father say, is naturally brave as well as generous and anything wearing the semblance of oppression he will fight until his last breath. That is why leaving his homeland in this way - being evicted cut him deep down to his soul.

When they sailed on the fleet of ships with the 13,762 passengers (many died along the way) on the twenty-nine ships for America in November of 1853, pride suffered and died. The pestilential atmosphere aboard the crowded ship created by a festering mass of squalid humanity imprisoned between the damp and steaming decks was more than a Scot could bear in those twelve weeks. The miseries of filth, water served out according to contract, foul air, and darkness amid hundreds of men, women and children, dressing and undressing, washing, quarreling, fighting, cooking and drinking made the voyage an endurance test never before experienced.

Even that could be endured for the sixty days for the promise of better things to come in the new land. One woman and her husband before they boarded, lived on three-half-penny-worth of barley for two days, another man, one morsel of bread for the day.

It was a bad time of the year to be sailing the north seas. Their ship was tossed about on the stormy sea like a cork and even John, who had sailed many times with his father on the seas north of The Orkneys, was feeling sick, trying to find somewhere to hang onto that did not roll about the lower deck. Most lay in their bunks too ill to care if the ship sank or not.

They looked forward to the quieter Hudson's Bay but soon discovered ice floes in abundance like little white islands on the ocean – treacherous jagged islands that threatened to tear a hole in the ship's side.

On deck one evening, as his mother, Jane, and sister Isabel huddled below decks, John and his father stood at the ship's rail. Wrapped in their precious blankets, Jane and Isabel struggled to keep warm. Denying themselves the trip up to the deck, they stayed to protect what food and water they had left and their few meager possessions from marauders.

As well, they tried to find a spot where they could get enough fresh air. The air that managed to seep into the stuffy hold was fresh but also, sweeping down from the North Sea, it was cold. The two rarely left the bunks the four of their family crowded into. At first Isabel was nauseated, but she was now used to the rocking creaking ship.

John and Andrew looked out over the ocean waves that rose as high as the ship and plunged it into the wake. They were both used to the tossing of a boat on the waves, and they tired of the sounds and smells below. As long as they were allowed, they remained on deck of the bucking, creaking vessel.

"Why did we have to leave the Orkneys then, Father?" John asked, unable to understand.

"Because greedy men wanted to replace us all with sheep," Andrew growled in his native Gaelic, his long sideburns greying under his woollen tam covering unkempt hair.

"But why were sheep better than us?" John asked in his confusion.

"Because we only caused the laird more trouble to feed and find gainful work. So many crofters rented the land and did not bring him any money; many could not pay their rent. But sheep was money. With very little help the laird could pasture hundreds of sheep. Those he could sell and ship all over the world for people who wanted the wool to keep them warm."

John nodded. "But where were the crofters to go?"

"We were too many for them, a big problem. No one knew what to do with us. All they could think of was to send us from the land to another land so they called in the ships. But no one wanted to go."

"I want to go father," John said brightly.

"Ye are young. The young accept change as a great adventure," his father sighed.

"First, I heard that we were goin' to go to America," John puzzled, "and then they said it was Montreal, Canada. But I heard the helmsman talking with the captain when I was on deck, and they did not see me behind the curls of rope. He said that only *some* were goin' to Montreal. They have more people comin' in than Montreal can find room for, so they said that all those from the Orkney Islands and North Scotland would be shipped to a place called York Factory on Hudson's Bay. It's a much longer journey, but the Hudson's Bay Company wants us. They agreed, the captain said, to pay for our passage and they will find work for us."

Andrew looked quickly at John with something like alarm on his face. "So now we find out who is payin' for our passage. The Hudson's Bay Company is payin' the shipping company. But why would they do that?"

"The captain said that they mostly want Orkney Islanders because we can stand the northern winters; we are tough, hard working, and eager, he said." John looked up into his father's puzzled expression that gradually became knowing.

"I think lad that we are about to get a new laird. It looks like the Hudson's Bay Company has bought some Orkney Islanders."

3

York Factory

Jane Lenny looked forward to this new land like a drowning woman looks forward to rescue. When she stepped off the ship, the reeking den she shared with dozens of both sexes, she felt as though she had been released from bondage. The wonderful ground that she began to doubt she would ever set foot on, she could not wait to reach. She and six-year-old Isabel shared the berth, nothing more than a shelf three feet wide and six feet long in their airless, lightless, noisome dungeon for two months, where cleanliness was impossible. But even this would be like a nightmare to her soon.

Now a new and wonderful world was opening to her. Green spruce trees lined the high banks above like sentinels. The tall, white, dormitory-style buildings formed a compound surrounding a wide-open courtyard. Below the ridge of trees on the bank above the wharf, the steel fenced-in yard faced them. This compound looked out on the ocean, whose waters lapped at the sturdy wharves that extended well out from shore where many boats were tied.

The first thing that assailed her, though, was the cold. It was November and snow banked the shoreline around Fort York, and up the bank to the tree line. It had always been cold and damp below deck aboard ship, so that she and Isabel were never comfortably warm in their narrow bunk under the skimpy smelly blanket.

Isabel's pinched little face that seemed to be all eyes surveyed the new land, and she shivered, pulling her light sweater around her long woollen dress. She had not been out of it for the sixty days of their voyage. A woollen scarf covered her red hair and was tied under her chin. The shoes over her black woollen stockings provided little protection from the cold as she stepped from the end of the wharf into the snow, for they were worn through and too small for her. But cloths tied around them provided a little more warmth as they tried to cover the holes.

Because of ice extending out from shore, the ship was anchored out into the bay, and small boats shuttled the Scots and all their belongings to the wharves. Few though the belongings might be, they were all that the immigrants had and were precious.

Men in buckskin clothing, tall moccasins, and fur hats herded the immigrants up the bank. Men, women, boys, and girls followed single file, trampling the snow into a solid path to the Fort,.

Before the gate, they passed several large canons, lined up aimed out to sea, an ominous echo of past battles waged to protect this entrance to Canada's North. Stories abounded about the struggles between the Northwest Company, and the Hudson's Bay Company, for supremacy in the race for the fur trade. But at this moment in time, hearing about this fight between companies for domination over furs was the furthest thing from the minds of the Scots whose only interest was to find a place out of the cold and snow – a place where there was food, fresh water, and peace.

At the gate to the fort opened to the troop by the sentry dressed in heavy fleece, woven woollen pants and fur hat, the new immigrants looked up to see a tall tower, at the top of which flew the red, white and blue stripes of the British flag. In silence, they walked the wide wooden boardwalk between the vertically placed pointed posts that directed them to the large three-storeyed white frame building ahead, their feet shuffling, scraping, and clicking.

Inside the building, they were led to a large hall filled with long rough wooden tables and benches. Sitting down wordlessly, the five-hundred-odd Scots crowded and slid into the benches, or stood lining the walls when the benches ran out. They faced silently ahead, waiting – waiting for someone to tell them the reason for their being there.

At last, a tall impressively dressed man, grey hair fringing below his beaver hat, walked briskly to the front and stepped up onto a low riser to address them. A hush fell over the crowd so that even if the man had not shouted his greeting he would have been heard plainly.

Another man in buckskins and fur stepped beside him on the floor below the riser facing the audience. He, they soon realized, was the interpreter. For the man in the beaver hat would be speaking English and the man beside and below would be translating his words into Gaelic.

"Welcome citizens of the British Isles to Ruperts Land," the man spoke loudly, then hesitated while his interpreter translated. "You have journeyed long to come to this new land. We hope that you will soon consider this *your* land,"

The man in buckskins stood straight and tall, expressionless and still, so that the audience of immigrants looked only at the man on the riser, almost believing that he was talking to them in their language.

"You will all be given winter quarters within the fort and some will be in the log cabins on the other side of the fort. You will assist in the duties necessary to feeding, clothing, cleaning, and keeping the place warm. As soon as you have seen the man at the desk along the back wall, he will assign you the quarters that will be yours for the rest of the winter."

There was a murmur and a restless shuffling. John, sitting on the floor at his mother's knee, looked about the crowded hall at the Scotsmen. Dirty, haggard, and hungry, their eyes glazed over, they began to feel like prisoners in a strange land not knowing the rules. Feeling their freedom sliding away from them was like trying to hang onto a handful of sand.

John shivered and pressed closer to his mother's knee.

"I know that you have left your country against your wills. Many have been independent landowners where you fished and grew your own food. You will again own a piece of this new land."

The faces around John relaxed slightly but still looked wary, unbelieving.

"First," the man shouted, "we must all work together and look after each other. Some of you women will be cooks in the kitchen, some will be in the laundry, and some will make clothing. Men will bring in wood to burn in the stoves, saw it and chop it up. Some men will hunt, fish, and trap to bring in warm furs that will keep everyone warm, and bring meat for our table. Some will tend the animals in the barns behind, milk the cows, and feed them. Everyone will have a job from the very young to the old. But all will take time in the evenings to learn and to understand the language, and the nature of this new country."

"We're cold, and we're hungry," a Scotsman yelled out in frustration. "And ye talk tae us about learning a new language and hunting for furs thah we know nothing about."

The man in buckskins turned to translate while the people around John and his family stirred restlessly and talked among themselves tensely.

"There is food in plenty for all. We prepared for your arrival. As soon as you are given the assignment of your quarters and given your work allotment, it will be served up in this dining room. Make no mistake; this arrangement is temporary. By spring you will have the opportunity, those who desire, to take a patch of land as your own. There, you may hew down the trees, build your own homes, plant your own gardens after the trees have been cleared and the stumps have been pried from the ground. But right now you have warm dry rooms here in the compound.

"While you are pumping the water from the well and carrying it into the fort, a well that others have dug so that you may drink, someone else is washing and carding the wool for the sweater to keep you warm."

Silence reigned, and the people began slowly to accept their fate. They would not lose heart or hope. Some day, they carried in their hearts, they would again win back the freedom and independence they once had enjoyed. Though some still longed to return to the country from which they fled, most accepted the new way. After all, they would be helping each other. They would all be working together to win back their pride and self-sufficiency.

As names were called out, they gathered up their belongings and reported to the man at the rough wooden table, pushing between people who milled about in confusion. Andrew led his family when he heard the man in buckskins call out, "Lenny!

"Fisherman, boatman," the man at the table told Andrew briefly as he handed him a slip of paper with the number of their quarters. "Wife and daughter in the kitchen – bakery. Son, John, working with the father."

Then they were shoved aside as the next in line pushed forward leaving the Lenny family to stare at the slip of paper and try to find where their space was located.

A man in a fur hat pointed them towards the door to the outside, and after the crowded stuffy dining hall, the cold air hit them in the face like an icy rag. They gasped and pulled their sweaters around themselves.

Shivering and stumbling, they followed a wooden sidewalk that bordered the large buildings forming a square about a centre open courtyard.

Following others ahead of them, assuming that they knew where they were going, the Lenny family dodged into the second building, hoping to escape the cold that made them cough and stung any exposed skin. At the door, however, a man in a great coat, looked at their number, spoke several unintelligible words to them, and sent them to the next building.

Out into the cold again, Andrew led his family, and they hurried down the wooden sidewalk, matching their steps to miss the spaces between the boards. Inside the next building, the man at the door accepted them and pointed to a door up the stair steps with another number on its door matching the new number that the doorman had given Andrew.

Tentatively, slowly, he opened the door that lead them into a large room divided into three small rooms by half-walls, open from the top of the wall to the high ceiling. The three small rooms were evidently dividing off two small bedrooms and one larger living area. The room was furnished very simply with cots, table and chairs and rough cupboards, meant to contain their belongings. There was one fairly large window looking out onto the courtyard, and in the family area was a large fireplace that would provide heat. The low, half-walls were built that way purposely so that the heat from the fireplace would spread over the walls into the bedrooms.

As the rest gazed about in a daze, Jane saw the bare bones of a challenge, and she saw it the way it would be after her hands had turned it into their new home. Before the fireplace, she would weave a rug of rags. Somewhere she would find material for curtains for the big window, and the bedroom doorways. A tablecloth would cover the rough table and she would make cushions. There would be pegs to hangs their clothes, and bright blankets would cover the sheets and bare mattresses.

Jane Lenny straightened her shoulders, whipped off the grimy scarf from her head, pulled back her dark red hair that was beginning to hang grimy and stringy, and for the first time in weeks, her eyes were bright sparks of light.

"John, go find us some wood and kindling to build a fire. We need to warm up. Andrew, go down to the man at the front and tell him we need warm blankets, two each, and pillows, and I want a bucket for water to hang over the fireplace. Ye shall set that up."

"Isabel go with him so ye can help carry. Find out when it will be time to go down to eat, and Andrew, find when Isabel and I must be in the kitchen to bake. Will it be tomorrow or perhaps this evening? I am going to find out where the leftover materials are put so that I can use some of it to make things comfortable in here. I will start tonight. John, ye run and scout out where everything is so that we can find what we need."

The family smiled. Their mother was about to show them how to make their 'quarters' their home.

Andrew was skilled with boat handling so it was natural that he become a fisherman, tugboat operator and pilot for other ships that sailed into the bay, but the factor had other plans for John. He was to help other young boys to herd and care for the animals that fed in the grassy area within the enclosure. If food became scarce, the men went out with scythe and gathered more to bring inside the enclosure. They dare not let the animals graze out of the compound lest the animals from the forest near-by: the wolves, the coyotes or the bears, carry them away. If the sheep, cows, and pigs attracted the wild animals the hunters soon moved in and shot them. The furs were valuable, and the hunters hardly had to move away from the fort to claim their prizes.

Another crew would tend to the hides, clean and cure them, for the women to turn into warm clothing or bedding.

Because this compound with its new influx of personnel produced all that its people needed it was aptly named a 'factory' but also, their leader and director was called a 'factor'. That was how York Factory got its name.

Those who were capable became the teachers or trainers of others. Isabel soon found herself training as a teacher, helping others to learn their lessons for two or three hours a day. Part of their education was learning from the factor's wife, who had only recently arrived from England. From her they would learn to speak English.

Jane, though she started in the kitchen and then moved to the laundry, soon found that her talents lay in sewing and working with hides and furs. Indian parties came into the fort to bring furs for trade but most of these furs were put away until the trading ships came in the spring to take them back to Europe. Not as many ships came through any more now that it was safer to move the furs south to Fort Garry to the United States through Chicago and New York. However, they still travelled faster from York Factory by ship.

Life on this part of the Hudson's Bay was hard. It was a cold and stormy outpost. Even inside the buildings of the fort with all of the heaters and fireplaces burning to capacity it was always cold. The hardy Scots, though they were used to the icy blasts from the north in The Orkney Islands, never seemed to get warm.

While most of the families worked into the communal life well, they looked to life beyond the walls of the fort. They were crofters and farm families who had owned their own simple quarters. Farmers longed for a piece of ground in this big new land with a chance to build their own lives in their own homes.

When the factor began to hear the rumblings of discontent, he gathered them together in the large dining hall. "Fellow countrymen of this new land," he shouted as his translator interpreted, "This winter will soon be over and many of you are talking of travelling and exploring farther west to seek your fortune or for adventure."

He paused for translation and then had to quell the murmuring. "You have to travel far for land to farm and for a climate that will allow you a decent season of growth. This is rocky, boggy land that is thick with muskeg and spruce and solidly frozen a few feet below all year round. All that it is suitable for is hunting, trapping and fishing. It will grow vegetables, though, for a short season of the year. Until then, if we run short of food this winter the Indians have sold us some pemmican and that will be our staple."

Factor Thomas Sutherland in his quarters the night before, spoke at length to his right hand and trusted interpreter Colin Spencer about how this situation should be handled. "The Hudson's Bay Company needs these people to stay here. We need to man those York boats up the rivers to the western fur trading posts." Sutherland paced the rough boards of his office floor, his hands clasped behind his back. His high silk scarf was wrapped high around his throat above his black, slightly threadbare suit jacket with the tails. This, they all recognized in him, was a sign of importance.

"But Thomas," Spencer argued, "what makes you think these men will stay? All of the other immigrants that came through here used this as a passage to the Red River Settlement, to the U.S. or Selkirk's land grants. What makes you think you'll keep them up here on this frozen shore?" Spencer was a soft-spoken man in his buckskins. He was dark-skinned mirroring his half-breed background, the product of a Scot and an Indian woman, but he was raised at the fort and spoke English with a Scottish accent. Cree, as well as Assiniboine he understood and spoke very well and was invaluable as interpreter when the Indians brought in their furs. He worked for 'The Bay' ever since he could remember, at the fort, travelling west in the York boats or bringing in food or furs to keep them surviving.

Sutherland stopped pacing and faced his right-hand man. He always listened carefully to Colin Spencer who knew more about what was happening at the fort and with the people who came here than anyone else. "Because," he informed him with a frown, "their families are here; their very young families and their old parents." He continued his pacing. "And because they are poor, they can't afford to travel further into a country that they know nothing about. These people are used to the cold and deprivation. To them this place is a haven, a future when their future was lost, a glimmer of hope when theirs slipped into darkness, independence and a chance for a place of their own."

"You know that Scots are fiercely independent and ambitious. How long do you think it will be before they discover that they can't grow anything in these short seasons? That the little shacks they build out here won't keep out the cold and the summers are so short that nothing will get a chance to grow even if the soil was thick enough to sink its roots into." Colin remembered others who had tried to stake out a piece of land and had cut down trees to build cabins only to have them sink into the swamp and muskeg. He shook his head doubtfully.

He agreed with the natives who shrugged and looked at these white fools as though they harboured bad spirits. They tried to tame the land, planting and cutting and building and they froze in their beds or else they wandered away.

"We need the young men to take the boats out west, to trade with the natives, bring back the furs, and to come home to their families. We need them to marry, to work together with their fellow men and women, to build a community together, to help each other and call this York Factory home. It must work! It will work." Thomas Sutherland smacked his fist into his palm and straightened his back. "The Hudson's Bay Company has invested a lot in this fort. They've invested a lot in bringing these people over here. They have an advantage over the other voyageurs from Montreal or Chicago. We can get the furs to market in half the time that they can. That was how the Hudson's Bay beat out the Northwest Company and they finally had to sell out to us. They could not take the competition. We can't lose the advantage now. We have got to move into the breach."

"Those big slow clumsy York boats," Colin shrugged and shook his head. "Compared to the fast light canoes from the South they are like sending an ox to carry a message instead of a racehorse. It is impossible that the Hudson's Bay boatmen could win the race with the furs."

"But," Sutherland laughed shortly and triumphantly, "that's just it; they did win the race!" Thomas' pacing had turned to strutting about the small room with its little fireplace and wooden desk. "The York boat is heavier and slower, but it is more durable. It can carry more than twice as much as the little southern canoes can. On the lakes it can be turned into a sailboat, saving manpower on the paddles and saving merchandise in the storms and high water."

"But what about the portages?" Colin insisted. "Carrying a canoe is nothing for a couple of voyageurs. They can walk for miles with it on their shoulders but I wouldn't walk a mile with a York boat – even with six men helping me."

"Ah, but now," Thomas stopped with his back to the fireplace, stretching his hands to warm. "The big Yorks don't go off the highway. The natives with their canoes and snowshoes come down to the forts on the rivers. The Methye Portage from the Churchill River to the Clearwater to gain the Athabasca Landing is a thing of the past. Having more posts and forts is the answer to bringing the furs out of the north down the Athabasca and the Saskatchewan that we travel – a water highway! Our only worry now is getting the manpower on these boats. The Hudson's Bay Company has got all the furs coming to them now. We have just got to get the boats up to the forts through the spring and summer. It is such a short time that the water highways are open and we do not have enough manpower here to operate the boats."

Spencer extended his long legs as he adjusted his position in the uncomfortable wooden chair. "So the young men in that group that you brought in are the ones in which you are most interested. Most of the people you brought over are kids or old men and women. They are no good to you."

"Oh, yes! Everyone has his or her purpose. Most of them are the keepers of the fort. Take young John Lenny and Norman Morrison, Alex Macleod and Cameron Monroe; they will be growing up into the trade, training under fathers, brothers and heroes like Alex Ross did. They will soon take over and be faithful to the Hudson's Bay Company and York Factory." Sutherland was convinced. If he could just convince everyone else, starting with Colin Spencer.

Colin nodded. *It could work. But come spring they'd be working with a lot of tenderfeet. They'd better start the training and education soon.*

4

Jack River House

The two York boats pulled over from the wide rough Nelson River to the smaller stream that led to Jack River House on the Hayes River. The Hayes was a quieter, easier river to navigate - made for the canoes and lighter boats. The big Yorks travelled faster up the wider, swifter Nelson, but they liked to pull into Jack River House even though it was out of their way and was more suitable for travellers who were heading south down the Eastern Shore of the Winnipeg Lake.

People stepped aside at the entrance to Jack River House and gave room to the husky fur traders. These men were a loud, wild sort, and no one that they wanted to stand up to. Not all of the occupants of the two York boats went up to the stopping house to spend their money on food, drink and whatever was offered up that day. At least two must stay with the boats to guard their cargo.

The voyageurs were going *to* the fur-rich West not coming back from it, so they did not have their boats loaded down with valuable furs, but they did have other precious cargo. Most of what was on board, wrapped in oilskin packs, was ordered by the factors of the posts out west: supplies of food, canned goods, traps, hunting supplies, guns, bullets, blankets, cloth, and salt to cure the fish and meat. Knives, trunks, tempting trade articles like beads, buttons, bright ribbon, books, pencils, barrels of rum, pickles, sugar, molasses, tea, pots, pans, canvas sacks, razors, boots, suspenders, bottles, tools of iron and needles of steel were also stowed on board. It was all valuable enough for a man to lay down a season's trapping of furs stacked as high as a man's rifle.

After York Factory had once been burned to the ground and the Northwest Company had sailed off with the entire inventory of furs and

25

trade goods, they would never again take chances. Even though that was many years ago and the Hudson's Bay Company had little to fear from the French or competitive fur companies, they were still cautious. Any white or Indian thief could make off with merchandise that was not carefully guarded.

Senior boatman McTavish and James Ross of the other York boat took the first watch. The other strapping young boatmen climbed the bank to the big house with its other small storage buildings behind it.

In high spirits, the men strode through the door with a shout of greeting to the owner of the house who stood behind the counter. "Badger Jack," Alex McLeod hollered loud and clear. "How air ye? We havena seen ye since last fall. Ye're a mite older, but just as handsome."

Jack Morton scowled at the young men bursting through his door. Looking over his glasses and under bushy brows, with a head of tousled hair that stood out at his sideburns greying but still dark, he looked for all the world, the young men thought, like a badger peeking out of his hole after a hard winter. Jack did not waste much effort in smiles. He was not there, behind his counter piled with various sales goods, in a popularity contest and these overgrown boys were not here to bring him anything he needed. He got his supplies from the south, Fort Garry at the other end of Lake Winnipeg. They were here to buy little, perhaps some pemmican to take along on their journey, and some of his deep fried scones and venison.

"I suppose y'ere lookin' fer a clean bed fer the night – tired ae sleepin' on the ground air ye? Well I can put all-o-ye up in the shed out yonder for a quarter each. All ye have to do is split that pile ae wood and I might consider givin' ye a blanket tae keep out the chill." Jack knew they would not be sleeping in his bunks or splitting his wood. They were after food.

"Och, we dinna naid beds," Cameron declared. "We'll be spendin' thae night in our bedrolls as usual."

"But we could sure do with some of those tasty scones ye make – if ye still know how to make 'em," John cut in, licking his lips, a twinkle in his blue eyes. John Lenny was tall and lean with that hungry look that would make any cook hesitate.

"Ye cook fer yerselves on the jairney west dinna ye?" Jack threw over his shoulder as he headed for the kitchen. "Why is it that ye need my food? Have ye noh got enough o' ye're own?"

"Waire savin' that for the jairney," Alistair replied for them all, as they followed Jack into the next room.

His Indian woman cook stood beside the big iron cook-stove that Jack was very proud of. It was delivered up the lake on a barge and had cost him a lot of money, but it was worth it. It was quite impressive. On top of the stove was a big iron pot, half full of hot fat.

Now Jack at one time used bear fat, but his customers complained that food fried in it was strong, and the odour of it cooking was not pleasant. The bear meat, though, was not bad. So Jack began to get in regular pork fat from the south. He also got in grain flour. That was the best treat of all. He made biscuit dough and dropped the spoonfuls into the hot grease. When they rose to the top and he scooped them out with his long-handled wire basket, they were the most delicious temptations that he ever put out. Sometimes he dropped the biscuit dough into hot stew or rolled them in flour and baked them in his oven and they got rave reviews. But the deep-fried tidbits were the most desired.

Several natives and Métis stood around or sat at one of the three tables that he had set up in his kitchen-dining-meeting area. They, also, had discovered Jack's 'Dough-Gods', as he called them, and made it a point to drop in often to see if Jack was making any that day. Jack's roadhouse was becoming a popular attraction.

But when the stoic Indian cook, Starbird, took the deep-fried treats out of the hot fat no one was to set a finger on one until he paid for it. Men brought in partridges, squirrels, fish, or ducks to trade or they paid the required pennies, if they had them. The boatmen usually had saved their pennies for the treats and gladly laid them down.

But eating was not all that went on at Badger Jack's. As evening approached, the entertainment started. Any music was welcome from passing visitors, and they were pressed into service. The Métis who were not familiar with the English tinged with Gaelic accented dialect could enjoy the music. It was universal. However, some Métis had been exposed to the dialect and could speak key words. Most of them had been exposed to French years before and spoke that with the combination of Cree or

Assiniboine. But in this northern area along the rivers, English was understood and spoken most.

They remembered that Alistair sang, and he often obliged them with his lilting tunes to the accompaniment of tabletop drummers, tapping, snapping or clicking. At this rhythm addition the Indians reacted with smiles and toe tapping or leg slapping.

John's best friend, Cameron, played a mouth organ and that brought eye-popping delight. They would dance around the tables with joyous abandon. When the Indians displayed their dancing they wondered at the Scots. How did they celebrate? Jack had translated that question to the boys.

At this, the boys grinned playfully and the next time that the boats came through from York Factory, John Lenny, and James Ross, Ewen and Willie MacRae, from the second boat, brought along their kilts and Scottish regalia. The natives and Métis laughed uproariously to see these men in skirts with their long skinny, hairy legs cavorting about, the sporran in front flipping and swaying as their legs displayed a Highland dance. They demonstrated the Sword Dance and the Highland Fling while Richard Chisholm expertly played a rhythm with his tambour drum. With mallet double whipping back and forth between his fingers it made a unique and pleasing sound causing the Natives to draw close to inspect. They were used to a much slower rhythm on the drum. This fast flipping back and forth of the little mallet had a very catchy rhythm that could not help but cause their feet to move in time.

John inherited his father Andrew's Highland outfit, which was their Scottish tartan and saw many demonstrations in its day, in happier times. Andrew also taught John how to play the bagpipes, though he did not play them well. But this need for music in the West encouraged him to practise until he became much better. At first, his listeners held their hands over their ears, but then they tolerated him if he was not too close. Soon, however, they began to appreciate his expertise.

If, at the Fort, they were introducing a dignitary, they got first Andrew, then a more talented John to pipe them into the dining room in regal style. His talent as a musician was beginning to be recognized.

Though the natives were startled at the loud brash music that drowned everything else out around it, they later recognized its potential as an instrument, along with the drums, to dance to and accompany the singing. Its distinctive drone accompanied some of their sad songs that Alistair did so well and that, curiously to the natives, brought tears to the eyes of the usually happy and rambunctious or stoic Scots.

The Scots were ready for them this time. The boys brought their Highland paraphernalia from the skirts to the pipes to the swords. And this time Starbird had brought her sister when she heard that the boys were on their way. Raincloud brought her dancing outfit and the men had their ankle bells, feathers and drum. It was challenge time.

"Mmmm these Dough-Gods air delicious t'day," Cameron praised. "I'll buy three more for along the way." As Jack took the pennies, a few more natives came in the door dressed in their feathers, paint, and bells.

"I suppose you boys are looking for free fries just for putting on a dance display," Badger grumbled in Cree though secretly he was prepared for just that.

"Rabbitskin pay for Spirit Doughs for everyone here," their leader stepped forth holding a finely finished doeskin, soft, pliable and ready for working into wearing apparel. Rabbitskin, his bare shoulders and arms bronzed and glistening, standing a half-head taller than anyone else there, laid the skin on the counter in front of Badger Jack and stepped back while making a grand sweeping gesture to all in the room.

Jack, not wanting to display how eager he was for the wonderfully soft, pale yellow doeskin, scowled but acquiesced. He had thought that there would be a trade for pemmican as usual, but this was a surprise. "Starbird, start another batch. After the dancing everyone will be hungry again. I accept your trade. Boys," he shouted out to the Scots, "Rabbitskin has bought deep fries for everyone here. But first their tribe will challenge the Scots in a dancing exhibition that no white man has seen before. Find a seat and move back."

Switching to Cree again, he addressed the tall brave they called Rabbitskin, "All right, friend, you're on first, and then the Scots will challenge with their tribal song and dance." This was to be a night to remember.

First Rabbitskin put fresh wood in the fireplace so that the flames danced high, licking the logs and scattering sparks of light. A master of showmanship himself, he nodded for the rest of the braves to join him.

Arms crossed over their chests, shoulder to shoulder, they turned fiercely painted faces on the audience as they stared haughtily toward the Scots. A hush fell over all as Raincloud turned down the lamps.

Suddenly, the still of the room was rented by a shrill war cry accompanied by a tremolo of voices. His six braves emitted sounds fierce and primal as a wolf pack at twilight. The seven braves whipped the blankets from their shoulders and from around their waists and stood in the flickering firelight in breach-clouts, feathers twisted into their braids, and bodies painted with bright slashes of colour. Chills rippled through the audience and they shivered.

A drumbeat began pounding like a great heartbeat and the Indians leaped into a stalking posture. They moved in unison, toes pointed and placed, then heel, down as their muscular bodies moved in exaggerated postures of stealth, eyes darting to left and to right. Arms moved slowly as if parting the foliage. Hearing the tempo of the drum quicken, the audience's tension built.

Soon the dancers were springing shoulder high, crouching, whirling, and swinging imaginary clubs, stabbing with their imaginary flashing knives. They imagined themselves swift, powerful, and fearless in attack, surprising the enemy with yips, grimacing wolfishly as they grappled with imaginary foes.

With a start, Badger Jack realized that this was no ordinary dance. These were warriors rehearsing their legendary war dance. They stabbed, spun about to kill enemies behind them while flashing their naked blades in the night.

Firelight gleaming on their sweating muscles, they leaped far off the floor, landing on the balls of their feet. Their hearts were fire, honey, and salt as they lived again the past. Arms arced as if with weapons as they leaped; then upon landing curled tight as a snake. They ended with a final thump of the drum and a fierce ululating cry as their hands thrust toward the ceiling, faces echoing their exertion, and chests heaving from the intensity of the dance.

Jack realized and so did many of the observers, somehow, somewhere deep inside their hearts, this was a dying dance of a changing people. Their bodies said what their mouths could no longer say: "Once our people were many. From sunset to sunrise our campfires shone like stars rained out of the sky. Then the 'whites' came. Our fires have dwindled. Our people are passing away as the snow on the mountains melts in the spring. We no longer rule the forest. Our hearts are twisted in sorrow for what will never be again."

The emotion of the dance so stirred the people watching that for a long moment no one moved, no one spoke. They were breathing as heavily as the dancers. Though most of the watchers did not understand the significance of the moves, they felt them and had a new comprehension for the past and its people. Then a thunderous applause erupted with clapping, lap slapping and foot stomping that seemed to rock Jack's stopping house.

Before they could recover from the last dance, one lone dancer moved timidly out onto the dance floor. It was Raincloud. She was dressed in a soft doeskin dress beaded and fringed, and beads threaded through her braids. Bells on her ankles and wrists added a gentle calming wistfulness to the stark violence of the last dance. The beat of the drum was quieter, more subdued, and moved with the bells.

Raincloud did a toe-point, heel-plant step as she twirled, raised her arms, and pantomimed many activities of an Indian woman. Her actions mimed the planting, the scraping of hides, the gathering of berries and grains but then the feeling of the dance changed as one brave slid into the scene with her. They moved about the area in an attitude of quiet pursuit as though pretending not to notice each other. As the dance progressed the two became closer and closer until without touching they were moving in unison, he behind her, pushing all else away, pushing all others away from pursuit.

Sometimes he would be the aggressor and sometimes she would be while he pretended not to notice or care, so busy with making and trying out a bow and arrow.

Suddenly, with a final flourish on the drum and an exultant ululating cry from the brave, he swept her up, holding her above his head on both palms while she hung limp as a water weed, before appearing to let her suddenly fall and catch her in his arms. Then he ran off with her to the laughter and applause of the audience after they had sucked in a fearful breath when she fell. The courtship dance had been well received.

As John and the other boys prepared for their dancing and songs in answer to Rabbitskin's challenge, John recalled stories that his father had told him about when the Scots were war-like Celtic tribes in the Scottish Highlands. Then they were clans and fought each other over territories and religion. When the hated British came to conquer them, ending in the Battle of Culloden, all the fight was gone from the rebellious Scots.

Their kilts, tartans, and dances were remembered, however, and many were faintly reminiscent of battles in the past just as the natives were today. The two nations were not so different after all! If the Scots could revere their Club and Sword Dance why could the natives not revere their 'Knife and Tomahawk' war dances?

But when the kilted Scots danced with their hairy legs and bony knees, their kilt flipping out like a pleated flag, the natives could not seem to take the dance seriously. They laughed and slapped their knees at the hilarity of it all. And when John played his bagpipes, they nodded and 'ah-ed' though its honking and loud bellowing made them back away, initially nervous. However, they came up to him afterwards, touched and squeezed the bag and wanted to blow into the mouthpiece.

John, though, closed his eyes as he played and smelled the heather, heard the sound of his mother and sister singing and almost felt the sea spray and the taste of salt on his lips. Then it was gone.

Though the natives could not understand a word of Alistair's songs, they sat and quietly enjoyed his pleasing voice and felt the song's distinctive rhythm.

The mouth organ was a different story. When Cameron started playing a Celtic tune he learned as a child, everyone was up on the floor dancing in the way their feet had first learned to move to music.

The Spirit Doughs, as Rabbitskin had dubbed them, disappeared from the platter as fast as Jack and Starbird could make them until they were out of biscuit dough.

Gradually, people drifted away to find their bedrolls for the night, leaving Jack to clean up and put away. It had been a great party, but the place smelled like a wrestler's sweatband. As he picked up overturned chairs and wiped up greasy fingerprints from the tables, Jack wondered again about the warrior dance. Was this a rehearsal for a showdown with the white population who crowded in, taking over all the land, depleting the furs and game and involving them in their confrontations as well as stealing their women? Or was this a prelude to their own tribal wars? It was well known

32

that the Cree did not get along with the Algonquin. The Assiniboine and Cree blood was shed in the past. Or was this just a dance for entertainment only? Jack stopped and stared into the dying fire in the fireplace. If the native tribes got together and fought for their rights, he wondered if they could beat back the steady push to the west.

5

Stolen Furs

As the sun climbed over the forest-wrapped hills overlooking the Nelson River, it found the sixteen occupants of the two York boats pulling hard against the strong current. They were out on the river highway by sunrise that morning. Summers were short; there was no time to lose. They had to make many miles upstream while the summer still lasted. This was their second trip West, although only as far as Cumberland House, since the river ice had gone out, but there was no time to rest yet.

"There's a wind comin' up," Campbell shouted out from John's place on the paddle. "Wai'll be able tae put up the sail by the time we get tae Lake Winnipeg." A great cheer went up from the other seven in the boat, including John. That meant that the men could relax on the paddles for most of the day while the wind did the work, carrying them along on their journey. "I'll come up and help ye h'ist the sail, John," Campbell offered. "Wai'll be able tae ride the waves all the way to Grrand Rapids."

That meant that Campbell did not intend on taking the side trip up to Norway House. *Well,* the weary rowers thought, *I guess we'd better take the wind while we've got it and not waste it with detours.* They were a bit disappointed, however. Norway House was the crossroads of the fur trade route. Boats sped, usually on wind power, from Fort Garry with supplies up the east side of the lake to Norway House where they divided the supplies. Here, one branch went to Norway House, Jack River House, Oxford House, and Rock House east up the Hayes River and another branch sailed to Grande Rapids, Cumberland House, and points west.

At Norway House the traffic was heavy. The Campbell Crew on their way east to York Factory made the mistake once of stopping off at Norway House with their boats loaded down with beaver pelts. They knew it was dangerous, but a storm on the lake forced them to make the stop before heading up the Nelson River, and hopefully quieter water. The waves were tossing the tiny York boat around like a cork on the frothy dark waters. Suddenly in the northeastern sky, black clouds boiled up and swept towards them ominously. Lightning streaked across the northeast and sometimes whitened the night in an eerie blaze of light.

"B'ys," Campbell shouted above the roll of thunder as he struggled to get the boat's rudder under control. "takk down the sail before she shreds." The huge canvas square billowed out and strained on the ropes while McTavish struggled to hold it steady. The heavy boat leaned dangerously low to the water on one side while the other side rode high at nearly a forty-five degree angle. The poles, anchored across the middle, extended out at right angles to the sail, serving as balance beams. At times, they touched the water and jerked the boat around nearly swamping it.

Glancing behind them, they could see that the York boat following them was having an equally hard time. They planned, when they saw the sun disappear behind menacing clouds on the horizon, that they would skirt the north shore of the lake and dodge into a sheltered cove if the weather worsened. The wind insisted on blowing them further out into the lake though they struggled to keep her on course. When they lowered the sails, they had to work harder on the paddles to pull against the waves, but when they raised the sail, the wind threatened to swamp them.

Gusts of wind drove the boat further away from the north shore, screaming in their ears so that they could not hear Campbell's desperate instructions. They were too busy just trying to keep the boat from heaving them over. At first John and the other Nor'westers feared that they would lose the valuable beaver pelts on board to the bottom of the lake. Then they were afraid that they would lose their own lives to the cold northern Ruperts Land lake. At last there was nothing to do but make a run for it and hope to reach Norway House without being blown across the lake.

Then came the rain. The thunder crashed overhead as though the very skies were breaking apart. The cold deluge swept over them like a waterfall, stinging and lashing them mercilessly.

Finally, out of the blackness a pinpoint of light appeared. "Pull hard! Left! Come around!" Campbell shouted over the din. "Wa'll miss the wharf at Norway House."

The pelting rain, rolling down their faces and down their backs, some blowing in under their oilskin jackets, was not letting up. With a mighty jolt the boat rode a wave up onto the shoreline, coming to rest against the bank and throwing them forward into the seat or balance beam ahead of them. Gathering himself together, John grabbed the rope and leaped out onto the shore, thankfully feeling the firmness of the earth under him.

They landed not too far from the main wharf and managed to pull the cumbersome boat to anchor it safely in the shelter of the quay. Men carrying lanterns met them and helped them onto the wharf while McTavish and Campbell secured the oilskin covers around the pelts and their supplies.

John, Alex, and Alistair ran along shore to see where the other boat landed and located it just across the little bay near another smaller pier. They damaged the front of the boat and moved the pier, but all were safe. Willie and Ewen Macrae, and James Ross were walking up to their necks in the lake pulling their boat as far into the safety of the shoreline as they could, without running it onto the rocks.

When all was secured, the many men who had come out from the buildings on shore with lanterns and muscle-power to help suggested that they come up to the Inn, get dried, and have a hot meal. The rain was still pouring down even though the lightning and thunder had moved off down the shoreline.

Happily, the bedraggled group followed the troop up to the lights in the inn above them on the bank. The atmosphere was warm and inviting, and the smell of hot stew and biscuits had the Nor'westers stomachs growling.

This was a busier place, larger and more travelled than Jack River House. Many patrons, Indians, Metis, and white, sat around the large area at tables in the dim light. They all looked up curiously and suspiciously at the newcomers who pulled off their wet outer clothes and sat in the steamy smelly atmosphere as their jackets, draped over the backs of their chairs, dripped little rivers onto the board floor. John, his soaked feet getting numb, slipped off his boots and took his socks out to the doorway to wring them out.

The difference between Jack River and Norway House was beginning to become clear. They served whiskey to any patron who could afford it, but there was no friendly atmosphere. Here they paid cash or suitable trade-goods for a bed, food, and drink and there was no entertainment.

"When we ait and dry oot," Campbell told his boys separately at each table, "Wai'll spend thae night under our tents and boats as usual. Their prices air tae high here."

The boatmen, after eating and drinking, felt a warm glow and were in no hurry to move out into the damp cool of evening. Their socks and boots sat around the fireplace drying while they sat barefoot looking around at the clientele.

A pretty Métis girl came by to see if they wanted more to drink, and a group of Nor'westers like themselves sat hunched over their drinks at the table next to them, looking tiredly into their glasses. A group of Métis stood in the corner covertly eyeing the crowd with faces partly averted. A powerfully built man with a black bushy beard and hair sweat damp and wild, sat across from them staring openly, while a young Métis girl stood at his shoulder shyly, waiting patiently for his instructions or direction. A trio of French Canadians stood beside the bar in their buckskins talking animatedly and at times angrily in their native French.

Patrons came and went through the big heavy wooden door, out from under the porch roof and down the steps, greeting others on their way up to warmth and shelter.

"The rain's stopped," Will Douglas, the steersman of the other York boat announced as he got up from his table and put on his boots. As the rest looked out the window, they could see the twilight glow on the last of the storm clouds and night shadows that crept in across the little bay and dark wharves. A fog was beginning to roll in to envelop the buildings high up the banks.

Will led the way and the others put on damp jackets to follow him. They would light fires along shore to finish drying out their clothes overnight. As soon as John and the rest of their boatmen found their boat, they prepared to pull it around to a quieter area away from the main wharf. McTavish spotted a place near the other boat.

"Will is gae'n to naid a little help to repair the front that was damaged when they ran into the pier," he told Campbell as he gave the boat a mighty push away from the mud of the shore.

"Whah the…?" Campbell exploded, pulling the limp oilskin canvas back, and throwing it across the seat. "Someone's been intae our packs." He rooted around, throwing back parts of the canvas in hopes that the cache would suddenly appear before them.

"Whah?" McTavish queried in disbelief. "We wairna gone thah long!"

"Thah canna be!" Cameron cried out as he ran over to the shoreline. "It was raining all the time!"

The rest hurried up to the boat wondering what all the fuss was about. This was unbelievable! How could it have happened? Then Will and his crew from the other boat were heard shouting from along the shore.

"Ach, my God! Nae!" Campbell groaned. "Noh them, as well!"

Both boats were robbed of all their furs and what provisions they had left. It was a crushing blow. All that they worked and sweated for in these past weeks – gone!

Guide Chisholm, Campbell, and Will Douglas began shouting orders. "Look for tracks!"

"Get up to the Inn and search every square inch."

"Ask anyone who maught hae seen anythin' strange durin' the storm."

"Cameron, find oot if anyone was on the wharf or walkin' along shore after we came inside."

"Willie and Ewen check up along those trrees. See if there is any sign."

"Ye b'ys check every buildin' up on the bank! They hae gottae be here!"

"There air nae tracks! The rain hae washed them all away if there wair any!"

"There would *hae* to be tracks! *Somewhere!*" Campbell was nearly frothing at the mouth in agitation. His red hair and beard stood out like a wolf's bristle and his eyes blazed fire.

They searched everywhere while Campbell, Chisholm, and Douglas, the captain of the other crew, with a backup of four husky Nor'westers, McTavish in the lead, stalked up to the Inn, threw open the door, and Douglas thundered a challenge to a startled roomful. "If the derrhy rotten divil's spoor thah stole our furs and provisions is in this room he hae beher start runnin' noo afore we tear him limb frae limb!"

The group stood in a frightful phalanx with their backs to the door, guns and knives drawn. Their rifles had been stolen with the rest of their provisions. McTavish was an awesome sight at the best of times with his giant-like stature. But McTavish carrying this much anger and a handgun to match was a chilling sight. His eyes shooting fire and the muscular group with him, brought the Inn to a standstill, struck dumb with shock and fear.

Albert Wilson, the proprietor, when the shock thawed his muscles, scurried out from behind the counter. "See here," he bristled with an English accent, "Of what is it that you are accusing us? And who are you accusing?"

In his heavily accented English Campbell repeated Douglas's accusation with some re-phrasing. "Someone in this room or at this landing has raided our York Boats and has stoolen our furs bound for York Factory. The furs noh belong tae us but tae the Hudson's Bay Company. The provisions, guns, clothing, and all belong tae us, and wai main tae get it all back, or naebody leaves this room or Norway House."

"My good man," Wilson tried to sound calm as he edged closer, "All of these people," he swept his hand encompassing the room, "have been here before you arrived and did not leave since you left."

McTavish swung about, aiming his pistol at Wilson menacingly, indicating that he not take a step closer. Wilson stopped abruptly and, with a shrug, raised his hands, lapsing into silence.

A murmur rippled around the room, and unfriendly eyes stared back at the Scots. The Métis' black eyes stared back with unflinching bitterness, veiling old wounds. The French Canadian group still recalled old battles when they were part of the competition, the Northwest Company who fought and stole openly from the Hudson Bay Company before the two companies amalgamated and the Hudson's Bay Company became the only fur trading company in the northwest. That was over forty years ago but it had been downhill in the fur trade for them ever since. The English and their Hudson Bay Company had the northwest trade sewed up. So these French voyageurs of the past found it difficult to feel sorry for the Hudson's Bay employees.

The group of Nor'westers returned the stares through bleary, whiskey-clouded eyes. Life was tough all over. They had just returned from Fort

Garry after leaving a boatload of furs and had turned around and headed back to the West with little to show for their labours after expenses were subtracted and a hard night of drinking and carousing that drank up the rest of their wage.

Chisholm's eyes bored into the big Nor'wester with the little Métis hanging by his chair, and the man stared back impudently, a slight smile twitching at the corners of his mouth.

"I'll wager that SOMEONE haire knows whah happened to those furs," Douglas shouted as he shook his fist in the air, clutching a knife, the blade flashing menacingly in the lamplight.

"So why are you standing here waving your toys around?" the big man rumbled. His smile made the hair raise on the back of the neck as his men turned slowly, half rising, spoiling for a fight.

"Now hold on there," Wilson rushed in. He did not want to have his establishment broken up again. "If you people are looking for a battle, take it outside. You Scots, I have told you," he whirled to face them, "that you are wasting your time in here. There were no furs taken in here and no one here has had the chance to go out and steal them. Your thieves are out there!" He pointed to the door.

For a long minute the standoff held the room silent until the Scots turned and left to the sounds of unkind laughter ringing in their ears.

The next morning before the sun was up, the Nor'westers rolled out of their damp blankets, their only shelter their overturned York boat. They had not put up their tents since they were missing and the boat, now empty, made an adequate shelter. They had taken turns sitting up, keeping watch for signs of prowlers.

After leaving the Inn the night before, they had done another thorough search of the area from the woods behind the inn to the storage buildings, nooks, and crannies nearby. They trooped up to the houses on the ridge and pounded on doors only to be greeted by disgruntled people who spoke to them in languages that they did not understand – Norwegian, Swedish, English and French. Not to be put off, however, they searched the grounds under the occupants' watchful and suspicious eyes. Nothing was found except a few hardened or moth-eaten wolf or moose hides. They could do nothing but to turn in for the rest of the night.

One or two sat up around the fire along the beach for awhile and talked. "I hae haird of this happenin' back in the days when the Northwest Company and the Hudson's Bay men were battling it out to see who would win the race bringing back the furs to the East coast, back before 1820. But this is 1863," Campbell complained, still pacing back and forth, chewing on his red moustache in agitation. This was the worst mishap of his career in the fur trade.

It was just a year or so ago that the 'Little Emperor', George Simpson, retired so it was no wonder that things would start falling apart. Simpson ruled with an iron hand.

"Things air changin'," growled Chisholm into his pipe as he sat on a log staring into the fire. "Hae ye noh noticed that things air changin' in the fur trade? Our haul was doon half ae whah it was last yair. There's just noh enough pelts tae gae arroond anymore."

"Thah's just it!" Campbell smacked his fist into his palm. "The Americans across the borrder on the Red River are likely payin' tae get the furs re-routed their way since thae supply is doon. They offer higher prices and all the whiskey they can pack away. They hae got steam powered river-boats and railway locomotives waitin' at Fort Garry on the Red River and they can move a lot maer fur than thae Bay's lumbering brigade of York boats! I think this is the beginning of the end for York Factory."

"If we stair clair ae thae south route and keep our furs movin' to York Factory, they can still get to Europe faster than thae Americans can get them there and thae French Canadians from Montreal as well. Those people over there still want their fancy beaver hats." Chisholm was calm, but he knew that Campbell and Will Douglas had to answer to Sutherland, the factor at York. This would be a loss that they had to make up.

As the camp put their bedrolls away and breakfasted on what they could find, rationed to last until they made it back to Fort York, John noticed a familiar form on the wharf. He was talking to the French Canadian crew that was preparing to head south to Fort Garry. *That's Alex Ross, one of Will Douglas's crew*, John observed. *I wonder if he's asking them about the theft. But we asked them last night, out on the dock. They had even let us search their boat and we found nothing.* John turned hurried footsteps toward the dock to join them.

Leaping up onto the sturdy board wharf, John made his way towards the trio, including Alex. "Good Marnin'," he hailed. "Looks like a great day out on the lake fer headin' out - enough breeze fer the sail."

"Good marnin'!" Alex smiled as he turned to face John.

The other two nodded with a curt, "Bon matin!" for John and Cameron had all but accused these French Canadian traders the night before of theft, and they were not feeling in a forgiving mood.

John and Alex were interrupted by one of the Frenchmen who advised Alex in French to get stowed on board.

"I will be right there," Alex called after them in French before turning back to John.

"Do I understand," John asked quizzically, "that ye air goin' wi' 'em?"

Alex was older than the young men in Campbell's or Douglas's boat crews, except for McTavish, and eight years older than John. He had signed on with the Hudson Bay Company after travelling west as far as Fort Garry looking for adventure. The fur trade was down to a trickle through Montreal at that time, and between the Red River settlement and the steamboat travel south down the Red River to the United States, Fort Garry was a land of opportunity.

At that time, 1855, Alex was a newly married man, and his wife, Sarah Francis, was expecting a baby. When he made a place for her in the west after he had made his fortune, he told her, he would come back and get her. In the St. Andre's Presbyterian Church where he and Sarah were married there was word that missionaries were travelling west. It was a call. After that, he heard that a group of nuns from the Catholic parish, the Grey Nuns, were going to travel far west to minister to, and teach the savages. Alex was fascinated with the idea of travelling ever since.

Alex told them as they sat around the campfires at night, what it was like in Fort Garry, the wild drinking and brawling, the fighting and the killings. He had no trouble getting on with the Hudson's Bay Company and joined a group of Nor'westers heading north, up the great lake to York Factory where he'd signed on, and was soon on a York boat for the Northwest.

John remembered Alex when he came back from the west. He remembered his brown rippling muscles as he helped the younger boys learn to become boatmen. He remembered his quiet, even-tempered manner compared to some of the other loud, brash, and blasphemous Nor'westers. Alex was a slender, light brown-haired Scot with startling blue eyes and a wide winning smile. He was patient with the fourteen-year-old, helping him learn through the winter and early spring the art of operating a York boat and the skills to become a Nor'wester.

John always knew that Alex was restless during the long idle winters in York Factory until spring sent him back up-river to the trading posts a thousand miles away, to the beauty and the excitement of the wild west. It was not until John, husky at sixteen, joined the Nor'westers on their trek west on the end of a boat paddle that he realized the reason for Alex's restlessness.

Around the campfire one night he revealed to his boat partners that he was married and his wife probably had their baby by now back in Montreal. He always thought that by now, eight years from the time he left, that he would be returning to get his wife and child and take her west with him. But at twenty-seven years old, he still had not made the fortune that he started out to find. The fur trade was dying in the west and he had not found a place for himself there.

"The Hudson's Bay Company, once they get ye here, doesna want tae let ye gae. They wanted tae hire men who were already married because they wair afraid that single men would take up wi' the native lasses. The Nor'westers would aither spoil the young lasses and leave, or else the Bay would lose the men to the Indian lassies and lose another boatman." Alex poured out his unhappiness as he stared into the fire. "And they wanted men who were older and more experienced so that they could entrust expensive merchandise tae their hands.

"But all I've really gained that I can return to my wife and child wi', is the ability to pull on the paddle of a York boat from mornin' 'til night until my muscles ached, and tae speak in three languages, French, English and Gaelic - nae fortune!

"But I hae found a branch o' the family," he waved towards James Ross, "that I didna know aboot. And I hae learned more aboot how I came to be on this side o' the ocean. I discovered why my father left Strathcairn in Easter Ross in Scotland. They left during the Massacre of the Rosses - the Highland Clairances. I remember my father telling me soomethin' aboot it. Hard ambitious men with writs of removal in Glencalvie in 1841 berrned the hames to the groond of innocents whose hearts were rooted to their hearths. It was just like your bard and historian, Alistair, sang aboot:

He is a poor craiture without responsibility,
Without honour understanding or shame.
Doubly judged for driving
Away the Rosses of Glencalvie

Wicked massacre to bring the sheep
Wasting and stripping the poor
They ship them to the colony
The Rosses of Glencalvie."

John remembered those words as he talked on the dock to Alex this warm July morning. He knew he was about to lose a good friend.

"I am laiving fer Montreal," Alex said simply. "This is the first opportunity I hae had tae gae hame. These French traders are headin' for Montreal after they stop at Fort Garry."

"But ye willna get paid for this trip," John argued. "Ye hae goh summer wages comin'."

"After this stop and losing the load, I doobt if my pay will amount tae much. That is how they keep ye. I hae goh tae escape while I hae goh a chance; otherwise I will be trapped for another winter. The fur trade is going nowhere fer me." Alex turned to go as he heard one of the voyageurs shout to him rudely in French.

"Thanks for bein' a friend and fer helpin' me," John shouted after him. And he watched as Alex, without good-byes or parting words, had sailed away to his real life.

John, like most of the other voyagers, was not anxious to take the side trip to Norway House this time. They had lost the furs and they had lost a friend. It was clear sailing to the west and Grande Rapids.

6

Longing for Cumberland

When the Nor'westers reached Grand Rapids on the west side of the big lake, it was time to take down the sail for the next stretch of their journey. They had time to eat their cold fries from Jack River, lean back, and have a break from the muscle-stretching rowing.

Grand Rapids, named by the voyageurs of the Northwest Company years ago, was virtually a falls in a series of steps. All the waters from the rivers of the west and Cumberland Lake drained into the mighty Lake Winnipeg and eventually on to the ocean through the Nelson and Hayes Rivers. For the canoes of the early voyageurs the portage was relatively easy, but for the heavily built York boats, portaging was virtually impossible. This was by far the most difficult step in the trip up-river, difficult but not impossible. The Hudson's Bay voyageurs had located what was called a 'water file' at the sides of each step and devised a way to avoid the roaring, plunging waters in the middle of the river and the jagged rocks and clutching overhead branches at the edge.

In the water file the current ran free with a 'v' leading into it. The steersman aimed the craft at the centre of the 'v' while the bowman at the front peered forward and pushed the vessel around the unexpected rocks. The paddlers pulled hard and pushed with their poles to mount the rushing torrent, avoiding the cauldron at the river's centre. When they reached a quiet backwash, the Nor'westers had to climb up the slippery rock with the tug ropes. By using the tumpline, the leather strap for pulling with their heads, across their foreheads, they scrambled up the edges of the cliffs, using whatever purchase they could to hold on, and pull the boat up the next water file.

The steersman and bowman were all who were left in the heavy boat that dragged and pulled against the straining backs of the Nor'westers on the banks above. Sometimes they were able to wind the ropes around trees or rocks along the shore to add more strength and to hold the boat steady until they manipulated the pull up the water file. It was perilous, painstakingly slow, and, not to mention, dangerous. One slip and one of the men could into the falls.

In the early days of the wars between the Northwest Company and the Hudson's Bay the York Factory boaters were continually sabotaged by the Northwest Company voyageurs who tried to delay and halt the boats getting to the fur trading posts first. They broke down rocks that gave handholds and footholds for the straining boatmen on the shore. They put obstructions in the way and shoved rocks into the water file, making another unexpected detour with nearly disastrous results. The Bay Company men sweated, cursed and groaned, but they persevered and gained the top of the falls. It often took nearly the entire day, and the men were too exhausted to go any further so they had to make camp at the top of the falls.

Finally, a peace was sought and negotiated. The two companies joined. It is fair to say that the Hudson Bay Company won the undeclared war. Even the governments of Upper and Lower Canada answered to the mighty Hudson's Bay Company. However, there was still opposition to the rich, fur trading company judging by the sniping and cold war that broke out now and then.

John noticed that Grand Rapids was busier, more populated, and better built than Norway House. It was a focal point in the trade. Just below the falls, right on the sheltered bay, almost another lake connected to the big lake. But the two York Factory boat commanders were not anxious to stop in for long. They were eager to get up the rapids while the weather was in their favour. It might be dark, they thought, before they make it to the top of the rapids. That disturbed the commanders. But it was too early to stop for the night. The boys ate when they had a break from the rowing during the sailing. The distance was eaten up as the boat flew ahead of the wind.

John was exhausted from scrambling up the slippery rocks pulling the heavy boat, the tumpline biting into his forehead, sweating and struggling to keep his feet.

While leaning against a tree slightly back from the campfire on the rocky beach, John chewed on the hardtack soaked in the pork and beans on his tin plate, nearly falling asleep in exhaustion before rolling into his single tent.

"Wai should be able to put the sail up again today to cross Cedar Lake. It willna take long to get up this short river between the two lakes, will it?" Cameron asked Campbell as he reached over to fill his plate with the last of last night's beans from the pot hanging on the tripod over the fire.

"It will noh be clair sailing until we make it up thae Cedar River. It is one of the most treacherous on this route," Campbell warned. "It's full ae rocks, and it's deadly swift. The waher takes quite a fall from Cedar to Lake Winnipeg. This is a low plateau through here until it gets to the even lower basin, Lake Winnipeg. But luckily, I know it lak the back ae m'hand."

"Wai naid the wind up tae fill the sail across Cedar Lake, though," Alistair reminded. "If it stays wi' us. Otherwise waill be rowin' across." Alec McLeod and Cameron groaned.

"There's always a lot of fish in that little stretch of river, though, clear cold-water rainbow trout. Waill hae to pull a couple of them in to fry up for tomorrah," McTavish cut in with his surprisingly high voice for such a big man. He cleaned his tin plate in the river, stretched and rubbed a full tummy.

"How long before Cumberland?" John asked. They all raised their heads to hear the answer to that.

McTavish pondered as he rolled up his bedding and took out his fishing line, placing it on top. "I woold say thrai days, dependin' on how fast the wind carries us across Cedar Lake."

Cumberland House, at the junction of the Saskatchewan River and Cumberland Lake was a favourite spot built on a convergence of routes. The big inn was always overflowing with voyageurs coming and going as well as natives, Métis, hunters, trappers, explorers and people who settled there to stay, setting up their shacks, their trap-lines and fishing posts. White Swedes, Norwegians, Scots and Irish settled there with Métis wives prepared to stay. Cumberland was on the edge of the light bush area, the separation of the plains and the great rocky shield, land that was not good for much except hunting and fishing.

Dousing the fire, Campbell said thoughtfully. "Aye, it is a forty-day pull frae York tae Cumberrland. If we get a good wind across Cedar we should make it in two or thrai days.

As they broke camp, the boys began to look forward to Cumberland House. This was their fourth trip West on the river highway and they had only gone as far as Cumberland. Mostly teenagers, having started out as voyageurs when they were fifteen or sixteen, they learned much, but still had much to experience.

The worst of the difficult rapids and pulls were behind them at that point. From there on, they hoped, it would be clear sailing.

Cumberland House was the hub of the West, the crossroads, the hive of activity from north, south, east and west. From there the river headed in a southerly direction through woods and more fertile land, where scrub trees began to grow tall and lush. Then suddenly one branch of the Saskatchewan veered off into the open prairies in the South.

Cumberland House was the largest and oldest inland trading post in the west. Indians and whites alike portaged and paddled south from the north country Churchill River route to Cumberland and accessed the Saskatchewan route. They brought loads of furs to trade with the factor at Cumberland House.

Settlers in squeaking Red River carts were beginning to arrive from the plains to this doorway into the lake and swamp country and the rugged and rocky 'Shield.'

As well as a prolific fur-bearing animal area this was a haven for bird life of all kinds and the lakes and rivers teemed with fish. Even a small herd of caribou headed through seasonally, followed by the Indians.

The settlement at Cumberland point was growing steadily. Even a steamboat arrived from points upstream causing much excitement as important Bay Company men took advantage of it to journey up to The Bay's most important post along the route to York Factory.

On their last journey the fur traders in their longboats having come only this far from York Factory, collected enough furs from the Indians and fur traders from the North Country to give them all they needed. This time, however, they planned to go much further inland.

In awe, the men wandered up the narrow muddy street as Indians carrying their cache of furs headed to the post. The pier where many other boats pulled in was crowded with shouting, jostling, purposeful men in buckskins and headbands, pushing for position. From the pier the street started and led right up to the overhanging bank. Along the street, log cabins with business fronts sported overhead sheltered porches and crooked wooden sidewalks. Businesses like a general store, carrying clothing, guns, blankets, and tools displayed their wares. Even a doctor had hung out his shingles.

Indian women sat along the wooden sidewalks with their wares for sale. Some were readying fringed moccasins, and beaded buckskin shirts, while some women were birchbark biting. The boys stopped to watch in fascination as the squaws folded the birch squares into a wedge shape, then bit and rubbed it with their teeth into designs and patterns. Delicate insects, flowers, birds and snowflake designs on the birch squares were displayed on a blanket on the grass to the fascination of the white population who stopped to stare. Fascinating stones were polished and displayed. Some stones that seemed to have streaks of gold, copper, and silver through them interested many explorers who tried their hand at Cree to find out where the stones were discovered. The next time they explored the stony shore of the river they would look closer.

The men gathered nightly at the inn to drink, watch, and listen to the local entertainment. John discovered the merry atmosphere when on a dare he piped the crew from the boat landing up to the inn. John heard that the Bay's iron-willed 'Little Emperor', George Simpson, had hired a bagpiper to announce his arrival by piping him up to the post. So John had pulled his bagpipes out of his pack and played the bagpipes from the boats all the way up to the Inn.

The act so astounded the people standing about that, after first standing back in wide-eyed wonder and fear, they smiled and clapped as they followed the men up to the inn. It meant that the party was about to begin. The crew of the York Boat felt like men of importance when people stood back to let them through.

The factor of Cumberland House came to greet them, smiling widely, and entertainment was quickly organized – food, drink and dancing. It was good business and brought in fun-lovers from up and down the street to the length of the pier. Since they had already honed their music and dance skills at Jack River, it did not take much urging to get them to perform.

That always prompted other dancers. The Indians performed their native dances as well as feats of strength and agility.

Singers, mouth-organists, and fiddlers were applauded for their entertainment. Even a button-operated concertina, that travelled many miles to get there, was played.

The boys were understandably eager to reach Cumberland House, the gateway to the plateau and high country – the end of the rugged, rocky, barren Ruperts Land Shield. They attacked the white-water rapids with a vengeance, mile after muscle-aching mile in the summer sun.

7

Camp Visitor

McTavish managed to hook a couple of fish so their mouths watered at the thought of dining on lake trout that evening.

Out on the lake, they had time to look around. Huge white birds with black wing tips and oversized bills sailed overhead and sometimes lit on a rock that protruded out of the water, waiting to catch their dinner.

"Thah is a pelican." McTavish observed. "Watch him dive intae the waher sometimes. There he gaes! See the fish he got. He can carry that whole thing in his beak until he gets tae shore where he can share the feast wi' his family.

"See, up there in that old dead tree along the shore? Thah is a bald aigle. He's hopin' the pelican will drop the fish on the rocks. Then hai'll swoop in and geh it. He doesna dive for fish but loves to eat them," McTavish pointed out to the boys who lolled back on their seats.

Leaning on one of the poles that gave the craft stability, the sail billowing overhead, John stretched out his cramped long thin legs and relaxed. If only the whole trip could be this trouble free and easy!

"Look over there," Alex Macleod pointed out. "Along the edge over there by that dead tree thah is bent over intae the waher. There gae two moose wadin' inta the waher." Alex was a slight, wiry voyageur who looked fourteen rather than his eighteen years. But his strength and agility belied has youthful appearance.

"The natives call him 'Wapiti'. He's laird-o-the-wilderness. Loves this swampy north country," McTavish volunteered.

"And there's a baiver family. One of them just slapped his tail on the waher to warn the rest that they hae company," said Duncan McKenzie, the huskiest and broadest of the rowers, a good three years older and more experienced than the other young men. "Thah is their hoose over there, that pile-o-sticks."

"We'll hae to takk doon the sail noo," Campbell shouted. "Here's the river, and waill soon be tacklin' the Big Eddy Rapids. Nae maer rest time! This stretch o' river below the rapids is so full ae jagged rocks thah ye hae tae thread yer way through. Some ae the rocks are just benaith the surface, thae most dangerous kind."

"Och noo, I remember this stretch ae river," Cameron called out as he adjusted his hat and strap under his chin and picked up his paddle, bracing his feet against the boat-rib.

Since Alex Ross had left the crew, John and Cameron had become good friends. They had been matched up as rowing partners. Cameron seemed to devote himself to making people laugh, especially John. Because John was such a serious sort, Cameron used to tease him into laughing.

John always laughed as though he were in pain. His eyes scrunched up and his shoulders vibrated. He sounded as though he was croaking, and swallowing his laughter. But Cameron loved to tell stories to the rest about John's bony knees and skinny legs in his kilt, and Alex would explode into mirth.

Then Cameron would force John into chuckling, telling him about how 'a pelican could hold more food than his belly-can!' John appreciated Cameron's sense of humor, but someone else in the boat did not. He knew what was coming when Cameron started his teasing aimed at Norman. John knew that Norman did not like being teased. But though John nudged Cameron and tried to head him off, he charged on.

"This was the place where Norman stood up to pee in the waher and we hit that submerged rock. He lost his paddle and took a nosedive into Duncan. We had to terrn aroond and go back for his paddle and then the boat started laiking. Way had tae pull ashore and lost a couple o'hours fixin' the bottom o' the boat." Cameron ended with a guffaw aimed at Norman.

Duncan MacKenzie, who loved a chance to make fun of someone else, chuckled loudly. His red hair and skin were like a flaming beacon and his distinctively loud laughter never failed to attract attention.

Norman Morrison made a face. He did not appreciate that being brought up, especially when he ended up wetting himself and Alex on top of it all. That was embarrassing, and was their first trip to boot. He felt especially embarrassed since he was always trying to prove himself. On this occasion he discovered that he could not make it to the next rest stop. Everyone laughed except Norman who swore to himself that he would find an opportunity to get even with Cameron.

Norman was a quiet, moody young man. He did not say much, just did his job rowing. He never complained or showed much emotion. Everyone knew, though, that there was a lot more going on inside that he revealed to no one.

John glanced warily at Norman to see how he was reacting to Alex and Duncan's hilarity. He had a feeling that Cameron should not have teased Norman. John was afraid that Norman would not forgive and forget this incident.

Navigating their way through the narrowing walls of the riverbed, the York boats were plunged into the struggle to conquer the perilous river that boiled and frothed around them, tossing them about. If they were not careful their paddle could strike a huge rock that suddenly rose beside them. They could not afford to break a paddle, especially if they lost half of it to the river.

The boys heaved and pulled on the paddles against the strong current. It was up to McTavish and Campbell to avoid obstructions, but sometimes one erupted beside them that they had to be careful not to strike with a paddle.

Chisholm, their trusted guide, had transferred to the other York boat on this leg of the journey, making eight on each boat. Jim Ross also went to Douglas's boat, making way for the broad shouldered, husky Duncan to transfer back to Campbell's boat to even the strength.

When, exhausted and weary from the tension and hard pulling, they stopped for the night. They could not wait to roll into their blankets after a meal of McTavish's fish. Their thoughts would wind themselves around the coming stop at Cumberland.

William Douglas's crew pulled into a little cove farther down-river from Campbell's but they were within shouting distance if need be. In this wilderness, danger was always just around the next bend. They often got together around the campfire to share food, talk or song. As darkness crept in on them, and Alistair's voice, accompanied by Campbell's booming bass, drifted across to Douglas's crew on the cool night air they were drawn like moths to the dancing fire. Soon the shadowed forms of the men from the neighbouring crew came wandering over to join Campbell's.

A misty rain began to fall as they finished their meal and put away the last of the fish for morning. Hurriedly, they set up their single canvas tents and burrowed in under their blankets while a whirling cauldron of grey cloud swept in across the rugged rock and stunted trees of Rupert's Land. Damp shirts soon dried with body heat as they slept. Rain pattering on the sloping tent above John and the gurgle of the water as it lapped the shore, prompted the heavy eyelids and sore muscles to relax.

Suddenly, a high-pitched shout of alarm and clatter of pots and pans caused the hair to raise up on the back of John's neck. Then a snarl of an animal ripped through the stillness.

John leaped up, knocking his small tent over and exposing his warm blankets to the rain. Trying to focus his eyes in the darkness, he backed towards the river. A huge black hulk loomed over the dying embers of the fire. Tangled around its claws was a white tent, and backing away before it was the shadowy form of one of their crew. Their stewpot, tin plates, cups, and cooking pots lay scattered near the dying fire under the beast's feet, and the rest of the crew, now out of their tents, was scattering along the shore.

A shot boomed from the direction of the York boat and a tongue of fire spurted from the barrel. John recognized the intruder as a grizzly and knew how vicious and unpredictable it could be. His bare feet felt the lapping of the river, but he also knew that the river was not necessarily a safe haven from a grizzly.

A roar of pain and anger brought the bear down from a standing position to all fours as it forgot about the flimsy human who crawled out from under the white canvas covering. Now it faced the new effrontery, the one that spat fire and pain at him. Before the bear could take another step towards the new assailant, though, another boom assaulted it. The huge beast felt a searing burn on one side of its head.

This was too much for the animal, and with a shuddering roar of pain it turned and crashed into the trees behind them and was gone.

Slowly the men edged back towards the fire, shaking with relief and fear. "Who the hell left the food out so that the bear could smell it?" Campbell demanded.

It was Norman who had the tent ripped off his body as the bear searched for more to satisfy its hunger. It smelled fish somewhere.

"Did ye cover up the fish thah was left over by puttin' it in the big pot and puttin' a board o'er it?" Campbell asked as he carried the gun he used and approached the fire.

"Aye," Duncan assured, "and I put it o'er there under thah rock."

"Whah aboot the leftovers? The pieces? Where did they gae? Who got rid o'them?" Campbell insisted.

Silence. Everyone looked around the eating area assuring themselves that bones, tail, and any other evidence had been disposed of, hardtack stowed back in their parfleches so that they could lunch on it later, protected from water or weather. The buffalo hide waterproof bags could be carried with their bedrolls and become their ration when other sources of food were done.

Shivering in the cool night air and with the shock, John struggled to remember. *Was it his fault? What had he thrown away?* In moments, the wilderness had become a terrifying place instead of the easy relaxed picture he'd had of it just yesterday out on Cedar Lake. One careless moment, one mistake, and one of them could have been torn apart.

"Whah was doone wi' the guts and fish scales when the fish were clained?" McTavish in his calm but surprisingly high voice had to pursue this.

"McTavish, the bear could hae smelled the fish cookin' and came down to investigate. Smells of cooking travel a long way," Duncan McKenzie, a more experienced Nor'wester tried to explain.

"Cameron and I clained the fish on the other side o' that rock nair the fire," Alex admitted.

"Thah was beside my tent." Norman spoke up in an aggrieved voice. He was sure it had been on purpose to attract the bear to his tent.

"I hae told ye," Campbell reminded patiently, "tae always clain the fish in the waher and flush away thae evidence and thae smell that would attract wild animals. Noo ye see why."

Norman scowled at the two young men, feeling wrongfully accused because the bear targeted his tent, which was now in tatters at the edge of camp, left behind by the retreating bear. One more reason to feel 'put upon' by these two friends who were now on his hit list.

"Wai'll hae tae be on guard thae rest ae the night," Campbell warned. "In case it decides tae reterrn. It depends on how hungry it is fer fish."

The rest of the night, the camp slept lightly as they curled up trying to dry and warm up their damp bedding. Norman, with McTavish's help, pulled what was left of his canvas tent around him and tried to settle down again. He moved to the other side of the fire, partly on the stones and the sand, feeling slightly safer. Campbell built up the fire to a high dancing torch, hoping that its size would discourage a return of their visitor.

John, however, was told that once a bear was wounded it became a very dangerous threat. The rest of the night would be sleepless for him.

All the next day while the young voyageurs put their backs into rowing up the thunderous, rapid-filled river, the uncomfortable misty cold rain tormented them. Their buckskin jackets protected them somewhat, but eventually the rain seemed to soak into their bones. Only the steady and vigorous rowing kept them from becoming cold. The blue-grey stone bluffs above the curving river and the steep walls hemmed in the tumbling water. The frothing dark turbulence increased the speed and violence as it thrashed and clawed at the rocks hemming it in, while the dismal weather seemed to complain apathetically.

With infinite relief, the two crews reached Cumberland Lake. It was as if the river suddenly released its angry claws on the York boats. The smooth water spread out as the rock walls retreated and the land flattened out towards the less threatening hills.

They had not stopped along the way for a break, for rest or food, not only because they were too busy on the paddles and the rocky shoreline was too uninviting, but Campbell spotted something on the hills to their left. Following them at a discreet distance, climbing the rocks and skirting the stunted trees that hugged the hills was the brown grizzly. Campbell nodded to McTavish and to the boys who looked up as they pulled over into a backwash.

"Look whah hae been followin' us from our last camp." He nodded towards the bank above. "He must be lookin' fer more fish."

"Or more lead poisoning," Duncan laughed.

It took no convincing for the Nor'westers, after emptying their bladders over the edge during the quiet water respite, to continue their steady pull upstream. They did not yearn to do battle with a persistent grizzly. They would gnaw at their hardtack on board instead.

Steering out to the middle of Cumberland Lake, they put up the sail and relaxed as the boat skimmed along with the breeze that rippled the water. On the other side of this lake, they were happy to recall, lay Columbia House Village, only a few more hours away.

8

Revenge

The Cumberland delta, a lush lowland choked with marsh grass, was, in the daytime, alive with ducks and geese. It became a maze of twisting waterways threading through the tall grass making it difficult to find the right channel to Cumberland House. Beyond that, to the north, lay mile after mile of muskeg, thick cranberry-covered moss, and spruce that sheltered the leathery evergreen leaves of which the natives made Labrador Tea.

The sun was sinking behind a bank of pink rimmed clouds as the lights of Cumberland beckoned them. Here the brown waters of the Saskatchewan River flowed wide and deep by the wharf where other boats and canoes were tied. Cumberland House stood upon the bank above, a log house with a British flag fluttering out front and a balcony built around its belly, looking as prosperous as it was.

"Air ye ready fer this, lad?" Duncan whispered hoarsely to John who reached for his packsack containing his bagpipes and kilt.

"Aye," John told him in all seriousness as he pulled his kilt on over his head and pulled off his trousers. His sash he put on across his shoulder. With his tam perched on his head, sporran hanging down in front, he scrambled up on the dock with his bagpipes. Their sister boat pulled in beside them, and all eight men leaped out beside the Campbell crew. Some had on their tartan scarves or kilts, one had a tambour drum, but they all wore smiles as they lined up behind John, ready to announce their arrival to the people of Cumberland House.

McTavish anchored the boats to the wharf and prepared to take the first shift on guard while the rest marched in a long line behind John Lenny. Tuning up his pipes, and pumping air into the slack bags, John sounded several honks and false starts before he swung into the 'Bonnie Bonnie Banks of Loch Lomond'. Marching stiffly and proudly up the slope, they sang in their Scottish brogue while the village people stopped to stare and then to cheer. People inside Cumberland House pushed out onto the balcony and steps to watch them arrive.

Village folk followed the troop inside where they passed Factor Hopkins' transaction counter near the door. Felt hat rakishly pushed back from his forehead and pipe clenched in his teeth, which were the same color as his yellowish-white beard, he straightened and stared. The factor had been dickering with a tall Métis over a stiff pile of furs. His youthful clerk dutifully writing down numbers in his book stopped, quill in the air, as the crowd pushed in. Hopkins smiled widely, still clenching his pipe almost rubbing his hands gleefully as he saw business booming.

The large tavern, to which the troop led the way, could scarcely hold everyone standing, let alone find seating room. But the patrons, who could not find chairs, sat on the floor or leaned against the wall. The evening's entertainment was about to begin. Rum was soon flowing freely from Hopkins' barrel for those who could not afford the price. Beer was also available. The Métis or natives could trade pemmican for rum or beer, but the hungry York boat crew chose the pemmican rather than the pricey rum.

The two boatloads of Scots managed to crowd around one table. There were as many native women there as there were white men. Old or young, they all crowded the dance floor area when a fiddler started playing his polkas and jigs to the beat of a tambour drum. A contest was soon urged for the best dancer of the jig.

This was something new. Settlers in Red River carts reached the settlement area between the forest, muskeg, lake, and the prairie. They brought with them a whole new way of life and customs from the Red River Settlement near Fort Garry south of Lake Winnipeg. The new people were quite a different lot from the Nor'westers, the fur traders, and the natives.

These Nor'westers were an unsettled bunch. They came one day and were gone the next. They took from the land and were gone down the river, away on snowshoe, or canoe to the wilderness. They never stopped long enough in one place to make a home.

The Red River settlers were a 'find', 'claim', and 'stay' lot. They staked a claim and proclaimed ownership, or future ownership on a patch of land. They began to clear trees and rocks, and they set up cabins that they swore to keep until they died. The squeak and squawk of their carts could be heard from a mile away, and their oxen that hauled the carts were serviceable enough to pull plows, later pushing the land into furrows and pulling stumps out of the ground.

When they arrived at Cumberland House, they realized that this was the end of the good land. From here on to the north and to the east it was a wasteland of rock, muskeg, swamp, and water. So they took squatter's rights on the rolling hills, valleys, and lowland to the south and west, bordering the prairie land.

Moving north, ahead of, with, or behind the Red River settlers were the Métis and the Indians who tried to escape the civilization in the south and east. Since the buffalo herds on the prairie were becoming scarce these people moved north into the forests looking for a new source of food and a new way of life.

When they called out for The Red River jig the floor filled up with mostly Indian women, some Indian men, and some white men. The Scots stretched their necks in fascination to catch a glimpse of this new dance, to see these new Red River settlers and natives strut their stuff.

The fast shuffling and tapping, stepping and kicking to the trilling and fast fingered licks on the fiddle excited everyone into a frenzy of hoots, clapping, and table slapping, cheering and foot pounding. One Indian leaped into the air, twisted and swung his legs about so wildly that a great wailing, hooting cry of appreciation swept through the audience, and they proclaimed him the champion dancer of the Red River jig.

This was all so foreign and new to the Easterners. This West was strange, but they felt a new sense of belonging, a part of it all.

All about them the room was heavy with the smell of wood-fire smoke, beer, rum, and sweat. In the dimly lit interior, Norman, with a glint of malicious mischief in his eyes, bent on revenge for imaginary wrongs, slipped over to the sidelines and spoke in that universally understood combination of hand signals, Cree, French, and English, to a young Indian girl standing apart from the others.

None of the Scots, except Duncan, who was in on the conspiracy that Norman had labelled a joke, noticed. Surreptitiously, Norman pointed Cameron out. The girl looked his way furtively, then disappeared out the door. A few seconds later Norman followed her, explaining that he was going outside to pass his water; whereupon Duncan stood up and told the rest that he was going to do the same thing.

They returned a few minutes later, smiling widely, but no one noticed. They were too busy watching the dance floor area where several settlers and fur traders were dancing with Métis girls. Boots and moccasins were flying, buckskin skirts swishing, and sweaty open-down-the-front flannel shirts, hung out of faded trousers. Two Indian girls approached the voyageurs at their crowded table and asked Cameron and Duncan to dance.

Cameron shook his head, but Duncan and some of the others boys urged him enthusiastically. "Aw, gae wi' her Cam," Alex teased, "Give her a wherrl. She wants to see those pretty knees of yours under your kilt oot on the dance floor."

"Coome on!" Duncan tugged at his arm. "I'm gae'n tae gi'e the Red River jig a try. Dinna ye turn the lass doon."

"Aye!" the others urged. "She willna bite."

"Show her some of ye'r steps while ye're at it!"

"Do the Highland Fling to the Red River jig."

With his reluctance fading in the fun of the moment, Cameron allowed himself to be led out onto the floor while the girls along the sidelines cheered and pointed to the bright kilt and socks to the bare knees. All of the Nor'westers clapped and cheered as Cameron danced some of the Highland Fling steps to The Red River jig music. Other dancers backed off smiling and cheering in appreciation of the display. When the dance came to an end, they would not let Cameron and Duncan leave the floor. They danced singly, they danced with another partner, and then another until the two boys finally begged off and sat down to mop sweat off their brows.

"Cameron, ye and Willie Macrae frae Douglas's boat crew have to take ye'r terrns on guard," Campbell told them gruffly, his face unsmiling. The two Bay Company foremen were scrupulous about not allowing their boys to fraternize with the Indian and Métis girls, and they were not going to relax that vigil now.

In contrast to the French and the Northwest Company men in earlier years of the fur trade, the Hudson Bay employers discouraged, if not downright demanded, the abstinence of fraternization between the Indian women and the voyageurs.

In earlier days French fur trade personnel found the Indian women comely and resourceful in the harsh winters in the west. Fairer of skin than the men, usually, travellers found them pretty and affectionate. Many voyagers would not have survived the severe climate but for these willing girls who provided them warm beds, meals and labour in helping to carry packs. In addition they acted as guides and translators.

When the Northwest Company, Hudson Bay Company and the French missionaries realized that the men were forming liaisons with the Indian women resulting in illegitimate children that were left behind when the men went back east, they became alarmed. Some of the men did form permanent relationships and marriage. Some even brought their families back east with them, but most of the women were left behind to return to their tribes or arrange alternate ways of life, when the voyageurs never came back to them. The Indian women, in return, expected free access to the trading posts and to provisions that the white fur traders enjoyed.

Missionaries, when they travelled west, performed many weddings to right the immorality that they discovered. The Hudson Bay directors of the fur trade tried to hold a hard line on these relationships. They had lost voyageurs who were not ready to return to their paddles, or who tried to find a place on board for a native female cook or camp slave.

So Campbell and Douglas on their respective crews followed instructions diligently by discouraging the straying of their boys from casual fraternizing. They believed in 'nipping in the bud,' any relationships from forming. The Nor'westers knew the rules. They either obeyed them or they would not be hired on the following trip.

Not too long after Cameron and Willie dutifully left to take their turns on watch, other voyageurs yawned and stood up, stating their intentions to turn in early. Seeing that Douglas was prepared to stay until the last crewmember had left the party, Campbell decided to also turn in. He reminded the young men that the York boats would be leaving at dawn so he recommended that the rest plan not to stay too much longer.

The canvas tents were set up, little patches of grey-white canvas on the trampled grass near the campfire. The boys had set them up with bedrolls inside before the music started while it was still daylight. Some of the voyageurs, though, seemed loath to leave the fire and crawl into the tents just yet. Cameron could see their silhouettes around the fire from his position on the pier near where their boats were tied. One of the shadows left the fire and started towards him on the pier. It was Duncan.

"Why dinna ye terrn in too, Cam?" Duncan told him as he walked up beside Cameron. "Ye were up ferrst this marnin' and my terrn comes in an hour. There's nae use in me gaen' t'slaip fer an hour and gettin' up then. I may as well start my shift noo."

"Thah is a fine idea!" Cameron answered in surprise. He could not remember Duncan ever being so generous and solicitous over his welfare. Duncan was usually trying to scrounge an extra hour's sleep instead. But he was not going to analyze the man's intentions at this point. He was suddenly very tired and sleepy, already feeling that bedroll folding around him. But he thought he'd stop off at the fire for a few minutes.

"Thank ye, Duncan. I'll reterrn the favour sometime." Cameron headed down the pier towards their fire and past all the other fires and camp crews on the beach.

About the same time, Norman, turning away from the fire and starting down the beach, met Cameron. "Everybody's raidy tae terrn in. Campbell's chasing us all away from the fire and tae our tents. Air ye coomin'?"

"Aye! Right ye air," Cameron switched directions after hesitating momentarily. "'Tis late."

"Aye," Norman remarked and veered towards his tent. It did seem strange to Cameron for Norman to walk out of his way, in the wrong direction to his tent, just to tell Cameron that everyone was leaving the campfire. But he shrugged and changed directions also.

As soon as Cameron knelt down in front of his wee tent, he sensed something amiss. He could not put his finger on it. As he put his hand on the flap to pull it back he heard someone stirring inside. *Someone or something's in my tent!*

He threw it back and jumped aside, waiting for an animal to jump out at him or someone to leap at him. Nothing happened. No one emerged from the tent. Cautiously he got down on one knee and peered warily inside. At first he could see nothing but blackness, but then a shadow stirred at the back of the tent.

"Who is it?" Cameron demanded. "Who is in here?"

There was no answer so he backed off a little farther and demanded again, "Coome out of there or I'll drag ye out." There was still no answer so Cameron hissed. "I hae goh my gun. I'll shoot." He realized with chagrin that it was an empty threat. His gun was inside the tent with the intruder and he probably discovered that by now. Why had he not taken the gun with him 'on watch'? A fine guard he was!

"No shoot!" a tiny feminine voice called from inside. There was silence. No figure emerged and nothing else was spoken.

After a long minute that seemed like several, Cameron slowly approached the tent again and stuck his head inside. When his eyes got used to the dark interior, he could make out in the dim light of the moon above and the fires nearby the slight form huddled at the back of the little tent. Dark eyes wide and luminous rounded in fright.

"Whah air ye doon here?" Cameron demanded, his breath exploding in relief. He was not sure what he expected, but this was the last intruder that he suspected.

"Doon here," she mimicked his words, obviously unaware of what his words meant.

"Ye canna stay in here. This is my tent. Ye hae goh tae gae!" He stared at the slight form huddled against the cramped wall. She was not moving.

"Nae gae!" she murmured and hunched lower. Then as he stared back in frustration and confusion, she pulled back the blankets and indicated that there was room for both under the blankets. *What was he going to do with her?*

"Ye canna stay here wi' me, lass. I canna hae ye here!" Cameron edged inside the tent on his hands and knees and tried to catch her by the hand to lead her out.

The girl misunderstood the intention and began rearranging blankets, spreading them out and patting them into place. She raised her head, patted her chest and indicated who she was. "Nenuthtu," she nodded and edged a bit closer to him.

"Ach, nae, nae," Cameron shook his head vehemently. The tent was barely big enough for one person to move around in on hands and knees, let alone two. "Ye canna coom wi' me." The girl had taken off her moccasins and her soft, fringed buckskin dress. Bare arms and legs reached out from underneath a skimpy undergarment and long dark hair fell enticingly over her bare shoulders partly covering bare breasts. This, he was suddenly aware of as she crept closer, as well as the musky smell of her body. Panic welled up inside, and his throat nearly closed on him so that all he could say was a husky, "I canna."

"I canna," she repeated in a low murmur as she moved underneath the blanket and caught his hand to invite him in beside her.

"Cameron," a voice outside the tent called out. "Is everything all right? Whah's the mahher wi' ye?" It was John. He had just come down from the inn and had walked by Cameron's tent, which was close to his own.

"John," Cameron called out in relief as he fought to disentangle himself from blankets, Nenuthtu and tent. Scrambling out from under the flap he stood up facing his friend very nearly vibrating in agitation. "Ye've goh t'help me."

"Whah is it?" John caught Cameron by the shoulders to steady him.

Donald Campbell and Norman walked up at that moment. Frowning in concern, Campbell asked gruffly. "Whah's gaen' on here? Do ye have someone in ye'r tent wi' ye, Monroe?"

Norman, without hesitation, knelt down beside the tent, pulled up the flap and with self-righteous indignation said, "He hae an Indian lass in there."

"Monroe, you know the rules. Ye canna use a native lassie this way. Hae ye got a death wish? Her family will scalp ye. Besides that, it's against Bay Company policy to take up wi' Indian women oot herre in the West. I ken it's a long time awa frae hame, but ye canna takk a willin' lass this way and cast her aside like an old bone when ye're doon."

"But I dinna ... I dinna ken she was ... I dinna ask her. I found her here in my tent," Cameron stammered lamely.

"It wa' those knobby knees – those temptin' bare legs that turned her head and made her gae crazy for Monroe," Norman teased laughingly.

Cameron swung around to face Norman who was grinning maliciously, and he started to object. This was out of character for Norman Morrison, it occurred to Cameron. Hi-jinks and teasing were not usually a part of his make-up. That was why it sounded more like sarcasm than it did in fun.

Campbell reached inside the tent and pulled the half-naked girl out by the arm. "Ye canna tell me that ye were noh plannin' soomethin' wi' her in this state of undress. Noo ye get her back up tae the inn afore her family finds shay's missin'."

"I didna bring her doon here. I didna gi'e her any invitation tae come tae my tent. But I know who is responsible fer this," he swung around to face Norman. "Ye did this! How would she know which tent wa' mine? Why did she pick me?"

Norman looked wounded and unfairly accused.

"And whah air ye doon here? Ye should yet be oot on watch?" Campbell demanded of Cameron.

"Duncan offered tae takk m'place so I could...," Cameron stopped in mid-sentence. "Duncan was in on it too. Else why would he do such a thing against his nature? Hay's niver offered to tak even a part o' a shift fer me. And he is always the one to play tricks on people. They were both in on it – Duncan and Norman," Cameron accused loudly, facing first Campbell, then Norman squarely.

Nenuthtu huddled, shivering and frightened, partly hidden behind Campbell who held her firmly by the wrist. Hunched, head lowered in disgrace, behind the wealth of dark hair that cascaded over her shoulders she tried to hide her half-nakedness.

Campbell, as though suddenly realizing that he was holding her captive, on display before more and more ogling eyes that strolled by to see what all the disturbance was about, turned towards the girl. He made a few signs and gave her a little push towards the tent.

In a hurry now to get away, Nenuthtu scrambled into the tent, quickly dressed, and grabbed up the little travel sack that she had brought in with her. Eyes now streaming tears, she hurried away up the bank, never to show her face before these white men again.

Donald Campbell turned eyes blazing fire on the young men standing before him. "If I find that aither ae ye b'ys hae been playin' tricks on each otherr and toyin' wi' this wee lassie's affections I'll publicly tak ye oot and hae ye flogged wi' yer troosers doon. I hae me suspicions aboot ye Morrison and ye as well MacKenzie," he included Duncan who had just strolled into the group.

"Me!" Duncan said in innocent surprise. "Whah did I dae?"

"And ye're noh oot of the line ae fire yet aither, Monroe" he turned his ire on Cameron. "Anyone who would involve a poor innocent wee lass's affections on a lark deserves tae hae their hide tanned and be tied ontae the paddles fer a week!"

Cameron and Duncan turned beet red for a moment and then white, while Norman gave Cameron an accusatory look of disdain. As he turned away, a smirk of self-satisfaction flitted across his lips. John caught it, in the half-light of the moon and knew exactly what had happened.

As the Nor'westers turned away towards their bedrolls, John caught up to Cameron who was about to duck into his tent. "If it's any comfort to ye, Cameron, I believe ye. I think Duncan just got caught up in the fun. He didna mean fer the joke tae go that far, but Norman got just the result that he wanted. I'd watch that one if I were ye!"

Cameron, too hurt to reply, almost at the point of tears himself, turned briefly and gratefully to his friend, squeezed his hand in a heartfelt thank you and ducked into his tent. John ached for his friend and wondered how a little practical joke had gone so wrong.

Whether Duncan meant to exchange with Cameron for the rest of the time on watch was neither here nor there at this point. Duncan bargained for it and he got it.

9

Native Confrontation

The next morning the Campbell crew broke camp and stowed everything aboard, pushing off in silence. The fun from their arrival to the time when they left the inn last night was gone and forgotten. The bruised feelings, harsh words, and wounded pride hung in the air like a bad odour. In contrast, the Douglas crew shouted and sang out noisily as they said their farewells and pushed off following Campbell's boat out against the current.

This was finally the famed Saskatchewan River that they struggled to reach and would finally travel into the interior. Before this, they came only as far as Cumberland House, loaded their furs and returned to York Factory. This time their boat would travel much farther – into the excitement of the West, in sight of the towering Rocky Mountains that they longed to see.

The broad, mighty Saskatchewan rolled towards them, brown and strong, challenging the muscles of the young paddlers pitting their strength against it. After the mouths of the Torch River and other small tributaries were passed, there was less water, and less turbulence. The flow of the river became lazier as the land flattened.

They just began to relax a bit on the paddles when towards evening they heard thunder up ahead that began to drown out the sounds around them. The voices of the cormorants that swooped across the sandstone bluffs towering above, the chirp of the blackbirds, and the squawk of the whisky-jacks, the grey jay the Crees called *wiskatjan,* soon became lost in the thunder of the river. It was the Squaw Rapids.

A lot of water boiled over these rapids, and the rocks were large and treacherous, but there was a wonderful water file to the side that the York boats could take without having to portage or manually pull the boats across.

"There's only one dangerous obstruction in this falls," Campbell shouted above the noise of the water as it plunged across the rise above them and pounded on the rocks below it. "Thah is the rock up there. There is some talk that they intend tae dynamite it and remove it frae the streambed. Thah'll make way frae the big paddle wheelers thah will be travelling up and doon this river tae Cumberland House soon."

"Aye! It will take a lot ae muscle power though tae pull us up through this file, ye ken" McTavish shouted from the rear.

"Hard on the poles b'ys!" Campbell boomed over McTavish. "Slack off a wee bit and the water will flip us or carry us back doon the way we came and intae the rocks below. Haive ho, m'lads!"

The boys fought with all the strength they possessed, but seemed to make little headway. It seemed to be a draw between the river and their muscle power.

"Harder!" Campbell shouted. "Come on ye slackers! Ye've goh maer strength in ye than thah! One, two, haive! One two! *HAIVE!* "

The bow of the heavy boat raised out of the water as a horse would buck and bound over a log. Campbell's rudder came out of the water giving them a momentary feeling of flight, before the boat plunged on top of the wave that rose before them. That was all that the craft needed, to ride on the wave into the next file. The crest was reached, and they were over into the calm water above. The force was still there. They could not rest yet. The might of the water ran deep below them, but the force behind the paddles shot them along against the current.

"OCH AYE M'LADS! WE DID IT!" Campbell boomed while McTavish scurried to regain control of the rudder again, and John his pole. John felt pushed beyond his strength and capacity. But that soon was replaced by a surge of pride in the group accomplishment as the boat charged through. It swelled his heart 'til he felt like a conquering hero.

"There's a widening of the river arroond thah bend. The river got squeezed into this narrah channel, but up ahead there's quiet waher. Wai'll stop there for the night." Campbell turned to tell them. "I'm stairin' for thah patch ae trees o'er there."

As they pulled into shore, they noticed the lush forest land of trembling aspen, jackpine, and white spruce, marching across the rolling hills. Small animals scurried away as they pulled into shore. It was beautiful country. But the men were almost too tired to enjoy it. Campbell pushed them hard but after last night they felt it was seemly punishment. The Douglas boat had a hard time keeping up.

Both boatloads decided to build one campfire and eat together. With Douglas's crew's urging they gathered for singing around the fire at dusk. Between Alistair and Hamish McCauley's flute from Douglas's crew, they sang until weariness overtook them. They sang the tale of the murder in Glencoe again while tears burned their eyes, and thoughts of home sat warm but sadly on their hearts. And they sang 'The Mingulay Boat Song,' 'The Rose of Allendale' and 'Gallowa's Hills'. Then, without announcement of intention, they drifted away to bed singing inside their souls:

"Ye'll tak the high road
And I'll tak the low road
And I'll be in Scotland afore ye."

It was a while before John fell asleep. Staring at the roof of his tent, thoughts bounced around inside his head and images tormented him. The image of the young Indian girl with tears streaming down her face, the moonlight on her small brown shoulders and nearly naked body wrenched his heart.

The cruelty of men who would chase families from their homes, burn them to the ground, to scatter people to the four winds on tall sailing ships to foreign shores, scraped his mind when he remembered how old and sick his father looked when he left York Factory.

The melodies the fiddlers played rolled around in his head, along with the images of the sweaty dancers pounding their heels on the floor. Then there was the look of anger and frustration on the face of his good friend Cameron when he realized what his fellow paddlers had pulled on him. All he'd wanted was for people to laugh together.

In the middle of his thoughts, a scream pierced the night. Feeling the hair raise on the back of his neck, he froze. Wide-awake, every sense alert, he waited. Maybe it was not a scream. Maybe it was more like a cry. He listened again but the night was deathly quiet.

Unable to wait and listen anymore, he knelt and peered out of the little tent into the darkness. A lone shadowed form was silhouetted against the smouldering glare of the dying campfire. Crawling out of the little shelter, he pulled on his boots, trousers, and shirt and made his way to the fire to join the only other person he could see on the beach.

As John approached, the man whirled to face him. It was Campbell. He was standing, staring into the fire. Without saying a word, John joined him also staring into the flames.

Finally Campbell spoke. "I guess ye haird thae wildcat screeching oot there."

John sighed with relief. "Is thah whah it was. I hae never haird a wild-cat afore – never saw one. I wondered whah it was." John looked warily towards the tall dark trees at his back.

"Aye! He's pretty close too. We'd better stoke up the fire to discourage him. I think I'll gae oot by the boats and warn Duncan. He should hae his gun wi' 'im if the beast decides to come doon intae camp."

"Who's next on watch?" John called after Campbell. "I dinna think I'm on until midnight taenight."

"Aye," Campbell threw back. "Gae t'bed and get some slaip. Dawn comes airly."

After throwing another log on the fire and watching the sparks sail up into the blackness, John inspected the dark tree line behind him from the safety of the blazing fire and hoped fervently that it was enough of a deter-rent to ward off wildcats.

It was with a feeling of awe that the Nor'westers emerged from the rugged rolling hills, the dense trees, and rocky outcroppings, to their first glimpse of wide-open prairie. It happened soon after the wide and full Saskatchewan divided into two, one leading upstream south and west, deeper into prairie land, and the other leading northwest into bush land again. The northern branch, was known as the North Saskatchewan. The river was not so wide anymore and the rowing was easier because the cur-rent flowed at a slower speed.

As they rowed northwesterly they glimpsed more signs of life. They stopped for the night at outposts where bands of Indians came to trade. At the point where the Battle River joined the Saskatchewan dumping more water in with a brown turbulence there was an Indian camp. It did not look to the Nor'westers to be a permanent settlement of Indians because the circular-shaped tipis with their colourful designs and pointed poles protruding from the tops appeared to be too light to last all year round.

"They air a huntin' party," McTavish informed the paddlers who slowed their pull and hesitated.

"Shall we pull intae shore?" John asked of Campbell. The children were already scrambling down the bank to meet them at the confluence of the two rivers and the adults were leaving their smoky fires to watch them as they approached.

"They may hae buffalo hides and pemmican tae trade wi' us," McTavish said eagerly.

"But whah dae we hae in reterrn?" Campbell wondered aloud as the band gathered on the shoreline. Most of the supplies were promised to Fort Pitt and Victoria Mission.

"If they hae been on a buffalo hunt they could hae fresh meat and pemmican. That would be fine travelling food," McTavish ventured. The Nor'westers were already salivating at the thought of a fresh roast of buffalo.

Pulling into shore, they were met by the smiling, eager children and the dogs. Campbell was scowling. He did not know if this was such a good idea. Behind them the men approached and stood beside the boats, arms akimbo, frowning at the sparse store of goods bundled inside the big bumboats, as they had named the York boats.

'Buffalo? Hides? Pemmican?' Campbell asked, signing.

After a difficult session of signs and misunderstood language attempts, McTavish and Campbell concluded that it had been a poor hunt. They had little enough buffalo for their own food and shelter, but if the Nor'westers wanted to trade for the bones the tribe would be open. What they really wanted, Campbell gathered, was whiskey or rum from the signs many of the men made. They were not interested in trading for trinkets. Perhaps the tribe might be open to trade old buffalo hides for guns and ammunition, the natives signed. That way they could kill the next buffalo they saw, and they would have new hides to trade. The hides were already made into tipis.

Standing beside their boats, the Nor'westers, particularly McTavish, Campbell, Douglas and Chisholm, tensed as the Indian braves tried to peer inside the crafts to see what they held. They looked in particular for rum kegs. Glowering at the white men, obstructing their way, they again signed their preference for guns, bullets, and rum, ignoring the blankets that Cameron, Willie, John and Ewen proffered.

"Shall we haul oot the ammunition?" Willie from the other boat asked Douglas in a hoarse whisper.

While the tense standoff silently held everyone at bay, the Indians edged a bit closer, crowding the Nor'westers closer to their crafts.

"I dinna think they hae anything tae trade for the blankets or anything else we maught hae tae offer," Campbell spoke quietly in Gaelic as he held the gaze of the leader of the group. "They air interested in rum, and they air hopin' we will offer them some oot ae the goodness ae our hearts. If noh, they air noh above confiscating it. I knew we shouldna come this distance wi' but two boats; more numbers would hae been more protection."

"We should meet up wi' the other boats in Fort Pitt but they're headin' the other direction. We naid more but we dinna hae them or men tae man them," Douglas said evenly, his words aimed at Campbell, but his eyes held the Indian leader's.

The Indians knew a smattering of English and French but they had no clue as to what these Scots were saying with their strange accent so they stared back, waiting for some indication as to what the white traders intended.

It had been a poor hunt. The buffalo had not shown their brown hulks in the thundering herds. The tribe needed the meat to make into pemmican. For the hides and all of the other trading goods that they had always had to offer to the fur traders, they needed the buffalo. Their bellies growled and longed for the taste of the meat. They travelled miles without a glimpse of the herds they expected. At this place where the rivers met, they expected to see sign of the huge beasts looking for water. But there were no signs. Where had the buffalo gone?

Campbell shook his head at the natives and half-smiled as he signed to them that they had no whiskey, rum, guns, or ammunition. As he did this, he spoke quickly, loudly enough in Gaelic for all of the paddlers to hear without facing them. The natives might know a little English but not Gaelic.

"Boys, pretend that you're about to look for more trade goods as you get into your places. We're goin' t'beat a hasty retreat while we still have our scalps on our heads when we jump in, and shove off. They don't have their canoes here to follow; they came on horseback to chase buffalo and they do not have their guns with them, so row upstream as hard as you can. Now!"

On that signal, the men heaved the boats offshore, leaped in, and pulled as hard as they could upstream and toward the far shore. The natives with a cry of outrage ran into the river a few steps and then scrambled up the bank to grab their horses. They would not shoot after the fleeing Scotsmen. Their ammunition was low, and they had to save it for hunting, but they might be able to head the Nor'westers off on horseback.

Pulling hard at each stroke of their paddles, the men put all the power at their disposal to outdistance the natives. In spite of the strength of the current pulling them back, and though they were loaded to the gunwales with supplies and trade goods, the boats shot ahead. Behind them, they heard the frustrated scream of Indians in hot pursuit.

They watched as the lithe brown bodies, muscular and graceful, leaped onto their horses, the blood boiling in their veins and kicked their mounts into pursuit. The hair rose on the backs of the paddlers' necks as they realized that the distance was soon narrowing between boats and horsemen, and they doubled their efforts on the paddles. The riders soon pulled abreast of them, but when the horses were urged to swim towards the boats they fell back and drifted further downstream. One or two horsemen kept up with them on shore and shouted cries of anger across the water, but the boats soon pulled further away as they headed north across the wide expanse of water that was both the waters of the North and South Saskatchewan.

The wild force of the waters as they joined was enough to give the horseback riders all the problems they could handle. They headed back to shore to save their necks and that of their horses. The muddy turbulence of eddies and under-currents were not something the Indians wanted to battle. This fight was not worth it.

Sweating and straining, the paddlers did not slack off in their efforts until many miles upstream. Not a word was spoken or a song sung. All they could hear was the beating of their own hearts, their heavy breathing, and the water gurgling under the hull of their bumboats. It was funny how they took for granted that all of the natives in this western country were tame and friendly. This was 1863 after all; the fur trade had been carried on peacefully for nearly a hundred years. This was their first encounter with bad feeling between white and Indian and it shook them.

Now they peered warily into the bush along the high banks of the river. They knew about the moccasin telegraph. Far ahead of them, up the river, other Indians could already know about the Nor'westers who refused to trade with the tribe downriver.

But there was no sign of any more natives along the way. Still, they pulled and rowed and poled the heavy craft as far inland and up the river as they could before hunger and nighttime overtook them. That night they were almost too tired to eat and barely had the strength and energy to put up their little tents. They accomplished many more miles in one day than they ever did in the days since they'd left York Factory.

10

Fort Pitt Storm

Even when they came to the Eagle Hills rapids, they crossed them in record time. In these rapids, the sharp rocks protruded above the river so high that there was no opportunity to skirt around them or find a file and go through them. The sharp rocks made that course too dangerous. They could not risk the rocks doing damage to the bottom of the boat causing the cargo to get wet from a hole in the bottom allowing the river to get into the boat. They also did not want to be laid up while everything was unpacked, spread out to dry, and the holes repaired, taking the better part of the day.

The boats were flat-bottomed, bowed at each end and up the sides. The amount of wood made the boats so heavy that it could not be portaged, but other fur traders before them found a way around that. They cut logs from the woods, round saplings that were put down across the rapids in front of the rocks. Then the York boat was pulled across the logs. Rolling and sliding, as the voyagers put their backs to the ropes attached to the bow the boats inched their way, 'tracked', across the rapids with the odd scraping against the bottom of the boat. The wooden sides were covered with moose skins for an extra insurance against a leak, and it also helped the craft to slide a bit easier. If it looked as though a rock, protruding above the log rolls, was going to gouge a hole, an oarsman used his sixteen-foot paddle or another pole to pry the boat away from the danger.

It was backbreaking work, hauling and heaving the huge boat onto the log rollers and pulling it across the rocks in the rapids. When they got the bumboat to deeper water, they stopped on shore for a rest and a bite of hardtack before starting off again.

Either because of the strenuous pull or from the nerve-wracking escape from the Indian tribe, John slouched down over his arms on his knees, too tired and sore to eat. His muscles twitched and vibrated. He would have thrown himself down on the rocky shore and refused to rise again but the twitching of his muscles gave him no peace. There was nothing to do but keep going, slacking off in the quieter water until the muscle tension eased.

"Come noo, all ye men o' the Narth'west! Ye'd better hae some'at tae eat. Ye canna rest long. We must get gaen' afore ye stiffen up. It's a long piece afore we stop for the night. Fort Pitt is two days away." Chisholm from the second boat paced the rocky shore, anxious to get rowing.

The weary voyageurs rose and dragged themselves back to their places in the boat. Callused hands gripped the paddles again and feet braced against the ribbing of the boat as the oarsmen prepared for the next stretch, punching their way into the unknown.

Fort Pitt welcomed them so eagerly that they soon forgot about the unfriendly reception farther south. The factor was glad to see them. He had ordered supplies and was told by the last boat that they would be along on the next boat. The Nor'westers would have liked to get rid of the two kegs of rum, but they were scheduled for Fort Edmonton. Ever since the confrontation with the Indians at the South Saskatchewan junction, they felt that the rum kegs were volatile. Between the rum, the guns, and the bullets, they felt these were not worth the work it cost them in extra weight and worry.

The Indian women crowded around the two boats and followed the voyageurs up to the factor's store. Many stood around inside the store feeling the merchandise, looking for something to trade for pemmican or furs. Pemmican was always popular with travellers, but the factor did not want to take in too much at a time.

"We expected to meet the four boats frae Edmonton here on their way back to Yark Factory wi' a load o' furs," Campbell commented to the burly factor with the stump of a pipe gripped in his teeth. "They must be delayed. Way didna mait them alang the way."

The factor was also Scottish as were most in the northwest. He could slip back and forth between Cree and English in an instant as well as recognize the broad accent that passed for English. From the back room, an

Indian woman stepped forth, and he gave her instructions in Cree. He then turned back to Campbell and Douglas. "Ye can unload the cloth, the blankets and the foodstuff over there. Wapatomi will look after it. I will sign the form for it and take it off the furs when the other boats come tae pick them up. Have ye got them all itemized?"

Wapatomi was fairly heavy on her feet with a wee one in a cradleboard on her back and another in her tummy. She waddled over to the sacks that the men deposited on the floor in the storeroom and took charge. The young voyageurs stared at Wapatomi. The factor had obviously not heard of the Hudson's Bay Company rule about not taking on a native woman, wife, or 'live-in'.

"Wapatomi," the factor called out to her, "when ye're finished there, bring these men coffee. They've travelled far." Wapatomi grunted and nodded.

"It looks like rain out there tonight. Probably a thunderstorm judging by the clouds rolling in," the factor told them as he peered out the window. "I suggest thah ye park ye'r tents under thah overhanging ledge and away from the edges. That's where the water runs down off the cliff. It becomes a rael river sometimes. If ye have an extra canvas cover ye'd best throw it over ye're tents in case it's hail."

Wapatomi brought in the tin cups with the steaming hot coffee then, and the men pulled up bundles, kegs, and stools, mouths watering for the taste of coffee. All they had along the trail was weak tea. Coffee would really taste good. As soon as they brought the steaming cup up to their noses, they knew that it did not smell like any coffee they ever had before. But after blowing on it to cool it to taste they sipped.

Looking at each other in surprise and just a little downturn of the mouth in reaction to the bitter taste, they telegraphed their disappointment to the host.

"Ach, ye discovered that this is noh ye're usual coffee," the factor laughed loudly. "It takes some getting used to. Wapatomi introduced me to it. She roasts these tubers and roots and crushes them up to a fine powder. When she pours hot water on a spoonful, it makes this grand drink, and it's good fer ye. It keeps the chills away – keeps ye frae gettin' the shakin' sickness and the diarrhea. It can even remove warts if ye soak it in the brew. She makes a good tea, the yarrow tea that keeps ye're teeth frae fallin' oot and ye're gums frae pullin' away. It's good fer washin' out wounds too. It can soothe a sore throat or settle an upset stomach. Wapatomi is a regular doctor. She can cure what ails ye."

The boys were having a hard time to choke down the bitter brew, but agreed before they finished their cups it was not all that bad!

"We'd better get set up for the night and eat our supper before the rain moves in," McTavish interjected after a glance at the gathering gloom outside as heavy clouds swept across the sky. The men hurriedly finished their bitter brew and headed for the door. They had not as yet covered and battened down the supply-laden boats.

Before their meal was finished, brief as it was, the wind started up and rumblings of thunder were heard in the west. The fire was scattered about by the wind, and sparks were flying around.

"John, deal wi' that fire. Tear it doon. The rain will likely put it oot nae doot," Campbell shouted as he, Norman and Duncan covered the boat and secured it. The other crew was doing the same. The others in the crew hurriedly put up their tents, wrestling with the canvas as the wind tried to tear the flimsy things from their hands.

"Come and help wi' this thing," McTavish shouted to Cameron and Alex as he and Douglas's crew tried to anchor the large canvas protective covering to the cliff wall behind them to make a large tent covering. The recess in the wall had been gouged out by countless river floods in the past and afforded some measure of protection. The high overhead bank that leaned out over them made a completely inadequate roof since the rain and the wind slanted in from the west, but it sheltered them on one side if they huddled against the wall.

Stakes were hammered into the gravelly beach, and the two canvas coverings were anchored at the front after spreading out over the small tents. The voyagers would have to crawl underneath it on their bellies, but at least it would slant down so that the rain would run off.

A crash of thunder and flash of light sent the men scurrying from their last minute chores to slide underneath the canvas for protection. But then the wind whipping at the edge of the canvas yanked it away from the stake and sent it flapping wildly in the wind. While the rain started pelting down upon them, two of Douglas's crew grabbed the flapping canvas and retied it to the stake. They tied both sails together to make the large cover but the sails billowed up with the wind and continued to yank away at the moorings.

A nerve shattering bolt of lightning and blast of thunder sent a hail of rocks tumbling down the cliff behind them. Some of the rocks bounced on the canvas and rolled off but thankfully did no damage. Some of the rocks that rolled to the beach below the canvas lip were as large as a man's head. Cameron and John looked at each other imagining what would have happened had they not the overhead protection. But they also wondered if the next strike would bring down bigger pieces of the wall. They did not like the thought of being buried alive under half the cliff. It was as though the very skies were breaking apart, and they huddled in expectation of the worst.

Rain pelted on the roof while several of the men held onto corners of the sail that wanted to pull out of their hands. Finally, the thunder and lightning ebbed away leaving in its wake a steady pounding rain. With the quieting of the wind, the men were able to tend to their bedrolls and pup tents. It was a close fit, putting twenty triangular shaped tents under the space, but the quarters were dry under their blankets, at least temporarily.

As the factor had warned them, streams rolled off the hill behind them, bound for the river, and trickled across the sand and gravel around them. One or two of the men ended up with wet blankets and had to move their tent out of the way of the stream. Others ignored the wet blankets and continued to sleep through the night.

By morning the rain stopped and the sun tinted the clear eastern sky above the tree-covered hills with pink. The Nor'westers woke starving, for they had not eaten much the night before. They smelled the wood smoke and knew that McTavish was up starting the fire. At Douglas's fire in the next camp, they smelled salt pork frying in the pan, and their stomachs growled in response.

Crawling out from under the canvas sails, hanging sadly limp and crumpled, John commented to Murdock Chisholm that they looked about like he felt, and he wandered to the bush to start the morning toilet. He circled the bank and climbed partway up the hill to find a log to sit on and spend some time in concentration. He could hear a sparrow tuning up as it approached the day in a gingerly fashion after the storm had torn leaves and branches from the trees above. How fresh and newly washed the day felt, but it would not take long until the Nor'westers changed that. The mosquitoes swarmed out of the grass attacking bare skin, the most of which was exposed on his rear end, so he ended that job as fast as he could.

Streams still trickled downhill and across the stones toward the river, and he followed them. Staring at the amber water rattling over the stones, he washed his face in the river and then observed his reflection in the water. Just a stubble of a fine beard covered his face, reddish like his hair that reached to his shoulders. He planned to leave it that way until his beard was as red and bushy as McTavish's and then he would look like a *real* voyageur.

McTavish always saw to it that the boys had a good breakfast before beginning the day. This morning it was salt pork and beans with some hardtack to soak into it.

"Well b'ys," Campbell announced as they ate, "the next trading post is Victoria Mission, two or maybe thray days away, depending on how well we make oot on the rapids. Let's get on our way! Maybe we can outrun the mosquitoes. Thah is the one thing that keeps us movin'."

11

Victoria – The English Fort

Victoria Mission was different from the other trading posts. Indians had tents set up nearby, and a large log building with a crudely constructed steeple and cross rising from above the front door was the most dominant structure. It sat on the highest point of land and could be seen from quite a distance up and down-river. Adding to its attraction, the cross was stained red and was a curiosity and an object of awe to the natives.

Methodist missionary, George McDougall, with his twenty-year-old son John, had established the mission and named it after Queen Victoria. With the help of the Cree, he and his son cleared land, built a church, which doubled as the school, and a small cabin. The Hudson's Bay took advantage of the strategic area to build a fur trading post. Indians from miles north, nearly as far as the Athabasca River where other unfriendly tribes from the north claimed territory, came south to the Victoria Mission outpost.

Sometimes there was a sea of tents set up in the clearing near the church, looking to trade at the post or to check out the curious building under the big red cross.

When the Nor'westers pulled their boats up to the newly constructed pier, curious natives also came down to greet them. Some of them approached with a few words in English that surprised the crew.

Crowding around the boats the Indians asked from where they had travelled and what they had in their big canoes.

"The natives are being taught tae speak English?" McTavish wondered aloud. "Who is taiching them? Whah is he doin' up hair this far narth?"

"Maybe wai'll find thah oot from the factor up at the trading post," Campbell answered as they started up the bank towards the log cabin with the British flag fluttering from the roof.

"Chisholm, preparing to follow Campbell's lead, indicated that the rest stay with the boats in case the Indians should get overly curious.

Tramping up the steps that climbed the bank, the men paused on the verandah to look out over the river and countryside below. It was quite a high vantagepoint, but the church with its tall red cross was an even higher viewpoint. Trees stretched below them as far as the eye could see: white and black poplar, spruce and pine. Lush valleys dotted the hillsides and steep riverbank. A small creek tumbled into the mighty river from the hills. The scene was breathtaking, peaceful, and the Nor'westers could see why the spot was chosen.

"Good evening," said a voice behind them. They turned to greet a husky, broad-shouldered man in his fifties. He had greying sparse blonde hair, a huge greying moustache, and an unkempt beard that had stains from the snuff that he chewed. "Are you from York Factory?" He asked in English He stuck his thumbs underneath braces that extended across an ample belly. With feet astride and wide chest expanded, he let the voyageurs know that he was the proprietor of the establishment.

"Campbell nodded in greeting. "The natives at the landing waire speakin' tae us in English."

"This fort is new, but I've been up in this north country for many years. My name's Henderson. Josh Henderson." He stuck out a hand and gave Campbell's and Douglas's a bone-crushing shake. "I used to be in Edmonton at the trading post there, but I was sent up here when this mission was built. It was an ideal location to trade with the Indians, and a friendly one. Come in!" Josh stepped back to invite the visitors inside.

"Campbell and Chisholm followed Henderson into the crowded quarters, looking around the dim interior with its rough board floor of split timbers. The two Scots viewed an assortment of trade goods. Stacked up on shelves behind the counter were canned goods, bottles of medicine, bolts of cloth, pots and pans, furs fashioned into hats, coats and mitts, Hudson Bay blankets, pipes, Indian fashioned buckskin, and various tools. On the walls and on the floor were kegs of nails, snowshoes, guns, Red River cart wheels, canvas, leather straps, and belts.

"The language of the fur trade now seems to be English. At one time it was French and in some areas, still is. But McDougall speaks English and is teaching the Cree to speak it. Much of Edmonton is English so the natives need to learn it to trade.

"By the way, you'll notice that there are no kegs of whiskey or rum in my post." Josh paused for effect. "That is because McDougall won't allow the stuff to be brought in."

"How is it that a man with a name like McDougall speaks and teaches English and not Gaelic?" Chisholm asked, still curious.

"His father left Scotland, and George was born in England and raised there." Josh moved around in behind his counter, a spot where he obviously felt most comfortable. "George, raised a devout Methodist, came into favour with Queen Victoria, and she sent him to the New World to minister to and teach the natives. He lived for several years in Upper Canada with the Indians. Then he and his family spent two years in Norway House on the Nelson River."

"Norway House," Chisholm echoed. "We usually stop there on our route. I remember seeing that building wi' the cross on top. He must hae built it and ministered there." Both he and Campbell also remembered that they had not had a very good experience at Norway House, the theft of all of their furs and supplies. "Things hae noh been gaen' well since he left there, I suppose."

"His wife and children are still there," Henderson remarked, wondering why Chisholm had made the comment. "He just came west with his son to prepare a place for his family before moving them up. We're all looking forward to it. We get very few white women up this way. There's Mrs. McDougall and her two daughters. I'm sure George would leave them in good hands." He left the remark almost like a question aimed at Chisholm and Campbell, but neither of the men enlightened him any further.

"But you are wondering if you can set up your tents and stay the night are you not?" Henderson came around his counter again and pointed out a spot up the bank from the pier. "You're welcome to join the camp meetin' up near the church tonight. Then you'll get a chance to meet George, his son John, and John's new wife, Abigail, and see George in action. It was supposed to be inside the church but the Indians are more comfortable outside on the grass around the fire. I guess they'll move inside come winter."

12

Preacher Under the Stars

After the voyageurs had their evening meal and set up their tents, they drifted up the hillside towards the high dancing fire between the tipis and the church. Coming out of his trading post, Henderson fell in beside them and accompanied them up to the camp meeting.

A platform had been roughly put together on which George McDougall was to stand to address the congregation. The Indians sat in double and triple rows in a circle around the fire, facing the platform, the women and children behind, the men in the front rows. Though they waited in eager anticipation, they were stolidly silent and stern.

The imposing George McDougall strode out onto the platform in his dark suit. Though slightly threadbare in spots and rumpled, it commanded everyone's attention. His face was handsome yet, though his black hair was greying, as well as his black beard that covered only the bottom part of his face, just a shock of black extending from sideburns to his chin. His hair was neatly combed away from his face and high white forehead. His nose was aquiline; his lips were full but unsmiling.

His eyes, however, were the most spectacular of his visage. They were a startling blue under straight black brows and when he looked at someone it was as though he looked right into their hearts and pierced their souls. He took the time to look directly at each and everyone around the fire, particularly the newcomers, the voyageurs. Though they settled themselves well back and to the side of the Indians, he singled them out with his direct gaze.

McDougall spoke partly in Cree and partly in English, slowly, clearly and forcefully so that no one would miss a word.

"My children." he began, "My dear children of the Victoria Mission. I bring you all greetings from the Queen, the Great White Mother across the wide waters. You are all welcome at this fire." Raising his hands to the sky he intoned: "The Great Spirit and his son Jesus Christ smile down on you this day and will as long as ye have faith in his teachings and his saving grace."

He turned then, and spread his hand, bidding his son to join him on the platform. "This is my son John and his wife Abigail." John was very much like his father though not as imposing in stature, and Abigail was slight in build, dressed in ornately decorated doeskin, soft and fringed. She was a Cree, the daughter of their beloved Henry Steinhauer, their own Métis missionary. To the natives she was more like a princess and must surely be like the Queen Victoria of which McDougall spoke so eloquently.

Both John and his father were well aware that Abigail lent the trio a credibility and an aura that was close to divine. Just that day an Indian woman had rushed to Abigail to summon her to a tipi where one of their women was having her baby and was in difficulty. Abigail was able to help. She learned many things from her mother, the wife of Steinhauer, since she was a medicine woman and Abigail also benefited from her father's knowledge of simple healing procedures.

A few days ago she, along with her father-in-law, was also summoned to the bedside of another woman with a skin ailment. They had thought it was smallpox, and the whole camp was thrown into a state of alarm. George was especially worried. Smallpox was the scourge of the West. If it got into his mission camp, that would be the end of it. A few years back the terrifyingly lethal disease that struck down so many Indians, depleted many of their numbers in many villages. The blame was laid at the door of the white population, especially Peter Pond when he explored and traded with them as part of the Northwest Company. George and his mission did not need that, just when the mission was getting established.

Abigail realized that the red bumps that covered the woman's face were a reaction to a plant in the area and her illness was the result of her terror. Calmly, Abigail prepared infusions to take away and cool the itch and soon the woman was back to normal. So Abigail and John were understandably held in awe and near worship.

George prayed with the people as their heads were bowed in front of him, and he read to them from his well-worn black leather-bound Bible. He told them of the coming of Jesus and of how true civilization originated with Christianity. Jesus, he said, would some day return to live among them. Finally, he spoke loudly in a voice that rumbled across the audience like the voice of thunder.

"And I say to you children of the Great Spirit, indulge not in the pagan practices of self-mutilation, idolatry and polygamy. In them, the teachings of this great book of His word are ignored, but remember his words and live by them."

It had just come to George McDougall's attention that a relative of one of the men had cut off his wife's nose, as was the custom, because she was believed to be an adulteress. McDougall was appalled and devoted the entire next sermon to the topic. He fought the custom of the Cree to allow themselves to be skewered through the breast skin and muscle and be strung up in the air for long periods of time, being supported only by this strip of skin. This was part of the Sun Dance ritual that warriors endured to receive pity for the tribe from the Spirit World. The form of self-torture came to the Northern Cree from the Southern Blackfoot. McDougall abhorred this kind of self-mutilation, this ugly and detrimental form of tribal ritual. To simplify his teaching he explained and gave examples, descriptions and demonstrations to many words until they understood clearly what he told them.

"Now, my children." He turned to include John and Abigail who flanked him patiently through the service. "I must tell you that my son John and his wife will soon be leaving us." At this point a murmur of disappointment rippled through his audience. He held up his hand and went on. "I know you have come to love and enjoy their time spent with you. I will miss them as well. They are going to start another mission like this one, farther south. They will be leaving by cart and ox tomorrow morning. I will bless their journey, bid them safe passage throughout until they find their new mission. If in your travels ye should meet, may you remember and wish them well. May we see them again soon."

They sang hymns at the end then. The Cree remembered many of the words and joined in. George's rich baritone soared above all of the others, a voice that seemed to boom out and echo across the river below, shaking the very ground at their feet. After this, they filed past John and Abigail to bid them farewell.

The voyageurs had a chance to shake hands with the trio and introduce themselves while Henderson stayed near to translate for anyone who needed it. Then they drifted away, back to their own dying fire and their tents.

Josh Henderson joined them for awhile at their fire to meet the rest of the boys and to talk. "He's a fire and brimstone kind of preacher with a voice like a branding iron if someone commits a sin. He's been fighting the Indian idol worshipping ever since he arrived." Josh held his audience spellbound as he recited the tales of George McDougall and his battle with the pagan worshipping of idols.

"But in trying to swing the natives over to his way of thinking he's done a lot of things that would make your jaw drop." Josh settled down on a log, spat out his quid of tobacco, and started in with his tale.

"Just south of here where the Battle River lies, is the place where you had the run-in with the hunting tribe. That is the river where so many lives were lost, Indian and white because of wars over firewater, buffalo, unscrupulous traders, and tribal warfare. It is also the place where a huge iron stone fell from the sky. It landed on a hill near where the two rivers join. The Indians believed that the stone was placed there by the Great Spirit. It was actually a huge four-hundred pound meteorite, made of iron so soft it could be cut with a knife."

Henderson could see that the voyageurs were sitting erect and leaning forward in fascination, so he took his time, drawing out his story. "Indians from miles around made treks to the stone and left spirit offerings. They cut away pieces of the stone and took the blue-grey hunk of soft rock. They shaped and tested out its usefulness. Some said the stone cried out when parts were cut from it so they had to also suffer if it was cut.

"Some say that the stone seemed to grow. When it first landed, the elders said, it could be lifted but now it was impossible. If suitable offerings were left or self-torture endured, they could take from the stone or be protected on their journeys from death, injury, or starvation. Prostrating themselves to the stone, they felt close to the Great Spirit and under His protection. They could beseech the spirit for His protection and feel strong and beyond danger.

"But one day the stone disappeared." Josh stopped and looked around at the faces lit by the flickering fire, eagerly awaiting the outcome. "Indian tribes for miles around, from the buffalo hunters to the fur traders in the North Country, from the Blackfoot to the Cree to the Peigans to the Métis all shuddered with premonition of disaster. The buffalo will disappear, their medicine and wise men predicted; there will be fierce wars and starvation. Already this is happening as the Indian tribe you met down at the joining of the Battle and the Saskatchewan discovered. They think the white man has caused the Spirit to take back his gift of the stone.

"But it was not the Great Spirit who withdrew his terrible stone," Josh Henderson told them ominously. "It was man! Two men! George McDougall and his son John! George regarded that stone as a pagan idol, and no man should worship an idol. He and his son left in the dead of night with the Red River cart, the same one that John will be taking to the South country to set up his mission, and travelled the one hundred miles south to the Battle River where the stone lay. With logs as ramp and pry, they rolled the huge stone onto the cart and took it to Fort Garry where it was sent to Upper Canada to be on display in their Methodist college.

Some Indians, who suspect that it was McDougall who moved the stone, thought it only proof that he was a warrior for his faith. Others, suspicious of this white man, who set himself up against the wrath of the Great Spirit, left the mission and melted back into the woods. Around their council fires they whisper that, like the buffalo, someday soon He will also disappear. The Great Spirit will abandon His people."

There was silence around the campfire as the Scots, their thoughts their own, gazed into the dancing flames. John was glad that they were moving on the next day. McDougall was certainly a clever and successful man in the job he had taken on, educating the natives and protecting them, but he did not agree with McDougall's methods. McDougall was taking a terrible chance. John was recalling the confrontation downriver where the waters of the Saskatchewan divided. However, he soon put it out of his mind as he climbed into his bedroll.

13

The Chief Factor's Plans

From Victoria Mission they headed southwest towards Fort Edmonton. Much of their load would stay there. That was the biggest, busiest fur trading post in the West. Paths by the northern tribes were being beaten to the biggest northern post, Fort Edmonton.

The river, still wide and full, was not as treacherous as it had been further east. Powerful arms shot the heavy boat forward and made better time. Edmonton counted its wealth in beaver pelts, and voyageurs set out daily from the flats for the East or farther west to Rocky Mountain House. Indians streamed in by foot from the north, east, and west with pemmican and furs to trade. Pemmican was a necessary item. All the travellers needed it for their travelling food.

With their food supply getting low, the Scots poured more strength into the paddles. They would make it to Fort Edmonton as early as the next day. Along the riverside the voyageurs caught glimpses of Indians and sometimes white hunters or settlers. It was encouraging. Civilization was near.

Now the Nor'westers began to sing, raising their voices together in joyful Gaelic:
"If a body meet a body comin' through the rye
If a body kiss a body need a body cry?
Every lassie hae a laddie. Nane they say hae I.
Yet all the lads they smile on me
When comin' through the rye.

If a body meet a body comin' frae the toon.
If a body kiss a body need a body froon

Amang the twain there is a swain I dearly love mysel'
But what's his name or where's his hame
I dinna choose to tell."

When they stopped that night as the sun was sinking below the horizon, they feasted on the last of their pemmican and fresh fish that McTavish took out of the river and cleaned before they docked the boats.

"Look over there!" Alistair pointed. "Up the bank." They all strained to see in the gathering gloom what Alistair was directing their attention to.

Then they noticed a thin trail of smoke spiralling up above the trees. A small cabin was tucked into the shelter of the trees, and a small newly cleared field suggested that a farmer had set down roots on this stretch of land next to the river. A little path threaded down the gentle slope to the water, and a man was dipping water from the river in a pail preparing to carry it up to his cabin on the bank above.

"Look up by the cabin. Thah is one ae them Red River carts thah they came West in," Cameron pointed out.

It seemed very small to have carried all of a family's worldly possessions and his family. It was no more than six or seven feet in length and the crude wheels stood six feet high.

"They came West in that?" Alex Macleod questioned in astonishment, remembering the rough journey they had with a boat and the time it took them. "Nae shelter frae the rain or wind?"

"Ach, they would be able tae put up a tarp from the sides like a tent tae sleep under," Campbell interjected as he moved up behind them. "But there would be noh protection frae the dust. I hae seen trains ae those Red River carts travellin' across the prairie kickin' up a cloud ae dust that could be sain for miles."

"And they had thae advantage o'er the Yark Boats," William Douglas commented as he joined them from the other camp. "When this river starts tae freeze over, thah is the end ae travel fer awhile. But the carts can travel in winter or summer."

"Never aisily, mind ye!" Campbell interjected. "I hae sain those carts bogged down in mud sae that they couldna move for days. But women are starting to come West wi' their men, and no matter how noisy those carts were or how bogged down they got in the mud the women refused to lave any of their precious belongings behind."

"Buh they goh haire!" Douglas rested his case. "And they hae found themselves a piece ae the West tae claim as their own."

John and Cameron ran down the rocky river shore and across the grassy, scrub willow stretch around the bend to meet and talk to the hardy farmer. When they returned and the man climbed the bank with his buckets of water, the voyageurs gathered around.

"Whah did he say?" Duncan wanted to know.

"Where did he come frae? Is that his land?" Alex asked.

"We dinna ken," John answered in disappointment. "We couldna understand a werrd he said." Suddenly the crew realized that this was only the beginning of their struggle to understand and make themselves understood. They were no better off with the white people than they were with the Indians.

They bedded down for the night in the shelter of the willows along shore. The river silt from former river flooding made a soft bed, and as their fire died to glowing coals, they listened to the night sounds and the river as it gurgled and whispered a few yards away.

Fort Edmonton was all that people warned them about and more. The deep canyon walls that the river threaded through soon pulled back into a protected valley. Along the top of the cutbanks marched the dark ridge of trees that stood like silent soldiers guarding the cliffs. Around a bend they were overwhelmed with the immensity of the fort. On top of a slope, on a plateau below steeper banks above were the walls of the fort. On the flats below the fort was a sea of grey-white tents and dozens of people, horses, carts, wagons and oxen. Lining the river were boats, logs that had been floated in from upstream and were in the process of being split into slabs, Indian canoes, fishermen and stacks of boxes, parcels, and packages on barges.

They searched for a spot to pull into. Finally, Campbell spotted a Hudson Bay Company man whom he knew and who waved him in to a spot where they could unload. Here, the York boats would be unpacked and the contents carried up to the Hudson Bay post inside the fort. The Hudson's Bay Company could not lay claim to Fort Edmonton – only a small building inside the fort where goods could be sorted, stored, and repacked to be shipped in other directions. The majority of this would go on an eighty-mile portage north to the Athabasca River.

At this point the Campbell and Douglas crews were finished with the contents of the boats. As soon as they carted the load up the hill inside the fort, their job was finished. They could relax for awhile and enjoy the bustling fort. They separated their personal baggage, and with it slung over their backs, they left to find the office where they would find out what would happen to them next.

Part of the Bay Company post was a food depot where Indian women pounded buffalo meat into pemmican that would go out with the next crews. More men were bringing in buffalo meat from their hunting expedition in the south. Others were coming in with sacks of barley, oats and potatoes slung over their backs. These would all be harvested and stored. It was a beehive of activity.

What stunned the York boat crew was that, as they feared, they could not understand a word that anyone was saying. The cacophony of sounds about them as they walked through the fort's wide gates among the processions of Indians, traders, and scouts from the south on horseback. All of that crowd and workers laden with heavy packages was both exciting and frightening.

Entering the office of the Hudson Bay factor, they stood facing Factor Stevenson's wide desk. He had white sideburns, an ample mid-section, receding hairline, and was in high boots and a dark, though worn suit. And he spoke with an English accent.

"Good work, boys," Stevenson praised. "You got the supplies here in good order. You will stay the night and perhaps tomorrow night in the bunkhouses here in the fort. Then you will have your new orders."

Douglas moved forward with his proposal for the chief factor. "I believe we still hae time to takk a load ae furs back doon the river tae York Factory before freeze-up. If we lave soon we can make it while it's still warm."

"You might very well have time to take another load back down East, even though it is very late in the season. However, I don't have a load for you. Nor do I have a load for the next two boats that are expected in here any day now. The last fur trading expedition that left a few weeks back had to be sent north to Athabasca Landing. From there they will have to portage over to the Churchill River to the Hudson's Bay. But before they do that, they will have to build new boats at the Athabasca Landing for the trip east. They will have to build the lighter canoes because the Methye Portage can not be managed with York boats."

The boat crew looked at each other wide-eyed, remembering the story that Campbell told them about his first experiences on the Churchill River and across the Methye Portage.

"They will be spending the winter with the Indians up there while they collect the furs and build the canoes. In the spring they will take the furs east on the dreaded Methye, the hardest part of the trip. They will not only be carrying the canoes, but the load of furs, and they will be sinking up to their knees in muskeg. No more easy trip for them!"

"So air ye sayin' thah ye will be sendin' us o'erland tae Athabasca tae spend the winter in the narth?" Campbell demanded in alarm.

"No, I am not saying that." Stevenson put up his hand in denial. "Your crew will be travelling further west towards the mountains as far as Rocky Mountain House. At one time we could count on enough furs to be brought into Fort Edmonton by the Indians. But either the Indians are not doing any trapping, or else there is another group that they are trading with; perhaps the Northwest Company has started up again. I am sending you to find out what is happening to the furs. We are getting half as many as we should."

"So way will still be on the Narth Saskatchewan River." Chisholm was visibly relieved. He knew this river like the back of his hand. Panic set in at the thought of discovering a whole new river system.

"You will still be travelling up the Saskatchewan, but you will have to build more outposts on the river and travel out from there. I want you to find those Indians and explore that country until you find out what is happening to those furs!" Stevenson struck his palm with his fist as he paced the floor, his mouth in a grim line.

"How can we get the Indians to trade wi' us if another fur trading company has started up in opposition to the Hudson's Bay Company?" Richard Chisholm asked in concern. Usually quiet and stoic this unflappable man was disturbed by this news. Like Campbell and Douglas he knew the North Saskatchewan River and faced every challenge without flinching. But this was yanking him right out of his comfort zone and into a strange new situation.

"It means making friends with the Indians–getting to know them and getting them to trust you," Stevenson explained patiently. "I'll need one or two of you to travel across country to Lac Ste. Anne to the Mission. I don't trust those missionaries. They all speak French over there and they've taught the natives to speak French and to accept their religion. This may be their way to yank the fur trade right out from under our noses."

Stevenson was getting fired up with self-righteous anger. "All the land out here west of us belongs to the Bay. No other company has a right to trade for furs but us. If the Northwest Company, under the pretense of being missionaries, are stealing them away from us, they've got a fight coming."

"I thought the Narthwest Company joined the Hudson Bay Company yairs ago," Campbell commented quietly.

"They never did like the fact that most of the furs by-passed Quebec and went either south to the States or else north to York Factory," Stevenson fairly shouted in his English accent, making the Nor'westers jump.

"We maught hae t'bairn the mission doon like the Narthwest Company did wi' Hudson Bay Company forts," Chisholm grumbled. "Thah will roust those French out ae there and send them back doon East where they came frae."

"Now be careful what you're doing," Stevenson cautioned a little more quietly. "The missionaries are well-loved by the Indians. They live right with the savages. They teach them and doctor them. And you know how those savages love ceremony and singing. That religion stuff was right up their alley. A couple of years ago they even brought a bunch of nuns up to the mission from Montreal. The Indians make their treks to the mission on Lac Ste. Anne just to see the white women in their grey garb."

"They sent a bunch ae women oot tae the West tae the mission?" Douglas was incredulous.

"But the worst of the bunch is a priest they call Father Lacombe," Stevenson started pacing again. "Here you have a young Catholic boy looking for wild adventure with a half-breed Grandma and an Uncle Joseph who worked for the Northwest Company. Now, I ask you? If that doesn't sound suspicious, I don't know what does!" He paused, facing them, hands outspread, his face red and his jowls shaking.

"It cood be thah he railly is concerned for the welfare ae the Indians and fer spreading the word ae the Gospel," Campbell remarked, himself a God-fearing man.

"If you believe that, you really are a fool!" Stevenson struck his fist against the desk with impatience. "Now he's not far north of Fort Edmonton on the trail to Athabasca Landing, and he's dug in for a long stay. He's established a church and a school to teach the natives to speak French and to read. They say he's even working on a dictionary in Cree. They're calling the place St Albert. I hear they're planning to move the mission with all the Grey Nuns. It looks to me like he's planning to rival Fort Edmonton and make that the central post from the prairies to the North country. That's where he came from–the prairies–from Red Deer–getting his nose into the buffalo trade no doubt. No wonder we've not seen many buffalo hides and meat coming from the south lately."

"I hear the buffalo on the prairie air gittin' scarce." Chisholm spoke up, recalling their standoff at the confluence of the North and South Saskatchewan rivers.

"Someone down there is trying to make us believe that," Stevenson nodded knowingly. "I don't believe it. Probably trying to get us to pay more for the hides and meat. That's what it's all about. Trade!"

There was a pause in the conversation as Stevenson moved around behind his desk and sat down. The voyageurs looked at each other a little baffled. Half of what they heard was confusing to them. Where they were to go next? They sat staring back at the chief factor.

"I'll find you bunks next door here inside the fort," the factor finally broke the silence. "You're free to roam the fort and take in the activities. There's a tavern at the end of the square, and if you go to the west by the river on the flats you'll find a two-mile racetrack. There'll be horseracing tomorrow. If the betting is a little rich for your blood, you can always watch the ponies run and bet between you. It attracts a big crowd. There used to be a whorehouse above the tavern until the missionaries shut that down after talking to the women.

"That's another thing that those damned missionaries did to us. They never thought but that was the only thing those women had to live on, with free room and board too." Stevenson was getting wound up again. "They even tried to shut down the race track, but they didn't succeed there.

The Indians were getting really excited about the races and were getting carried away with the betting. That's what the missionaries were complaining about." He threw up his hands in disgust.

The Nor'westers began talking in low voices in Gaelic about their chances in the future fur trade as they had been doing.

"By the way," Stevenson spoke up as the troop headed out the door to look for their bunks. "While you're up in Ruperts Land you'd better stick to speaking English. Not many in the fort will be able to understand your Gaelic."

14

Sight Seeing and Entertainment

Depressed and tired, the Scots headed in the direction of the bunk-house. Then they began to be interested in the 'Big House", an eighty-foot, three storey white frame building in which lived Factor Stevenson and before him the other chief factors of the fort. It had genuine glass windows and had a gallery running around its circumference. It was the biggest building in the compound.

Around the inner edge of the fort's wooden slab walls were bunkhouses for employees, usually Bay Company personnel who worked in and around the fort. Other buildings such as store houses, sorting and workhouses, barns and equipment sheds, offices, places of business, blacksmith, harness-making shop, cafeteria, tavern, and trading stores were spread out in seemingly haphazard fashion across the square. Some wooden sidewalks led from one building to the other and some were dusty paths across the well-trampled surface. Ruts, clods, and bumps suggested that it had recently been very muddy. Deep tracks were left by carts, buggies, horses and people's feet.

Inside the dark interior of the bunkhouses that were windowless and bare except for narrow bunks against the wall, and a small barrel heater, the men deposited their packs. They never carried much. They were not allowed to, because they had to be prepared to haul supplies to and from the York boats.

They then set out to explore the fort in its entirety. People swarmed by them, not knowing or caring who they were and many talking in strange languages. The Scots were able to recognize many words in English, but most were not yet comfortable with the language.

Suddenly, their heads swung around as one when they heard some-one nearby speaking Gaelic. Stopping to locate it, they noticed two young fellows about their age. Impulsively, before they could stop him, Alistair hurried over to join the two. While they waited for him, he spoke quickly to the two men. Finally, he returned, and John asked eagerly, "Whah did they say?"

"They left the fur trade," Alistair told his friends. "They are both look-ing for jobs here in the West, and then when they save enough money, they are gaen' tae buy property and settle doon. Only, they want tae head south to the prairies. They want tae haird cattle across the barder from the United States, on horseback. They plan tae be cowboys. They might even get a chance, they said, tae chase the buffalo hairds."

The voyageurs stared at Alistair, then turned and headed on their tour in silence, each busy with his own thoughts. Thoughts of chasing from the back of a horse a lunging, pounding mass of shaggy, dusty brown, hairy animals, hurtling across the prairies while the ground rumbled under their feet, filled their minds.

But that was a big step, they suddenly reasoned. Without the Company looking after you, how would you even get there? How could you be sure that you would get your job? How would you live until you got there? None of them had even ridden a horse. They did not know anything else but the fur trade.

Other strange voices speaking strange languages passed by them until Cameron called out, "Look, there's a Scotsman with a business up here in the West." It was a sign on a fur curing and tannery building with a false front in white boards, and log cabin behind the false front. The sign read, "Furs Cured and Tanned, W.D. McLean, Proprietor."

"I'm thinkin' thah he can spaik Gaelic. Wi' a name like McLean, he has to be a Scotsman," Alex threw over his shoulder as he lead the way towards the building and up the step to the porch.

Alex called out an Orkney Island greeting and started talking enthu-siastically in Gaelic. "It's good to meet a fellow Scotsman. Have you lived here in the West long?" he asked. The man stared at them and shook his head in confusion. He could neither speak nor understand the language of their birth.

John came forward then and indicated the skins hanging on the wall in various stages of curing. In his heavily accented English he told McLean that he wanted to know how McLean had done that. There was a bearskin tacked to a board stretching. And there were muskrat hides, one of which McLean took off the wall and turned over, indicating that it had been carefully scraped and dried. Another skin he brought forward to show how soft and pliable it had become with tanning. When McLean asked John in English if he wanted to buy the skin, John shook his head and pulled out empty pockets sadly.

The man hung the furs back up on the wall briskly, realizing that these boys were only curious. After looking around the little shop and feeling the texture of the furs, the Scots drifted towards the door.

"How cood he hae a Scottish name and can noh understand the Gaelic tongue?" Alex mourned sadly.

"There's a good many paeple in Scotland who grew up in the south under the British who never learned tae speak Gaelic. They went tae British schools and grew up under the British monarchy. And there air some whose parents brought them o'er to Narth America a century agae," John said sadly. "I guess Stevenson is right. If we're gae'n tae stay here in the West for any stretch ae time, we're gae'n tae hae tae learn tae speak better English."

The sun was setting and the stars were beginning to shine as they made their way towards the far end of the fort. They could barely see the path ahead of them but the lights in the windows felt warm and inviting. Behind them and against the far wall, there were clusters of lamp-lit cabins. As they had been directed, they located the tavern and opened the worn and stained door.

The smell of smoke, sweat, and beer assailed them as they pushed inside. Men sat hunched around tables while the smoke curled up and clung to the ceiling beams, choking the illumination of the oil lamps suspended there. A soot-grey gloom obscured the air, stinging the nostrils, but the young Scots pressed forward into the noisy, heavy atmosphere until they reached the long bar. Behind the bartender there were rows of bottles and a barrel of beer tipped on its side with a tap on the bottom.

"What'll it be?" asked the bartender in English. The voyageurs were unable to buy anything so they shook their heads and gazed around, wondering why they had come inside.

Then music started, and the Scots looked over the heads of the seated patrons and spotted an upright piano across the room. Beside the piano was a stage about three feet above the crowded floor, and as they looked up, the curtains parted revealing three young ladies. They were dressed in frills, ruffles, and lace in bright colours but their arms were bare and their legs were covered with lacey-looking webbed stockings. The shoes on their little feet were high-heeled and pointed, and the beads around their necks hung down to their middles.

They were enough to take the breath away, and the boys stood and stared until the men at the tables behind them hooted at them to get out of the way. So they moved against the wall in the shadows.

The girls, dark-haired and dusky, were likely Métis, and they began to sing with sweet clear voices almost unheard over the whistles and cheers. It was hard to make out what they were singing.

After the song, they began a lively dance where they kicked their legs as high as their heads and swung their beads with one hand. At the end of the dance they swung around and flipped up their skirts showing a ruffled bottom above long black-lace-stockinged legs.

Then the girls ran off-stage flipping their skirts to the cheers and hooting of the men at the tables. The Scots felt their ears burning and their hearts racing. They had never seen such a startling, exciting display before. They found themselves cheering and clapping along with the rest.

But then men started pushing in front of them and trying to move around them, so they finally made their way to the door. Pulling in great breaths of fresh air, the wind giving their cheeks a cool kiss, they headed for their bunkhouse as the shouting and tinkling of the piano faded into the distance.

Back on the river again heading upstream, the crew of Scots felt at home. This sixteen-foot paddle in their hands almost felt part of them by now. Muscles bunched, extended, relaxed, and stretched comfortably as the boats shot forward. This end of the Saskatchewan, they discovered, was easy and almost rapidless.

With their York boat loaded down with winter supplies and materials needed to build themselves cabins in the west, as well as warm clothes and blankets from Fort Edmonton, they were ready for a winter in the woods.

John's heart was filled with trepidation, however. Facing the unknown was like that. Sometimes he was filled with a feeling of adventure, and sometimes with awe and fear.

When they stopped the first night, Campbell and Douglas spent a long time counselling the men.

"Ewen and Willie McRae," Douglas began the instructions as the whole crew gathered round, "Ye'll be stationed haire. Ten miles on aither side o' the craik is ye're terrritory. Up on thah bank overlookin' the river ye will build ye're post. Ye'll trap and patrol thah stretch all the way up tae the lake. Let the Indians understand that ye'll be there all winter tae trade wi' 'em. Then they dinna need tae takk their furs all the way tae Fort Edmonton."

"John, ye and Alex will be dropped off at the spot where the White Whale Creek meets the river," Campbell spoke next.

They sat around the campfire after eating their meal and their tents had been set up for the night. The sparks from the fire dancing into the air like fireflies proclaimed their freedom.

"This here's an impartant post," Campbell told them. "Thah creek leads to White Whale Lake and the road leads frae there tae the Mission at Lac Ste. Anne. The missionaries preach tae thae Indians who hae beaten a path tae their door. Just keep an eye oot tae whah is gae'n on there. Whah air the missionaries doon wi' the furs that the Indians air bringin' in? Whah air they offerin' fer them and whah air they givin' the Indians that keeps them retairnin' to the post at White Whale?"

Campbell and Douglas continued with the placement of the crew all the way up the river until Rocky Mountain House. "Wai'll be at Rocky Moontain Hoose," Douglas added "and wai'll be comin' doon tae check on how ye'r doin' and seein' if ye're needin' anythin' frae time tae time."

"But the first thing ye hae tae do, ae course, is tae build yerself a cabin. Be sure tae mount thae flag high above the roof on a pole so it can be seen fer miles aroond and the Indians will coom in out o' curiosity," Campbell urged.

"And," Chisholm spoke up, "the idea is tae trap and hunt the baiver, the bear, the otter, and the martin whene'er ye see them. Dinna ye wait fer the Indians tae bring them in tae ye."

"Oh, and at nights ye'll have tae skin the animals, flesh them, and stretch them ontae boards thah ye'll cut tae fit the hides." Campbell dropped into the conversation. "Then when they air ready they hae tae be tanned."

John looked up with alarm at their leader. They had never been taught how to do this. He recalled their visit to McLean's tannery in Fort Edmonton and wished that they had stopped longer to find out how it was done. Now they were expected to do this with the hides they gathered.

"Sir," he addressed Campbell. "We hae never been shown how tae do this skinnin' and stretchin', let alain the tannin'." The others also murmured their concern in that regard.

"Och, wai'll be doon to help ye wi' thah," McTavish assured them. "Just dinna leave them tae long afore ye do the stretchin' and skinnin' or ye find ye canna do a thing wi' 'em. Ye could ask the natives–they all know–they could help ye. Dinna worry lads! Ye'll be fine!"

The next day towards evening, Alex and John and their bundles of supplies and personal effects were deposited on the riverbank opposite the spot where the creek emptied into the river.

"I recommend that ye set up ye'r trading post on the south side ae the river. It's sheltered and ye can get the Indians comin' in frae the south as well as the narth," Campbell told them. "Wai'll likely be back in tae weeks time. Ye're goin' tae need a canoe tae gae across the river so thah will hae tae be built after the cabin is finished. Ae course by that time thae river maught be frozen o'er so ye'll be able tae walk across."

He grinned and the rest pushed away from shore leaving John Lenny and Alex Macleod staring after them uneasily. Feelings of inadequacy overwhelmed John. But inside, he knew that this was the wilderness challenge that each pair was about to face. It was a challenge to see which team faced it the best. John Lenny and Alex Macleod were not about to lose the race. They would excel or die in the attempt. That thought frightened John more than any challenge so far. They gritted their teeth in determination as they lifted the bundles to their backs and headed up the bank.

15

Adolphe

About the same time that the voyageurs were heading west to ply the fur trade in Canada, a teenage boy in France was building fancies of his own. It was not because he was dissatisfied with his life. He loved his family, his three younger sisters, and his mother and father. He was happy living in the small French village, and he attended school every day. As a matter of fact, his parents were very proud of him.

After school he played marbles on the sidewalk, rolled a hoop with a stick, and talked with his friends of what they would do when they grew up. Adolphe's friends wanted to join the French Foreign Legion and travel across Europe and Asia. One wanted to be a sailor and sail across the ocean – maybe even as far as India, and another of Adolphe's friends wanted to work on the railroad. The less adventuresome just wanted to work with their fathers with the grape vines and make the very best wine that Reims produced so that they would become rich.

But Adolphe, a quiet studious boy, always a very devout Catholic was content to serve as altar boy in the neighbourhood church. He went every day to help Father Baptiste Moulin.

Now sixteen, he had not changed his mind about serving the church. He loved Father Baptiste, the young priest who had led their congregation for these past three years. Father Baptiste took him under his wing, trained him, and taught him so much about his beliefs. It was because of this gentle and caring man that Adolphe decided to go into the priesthood.

"You are still so very young, my dear young friend," Father Baptiste told Adolphe one day as he helped to polish up the receptacles after Mass. Most of your friends have decided now that they are fourteen, fifteen and sixteen, they are too old to serve as altar boys, but you are the devoted one. What would I do without you?"

Adolphe would puff up and smile, his determination to be a priest like Father Baptiste strengthened. "Do you wish me to go with you to the lacrosse field today to help with the training?" he asked. "I am quite good in the goal but I could help the younger ones with their training if you would like?"

"Adolphe Perrault, you are good at everything you do. But your father expects you home to help him in the wine field. He already thinks that you spend much too much time here at the church," Father insisted as he patted him on the shoulder. "Your Father may have other plans for you, and you are too young to decide what the rest of your life will be like. You have much to experience."

Adolphe straightened his slight body as tall as he could muster, pushed back the hair that tended to curl around his ears and complained. "I am only seven years younger than you are Father. How old were you when you decided that you wanted to spend your life in the service of the Lord?"

"It is true that I started my training at a young age, Adolphe. I promised my father at his deathbed that I would fulfill his dream for me. But I had many unfulfilled dreams of my own. Would that I were back at your age facing the rest of my life and taking time to explore many other avenues for my future." Father Baptiste sighed as he turned Adolphe to face him. "Are you certain that you want to make up your mind now?"

"I am certain," Adolphe insisted with tears beginning to burn his eyes and a lump to form in his throat. "Do you not love the Lord as much as always, Father?"

"Ah, *oui*," Father Baptiste assured him as he again busied himself with the papers on the pulpit. "But it is not right that I should be your best friend while you turn your back on all of the friends you always played with, and all of the happy games you enjoyed together."

"Do you not want me here with you, Father? We have had many happy times, and we have had many wonderful talks. We shared so much, and I have learned so much. None of the boys can talk to me of such wonderful things. No one else can tell me such interesting stories about the world and the people you know about."

"Oh, my dear friend, of course, I like to have you here. If it were not for you, my life at this parish would have been lonely indeed. This is my first placement. Your friendship and devotion have been a Godsend to me. But things do not always stay the same. I will not be here at this parish for the rest of my life and neither will you."

"Where will you be going?" Adolphe demanded in alarm at the thought of losing his friend.

"Who knows!" Baptiste spread his hands and shrugged. "Wherever God sends me! I am his servant. I do not know what He has in mind for me but I am ready to do his bidding."

"As am I," Adolphe said with finality, facing Father Baptiste, tall and straight as a soldier.

Young Father Baptiste laughed as he put a hand on Adolphe's shoulder and walked with him to the door. "I hope you are as eager to help your father with the picking of the grapes. Your sisters will be looking for you to come and help. They will be calling you a shirker, running from work when the job is waiting."

"You want to train as a priest?" his father thundered. "I have been training you in the art of making wine. You will be taking over the business after I am gone. After all, you are the only boy in the family. You have much to learn. We have the best wine in all of Reims. I knew it was the wrong thing to let him spend so much time with Father Baptiste at the church." Louis aimed this last remark at his wife, Marie, as he wiped dinner from his greying moustache. "It was fine when he was a small boy to serve at the altar, but he is ready to leave school and needs to take his place following his father's lead." He leaped from his chair at the table and paced the floor of the small kitchen.

"Now, Louis, the boy must make up his own mind about his future. Would you rather that he joined the Foreign Legion and marched off to war?" Marie reasoned. "The priesthood is a good thing. We've raised our boy to be good–to be God-fearing, and to help others."

"He can do that without being a poor priest the rest of his life." Louis pounded his fist on the table while Marguerite, Cecile and Louisa jumped in fear. They knew their father to be irascible at times, but he was not a violent man, at least not with them.

107

"I already know much about becoming a priest. It would not take long to learn, and I could train under Father Baptiste," Adolphe said quietly. "I could do this while the grapes are not yet ready to harvest, or after they are finished. There is a quiet time that you do not have much to do …."

"*Mon Dieux*! He talks foolishness." Louis threw his hands in the air and stalked out of the house, slamming the door behind him.

"They said he's leaving tomorrow," Louisa prattled excitedly to her mother. Adolphe caught the bit of the conversation as he came in the door from the winery.

"Who's leaving tomorrow?" he asked with little concern, as he set down the case of empty bottles for his mother to sterilize.

"Father Baptiste," Cecile told him, anxious to have her voice heard.

"I am telling the story," Louisa argued, pushing her older sister aside. "A new priest came from Paris to take his place. He was at the church to-day for our catechism class, and he said he would be taking over for Father Baptiste. I forget what his name is." She turned hesitantly to her sister.

"Do not look at me. You are telling the story," Cecile crossed her arms and turned up her nose.

"Well, anyway," Louisa turned back to the astounded Adolphe, plant-ing herself stolidly in front of him, "the other priest said that Father Baptiste would be travelling far over the ocean to Quebec, in Lower Canada . He said it was a calling."

"*Qu'est que c'est?*" Adolphe shouted, nearly dropping the bottles. "That can not be! He said nothing to me when I saw him last."

"It must be true," Louisa plunged on. "Father Baptiste was right there, and he nodded. He even bid us farewell, and we wished him bon voyage."

Without a word to any of them Adolphe turned and charged out of the house.

Barging into the church office Adolphe surprised Father Laroche at his desk. "Ah, *pardonnez-moi*," Adolphe excused himself. "I thought that I would find Father Baptiste." Adolphe flushed with embarrassment at hav-ing barged in unannounced as though he had a right, and began backing out in confusion.

Father Laroche, an elderly priest who was balding and grey around his ears, looked up with a frown. "Father Moulin has gone to the rectory to pack up his things to leave tomorrow."

"Then he is really going?" Adolphe blurted out. "He is leaving as priest of this parish?"

Father looked up over top of his glasses without a smile or sign of welcome, his nibbed pen just dipped into the inkwell poised above the book into which he was writing. "What is it that you wished to discuss with him, young man? Is it so important?"

"I was just…. I just wanted to…. I wished to say bon voyage to him before he goes." Adolphe's young voice cracked, and he flushed again.

"As I said, he is in the rectory packing so he is very busy. I am not sure he will have time for you." Father Laroche went back to his writing as though he had no more time for this crude young man in rough and stained clothing, who had so rudely interrupted him, demanding to see Father Moulin.

Quickly, Adolphe backed out and quietly closed the door. Turning, he ran down the steps, out of the church door and in a few long strides reached the rectory door. This time he knocked.

The minute that Father Baptiste opened the door the words tumbled out of Adolphe's mouth. "You were going to leave without seeing me. You were going to leave me and go far away so I might never see you again, and you did not tell me?" Adolphe stopped with a lump in his throat that would not let him go on. He just stood there on the stoop looking abandoned and forlorn.

"Come in, Adolphe," Father bid his young friend sadly. When they were inside and Adolphe followed Baptiste down the long dark hallway with its polished mahogany walls, he went on. "There was no time to talk to you. It all happened very quickly and besides, you were very busy with the grapes. I did not want to take you away from your father at a time like this."

"This is more important; the grapes can wait," Adolphe complained. "Are you really going to take the big ship to Canada?"

"Oui, Adolphe." Baptiste told him sadly. He turned to face his friend as he reached the study. Boxes partly filled with books and various articles were strewn about, and he picked up one to continue filling it and tying it with strong string.

"Why are you going *now*–in the middle of your term of service here?" Adolphe looked to see that Baptiste was packing one of their favourite books, the one about when the *word* was spread to France and about the Franciscan Friars who helped build the beautiful Abbey of St. Michel. Father Baptiste visited it and promised Adolphe that some day he would take him to explore the huge castle. Now Adolphe would never go.

"Please understand, Adolphe," Father Baptiste caught his shoulders and looked down into his face, "I knew that someday I would be sent to another parish. I told the diocese that I would be willing to take an out-post. The younger priests often are sent to foreign lands. I was very excited to get the opportunity to go to the New World, especially to Quebec where French is spoken. The Lord is speaking to me. He wants me to take this placement. This is his plan for me. I knew it the moment that the bishop told me about it. I could not miss this opportunity for it comes once in a lifetime. I can serve Him in a way that no other can serve. I know this."

The intensity in Father Baptiste's eyes and in his voice gripped Adolphe, and he was touched by the same fire. "Let me come with you, Father. Let me share this opportunity to discover this New World with you."

Baptiste dropped his hands from Adolphe's shoulders and turned back to his packing. "Oh, Adolphe. You can not come with me. You are only sixteen. Your family needs you in the winery. You are the eldest. Your father needs you to take over the business some day."

"Father will be in the winery for many, many years. It is his life. But it is not mine. Perhaps, Father, this is the Lord's way of telling me that my future lies in the New World, in Quebec. I feel it in my heart, Father Baptiste. I feel it here," Adolphe put his hand over his heart, his eyes burning and his throat aching with the passion that swept over him.

"It is out of the question, my friend. I can not make that decision. The decision would have to be made by the diocese and your family. Perhaps some day when you are grown to be a man; if you still feel this way, you could join me in Canada. But I can not make that decision. A change like this can not be decided so quickly and casually. No, I will not be responsible for the change in the direction of your life on the spur of the moment. Non, non, Adolphe! It can not happen that way."

"Then there is nothing for me to do but say farewell and bon voyage," Adolphe stuck out his hand, abruptly backing down and becoming formal and final.

Impulsively, Baptiste turned from his packing, caught his young friend in a big hug, kissed him on both cheeks and steered him towards the door. "Farewell, my special friend. I will not forget you, and I will write and let you know all about the New world. Now, I must finish my packing. They are coming to take my boxes to the railroad station tomorrow morning at seven."

"May I at least accompany you to the railway station to see you off?" Adolphe asked as he went out the door.

"Of course. If your father says that it is all right, you may ride with me in the cart to the station and return with the driver. He will not mind as long as you help load and unload."

"I shall be over here tomorrow morning before seven to help load. *Merci*!" Adolphe turned his steps towards home.

On the way to the station, both chatted amiably in the easy way they always had. The topic of the New World did not come up. Adolphe was in the cart with the driver when Father Baptiste came out of the rectory, firmly closing the door for the last time behind him.

On the station platform, Adolphe bid his friend a hearty, happy farewell with smiles and best wishes before telling him: "*Mon Père* wishes me to check on the wine that was delivered to the station last night to be sure that it all got on board. So I must check on it before they finish loading. If I do not see you before the train departs do not forget to write. God go with you!"

"And with you," Baptiste called after him as Adolphe hurried down the platform.

The night before, Adolphe carefully put the wine shipment together. The kegs and barrels for Canada and the bottles for shipment to Paris, Adolphe loaded. The large barrels that would be loaded on the ship would have to be carried by wheeled carriers. They were very heavy and could not risk being dropped and spilled. Great care was taken to avoid them being split open or even banged lest they spring a leak. That happened before and Louis was irate at the loss of the valuable wine as well as the costly container. One barrel Adolphe selected very carefully. It was unusually large but it had something that none of the other barrels had–a not easily detected little hole in the side. *And it was empty!* Empty that is, except for a smaller keg that was buried inside so that it would not seem as though the barrel had been loaded empty by mistake.

Adolphe hung around the barrels ostensibly to check them out thoroughly for leaks or faults. He helped to load them, and *that* the railroad worker appreciated. The labourer knew that the wine merchants were very concerned about care in loading, but none ever came to help load the barrels onto the railroad car before. Concerned about loading other things, the station attendant did not notice that his helper had not come down from the car before the boxcar door was closed.

Adolphe took the small barrel out of the big one, threw in his little satchel that he had stowed inside, and again tried out the fit. He crowded into the small space, thanking the Lord again that he was short and of slight build, pulled the lid down over himself, and hooked it inside with the hooks and eyes that he installed the night before.

A small pinpoint of light pierced the darkness but Adolphe hoped it would be enough. *So far so good*, he thought, with his knees under his chin and his head bent down into his chest. He could even change positions, he decided, as he squirmed around with difficulty until he was curled up in the fetal position, his back rounded to the shape of the barrel. It was going to work. He must get on that ship.

But he need not spend all of his time in here. He felt the jolt as he realized that the train was pulling out of the station. He could take this opportunity to walk about, getting as much exercise as he could, while he had the chance. There was not much room to move among all of the barrels kegs and boxes. He carefully clambered over top of them to maneuver his way around, but he soon found a spot by the door where he could peer out of a crack and watch the French countryside fly by.

Father Baptiste waited as long as he could on the station platform for Adolphe to come, but as the warning whistle sounded he hurried on board. Eyes searching the platform from his seat, he craned his neck to catch sight of Adolphe for a last-minute wave, but the train pulled slowly away with no sign of his return.

That surprised Baptiste, knowing how much Adolphe wanted to see him off. He never broke his word before. However, there be some problems with the wine shipment, Baptiste decided. Or else the cart driver had to return and could not wait for Adolphe to bid long farewells. After all, they said all of the good-byes that they needed to.

Adolphe was much more accepting of this move today than he was yesterday. Baptiste was glad of that; he felt so uncomfortable with Adolphe's reaction to his leaving. And so guilty! He lay back in his seat and closed his eyes, wondering what the New World had in store for him.

16

Stow Away

Finally, the bumping, bashing, rolling, and jostling stopped, and Adolphe finally breathed a sigh of relief. At times he thought that he would never be able to stand it. His muscles were sore from bracing himself against the edge for support and his skin and bones had been smashed so many times that he thought he had to cry out in pain.

He was so dizzy that he thought he would be violently sick. He had the frightening sensation of weightlessness as a crane swung his barrel out into the air. Swinging back and forth like a pendulum, it lowered him into the hold, and he came to an abrupt and jarring stop when the barrel reached the bottom. Two or three times he nearly changed his mind, opened the lid and screamed out, 'Stop! Stop! I am in here. I fear I am going to die. I can not stand this!' And at other times he felt he could not breathe and was about to pass out.

The stevedores loading the ship complained at the weight of his barrel and dropped it on its side, swearing loudly. In anger, ignoring the signs on top saying '*This End Up*,' and '*Handle with Care*,' they rolled the barrel along, kicking it before them. Once, he was standing on his head for so long he was in terror that he would be left that way and not be able to get the lid open. But they finally moved his barrel with all of the others to the hold of the ship where they would stay until the voyage was over.

All of the time that he found himself hanging upside down, he was in absolute terror that they would stack other barrels on top of his so that he could not get the lid open. What would he do, he agonized? He imagined himself struggling to get the lid up to no avail and screaming until his lungs ached with no one to hear. The thought nearly made him tear open the lid and leap out to freedom, exposing himself as a stow-away, but he gritted his teeth and swallowed his panic.

He prayed: *"Dear Lord Jesus, Forgive me for this willful action. Please let me live. Please let them find me before I die!"* Ceaselessly, he prayed, trying to block out every fear from his mind, *let me live and I will follow your will for me. Thy will be done! Thy will be done! Please, Lord God! Let me live! Why did I do this? Will I ever see daylight again?"* Then he cried and he didn't try to be quiet any more. He sobbed until he realized that the barrels no longer moved except for a gentle sway back and forth. He was right side up, and he could hear no more voices, just the loud throb and hum of the ship's engines.

So sore that he could hardly move, he undid the hooks holding the lid, and pushed tentatively against it. It would not move. He pushed harder but it still would not move. In a sudden panic, he forced his hands and shoulder against it while pushing with his legs and emitting a shout that erupted from his very soul. It moved slightly letting in more light and causing the smaller kegs that were sitting on top of his barrel to tip and sway.

Encouraged and in desperation, he pushed again and this time the barrels tumbled aside and rolled across the other barrels. Painfully standing inside his barrel, he noticed that his barrel was near the edge of the others and only two kegs covered his.

Nearly sobbing with relief, he dragged himself out and climbed down to the floor. Rubber-legged, wobbly, and dizzy, he leaned against one of the kegs until he felt that he could breathe normally again. Hearing voices approaching, he limped behind the barrels and crowded into a space.

The sailors did not stop, however, but continued about their duties. Adolphe heard one of the men say as they moved away. "The anchor has been pulled up and the gangplank has been taken in. We are ready to ship out to sea."

"Has all of the cargo been checked to see that it is securely in place," said one of the men who seemed to be in a position of authority. "If any of these barrels of wine roll around while we are out on the rough seas it could be disastrous. See to it that they are strapped around their circumference and across the top."

Adolphe had a moment of panic. They could not find him *now!* Now that he had gone through so much to get here! They could put him off the

ship before they even got out of the harbour. He should not have come out
of his barrel so soon. Stevedores would be swarming all over the cargo and
find him. He should climb back into his barrel, he told himself, but even
as he thought it, his mind and his whole body rebelled against it. Instead,
he moved farther back behind the barrels until he found some boxes and
cases. Forcing himself into a crevice between them, he huddled in fear
while the men went about strapping the barrels together.

But his imagination tormented him. He recalled that in his panic to
get out of his enclosure he left the empty barrel with its lid off and his
satchel inside. The men would surely find the two loose barrels that rolled
aside, and then upon investigation, they would find his hideout and know
that a stowaway was on board. They would not pull out of port until they
searched and found the culprit. The scenario burned in his mind as he saw
himself being dragged from his hiding place and being hurled from the
ship.

Hardly breathing, he dare not even twitch in case he was discovered.
After what seemed like many pain-wracked hours, the men finished their
job and were gone. They had not discovered the open barrel. After climbing over the barrels with their strapping they had not found the damning
evidence.

By now, he could feel the movement of the ship as it left the harbour,
and he could hear the giant engines roar into action with deafening results.
The smells down in the hold were almost too much. The French shipped
cheeses as well as the wines. Adolphe could smell the overpowering odour
of Roquefort coming from one of the crates near him. Cotton, wool, linen,
and lace were sent to the New World as well as jewellery, perfume, cosmet-
ics and furniture.

The hold was crammed with materials for Quebec. And there was the
smell of fuel used by the engines. No wonder that the cheese and any other
foodstuffs had to be wrapped and crated so tightly! His head swam.

After the men were gone to another area of the ship, Adolphe squirmed
out of the hole he found between the packages, scrambled up to replace
the lid on the empty barrel, and to retrieve his satchel. Rooting around, he
made himself another hiding place behind other packages, found a tarpaulin that covered some cases, and made a bed. Digging into his satchel, he
pulled out some bread and sausage that he took from home, drank some

wine from the goatskin bag he had, curled up in the tarpaulin, and fell asleep to the rocking of the ship.

When he awoke, it was to the creaking, bucking, rolling, and diving of the ship. The waves outside must be very high because the ship seemed to climb as though up the side of a mountain and then to dive into the valley on the other side. If it was only the climbing and diving it would not be so bad, but it seemed to tilt to one side and then the other as though it might roll over. Then something would hit the side of the ship like a giant fist and the vessel would creak and groan in complaint as though it would come apart.

Things would come sliding across the hold and slam into the cases and boxes he hid inside. He feared that he would be crushed. Dragging his tarp he crawled out of his hole and tried to locate, in the darkness, a safer hiding place. In doing so he staggered about, falling against, and on top of other cargo.

Giving up on that, he located an area behind some boxes and against the wall. Here, he wrapped up in the tarp, leaned against the ship's side, and braced his feet against the crate in front of him. Tipping and rolling he tried to fall asleep again.

But soon he began to feel ill. He felt dizzy and his head ached. Nausea overcame him, and he turned to empty his stomach on the wall of the ship at the base of a beam. Up came the bread, the sausage, and the wine but he felt no better. Several times he vomited, and still he retched when there was nothing else to come up. He never before felt so utterly miserable in his life.

When the dim light of day filtered its way into the hold, he hung there, too miserable to crawl back into hiding. He did not care if they found him. Let them throw him overboard. He no longer craved life.

When the storm abated, the ship calmed in its rolling and diving, but Adolphe still felt so ill he could not drag his body back to his nest. *At least*, he thought, *I will not need food for the journey*. He felt he would never feel hungry again.

But he was wrong. After a long exhausted sleep, he awoke in darkness so thick that he felt he would smother in its fold. He was cold and shivering, but he was hungry. Weak and trembling, he found his way back into his original hideout, hauling his tarp behind him. He rolled inside it, ate some more sausage and bread, washed it down with the wine and was soon asleep again.

Days went by, Adolphe did not know how many, and the ship still sailed on. He began to feel better and braver so he started to explore his self-imposed prison. Whenever he heard anyone coming, he dove into a hole or corner to hide. Because it was so dim in the hold, it was difficult for anyone to see him. However, he could see just fine. *When I get out of here into the light of day*, he thought, *I will feel like a mole.*

Adolphe started to feel satisfied for overcoming the ordeal inside the barrel trap, the storm and resulting seasickness, avoiding detection and the tossing on the ocean without being sick again. Until one day he opened his knapsack and after rooting around, came to the realization that he was without food or drink. *How much longer will this trip last*, he wondered!

By the next day, his stomach was groaning, and thirst was gnawing at him. There was no water and the cheese and wine was crated up so tightly that he could not get inside without tools.

'*Why can I not*,' he asked himself, '*slip upstairs when it is dark and find what I need? How will they distinguish me from the other passengers anyway, even if I go up in the daytime?*' Thus inspired and driven by hunger and thirst, he made his way cautiously up the first flight of steps. This was a lot bigger ship than the old sailing ships that possessed but two levels, he discovered. This was one of the first passenger and cargo steamships to ply the ocean waters. It was a lot larger than he thought.

On this level, were many doors and a long hallway. He tried one door. It was locked. So was the next. A sign on the door said '*Crew only.*' Then he climbed up the a flight of stairs to the next level. Here was another long inside hallway with doors on both sides. He suddenly realized how vulnerable he was out in the open hallway with no place to hide.

Then he ran for the next level. This one was different. Here, he found the dining room. Because it was dark, no one was inside. Just as he was about to enter, a white- coated cabin boy entered and began to set the tables for the morning. Heading in the other direction, he saw two double doors, and he opened one, entering cautiously.

The first thing that Adolphe saw was a large pitcher of water standing on the counter and he made for it. He swilled down several mouthfuls, half of it running down his shirtfront in his eagerness. As he lowered it, he noticed loaves of bread fresh out of the oven, and he made for them, his mouth watering, remembering the taste of his mother's home-baked bread.

Before he could grab a loaf and make a quick exit, a hand reached over his shoulder and grabbed his wrist. Though he struggled to free himself and escape, the cook's grip tightened and held fast. When he realized that he was caught, he quit struggling and tried to bluff it out.

"I became hungry. I slept through dinner and thought I would come for a snack before bed time." Adolphe tried lamely.

The cook was a big man with a round belly and red face. His arms were huge, and his eyes were an icy blue. Towering over Adolphe, his big arms crossed, he asked pointedly. "What is your cabin number, son? Guests usually do not come down to the galley looking for food, and they do not drink water out of a pitcher."

Adolphe cast around wildly for some place to run and hide, or some excuse for an answer. "I am not one of the regular guests, I ..."

"You are a what? A cabin boy, perhaps? A deck hand? A rat catcher from the hold?" The cook bored a hole through Adolphe with his piercing eyes.

When Adolphe stared back at him, feeling like that rat caught in a trap, the cook went on triumphantly. "You are a stowaway, are you not? How did you manage to escape being found for so long? I can bet that you are quite hungry by now. Come with me. I am taking you to the captain. You can tell him all about it." The cook grabbed Adolphe by the arm and steered him up the next steep, narrow flight of stairs to the captain's cabin.

He had been congratulating himself on going undetected, and thinking he was home free. Now it was all undone. They would send him home on a return ship and he would be disgraced. Somehow, though, as he sat on the bench outside the captain's cabin, with a waiter not much older than he himself guarding him, waiting for the captain to come out, all that he could think of were rats. He had been sharing quarters with rats in the hold and had not seen one. Obviously they were better at hiding than he was.

After what seemed like an hour, the captain opened his door and invited Adolphe inside. Though he was a severe, unsmiling man, the captain was handsome, though greying slightly at the temples. A tall man with striking good looks, he had deep frown lines on his forehead, and, Adolphe thought, would have been much more handsome had he smiled more and frowned less.

"So, my cook tells me that you are a stowaway. What would bring you to do that? Are you running from the law?"

"*Mais non!*" Adolphe denied vehemently, shaking his head. "I wanted to go to Canada with my friend Father Baptiste but no one would allow me to go so I thought I would find my own way." Slouched in his chair in front of the captain's desk in utter dejection, he wiped his sleeve across his nose. Suddenly feeling like an errant ten-year-old, he straightened and looked the captain squarely in the eye. "But if you will allow me, sir, I could pay my way by working for you in any way you wish, for I feel I was meant to go to the New World."

The captain's expression softened, and he came as close to a smile as anyone on board would see. Suddenly he got up, went to the door, and called the young waiter who had been his guard.

"Paul, will you please bring Father Baptiste Moulin to my office."

Adolphe sat up in his chair, his eyes wide with alarm. "Do you have to do that, sir? Father Baptiste will be so disappointed in me."

"He will need to know sooner or later that you are on board, *n'est pas?*"

Acquiescing, Adolphe sat in submission with his head hanging as they waited for the waiter to get Father Baptiste out of bed.

No one told Father Baptiste the reason that he was being summoned to the captain's cabin so it was a shock to step over the entrance to see Adolphe in the chair, his head lowered and his shoulders slouched.

"Adolphe!" he gasped. "What are you doing here?"

"I gather you know this young man," the captain said to Baptiste. "He was caught in the galley early this morning before daylight, trying to steal some bread. I gather he has been starving while stowing away in the ship's hold."

"*Mais Non*, Adolphe! Why? Why did you run away? Your parents and your sisters must be sick with worry." Then Baptiste turned to the captain as Adolphe still sat looking at his hands in his lap, too ashamed to raise them to meet the hurt in his friend's eyes. "Captain Chartrand, I will contact the Perraults when I get to Montreal to let them know Adolphe is all right. I will pay Adolphe's fare. If you do not have another cabin I will share mine."

"Or we could set up a hammock in the hold," the captain said with a slight smile twitching at the corners of his mouth.

Startled, Adolphe looked up at the captain and realizing that he was teasing, hung his head again to hide his flushed cheeks.

Out on deck that evening, the two friends stood at the rail gazing out across the rolling waves with the moon painting a trail across the water. "I did not know that this trip could last so long," Adolphe complained. "And there is still no sign of land."

"There are many more days of travel before we get to the new world," Father Baptiste sighed. "You would not have made it on a bottle of wine and a roll of sausage."

"I am glad I got caught, then," Adolphe said. "I much prefer riding up here on the deck, if it was not so cold. When I get to the New World, I will get a job and pay you back for my passage, Father. I promise. I may want to be a priest some day but I will work at any job – and I am very strong. I can work for my keep. I also feel a calling in the New World, Father. I want to stay there where you are."

17

White Whale Creek Landing

John and Alex put so much into this area along the White Whale Creek that it was beginning to feel like home. The first year that they came, dumped off on the shore with little to sustain them, the two at first felt anger and a little fear. Determination to not let the land beat them set in, and they persevered.

Years later, the summer of 1869, after another gruelling trip by York boat West, the voyageurs again returned to their posts in the Northwest. The dangers of the roaring plunging waters, the jagged rocks, and the clawing overhanging branches were behind them. They felt the North Saskatchewan was their home.

John and Alex, assigned the post on the White Whale Creek, remembered that first fall and winter vividly. Their assignment was weeks of struggle.

"How do they expect us tae build a cabin, prepare for winter, build a canoe tae cross the river so that we can travel up the craik tae White Whale Lake, spy on the mission, and attract the Indians tae our post tae trade wi' us?" John leaned on his axe, already tired at the thought. "All afore spring!"

"Noh to mention the fact thah we're expected to cover this whole area bordering Duncan and Cameron's further upstream. We're expected to hunt for our food and for furs for the Hudson Bay Company," Alex slumped against a poplar tree.

"T'be sure, and if we hae any trooble, tae contact the nairest native and hai'll help shoo us how it's doone," John mimicked.

At that moment, it started to rain, a light shower, but enough to spur both boys into action. "The first thing wai've got to do is build oursel's a shelter, and we'll let everything else take care of itself as we need." John led the way up the bank and began clearing a flat area of trees.

While John cut down the trees, Alex de-limbed them and cleared the sight for the structure.

The sun was setting, and the two men were starving before they finally quit and turned their attentions to more immediate concerns. Pemmican was in short supply, but they needed to fill their stomachs now! They would replenish the food supply later.

Rocks were gathered for a fire-pit and a tripod built over it to heat water in their only large pot. The moon was coming up by the time they gathered spruce boughs for bedding under their tents.

The cabin took two weeks because time was taken away from it to hunt down some meat. A deer was downed with one shot, and they took time off the building to cut the meat into tongue-shaped pieces to dry out over the fire. That took both all day. They dare not leave the meat because already it was attracting little camp thieves. John brought down a wolverine and Alex a weasel. They had to take turns sitting up to guard the meat against predators and keep the fire going. Alex was wakened with the boom of John's gun. He shot a bear.

They preserved what they could of the meat and the hide. The bear strung up from tree to tree was skinned and the hide scraped, when they had another pair of visitors. Two Indians suddenly slipped in as shadows on John's periphery. Appearing noiselessly, unannounced, the buck-skinned pair stood silently waiting to be invited to the fire.

When Alex bid them to come forward, he began talking to them but got no response. Then they spoke a few words, but the two Scots shook their heads and shrugged. So they began to struggle with sign language and there was immediate success.

One of the Indians pointed to the bear, and John indicated that he shot it because it was trying to steal meat that they were drying over the fire. Alex indicated the same thing with the wolverine and weasel.

When the Scots displayed a willingness to learn to express themselves in Cree, the Indians seemed to be only too happy to comply. John indicated that they wanted to learn how to prepare the hides, and if the Indians would show them how and teach them how to speak Cree, they would give them the hides and some of the venison jerky.

The Indians nodded vigorously and set about to teach these stupid white men how to survive in the wilderness. They saved the fat of the bear and split it, half-and-half. They took the brains and rolled them up with the scraped bear hide. And they divided the heart and liver between them as well as other salvageable parts.

The rolled hide must stay that way for two days, and then they must unroll it, they'd indicated to Alex. The Indian then signed that the hide would not go stiff and would be pliable. The deer hide must be smoked over the fire after being scraped on both sides and treated with the brains. After that, it would be ready to cut out moccasins. The fur should be worn inside to make them warmer for winter they demonstrated.

Every day, the braves came to teach them, and they were fascinated with the cabin that the young men were building. Every day the Scots learned more and more about the language. One day the Indians brought an older woman with them, indicating that she was their mother.

The woman showed them how to make pemmican. She picked some berries along the way and pounded together on a flat rock the venison jerky, the berries, and some of the bear fat. It was then cooked on top of the hot rock. Although not as good as some they had tasted, made from buffalo meat and lard rather than bear fat, they helped make it, so it tasted fine to them.

They were learning to speak Cree more and more. Each time the men came over, they could carry on a better conversation. The natives even helped with the building of the cabin and were fascinated with the construction. With the axe, John and Alex split a heavy tree into planks that were used for the floor. The Scots taught the Indians about splitting logs into slabs by the use of axe and wedge. The Indians observed them splitting the log down as far as they could with the wedge, then cutting it off at that length and starting again.

The timbers were laid down crossways on the ground, and the slabs were placed over top to make a rather imperfect floor, but it did get them off the ground.

The roof was a simple one-way slant, having the front higher than the back of the cabin. Saplings were tied across, then slabs were placed over them, and then bark to keep out the rain. It was not altogether foolproof because rain did get in, so they lay sod pieces over that.

The Indians decided that their tipis kept the rain out better. The young men thought that over and decided that over the sod, the next layer would be hides, when they got enough of them to fit.

The Indian pair, whom they discovered were brothers, told them that their names were Gabriel and Paul Beaver. The names, they said, were their new baptised ones from the Mission. Now, Alex and John knew that the Indians trusted the Missionaries enough to allow their names to be changed. Did they bring furs to them for trade as well? They must encourage them to bring the furs to them to do so.

The next project that Gabriel and Paul helped them with was the canoe. For that, they needed more hides so the four of them went hunting. This was the Scots opportunity to strike up a trade agreement. As they learned more of the Cree language, they were able to let Gabriel and Paul know that not only would their company trade goods that they needed with them, but also with the rest of the Indians they knew. They discovered that the whole band went once a year to Fort Edmonton to trade.

When John finally got it across to them that their Hudson Bay Company leader was concerned that there were not as many furs coming in as there used to be, Gabriel and Paul shrugged not quite able to understand the problem. So the Scots dropped it and urged them to bring the furs to them. Then they could get supplies like bullets for their guns, rifles or tools, cloth for the women, sacks to carry what they needed, iron pots, knives or matches.

After that, more people came to their door, but so far, only from the south side of the river. When they learned more of the language they would be able to travel north as far as the Mission.

John marvelled at how much they had learned that season! With their hunting and with the Indians who brought in their furs that winter they had a load to take East by spring. Not as many as they had hoped, but enough to make the trip worthwhile.

But the winter was not an easy one. The two Scots were not prepared for the bitter cold. Blizzards howled around the little cabin and through the cracks between the logs that they had tried to stuff with moss. They layered all they could inside their moccasins, but their feet were nearly frozen when they arrived home from a short hunting expedition. Their boots, which they had worn through all of their former expeditions to the West, were even colder. They were showing wear, and the soles were becoming thin. Some of the furs that they harvested and had hanging on stretching boards all along their walls, they turned into covers for their bodies and for their beds.

The cold crept in at night on icy feet. Glowing red, the little stove that was used for cooking and heating, with the short chimney that went out of the side of the house was no match for the cold. Two feet away from it one nearly froze. Everything was done as close to the little heater as possible. They ate, they slept, they worked their furs and hides, and they changed their clothes as near the heater as they could get.

The wood was brought inside and piled along the wall so that it would be dry. They would freeze without it. Sometimes they were forced to use green wood before they got wise and brought dry deadwood from the forest. The green wood, they discovered, burned so slowly with so little heat that it was ineffectual. They had to keep cleaning the thick soot from inside the stovepipes.

Winter slowed the hunting and trapping. Animals stayed holed up in a storm or in the bitter cold – even the smaller animals like the beaver, mink and rabbit. They found nothing in their traps, and the tracks they followed were wiped out by the wind that drifted in over them, obliterating them. The wind swept across the open spaces and made drifts that were difficult to wade through, and in the bush, fallen timbers in the snow were a hazard underfoot.

They melted snow for drinking, washing, and cooking. All water was used sparingly because the container they had to melt water was small. The large one was traded to the Indians for furs.

The cabin had no windows, and the door did not fit well. Spaces around it let in the snow that drifted across the floor to their beds that were on the floor near the stove. Sometimes in the grip of a storm, the wind shook their little cabin like a cat would with a mouse, vibrating the door and threatening to shake it off its leather hinges. The stove gobbled up wood as fast as they could stuff it in.

To save washing, they turned their plates over on the crudely constructed table, the only piece of furniture they had in the first year. That also discouraged the mice that sometimes ventured out across the floor, anxious to share the warmth of the cabin. The next time the boys wanted to eat they used the same plate. In the summer the same tactic kept the flies off the plates. The cans of beans were frozen and so was the water in the pail against the wall.

No longer could they think of anything to say to each other. One evening, when it was so cold that trees cracked like gunshots and the stillness outside was broken only by the yodelling song of the wolves across the river, the two men sat in silence next to the little stove.

Working and re-working a rabbit skin that was going to be a re-lining for his moccasins, John looked over at Alex who was whittling on a stick with his knife trying to make a whistle. "Nae offence, Alex, but I hae become tired of ye're company. Ye hae nae said a word tae me all day."

"I dinna hae anythin' tae say. I said everything there wa' tae say." Alex stopped his whittling and looked up in surprise. He sat on a simple three-legged stool and cast around for something to say. "If this cold snap keeps up wai'll be stuck in thae cabin tomorrow, as well. We will noh be able tae trap again. I froze my fingers last time we went away far frae the cabin and we didna see a thing anyway."

"I didna mean talk about the weather," John complained. "We talked that one oot."

"Well, I could say thah it's too bad we canna get up tae the mission and see some other paeple. They'd be interestin' tae talk aboot. But it's a mite far in the cold. I could say that we havena seen Gabriel and Paul fer a long time and I cood say that it's a shame we didna start tae mark the days so we'd know how many days afore spring, but we didna remember tae do that."

"I know, Alex, I hae discovered why most of the fur traders that stay up here over winter aither go crazy or they tack themselves an Indian wife," John mumbled half to himself. "Noh thah ye ain't good company, and I fer cairtain wouldna wanna do all this aloone, but ...."

"I ken," Alex sighed. "Thah wee lassie – whah wa' her name? Nenuthtu that crawled into Cameron's bed thah night could crawl intae my bed any time she wanted. I wouldna chase her oot. I dinna care if the Company does tell us 'Nae tackin' advantage ae thae Indian women!' She could help warm up my furs tonight."

"And she would always be here keepin' the fire gae'n and haein' a hot meal ready when we goh hame frae the trap-line." John carried on the fanciful reverie.

"The only trooble is," Alex went back to his whittling. "I havena seen any ae them comin' aroond lookin' fer a warm bed tae crawl intae."

"Weell, make nae mistake, we havena exactly been verra far away frae the cabin. I think they all maest be up tae the mission."

"I wonder if Gabriel and Paul hae any sisters."

"Or wives?"

"If they hae they will be careful noh tae bring them near us." Both men fell silent again.

"Say when air ye gae'n to play yer bagpipes again. That would fetch them all a-runnin' – just oot ae curiosity," Alex suddenly broke the silence.

"They will noh work when it's this cold and my lip would likely fraize tae the mouthpaice."

"Ach well!" Alex tried out his whistle. "It'll soon be spring and we'll be gone frae here."

18

The McDougalls at White Whale

They weathered that winter and the York boat came for them in the spring. The long journey was made to York Factory, and they greeted their relatives with enthusiasm. John worried about his mother. She was not feeling well with a bad cough that would not leave her. His father was still out on his fishing boat every chance he got, but was slowing down and could not do the things he did so easily before.

His sister, Isabel, however, married a fur trader. They left York and caught the boat south to Fort Garry. No one was very happy about losing them but the Bay Company, promised her husband a placement within the company in Fort Garry in distribution and dispatching.

The Nor'westers had not long to visit with their families before being dispatched to the West again. The placement over winter of the fur traders in the posts along the river, and getting out there with the natives, learning the language, hunting and being involved with the fur production from the bottom up, was a good idea. The Hudson's Bay Company employers planned to continue that policy. More furs definitely came in because of that bold action.

However, the amount was down from what it was, so the policy was rigorously pursued, and the Nor'westers were sent back the next season with little time to lay over and rest in between times. They were instructed again to watch for signs of other fur traders, and signs that the missionaries were not only ministering to the natives, but trading with them as well. Furs were trading hands along the way.

None of the crew saw anything unusual. John and Alex reported the day they finally trekked up as far as White Whale Lake to see what was going on. As daylight waned, they realized that they would spend the night before trekking back. Their snowshoes shuffling along in the snow, they followed White Whale Creek half the way, until they met a fairly well travelled trail. This was the Lac Ste. Anne Trail. Even in the winter it showed signs of traffic: horses, sleighs, travois, and snowshoes, but it was not as busy as it was in the summer time. It was comforting, though, to see signs of humanity.

At a fork in the trail, instead of taking the right one to the nearest stopping house, they took the left toward the lake. They could see it from a high hill overlooking the trees. If need be, they would hike back to the stopping house, but it was important for them to get to the lake.

Here they discovered an encampment of Métis and Indians who were wintering near its shores. Many of the young boys were fishing through the ice of the lake and were heading in with their day's catch. The two fur traders stood watching two boys carrying their fish home as the sun set behind the icy pink haze on the horizon to the southwest. Seeing the big white fish strung together through the gills, John and Alex's mouths watered.

"Trade for fish?" Alex approached one young boy who shied away from him, uncomprehending.

"Trade?" John pursued holding out a jackknife and indicating with the other hand the fish.

The two boys looked at the knife displayed on John's mitt and their eyes widened, but they hesitated to reach out and touch the shiny prize. They looked into the faces of the strange men and then back to the fish; John nodded again.

"Henri! Jean Felix!" A female voice called, and the traders turned to see a girl of about twelve years approaching along the top of the bank. Behind her was an encampment of hide-covered structures with the smoke curling up from the opening in the roof. Their homes were in a circle, temporary structures built of poles and hides. Resembling tipis, they could assemble and disassemble them quickly and easily. The floor was raised on poles and spruce branches that were covered with fur, and the fireplace burned in the centre, allowing the smoke to travel upward through the smoke-hole.

The inability to make themselves understood frustrated John and Alex. "We hae tae spend more time with Gabriel and Paul and learn to speak more Cree," Alex sighed. "Even if we ask the questions that the Bay Company wants tae know, we canna understand the answers."

The two boys retreated hurriedly towards the girl who put them behind her in a protective gesture. *This must be the older sister*, John decided, as the girl with head erect faced them defensively.

She was small and slight of build with thick dark hair pulled back into two heavy braids that fell down in front of her shoulders nearly to her waist. Brown eyes sparked a challenge that told the visitors not to approach the boys further.

"Friend," John spoke the word that he remembered from Gabriel and Paul and put up his hand palm facing forwards.

"Trade," Alex spoke another word that they had learned before any other, and John again opened his hand displaying the pocketknife and pointing to the fish.

Pushing the boys ahead of her, the girl beckoned the traders to the encampment in the shelter of the trees. The night shadows were approaching, but the brightness of the rising moon on the snow made the path to the encampment as light as evening.

A fire burned in the centre of the circle of homes, and it danced high into the air, scattering sparks that sailed up and finally descended as black spots on the snow. In no time, twenty curious people surrounded the men as the girl led them to the firelight. A babble of voices demanded answers from them, and they spread their hands in frustration.

Suddenly, a familiar face emerged from the crowd. With a shock of pleasure, they recognized George McDougall whom they had left behind two years ago in Victoria Mission. "So it's the York boat Scots from York Factory!" he said to them and the familiarity felt like a warm hug.

Slowly, haltingly, McDougall introduced the men to the assembly. Then he turned to John and Alex explaining, "These are not Cree. Speaking to them in Cree would be difficult for them although many of the words are the same. They are Stonys from the lost tribe of the southern Assiniboine. Actually, they are from Lac Ste. Anne, and having been taught French in the Mission there, it would be better for you to speak to them in French.

My French is very limited so that I speak to them in a mixture of Stony and Cree.

"However, they are more Métis than Indian in this tribe. This is a temporary encampment for them. They are just here to hunt, fish, and trap and will then move on."

"We canna speak French either but we've been tryin' tae learn Cree," John told George McDougall.

Then another man joined them at the fire, a white man. "Oh," George interrupted, laying his hand on the shoulder of the man who stood beside him. "This is my brother, David. We have been considering the idea of setting up a mission on White Whale Lake. My brother and I travelled out of Fort Edmonton to explore this area and to meet the Stony tribe along with the Métis. David has a lot more experience with the language and has been teaching me."

David McDougall was a younger man with dark slightly greying hair that curled around his ears. Unlike his brother, George, he had no beard and possessed striking grey eyes that, also unlike his brother's, radiated good humour and friendliness.

"David is not a missionary but a trader," George went on in explanation. "Since the Stony language is closer to the Assiniboine tongue of the Indians on the prairies to the south he has come to help me learn the language and establish a base out here in the northwest."

The young Scots caught the term 'trader' in reference to David, and it rang warning bells for them.

"Trader?" Alex interrupted. "He's noh tradin' fer the Hudson Bay Company; we would hae recognized him."

"The Hudson Bay hae the fur trading rights on all of the lands in this area, ye ken." John added pointedly as he held David's clear gaze.

"Oh, no! Let me explain," George hurried to qualify his statement while David looked on in confusion. "My brother does not trade in furs. He is from the prairies. The only furs down there are buffalo hides." George McDougall's big voice and piercing gaze soon held everyone's attention as they always did. Startled, the Métis looked from one to the other, wondering if there was some dissention in this group of whites. "My brother, David," George went on, "is up in this part of the northwest, first of all to help me establish an understanding with the natives, and then to enlist my help."

The Scots relaxed. They were sure that they found the leak. They thought they found out where the furs were going that were not coming to the Hudson Bay trading posts.

"David and I are driving a herd of cattle south to the prairies as soon as he can make arrangements and as soon as he helps me establish a centre out this way. So far, the Catholics have a hold on the area around Lac Ste. Anne and have a long established mission there so we want to do the same on White Whale. Some day I hope to have a mission, a church, and a school.

"All of these Métis," George waved a hand to indicate the curious around the fire, "have been baptised by the priests either from Lac Ste. Anne, when the mission was there, or from Fort Des Prairies in the Red River Settlement. They travel for miles to have their marriages and their births registered and blessed by the priests in Lac Ste. Anne or St Albert. It is time that we offered them an alternative."

At this point, David and George directed their words to the Indians that gathered close, curiously wondering what the strange conversation was all about. Now David did most of the talking and the Métis and Indians listened with rapt attention. In his evangelizing style George McDougall raised his hands and his voice as David translated and George prayed over them and sang in his booming melodic voice, that never failed to fascinate the natives who swayed and moved with him around the fire. The Catholics may have had a head start but George was doing his best to narrow the gap.

Afterwards, as the Métis drifted away to their little homes, George and John escorted the Scots to the tipi that they had set up for themselves in the same style as the natives. They always stayed with the natives that they visited, and while there, George would be getting his crash course in learning the language of the natives.

As the four of them sat cross-legged on the raised bed platform and pulled their Hudson Bay blankets around themselves, they stoked up the almost smokeless fire in the centre until it glowed with heat.

"You are welcome to stay the night with us," George offered, and the two fur traders accepted with gratitude.

As they talked before turning in, George and David began to give them help with their English, and translating to Cree. Their heads swam with the effort. They were trying to practice better English, learn the Cree language, then the Stony, and George broke the news that to speak the recognized language of Indian and whites in this area of the northwest, they should be learning to speak French. As well, they were still no closer to learning what was happening to the furs around here.

"Since you left Victoria Mission," George McDougall told them, "my wife and daughters joined me. My wife is a teacher, and she has devoted herself to teaching English, among other important things, to natives and whites alike, especially to Scots like yourself. I came down to Fort Edmonton to establish a mission. It is long past time. I know it will be a challenge. The fort is a den of iniquity. The drinking, intoxication, the whoring, and gambling that is carried on is shameful. Not only in the taverns is there fighting, dancing and drunkenness, but it spills out into the streets so that you can hear the screams, shouting, and laughter until all hours of the morning. Sex has become a sport and a trade, and Indians are being debauched and traded like a commodity. Every missionary, be it Catholic priest or Methodist minister, has been ignored, laughed at, or run out of town. No one has yet been able to instill a conscience or get some trace of civilization started.

"But I plan to make it a challenge that I can not turn away from. I am going to build that mission in Fort Edmonton. Not only that, but I plan to bring my family here. It will some day be a place where decent women can walk the street and get respect. It will some day know the Lord!"

At this, George's voice boomed out, and he raised his hands in defiance. John and Alex wondered at this man's tenacity. They hoped that he would succeed in taming Fort Edmonton, that he would win where other missionaries before him had fled, but they had little confidence. He was planning to build a *mission* in the middle of a ferociously rough-hewn settlement where wild sled dogs howled through the night in the winter, bottles crashed in the taverns, and men died nightly in mysterious circumstances.

As they rolled up in their warm blankets and robes curled near the fire, they listened to the wolves howling in the distance. They wished him well. George McDougall was a brave and determined man, but they were glad that they were not facing the task ahead of him. They much preferred their job.

19

The Oblates of Mary Immaculate

Adolphe could not believe that it was eight years since the day he stole away aboard the ship that sailed with Father Baptiste. He remembered that autumn day when they stepped ashore at Montreal. The thrill of stepping onto a new land, and the houses climbing up the cliff, was as though he discovered the land himself. The trees were a blaze of colour along the wide river called the St Lawrence, but already there was a nip in the air, warning that winter was not far away. Father Baptiste warned him about the winters in Canada.

A delegation of black-robed priests and nuns met them at the dock, and he stuck close to Father Baptiste as they clasped hands formally. When the delegation raised eyebrows questioningly after glancing at Adolphe, Father Baptiste introduced him. "This is my friend, Adolphe. He hopes that we will be able to find a place for him in the New World. After travelling far across the ocean from his native shore he is understandably a bit lost. Perhaps we can take him under our wing and help him to find a new direction."

Baptiste, with a hand on Adolphe's shoulder, smiled down at him and the bishop who stood ahead of the other priests looked at him long and hard, not speaking. Bishop Constantine was elderly, slightly stooped, and white bearded. Adolphe trembled under the intense gaze but lowered his eyes, saying nothing.

Finally, as Adolphe was beginning to wonder if he was about to be turned away at the docks, Bishop Constantine nodded to one of the other priests who came forward and took his arm saying, "Come with me, my son; I will see that you have a place among us."

Adolphe was not happy about being separated from his friend, but Baptiste smiled and nodded. "Go with him Adolphe. He will get you settled."

Up the hillside, they tramped until they came to the big church at the top with the tall front and steeple, and the bell. It was the largest church he ever saw and the living quarters behind for the priests was two storeys high, built solidly of wood and stone. The nunnery was connected to that, a large structure that acted as hospital, kitchen, living quarters, and chapel. This was where they found room for Adolphe.

The halls inside were dark, cold, and echoed every footstep. Creaking passages led him so far away from his room that he sometimes became hopelessly lost. Never had he felt so far away from home, so lonely, and in such a foreign place. Though he tried to find Father Baptiste, he could not, and so he tried to content himself with his room, the courtyard, the dining hall where he ate with the nuns, and the chapel where he went with the nuns for prayers every morning.

At long last, Bishop Constantine sent for him, and the priest who led him to his room escorted him; he could never have found his way on his own. He sat quietly in the bishop's office waiting, hardly breathing, before the bishop raised his tired eyes to include Adolphe.

"I understand that you followed Father Baptiste to Canada against the wishes of your parents," he began, laying his quill pen down on the blotter on his desk.

"*Oui, Monsieur* – Father – Bishop Constantine," Adolphe stammered. Not knowing what else to say, he again fell silent.

"You are sixteen years old, are you not?" He pierced Adolphe with a blue gaze.

"*Oui*, Bishop Constantine," and again he fell silent.

"You may address me as Father." A long pause and he again spoke. "Since you do not have the training or education you can not be a priest and you are too young to be a lay brother. There is no place for you in the seminary. All of these priests will in time be sent to different parishes where they will minister to the people, either in Upper Canada or Lower Canada or in the West. It could be with the Indians where you would be asked to face dangerous situations for a boy your age."

"Oh, I do not mind! If Father Baptiste is going out west on a posting, I could be very useful and helpful. I am strong and resourceful and I ...."

"Quiet!" the bishop raised his voice in reprimand.

"I am sorry, Father. I did not mean to ..."

"We have decided," the bishop said unemotionally, "that you must select a trade. The Oblates of Mary Immaculate will sponsor you and pay for your training. You may come back here each evening after work for bed and board. We will supply your clothing and other needs as long as you assume duties around here that the nuns will assign to you. Is that clear to you?"

"Oh, yes, Father, that is quite clear. I thank you."

"When we have found a place for you we will call you." The Bishop dismissed him. Adolphe backed away hurriedly.

First, he decided to explore more of his surroundings. He stole into the chapel with its high domed ceiling, its rich mahogany pews, and high altar. He gazed at the huge cross with the Christ figure, the painted windows, and wall hangings. He listened to the echo that his footsteps made on the polished floor, and he smelled the incense and the musty smell of old books. Perhaps some day he would go on to train as a priest, and all of this would be familiar to him. Now, he seemed to be on the outside looking in.

He had to find Father Baptiste. Suddenly, he felt very lost and alone, like a wanderer adrift on the open sea with nothing but a life raft underneath him. Father Baptiste would know how to help him find his way.

Adolphe began a search of the entire grounds, all of the buildings, even all of the rooms if he had to. The three storey living quarters connected to the church must be where he would find him. Since he could not find the entrance outside after circling the huge building twice, he decided that the priests must gain access from inside the church. So he began a thorough search.

Finally, in the lower level, next to the wine cellar, he located a huge door with heavy iron hinges. Determined and with heart racing, he turned the handle and pulled the door open. He was met with a long dark hallway and the musty, dank odour. Suddenly he was seized by a frightful thought. *'What if this didn't connect with the priest quarters but is an escape tunnel to heaven knows where! Perhaps in the early days in the war between the French and the English it led to a secret passage to an underground route to the river and, in the past, a waiting boat. How long would the dark tunnel be?'*

Just in time, he ran back and caught the heavy door before it closed. Hesitantly, he stood at the entrance not sure whether to go back or explore further.

Curiosity soon got the better of his hesitation. He found a candle and a light from an upstairs fireplace, gathered up a book to prop the door ajar, and set out down the long dark hallway. With his heart in his throat he continued until he saw a door at the end of the hallway. He breathed a sigh of relief when the door pushed open as he turned the handle. Entering the wine cellar of the building, he held his candle high exploring, and came to stair steps.

Blowing out his candle at the top of the stairs, he entered a small vestibule that opened into a lower hallway and also to another set of stairs to the next floor above. He had guessed right, he congratulated himself. *One of these rooms must belong to Father Baptiste, but which one?*

When he heard someone close a door on the second floor, he quickly backed into a dark alcove that held galoshes, raincoats, umbrellas, and brooms. Peeking out of a crack, he watched a priest whom he had not seen before, come down the stairs in his black robes and pass down the hallway.

Deciding that the coast was clear, he stole out and headed down the hallway on the first floor. No names were on the doors, only numbers. Finding Father Baptiste was not going to be easy. Maybe if he waited long enough and was able to hide cleverly enough, Baptiste would eventually come down. A door was open at the end of the hallway, and after discreetly peeking around the corner, he discovered a long table with a sideboard and shelves. *'This must be the dining-room,'* Adolphe decided. Eventually, Baptiste would come to his noon meal. He would find a hiding-place until then.

Across from the dining room was another open door. Cautiously, he stole inside to see long rows of bookshelves. *'This must be the library. I can easily hide in here behind shelves and piles of boxes and books. And it's just across from the dining room! How fortunate!'* There was a window from the library into the hallway!

After wandering the aisles of the library, cautiously peering around the end of the shelves, he found one priest sitting at a table engrossed in reading.

When he saw through the window into the hallway, four of the grey-robed nuns approaching, carrying trays of dishes and food, he realized that all of the priests would soon be coming to the dining room to eat. Again Adolphe congratulated himself. Soon he would see Father Baptiste.

As the priests trooped into the dining room, he studied each face, each form. No one was familiar. '*How can this be?*' he demanded of himself.

Suddenly, he nearly jumped out of his skin. A hand caught him firmly by the shoulder. Wheeling around, he came face to face with the priest who had been reading at the table.

"How did you get in here, *jeune homme?*" the priest demanded in a quiet voice, but with a frown.

"I – I – I am looking for Father Baptiste. Does he stay in this rectory?" Adolphe tried to still his pounding heart and panting breath.

"Come with me," the priest told him and steered him out the door, down the hallway, and into a small office beside the dining room. "We will be right back," he said as he exited.

With a sigh of relief, Adolphe relaxed and waited. Everything would be all right when Baptiste came and explained to the priests. They would all understand why Adolphe needed to talk to him.

When the door opened again, it was not Baptiste who was with the priest, but Bishop Constantine, and his brows were knit with a heavy scowl.

"So, you do not listen very well when you are asked to wait patiently while others try to help you," he growled at Adolphe, and Adolphe trembled. "Again you steal in where you are not supposed to be, just like you did when you stole a ride here on board the ship."

"*Excusez-moi*, Bishop Constantine. But I must find Father Baptiste. I have not seen him since I got here, and I need to talk to him," Adolphe ended lamely.

"You will not find him here. When you left your home in France, you thought that you were old enough to be on your own. Are you not old enough to make your own decisions without talking to Father Baptiste? What is it that is so important that you can not talk to us?"

"I do not know what to do next? What – what – trade I should take. Will I always be living in the little room at the nunnery?"

"I will soon be telling you how you will be fitting into life here – unless you are considering running away to take your chances with the Indians in the West?" The Bishop scowled down at him, and Adolphe bent his head contritely. He had no answer, and he felt tears burning his eyes and a lump in his throat.

After a long pause, Bishop Constantine, with a quieter tone, spoke the words that sent Adolphe's world crashing to the ground at the bishop's feet. "Father Baptiste has gone. He has accepted a calling out West, and you could not have accompanied him."

"Where? Where has he gone?" Adolphe demanded, sitting bolt upright in his chair. "Why did not someone tell me?"

"That is not for the likes of you to know!" the bishop bellowed. "Where he has gone, no young boy could go. You have a lot of growing up to do before you are ready to face the hard life of a priest in his placement. And tomorrow you will either start that training or return to France. Which do you choose? The Oblates of Mary Immaculate can pay for your sponsorship here in the trades or they can pay for your return trip to France. Which do you choose?"

After a long pause, his head spinning in confusion and sorrow, Adolphe spoke softly. "I will stay."

20

The Mission on Lac Ste. Anne

Each spring Alex and John took their furs and met the York boats from Rocky Mountain House heading back to York Factory. Every fall they returned to their shack along the North Saskatchewan. The Hudson Bay Company flag now flew from their roof as a signal to all who plied the river or who travelled overland on the many trails, that they could trade their furs for whatever they wished without having to travel the long distance into Fort Edmonton. The other posts along the river did the same thing until they reached Rocky Mountain House, the end of the line.

Rocky Mountain House brought in furs from a wide field and kept many fur traders busy. They searched for the furs, contacting nine different tribes from all up and down the mountains. The traders also had to hew timbers to make new York boats that they either traded at Fort Edmonton, forts along the way, or took all the way back to York Factory with them.

Alex and John, with the help of their two friends, Gabriel and Paul Beaver, who came to their post quite often when they were in the neighbourhood, explored and became familiar with an area further afield every year. They even made crude maps. The Beaver boys helped them learn more Cree so when people came to their trading post they were able to talk to them a little and understand what they asked for.

The traders could not, however, find any evidence that furs were being traded to a rival, usurping company. The boys, and eventually all of the traders up and down the river from Fort Edmonton to Rocky Mountain House, finally had to accept the fact that there was no longer abundance of fur bearing animals. They had to accept the fact that the area was depleted of furs. The traders at White Whale Creek would walk all day without evidence of a bear, mink, otter, muskrat, or weasel. Even big game was in short supply. Where were the moose and the deer? The Indians and the Métis also asked themselves that question. They needed the moose for their canoes and tipis and the deer for their clothing and moccasins. But even of more concern was the meat the animals supplied.

John and Alex also began to feel the lack. They eagerly awaited the Indians coming in with their furs and the pemmican. The Métis and Indians needed food as well, so they were not trading it away. The stock of blankets, axes, and guns sat piled up in the corner, unmoving, while everyone searched for the animals to no avail.

It was 1869, and the fur trade was grinding to a halt. At first, John and Alex haunted the trail from White Whale Lake to Fort Edmonton hoping to divert the trade their way but the travois and pack animals were not carrying furs or hides to the fort. After a long hunting foray, they headed home, up the trail, back to their camp to make use of a meager catch – lucky to have enough to last them the rest of the winter.

During a mild stretch that winter, the two Bay Company traders planned a trip north, up the trail in the direction of White Whale Lake again. They thought they would stay at a stopping house and make the long trek to Lac Ste. Anne. They had to see if the conditions were the same further north as they were along the North Saskatchewan.

Their only problem, they would have to leave the post unattended unless they could get someone from another river post to take over for a time. Even though there had been no traffic into the trading post for two weeks, they still had to see that the post was manned. They also were not happy about letting everything freeze in the cabin. Their canned goods were down to bare minimum, but after they packed some along with them, they could bury the rest in the cellar. Their food supply was low. With none to trade, there was only enough to tide them over the winter.

As it happened, they had a visit from Duncan MacKenzie and Murdock Chisholm, who trekked all the way from Rocky Mountain House on snowshoe after stopping at the different posts all the way down.

The old friends had a happy reunion around the heater that night trading bits of information and smoking their pipes. Even if food was in short supply tobacco was not.

"If one o' ye cood stay fer a time, John and meself cood make the trip up tae Lac Ste. Anne thah we hae been plannin'," Alex spoke up after the four of them had finished off the last of the hardtack and beans and lit up their pipes. "We dinna lack to leave the post empty that long."

"We came tae help and see how ye were farin'," Murdock nodded.

"Tae be sure, there's one more post further down-river that we hae tae get tae and then wai'll be back, if ye can wait 'til we retairn," Duncan told him, as he moved his wet steaming leggings back from the heat a bit.

"Thah would be Hamish McCauley and Willie Macrae," said Chisholm. "We're mainly looking fer word aboot how the trade is doing - any better than last yair, and hae ye enough food supply?"

"Noh a lot o' variety as ye noticed, but we should make it 'til spring," John replied. "How air things up at the Hoose?"

"Aboot the same as here," Murdock stretched out his long legs towards the fire, enjoying the heat and relaxation. "We just finished buildin' two more Yark boats, but there'll be little use fer them if the trrade does na pick up."

"Sutherland hae finally accepted the fact that there's practically nae fur bearing animals left up in this country. We hae been bringin' in a few baiver every spring but it's a drop in the bucket tae what we used tae haul back."

"Well, we hae been tryin' to tell them thah fer the past three years, but they keep sendin' us oot here."

"It's their superiors in England and Montreal that they hae tae convince and now it looks like they air convinced," Duncan ended.

"Whah d'ye mean?" Alex leaned forward curiously.

"Well, all these years the Company hae been fightin' in the East fer the fur. The government in the East finally granted the company exclusive rights tae trade in this whole narthland. Now we goh word thah the Bay signed deeds of surrender tae holding rights on many, many miles of Ruperts Land fer the sum of three hundred thousand pounds."

"Who did they sign away the land tae?" John wanted to know. "Whah aboot the trading posts and our trap-lines?"

"Och, they hae kept the rights tae forty-five thousand acres covering the land aroond their trading posts and, I hear they resairved millions, huge tracts of land! It went to Upper and Lower Canada. They say thah soon the Red River Settlements will be part of Canada as well."

"So whah about Ruperts Land? Is it bein' taken over by the eastern government as well?" Alex wanted to know.

"The East has no interrest in the savagery of the West. When they canna get any more furs out o' this land they'll likely give it back to Ruperts Land." Chisholm seemed confident.

"This belongs to the Indians out here. Whah aboot them? How can the East claim the land by payin' the Hudson Bay Company?" John puzzled about the arrogance of governments.

"There'll be trouble o'er this," Chisholm nodded knowingly. "The Indians figured that thae Bay was just here tae trade wi' 'em, noh tae claim their country."

"We'll find oot when we get tae Lac Ste. Anne," Alex said ominously. "If they hae even heard anything. The French in the mission will be hearin' aboot it. In Upper Canada the French will be happy to get the rights away from the Hudson Bay. Since the Narthwest Company died all they hae up here are the missions."

"Even if there air very few furs back here?" Duncan was doubtful.

"They'll be happy tae claim anything thah doesna belong to the Hudson's bay." Alex laughed. "But we'd better get tae bed so John and me can get an airly start. Ye'd better hunt fer a rabbit or somethin' tomorrow; there's nae meat left. Check my traps doon by the craik. I havena even seen a deer in so long that I forgot how venison tastes."

It was late the next night when Alex and John arrived at what would some day be the mission house on White whale Lake where they stopped with the Indian band the first time they were up that way. They knew that the band would be gone by now. The natives did not stop anywhere too long. However, from the top of the hill they saw the black dots that were people out on the lake ice fishing. *Ah, for a feed of fresh fish*! They travelled a long way that day at a mile-eating pace. John and Alex with their long legs and their capability on the snowshoes covered a lot of snow-covered trail in a day. But they had pushed themselves to their limit up the well-travelled trail to the mission house.

This was the spot that would some day be the Methodist mission as George McDougall planned. The building was started, just a shell of logs and a stone fireplace that McDougall and the natives put into place, with a roof of saplings and bark. No one was around. The natives with their sapling and hide tipis had moved on, but they would use the little clearing again the next time they came through. Alex and John used the bare cold building as a protection from the elements, made a fire in the fireplace, and warmed their food over it before curling up into their bedrolls for the night.

Early in the morning the two men set off again for Lac Ste. Anne Mission. The trail was clearly marked and showed the tracks of horses, travois, and snowshoe as well as dogs and dogsled. This was the main trail from Lac Ste. Anne to Fort Edmonton.

However, no traffic was seen on it. The only indication of life along the way was a beaver pond where recent activity of trappers dug beaver or muskrat out of their winter houses that rose like little hay mounds out of the middle of the pond.

"I wonder where they took the baiver pelt tae trade?" Alex mused. "Probably tae Lac Ste. Anne."

"Maybe tae Fort Edmonton," John speculated. "But then, thah's a long way tae go with a few pelts."

"And, o' course, they would hae tae prepare them. It depends on how many they trapped afore this," Alex said. Evidence of snares put up for rabbits or weasels they saw, but they were old and it did not appear as though there had been any harvest.

The two pushed on with more effort and speed as a sudden squall picked up from the north throwing pellets of stinging snow into their faces. Collars were pulled up, fur hats pulled down, and scarves muffled their mouths as they bent their heads into the storm.

They reached the Lac Ste. Anne Mission as darkness began to descend on the tired pair and they looked forward to the warmth of the stopping house, people, and hot food.

The first thing to startle them was a low stockade surrounding the village inside. It reminded them of the stockade around Fort Edmonton except that it was not as tall. The two men pushed open a gate that swung on leather hinges. The gate was made of poles laced together with rawhide thongs, and they were hesitant at first to enter for fear that it was meant to keep them out.

However, they entered and pulled the gate shut behind them. *How strange this was*, they pondered. It soon became apparent why the stockade was constructed. A dozen dogs bounded towards them causing them to close the gate quickly between them and the mangy mutts. Thwarted by the closed gate, the animals soon went back to the food of fish scraps that were thrown over the fence to them.

After a glance at the dog sleds nearby, the two young men realized why there were so many dogs and why they were housed outside the stockade. These pulled the dogsleds, the winter form of transportation from Lac Ste. Anne to Fort Edmonton, St. Albert and beyond. The dogs soon raised a howl and racket that brought people running to meet them.

John and Alex stood for a moment staring about, taking in the unfamiliar surroundings. A settlement of thirty log shacks was spread out in a haphazard manner, mostly along the shore of the lake. On the highest point of land stood the mission chapel with its tall spire, its purpose obvious to every visitor.

The biggest building and the most dominant with its wide front, railing veranda and flag floating high above it was the Hudson Bay trading post. But before they could make their way toward it, they were suddenly surrounded by half the village folk, most of them children. Little round brown faces peered out from under dark hair and furry hats of squirrel and rabbit. The children stared at the strangers, not speaking until older teens and adults joined them.

One spokesman asked them a question that they thought must be either in Cree or French and the two Scots spread their hands and shrugged.

Hopefully the new arrivals asked the spokesperson, a young man in his late teens, a question in Gaelic and they all looked at each other puzzled. Alex tried a couple of Cree words that he had recently learned: "*Na-na-chap-han-ni, O-so-no-ni-hih*," and got a reaction. There were smiles and nodding and more chattering all at once, while they pointed to the post. But Alex was not sure what the answer meant. However, followed by the entourage, they made their way toward the trading post.

Leaving their company behind, they mounted the two steps into the post and were confronted by a large ruddy-complected man in his fifties. He had a reddish beard, a big head of hair, and a round belly that was accompanied by a commanding hearty voice.

"*Comprenez francais?*" he asked them in his booming voice as he stepped forward to shake hands. When they shook their heads, looking confused, he switched to English.

"So, we have a couple of Scots here, have we?" He laughed in his big booming bass after hearing John and Alex's reply. "My name is Andrew McGillivray. I'm the factor here at Lac Ste. Anne. What are you doing in these parts?" he asked. Andrew had been speaking French or Cree for so long that his English was rusty.

John and Alex sat down on two kegs beside the heater in the middle of the store. Andrew offered them a cup of coffee from a bent-up, blackened pot that seemed to sit eternally atop the heater or was pulled to a back corner of the stove when it was just meant to be kept warm. "We air verra glad," John started off as he pulled his boots off to toast his toes in the heat, "thah ye can speak English. We were noh farin' verra well wi' the few words ae Cree thah we understood."

"If you are goin' to spend any time in this area you'd better learn to speak French or Cree – both would be handy." Andrew sat down with his cup on a block of wood that had been cut in such a way that it fit his bottom completely.

"How is it thah a Scotsman lives oot this way in French territory?" Alex asked after a swallow of the black coffee that was strong and bitter after sitting all morning in its dregs.

"In the beginning this was a Northwest Company post. When it was built by the French voyageurs, the missionaries followed. Or maybe it was the fur traders that followed the first missionary post. I don't rightly know."

Andrew McGillivray leaned against the back of his wooden block and lit up a pipe. As an afterthought he offered the two young men some of his tobacco. They accepted happily and took pipes out of their pockets. "It was said that Father Thibault founded this mission in 1842, the first missionary in this part of the country, but I know the fur trade was all over this area for fifty years before that. They mostly built the trading posts on the rivers.

"The Northwest Company was first out this way. That's why the French names can mostly be found. They married or took Indian women and a lot of them stayed around here. Members of this whole settlement on Lac Ste. Anne are descendants of those first French voyageurs and Cree women.

"It was not until just a few years ago that the Hudson Bay Company built this post at Lac Ste. Anne. It was Colin Fraser who was the first factor. Because he knew the French language so well, after having a part French and part Cree mother, he was the ideal person to send out here. I learned to speak the language from him and that's why they sent me out here. They sent him on to Jasper House."

"So whah is thae fur trade like oot here noo?" John asked bluntly.

"And the animal abundance or noh?" Alex asked leaning forward eagerly, glad that the subject, the main reason for their coming this far, had finally been broached.

"I can see that you are wondering the same thing that I was worried about," Andrew finally answered with a frown. "It is true what you have no doubt been suspecting. The animals are no longer here in the abundance that they were when I first arrived in this country as a lad. Not only are the fur-bearing animals in short supply but the deer, the moose—all of the animals. Colin Fraser trekked back this way last winter to see how we were faring here since he left and told us that it is the same story all throughout the country.

"Colin spoke to the Blackfoot south of the Saskatchewan and it is even worse for them," Andrew went on. "Trade and horses made the Blackfoot powerful. At tribal festivals they were rich and free as the Great Spirit intended them to be, they told Fraser, but now the buffalo have all but disappeared. The plains Indians swept across the prairie like lightning, but now they have resorted to trading and eating their own horses.

"Their women were rich in buffalo hides, meat and tools, he said, but now they sicken and die. There is a change in the wind," McGillivray spoke ominously. "And it is spreading to the north.

"But Father Remas foresaw this happening years ago. This is why he has been trying to change the people's thinking. Here, in Lac Ste. Anne, they raise cows, pigs, potatoes and turnips, and barley in the small fields that they have learned to sow and reap.

"But wait," Andrew raised his hand. "I will bring Father Remas in to meet you and he can tell you all about it." He hurried out the door, and in a few minutes came back with an old priest. Father Remas was white-haired and bent over like a question mark. His face was wrinkled and browned from the sun, his white bushy eyebrows standing up into wings, but his face was kindly, though his eyes were starting to dim.

He spoke to them in French as he shook hands warmly and Andrew translated. "These are his beloved people. He will live and die with them.

You are welcome to stay a few days, and he will show you around. He invites you to eat with him this avening at his small home behind the chapel.

"When I first came to this country," Andrew translated, "it was to slash our way through the densest forest where the ground was boggy and rotten, thickly covered with fallen timber. Now there are trails all over. Game was abundant and starvation was unknown but now things are changing."

"The Indians," Andrew added on his own, "would not stay in one spot and settle down. They have always roamed around and followed the game. All of these people in this settlement are Métis. They could be convinced to settle in one spot and raise their food, to cultivate the land and scatter the seed – to wait for it to grow."

"The cattle took much care and the Indians did not like the taste of the domesticated cow. The milk was for babies, they thought," Father Remas added and Andrew translated with a laugh. "But the Métis grew to like it, and they did not mind the work of agriculture."

"*Venez, venez*! I will show you." Father Remas beckoned as he shuffled out the door ahead of them, leaving the two Scottish lads to quickly pull on their boots and coats and follow.

Father Remas proudly took them to the barn where five cattle, two horses and five pigs were cared for by the whole village in turn. Hay was stowed in the barn under Father Remas' direction and the bins and sacks of barley were available for any of the women to use.

"They would," Andrew translated, "scoop the barley intae lukewarm water tae soak. Then they would put the softened grains intae a smoothened out block, pound it with a mallet until the husks were off, and then use the grains in soup or for bread or pemmican. Or it could be fried until black and then ground up for coffee."

Father Remas limped about the village painfully but proudly pointed out how they made soap with grease and ashes. Tiny long roots from the muskeg were used to sew together pans, berry baskets, and pots. Over the seams, he pointed out, heated spruce gum sealed the leaks.

"But the Métis are happiest with the whitefish from their beautiful lake," Andrew added. "They don't miss the deer and the moose so much as long as there are plenty of fish that can be caught in the winter through the ice. Thousands of fish in one day have been taken from this lake. Not so many at one time any more can be caught but at least they have not been depleted."

Father Remas led them down through the village and showed the men the homes where the Métis families lived. One, in particular, they stopped in front of. It was newly constructed of hewn spruce logs. Two windows were cut into the logs and rafters made of poles placed three feet apart were covered with bark and anchored with pins made of wood. No iron nails were used. They were too expensive.

Father Remas hailed one of the young men who appeared in the doorway of a home, which was just in the process of construction. "Jean Baptiste," he called out and the young man came out to greet him.

As the two talked, Andrew translated. "The house is nearly finished. The open fireplace, which they call a mud stove has been built, and the chimney, which was built of clay and hay plaster, is dry. There will be a party this evening to dedicate it and celebrate the finish. You two are invited as well as all of the neighbours.

"We would be glad tae attend," John spoke for both of them.

21

House Warming

After a supper of whitefish cooked over an open fire, potatoes taken from the cellar, and milk to drink, they felt pleasantly full and contented. "If we are going to go to the celebration of the new house, we will need gifts," Andrew announced as he pushed his plate away at the little table in his kitchen. His wife, Rose, a Métis woman, who spoke very few words and only when answering a question, picked the dishes up and took them to the corner cupboard, where she washed them in a basin of water. When she was finished with her duties, she melted away again, sitting on a low bench in the corner.

"We hae nothin' to gi'e," John spoke up unhappily. "Perhaps we should na gae."

"Of course you should. Not going after an invitation would be an insult. This couple has just been wed by Father Remas two days ago and this is their first home, built by his own hands with help from the neighbours. They are a young couple whose parents are also in the village. They grew up nearby to each other and there is much to celebrate. We'll find something for you. Have ye a knife that you could part with? Or maybe a blanket? How about a trap, or an article of fur? Iron articles are always popular. They will need iron that can be bent into hooks to hang pots over the fire. Old pieces of guns could be dismantled and used in that way. Come into the storeroom and select something if ye like, and maybe ye can trade wi' me for it or a promise of something next time ye come doon." That was very neighbourly of Andrew. The more he talked the more he fell back into the old accent that had not been forgotten, just buried away for a time.

So, in high spirits, the group headed out, minus Father Remas who felt he was too old for the partying, and besides, he was not feeling particularly well and planned to crawl into his bed as soon as he finished his evening meal. Rose, however, did go, loaded down with food for the party.

When John and Alex saw the number of people who arrived they had serious doubts about how everyone would fit into that small cabin. But it appeared everyone planned to crowd inside whether there was room or not.

Inside, all managed to find a place to sit on the floor for there was not one piece of furniture. There was not even a bed! Blankets for sleeping were rolled away and so took up no room. They had no use for table or chairs either. All that existed in the little cabin was the corner fireplace, which was raised above the ground on poles and plastered well into the floor.

One of the men brought his fiddle. He was always popular at a party. Another brought a flat tambour drum on which he beat a rhythm for the fiddle. The recently married couple among the circle of guests was all that was standing and they received the gifts seriously and matter-of-factly, nodding in appreciation to the giver. Then a jug was passed around for all to sip from. John supposed it to be homemade wine. Since there were not enough cups everyone drank from the jug.

As the jug circulated, the music started up and since there was no room to dance, all just slapped a rhythm on their legs, clapped or tapped their toes. One Métis man beat out a rhythm on the rawhide calfskin that covered the window since there was no glass.

Many husky voices shouted out André's name, encouraging him as he played his fiddle. It was homemade, a cleverly fashioned instrument made of strips of wood bent, shaped and glued together. The strings were made of the sinew from the back of a moose, the bridge of bone and the hairs of the bow was horsehair. Tree-sap of the black spruce provided the rosin for the bow and the wood was polished to fine perfection.

André held it to his chest and sawed off a merry tune to the drum accompaniment while all cheered with enthusiasm. The tune was jerky and the bow scratchy, but this was the music that stirred their hearts. When he had played all that he knew, he started over again, and this time people added their Cree words and high native sounds passed down to them from generations past. Then they switched to French songs learned from voyageurs and missionaries.

Some of the gifts neighbours brought were food offerings for the party. Rose, along with other Métis women, cleared back some legs in the centre of the floor to make way to set out some of it. A white canvas sailcloth was spread out on the floor, picnic style, and a white cloth, in honour of the happy couple, was spread on top. On this they set a large flat basket holding pieces of smoked fish, pemmican, barley-bread, and barbecued meat that was cooked under hot coals of wood. The only cupboard for dishes was a small three-cornered shelved one that held their few dishes and the gifts that were brought. It occupied a space in the corner and was the only furniture other than the stove.

The music, the food, and the wine, along with the happy feeling of closeness and friendship gave everyone a warm feeling of togetherness. The two strangers could feel it and felt a part of it. Alex developed a fondness for the fiddle and the brew in the circulating jug. He moved beside André so that he could watch and learn.

Next to John, a game was started and, he began to take an interest in it. The fire in the mud stove nearby threw enough flickering light over them to see to play as well as to give heat, although the closeness of the bodies in the room also provided heat. A big slab of wood was stood up perpendicularly in the deep stove and provided light as the flames climbed up its length. Since John could see no lamps or candles, he assumed there were none.

Sitting cross-legged on the floor next to him playing a game with their hands was a young girl and a younger boy. They were not allowed to sip from the jug so they amused themselves with the popular game. The boy would close his fists behind his back, then bring them out while the girl would guess which hand the prize was in. When she guessed wrong he crowed in exultation, took one of her little many sided beads that she pulled from the pocket of her heavy, cotton flannel skirt and displayed in a little pile in front of her just opposite the young man's neat little pile of beads. John, with his back against the wall, eased forward, past the shoulder of another young man so that he could get a better look at the game in progress.

This time the girl exclaimed, "Ha!" and took a bead from the young man's pile in front of him as she captured the little block from the boy's hand. She guessed the right hand containing the little square of wood and won the prize - one of his beads from his pile. The beads were made of glass, or wood and had holes drilled through them so that they could be strung together or used singly as they were doing. They were round or square or many-sided if they were made of wood, and polished.

If he were being honest with himself, John would have to admit that he was as much fascinated with the girl as he was with the game they played.

Her dark hair was long, falling loosely over her shoulders and shone with a reddish glow in the firelight. Her face was small, and her eyes sparkled impishly as she won another bead from her opponent. Her smile was radiant and caught John's immediate attention.

Sensing John's interest in them, the pair looked up at him and the game ended for a moment. Suddenly they were both shy. The boy lowered his eyes to his pile of beads, but the girl returned his stare, that spark of curiosity dancing in her brown eyes with their flecks of hazel.

"*Mon frère, Henri*," she introduced her brother and then she pointed to herself indicating her name, "Lucy."

John reciprocated and introduced himself giving his full name "John Lenny." She nodded, smiling.

With signs John indicated that he would like to play the game. She moved to face him, her knees boldly touching his legs that were crossed in front of him, and indicated with a raise of an eyebrow what he had to wager since her previous opponent quickly rescued his precious winnings. John had no beads, and he cast around in his mind what he could possibly put up with any value. Suddenly he remembered the little beads sewn and twisted into the fringe of his jacket. He took it on trade for a gun from an Indian who needed a gun and bullets from the trading post. Since the room was getting warm, especially sitting next to the clay stove that threw a lot of heat as well as light, he had taken off his jacket and was sitting on it.

Pulling his jacket out to display it, he pointed out the tiny beads that the Indian squaw used to decorate the jacket. These were a lot smaller than her beads, but they were all he could think of.

The girl looked at them closely before looking up at him and smiling that radiant smile of hers. She nodded and they both set about to undo the beads from the jacket. Immediately she discovered how they were put in and began expertly undoing the fringe from the beads with her adept hands. Clumsy hands were not made for undoing the beads so he held the jacket front while she deftly untied them, separating them from the sinew that fastened them to the fringe.

While she bent over the task, he marvelled at her beauty. She was only about sixteen years of age but she seemed so mature, so bold and self-assured. The saucy toss of her head and the well-developed form of a woman unnerved him.

When all of the beads were removed, she poured them into his palm with a triumphant smile. Then she sat back ready to play the 'game of hands'. Indicating that he should set his handful down onto the blanket, she made a nest for them so that they would not roll away.

Putting her hands behind her, she made a pantomime of shuffling the wooden game piece from hand to hand and then displayed both little brown fists before him, bidding him guess which hand held the square. Looking boldly into her eyes for some clue as to which fist to choose was the best part of this game. However, it became even better when he chose the hand, not by pointing at it or touching it with one finger as was the custom, but by taking the smooth fist in both of his big hands and peeling the fingers back.

"*J'ai gagné.*" she crowed with a gleeful laugh showing her empty palm. Then she reached over and confiscated one of the prized beads. Now the brother, Henri, moved in closer, losing some of his shyness. He laughed with glee to see his sister winning the stranger's betting pieces.

The next time, John began to decipher his opponent's tactics to throw him off the track, and he won twice in a row. The smile disappeared from the girl's face. She began to worry, imagining herself losing all of the wonderful beads. He won his bead back and another one of hers. Her opponent had taken one of her prettiest beads.

Chewing on her lip, she tried to decide in which of his callused fists the elusive game piece was hiding. His hands were large, and she could find no clue in his face. She chose badly and he took another bead. By now all traces of sparkle in her eyes was replaced by worry. She was losing!

This would never do, John thought. The beads were of no use to him. Now that they had been removed from his jacket, they were of no more value, except as a means of continuing the game with this fascinating girl.

When he pulled his fists out next time he squeezed the one with the wooden block a little tighter. Lucy looked at it warily. This could be a ruse to get her to pick that one. Henri had tried that one on her. She chose the other one and lost one more bead when the fist came up empty. She swallowed, and her eyes glistened with close to the surface tears as he reluctantly took another bead.

Henri now crowded in to try to get her to let him bet her pieces. He was sure, he argued with her, that he could recognize the man's tricks. But she turned on him in irritation. "*Non, non Henri!*" she insisted. "*Allez!*" These were her beads, and this was her game. She would win them back.

Now John had a dilemma. How could he get her to choose the right hand so that the smile and the sparkle would return to her eyes?

Displaying his hands, he deliberately looked at the fist with the game piece, but when she looked into his eyes, he looked away pulling the hand back just slightly. Like a coyote pouncing on a mouse she knew she 'had' it. Impetuously, instead of carefully pointing at his hand, she grabbed his strong hand as he had done with her and peeled back his fingers.

"Ha!" she cried out proudly, looking at Henri with a disdainful flip of her hair. Retrieving the game piece, she selected her favourite bead.

The confident smile back, she put her hands behind her back again and tried a new tactic that would really throw this stranger off the track.

She won several times in a row and was flushed with victory when she realized that she had more of an audience than her brother, Henri.

Since the jug of wine was empty the others were turning to other forms of entertainment. They were cheering on the game and looking for partners of their own to start up a new game. Who had another gaming piece? Looking around, John noticed that several others were also playing the same game in little groups around them. At that moment, Factor McGillivray appeared, standing over them unsmiling.

He spoke in French, but John could make out that this kind of wagering was against the rules of the village. Pére Remas would not like this, John gathered, as the name was brought up and others hung their heads. The wine was not allowed either, after an incident that had happened in which a fight started and people were hurt.

"Lucy," he scolded her, "*Est-ce-que c'est les grain de votre chapelet?*"

John suddenly realized that the factor was talking about Lucy's rosary beads. She had taken apart her rosary to mix them with her other beads!

The door opened and in came Father Remas. The whole room went quiet while the priest spoke to them quietly but severely. Sitting down beside John, Factor McGillivray explained, "We had several incidents in the past having to do with liquor and the *'Jeu des mains'*. Under the influence of the firewater, some of them gambled away everything they owned. They broke into the trading post and stole from the factor before me. They fought each other and beat their wives. At the council, they agreed not to play the game of the hands any more and not to drink intoxicating beverages. Père Remas called it his 'Temperance Society', and they all swore to follow the rules. Things have run smoothly since then, until now! They thought that since this was a celebration of a couple's first house that the wine was not as bad as the hard liquor."

"But it wa' an innocent game wi' the children!" John was incredulous.

"That's the way it starts. Unfortunately, it was not stopped completely. The children learned the fascinating game from the adults and have been playing it in their groups with sticks and now beads. Lately the adults have been turning a blind eye with the children, thinking as you did: 'They are just children! It is all so innocent!' But you see what it caused Lucy to do. She took her sacred rosary beads apart. Fortunately, it was a small amount of wine for a large group, and they were not driven to fighting or angry flare-ups."

John noticed that Lucy was given a private lecture by Father Remas. Her head was bent, and tears dropped onto her hands that were folded in her lap. Then she nodded and moved back towards John and Henri. Father followed her, his hand on her shoulder.

Kneeling down again in front of Henri, she apologized and returned the beads she had won from him. Then she turned towards John. Cheeks flushed, eyes downcast she recited her apology to him, *"Je repent, Monsieur Lenny,"* she murmured. Then she poured the beads that she had won back into his hand.

"Ou et votre maman?" Father Remas asked the girl.

"Maman est malade," Lucy told Father. *"Et Celestin, et Alexandre."*

"Qu'est-ce que c'est?" Father Remas seemed to be alarmed. Both he and Lucy left abruptly, leaving John puzzled.

"Lucy told Father Remas that the reason her mother was not at the party was that she was ill and so were her little sister and brother, Celestin and Alexandre," McGillivray said, frowning

Alex, feeling a little light-headed and happy, wandered out of the cabin behind John and the factor, whistling one of the tunes that the fiddler played. "John," he said as he moved up beside his buddy, matching his wobbly stride with John's, "I hae made up me mind. I'll be makin' mesel' a fiddle. That will be a good thing to whittle on over the winter. I hae seen how tae do it and I'm cairtain that I'll be able tae play it. It's just a matter ae practice."

"Mmmm," John replied noncommittally. He stuffed his hand into his pocket and met with a handful of beads. '*Now what am I going to do with these?*' he sighed. "Just carry on up tae bed at the factor's cabin," he told Alex, "I'll be right back." Then he turned on his heel and headed downhill toward the Métis village again.

Curious villagers eyed him as he met them or passed their houses, and he wished that he could speak the language. How was he going to find the right house? Finally, he met a man that he recognized from the party. "*Le maison de Lucy?*" he asked, hoping that he had remembered correctly the word for 'house'.

The man pointed, said a few words that John did not understand, and carried on. The tall chimneys extending above the houses issued smoke and sparks that spiralled high into the evening sky. They built their chimneys tall so that sparks did not set the roofs on fire. Any sparks that did land, however, winked out on the snowy roof.

John turned towards the house that the man had pointed out and met with thirteen-year-old Henri and another boy of about seven whom Henri called James. They stood seriously as though barring the door, making no move to find out why he was there.

"Lucy?" he asked simply

Henri spoke quite a few words that John did not understand, and John shrugged, repeating his request to see the boy's sister.

The door opened then, and Father Remas appeared, looking very serious, a pained expression on his face. Looking past Father Remas, John caught sight of Lucy, with a three-year-old clinging to her skirt and a year-old wrapped in a blanket on her hip. She jiggled the baby up and down trying to soothe him while tears traced dirty rivulets down his cheeks, and his nose ran with mucus.

The house was lit only by the fire in the corner mud stove. When the door opened, the cold rushed in upon the blanket-wrapped people lying on the floor since they had no beds. Nine people lived in this little shack, including the parents, John realized. Two little boys and their mother were sick, and Lucy was attempting to look after them. Overwhelming pity assailed him.

The largest form on the floor, obviously the mother, started to shiver violently and moan with pain in her legs and back. Lucy reached quickly for the door and closed it to keep out the cold. It would not stop the violent shivering, however, until Lucy's mother began to burn again with a high fever.

With a hand on John's arm, Father Remas turned him, and they headed back toward the little church up the hill. Since Father Remas could not speak English and John could not understand French very well, they walked in silence.

As they entered the trading post they met McGillivray and Alex who looked at the pair curiously. Father Remas explained the situation for a long while to the factor, and without further remark or salutation of goodnight, he left hurriedly.

"Thah's it!" Alex remarked with vehemence, "we hae just goh tae learn French."

After Father Remas closed the door, McGillivray faced them gravely. "Ye must leave here first thing in the morning," he announced.

The two young Scots were thunderstruck. "Why? Whah hae we done? Sure we dinna ken the customs, but we dinna think we ha' done anythin' verra wrong," they asked, not waiting for the other to finish.

"It's not what ye did." McGillivray shook his head with irritation. "There is sickness here. If ye don't leave right away ye may not be able to. The smallpox has come to our village. We are no strangers to it. The last time the epidemic came, it took many Métis lives. Father has gone to see how many Métis are sick. The white blood that flows in their veins may make them stronger to face the disease, and we still eat well. Many in other villages do not.

"Many of the elders in the village well remember the last epidemic and they will be terrified. Some may want to run away, but we can not let them go to spread the disease. We have to quarantine the whole village. That is why ye must leave first thing in the morning before others know what is happening." Factor McGillivray paced in agitation.

"One more thing!" He stopped and faced John looking him squarely in the eye. "Father Remas could see that ye have developed a fondness for the girl, Lucy. She has none of the symptoms yet, but if she stays, looking after her sick brothers and sisters, trying to be the second mother, she will also sicken and die if this is a killer epidemic as it was before."

John was completely taken aback. He stared in astonishment. Was he asking John to take Lucy with them when they left in the morning?

"She is too young to be a sacrifice to this disease. And she is smart as ye could see. Would ye give her a chance to survive this sickness? She could look after ye well, cook your meals, keep your cabin warm when ye are away and she could teach ye to speak both Cree and French. Ye know how handicapped ye are, being unable to speak the language of this part of the West." Factor McGillivray, in making his impassioned plea to John could not have known that John was convinced before two words had escaped the factor's mouth. McGillivray was right. This girl coming to live with them was a perfect idea.

"But," John hesitated, "will she want tae come? Will she be afraid?"

"It was her idea. Father said that she will be ready if ye want her to come."

The brave girl would leave her mother and father, the familiarity and comfort of her home and village, her friends and her brothers and sisters to follow them into the unknown–almost complete strangers! Alex's eyes widened and he stared at John. On the surface this sounded good, but he did not know what problems this could present for them.

"And Father Remas agraid tae this?!" John shook his head in disbelief.

"In one native village during the smallpox epidemic of 1779 and 1780 nearly the entire population was wiped out. If he can save one person, he will do it," the factor nodded.

"But whah aboot ye? Whah aboot the priest?" Alex spoke up. "Maybe ye should run as well."

"No, I will stay and so will Father Remas. They depend on us. It is our job to help. This is our village; we will not abandon it. These people are our people. Father Remas taught me that," McGillivray said with finality.

"We will do it gladly," John agreed without so much as a glance at Alex. "She will be safe wi' us."

22

The Faithful Followers

Adolphe was finally on his way. It seemed as though he was marking time these past years since he first arrived in Quebec City. For six years he lived at the convent of the O.M.I., the Oblates of Mary Immaculate, with its long dark hallways, and the nuns who moved like silent ghosts up and down its length. He worked as a carpenter apprentice in the city and went home each night to sleep in his little room. The nuns brought his food and clean clothes and reminded him of the chores he had to complete.

His only contact with the priests was in the church where he served as altar boy and the classes that he attended with other boys his age. His lessons were mostly topics he had studied in France, but occasionally he got to go into the library and pour over books that they allowed him to read.

He worked hard at all of his tasks no matter how menial. His selected trade as carpenter, though, was always second in importance to his real life's ambition. No one, however, heard that from him. He did as he was told, bided his time and learned. Then in 1868, after six years of learning his trade they pronounced him a 'tradesman'. At twenty-two he was no longer a boy, but a tall and husky man, too old to be living in a convent full of nuns.

He said as much to the bishop when he asked for an audience and displayed his certificate of accomplishment in the trades. He felt that the bishop had forgotten him and had no idea why Adolphe was showing him this document about his experience in the trades.

"Very soon, my boy," he nodded sagely when he finally realized what this visit was all about. "You will get your chance to prove yourself."

Only a few days later, while Adolphe was working on a new house under his old instructor, Bishop Constantine found him and asked him to come to his study when he got off work. Adolphe knew that something was afoot when his instructor handed him his pay and shook his hand in farewell. *Why had the Bishop not told him of his plans instead of his instructor?* He pondered this, but he shrugged and accepted it as he had always accepted the surprises in his life.

In the bishop's study his joy knew no bounds when the bishop announced that he would be leaving the next morning. With thirteen other recruits, he would accompany the newly installed bishop of the O.M.I., Bishop Grandin, to his new post in the West, the mission built by none other than Father Lacombe at a place named for Father Lacombe, St. Albert.

Their journey as far as Fort Garry was uneventful, although a great revelation to Adolphe. The transportation by water through the Erie Canal and across the Great Lakes was a matter of riding on the large supply boats that ran by steam power and not by paddle as the voyageurs did in the early days of the fur trade. The journey was long with several stops. There was much settlement along the St. Lawrence River and the wide lakes that fed it. However, Adolphe never dreamed how wide the Great Lakes were! He did not see land for three days and only touched onshore for cargo or fuel. The passenger freight boat travelled across the biggest lake of them all, Lake Superior, and Adolphe experienced storms and rough water just as though he were out on the ocean. It amazed him that voyageurs in the past travelled this same route in small canoes loaded with furs.

When they finally stepped ashore at what had once been called La Grande Portage, Adolphe knew that this was where the voyageurs hoisted huge packs on their backs and travelled overland to set their canoes in other rivers that carried them further west.

His group, however, would be travelling to Fort Garry by wagon train so that they could transport all of their cargo and personal effects. Canvas covers were arch-ribbed over them and the cargo to keep them dry. From there the travel was not as smooth and comfortable. It was dusty, noisy, and slow.

Fort Garry, which was soon to be called Winnipeg when the new province was part of Canada, was the beginning of the Wild West. The lawlessness, the mud streets, the horses and carts vying for room with the fur traders, the Métis, the well-dressed land speculators, the drunks from the taverns, and the property owners, prompted the travellers to leave this frontier town as soon as possible.

They lost no time in discovering that the best way to travel west was by Red River cart. A regular 'Fur Trade Route' they were told, led from the Red River at Fort Garry to Fort Edmonton. The Red River carts were made by the Métis people at Fort Garry and were relatively cheap. It was not recommended that horses pull the carts, however. Horses would not be able to stand the noise the carts made and would react badly. It would be better to buy oxen to pull the carts. The oxen were tough enough to be able to make the journey and stand the strenuous pull. Then they used them when they got there for farming the land.

It was not until the party set out that they realized the truth of that statement. The trail to the west was fraught with pitfalls. When it rained the rutted trail ahead turned into a swamp. Boggy mud-holes sucked the wheels down till they were nearly submerged and the cart had to be unloaded a few hundred pounds at a time, taken to a higher, more solid stretch while pry poles were used to dig out the cart, and the oxen pulled it through.

All the men sweated over the portaging, prying, and digging, mud-caked, sweat-soaked, weary, sunburned and mosquito-tortured from morning until they flopped into tents at night almost too tired to eat.

The next day the sun beat down on them so mercilessly that they did not know which was worse: the frying sun and the choking dust, or the soggy mud rutted trails and the drenching rains. They did not know which to hate more – the mosquito-tortured nights in the tents or the merciless sun in the daytime.

Day after day, they got up to face another prairie test. A thunderstorm would roll over them while they hid underneath the dubious shelter of the carts and tarps with its crashing thunder, frightening lightning, and violent hail. The oxen in terror would have run off until they found them mired in a bog.

Another day it would be the wind trying to tear them apart. Or the oxen would be a solid mass of black flies that tortured them to distraction until they had to stop and start a smudge of the carefully gathered wood along the way. Out on the open prairie there was very little wood. They gathered up what they could for their campfires at night. The Métis recommended that they burn the prairie buffalo chips so they watched for them as well.

Worst of all, it seemed, was the continual screech of the carts. They had several carts to contain all of their belongings and the screech could be heard for miles if they did not see the cloud of dust coming first. If they used grease for the wheels it would clog up with dust and mud and would not turn so it had to be greaseless.

A flat platform with sides built up into a box was carried by two unusually large wheels with a poplar-pole axle and a shaft to which to yoke the oxen. The wheels were big enough to roll easily over bumpy terrain and thick mud. They could be easily removed, and the cart platform could be covered with hide lashed to the bottom of the cart so that the load could be floated across a river.

Trails branched out everywhere. Inevitably they took a wrong turn and by the time they found someone to ask the direction, they were many miles off course.

On one particular branch when they realized that they were off the trail they noticed signs of life. From a sod shack with its stovepipe extending above the sod roof rose clouds of smoke, dense and pungent from burning cow chips or buffalo bones. Here they stopped to ask if they were on the right trail to Fort Edmonton. They were not, and had to turn back and get on the right trail again.

In spite of the deprivation and torment, the younger men, Adolphe's age, seemed to thrive on the new experiences. As darkness closed in at nights, they rolled into their tents crowded with at least six men and were asleep in seconds, tired but grateful. When the coyotes howled their mournful cry and mosquitoes whined about their heads, they slept.

Bishop Grandin was nothing like Bishop Constantine, and Adolphe, as well as the others in the group, soon grew to love him as a friend as well as their religious leader. He was a lot younger than Bishop Constantine and thought nothing of getting down with the others with a pry-pole to dig the cart out of a mudhole. He dressed as they did in his worn flannel shirt and pants, braces and scuffed boots. His black priest garb was for church ceremony and not for the trail, he had told them smiling.

Five other young men in their early twenties, brimful of adventuresome fire were eager to tackle the enormity of the West. Three of these were priests of Bishop Grandin's band of missionaries, Father Lariche, Father Leduc and Father Blanchet. Others considered part of the bishop's band of missionaries were, like Adolphe, lay personnel in training.

Father Lariche was Adolphe's favourite of the band of recruits. He was as strong as a horse with powerful arms and muscular frame. But he was friendly with an infectious smile and a ready word of encouragement. In Quebec, he had trained to be a prize fighter and was also an accomplished acrobat. He did not let these talents go to his head, though, or use them to overwhelm or dominate others. He was always the most friendly of all the missionaries.

Of the seven other men, three were secure, plodding faithful followers of the church but older and apt to tire more easily. They chose to be cooks, laundry, and camp set-up personnel. One of the priests, Father Blanchet, was trained in herbal medicine and his devotion to Bishop Grandin's care and health as well as the rest of the camp was commendable. He was slight of build and seldom spoke except in answer to someone's question. He always seemed to be in deep thought.

The other two travelling with the Grandin party, Fathers Grouard and Paul had experience with guiding, were part of the faithful thirteen, and trained in the priesthood. In the West the Bishop would find them a placement, a parish of their own. They were willing, capable, reliable, and valuable members of the team but they were addressed as brother.

When the carts squealed up to the gates of the famous fort after crossing the river at a near-by ford, their first thought was to find comfort, and decent food, for their supply dwindled to salt pork and a few potatoes. It was becoming cold at nights since they began their journey many weeks ago.

After asking around the fort, Bishop Grandin found that there was a Methodist church on the crest of the river bank, but a Catholic mission was not within Fort Edmonton. It was north of Fort Edmonton, Ste. Albert Mission.

After checking in with the Hudson Bay factor to be sure of the route, they carried on. The bustle and busyness of Fort Edmonton with the crowded comings and goings was soon left behind the fort walls, but they would be visiting again soon when they were ready to build a church within the fort walls.

In late September 1868, after travelling for two months they found the log church surrounded by a Métis and French settlement. Adolphe and the rest of Bishop Grandin's faithful recruits got the Bishop here safely.

While Father Lacombe served in the South his first school in the West had a new Bishop. The previous one, Father Moulin travelled south as well, where he was desperately needed.

It was soon determined that young twenty-four-year-old Father Lariche who had travelled with them from Quebec would take over in Fort Edmonton. The rest would go with Bishop Grandin at St. Albert, except for two of the faithful thirteen who would stay as lay brothers with Father Lariche.

Adolphe did not want to show how disappointed he was that Father Lariche would be separated from him. He felt as though he were losing Father Baptiste all over again. *But,* he thought, *he will not be far away. St. Albert is not far from Fort Edmonton.*

Adolphe felt proud to be included in the group of thirteen faithful followers. He heard about the famous Father Lacombe for whom the mission was named and he was looking forward to meeting him.

The little settlement along the Sturgeon River was populated almost totally by Métis. Their little houses were clustered along the river in the peaceful valley, below the surrounding hills. Trees grew in abundance and the fish from the river was a staple in their food as well as small gardens, but there were few fields to grow grains. They still lived the life of hunting, fur trading, and gathering of berries and grains. Many times now, however, their hunters came home empty handed, and they feared the coming harsh winter.

On the hill overlooking the settlement below was the church mission school, its connecting dormitory housing the Grey Nuns from the Sisters of Charity in Montreal. This was where Bishop Grandin and his party headed.

The log church was small, and the dormitory was not much bigger. The Grey Nuns lived a frugal, very austere life in a few small rooms. Already two or three were crippled with arthritis from living in cold, draughty, and damp conditions, but tough and determined, they had a job to do and carried on resolutely.

When the Red River carts pulled up the long hill before the mission house, eight of the Grey Nuns of the Sisters of Charity hurried out to greet and welcome the high ranking newcomers. "Your Grace," they murmured with heads bowed, curtseying low.

One of the women, older than the others, with face lined and hollowed, stepped forward. "I am Mother Superior and this is all that is left of our original group who moved here from Lac Ste. Anne. We are grateful and happy to receive you, Bishop Grandin. Your reputation precedes you and your addition to our humble mission is very welcome. Father Lacombe, himself, has gone to the prairies with the Christian Cree Chief Maskapetoon to sue for peace. There is much trouble in the south, much starvation, and bad feeling between the Indians and the white people."

"Thank you, Mother Superior. We would be eternally grateful if you could provide us with food and a place to sleep." He looked askance at the pitifully small dormitory and then added, "But of course as long as you have a hot meal we have been used to sleeping in our tents; we can do that until we build larger quarters."

"Ah, *certainment*," Mother Superior hurried to say. "You may occupy Father Lacombe's modest quarters behind the church and," she added apologetically, "your party may set up their tents in the shelter of the stables or in the loft. You may put your oxen in the fenced-in area behind the barn."

The nuns scurried around getting a meal together, which they set up inside the chapel. "As you can see, Bishop Grandin, the chapel has been converted to serve many purposes from dining area to meeting area to schoolroom. Since Father Lacombe established his school six years ago, we have been teaching and instructing what Métis we can convince to come in our doors. They trusted Father Lacombe, but since he left, only a few have come. This is the table they sit around to learn - when they come." She indicated the table that their meal of bread, potatoes and fish were set upon. Mother Superior covered it with her special white tablecloth, and set out all of their glass dishes.

"Here is Father Lacombe's Cree-French dictionary that we have been using to teach the Métis the language. And here is his book of pictures and numbers. He has only two copies so far, so as you can see, it is much thumbed up. We have also been trying to teach them simple cleanliness." She pointed out the basin and towel.

"How have you found the lessons going, Mother Superior?" the Bishop asked as he helped himself to a portion of steaming fish that had been baked in their outdoor oven. Then he passed the dish down the line to the other men in the party.

"The attendance has been sporadic. In the summer, they are often away on hunting and foraging expeditions, but in the winter they come if they are cold or hungry. We always have something for them to eat to entice them to come." Mother stood to the side while the other nuns with their grey cloth mop caps covering their hair passed around the food and took away the empty plates.

"Lately though," she said slowly, "there have been more and more people crowding into our village. There are new tipis or cabins every day. Hard times and hunger is driving them in from other areas where hunting is poor, and they are hoping that we can help them. To tell you the truth, Bishop Grandin, our resources are sadly depleted, our gardens and our food store. They seem to feel that if they move into our settlement that we will help them. Some of them are sick with tuberculosis and pleurisy. They expect us to do something for them." Mother Superior threw up her hands helplessly and sighed deeply.

When the women had gone, the men sat around the large fireplace, which was all that the church had for heat and light and talked as they gazed into the flames.

Father Blanchet, the quiet and serious young man with the interest in herbal medicine and the training as a doctor, spoke out of the silence. "All of these people who have settled in this valley are no longer Indian, and they are not white. For one hundred years their women have formed alliances with the fur traders at no advantage to them. It is important that we do all that we can to help. These Métis are their children. It is up to us to make up for a generation of hard hearts and ignorance."

"In this land of plenty, the buffalo and the moose, the land to grow things it is impossible that there should be starvation," Bishop Grandin shook his head sadly. They had much to do.

23

Smallpox and the New Red River Settlers

Adolphe was busy with the building of the new mission. The old log church was to be replaced and a big new residence, hospital, school and a new church would be built beside it on the hilltop. When Father Lacombe came to spend a few days with them before continuing his missionary duties elsewhere, he impressed on them how important it was for Bishop Grandin and his core of priests and brothers to continue the work with his children, the Métis in the settlement. The new mission must be built to accommodate all who came.

"Continue my school," were Lacombe's parting words were for the bishop. "Be sure my people are fed and cared for. It will get worse up here for them soon. Lead them to the Lord. Use my dictionary of Cree translations to help them understand." Then *Arsokitsiparpi,* the Man with the Good Heart as the natives called him, was away again.

Adolphe admired the selfless man who impressed on the Métis of the village that it was important to help these new men of God to set up the building. Tirelessly, day after day the Métis men sweated beside Adolphe the following winter to cut down the trees and haul them in with the use of the oxen to the site of the new mission house. In turn, between the Oblates of Mary Immaculate and the community elders, they saw to it that all of the people were fed. Hunting parties brought in meat and storage houses were used to capacity.

Adolphe's experience as carpenter came in handy, and he became foreman of the job. As the job progressed and the building took shape, the Métis men began to understand and appreciate what was happening.

171

But by spring, 1870, it was obvious that something insidious was creeping into the newly formed village founded by Father Lacombe. At first it was the news that some of Adolphe's workers could not make it to the job because they were sick. Then he heard that the whole household was sick. Neighbours were sick as well. When Father Blanchet was urged to come down to help, he discovered high fevers, and skin badly swollen on the faces, hands and feet. Some faces were covered with large pustules and boils. These were spreading and breaking under the skin making patches of red or black. Severe headaches, vomiting, and fits of shivering affected others as Father Blanchet went from dwelling to dwelling.

Hurrying back uphill to the temporary living quarters the priests and brothers put together while building the new mission house, Father Blanchet covered a kerchief with an antiseptic solution to put across his face and gathered up what he could to treat the afflicted. In his heart, he knew that any of his herbs or emollients would be useless to treat this problem. This was smallpox. Father Lacombe told them about this problem spreading over the Blackfoot on the plains, but now it had come to their village.

"How has this happened?" Bishop Grandin demanded. "Where did this come from?"

"Do you recall the group that arrived from Fort Edmonton just a week ago?" Father Leduc reminded them. "They settled with the L'Hirondelle family by the creek. A home was started for them, and when the youngster came for food, he said that his mother and sister were sick." Father Leduc was responsible for food storage and distribution and now that spring was here he was worried that provisions were low and the supply wagon had not yet come from Fort Edmonton.

"No one is to leave the village," Bishop Grandin ordered, "And no one is to be accepted in. All sick must be taken to one dwelling to be cared for. Anyone who has no sign of the disease must be quarantined from the rest. The old woman that disappeared yesterday, the one they said wandered away–she must have been sick. Perhaps she went away to die! This is serious. How many are sick?"

"I know not," Father Blanchet admitted. "Many I believe."

"*Pére Blanchet*!" a little boy shouted breathlessly as he ran up to the front of the church and the three priests hurried to the door. "*Mon mére est mort*! I can not wake her and her skin is black."

"The Black Pox," Father Blanchet shuddered. "We must hurry or everyone in the village will die."

By the beginning of summer, most of the village was infected with the disease. A runner from Fort Edmonton, from Father Lariche, was stopped on the edge of St. Albert and told that no one was invited in. He wanted Father Blanchet to come or send medicine. Father Blanchet met him and turned him back with disappointing news.

"I have nothing for you. I can not help those down with the disease. I can recommend treatment, only, but it will not cure the smallpox, only make it a bit easier to bear. Bishop Grandin is even now at a burial ceremony for three members of the same family. I was not able to help them. One man with a mild form of the disease who survived except for scabs and loss of some of his hair had refused any help from me.

"So far, even though I have been with the infected, trying to help, I have not developed the disease. I believe that it is either because I have been careful with cleanliness or else our white skins make us less vulnerable to the smallpox."

Father Blanchet slumped wearily. He was roused out of sleep for nights and called to bedsides to put his infusions of herbs on the infected and order antiseptic washes for the uninfected. Sometimes the diligence worked, and a few survived, even though were exposed. It was like a wildfire that hopped across a forest sometimes burning to the ground and sometimes leaving whole areas untouched.

"*Non*," the runner from Father Lariche insisted. "I do not believe it is the colour of the skin. A man who came for help inside the fort told us that the holy man whose name was McDougall lost two of his daughters to the disease. They called him a Methodist. He just built a big mission house on the bank overlooking the river at the fort."

Father Blanchet shrugged. "If anyone got the disease after exposure, it would be me. Why did we all not come down with it?"

"Fort Edmonton is rampant with the disease, and people are dying left and right," the runner replied sadly.

Before the summer was over, the epidemic subsided although there was still the odd report of illness. The quarantine on entry into St. Albert was still in effect, but the supply wagons were allowed in. Due to the epidemic, there had been little planting and hunting for meat–partridge or duck. The village was dangerously low on food again. Gradually there was now evidence of berry picking, pemmican making, fishing, and snaring of rabbits.

One day, as Adolphe hammered and sawed on the construction of the mission house, he saw a small cavalcade of Red River carts coming down the hill on the south side of the village. They crossed the little bridge that Father Lacombe had urged the village folk to construct in the early days of the village's birth, and started uphill towards the mission. He wondered at people still travelling in view of the smallpox epidemic, that had curtailed all travel for so long.

Curious, Adolphe lowered his hammer and watched them approach. After labouring up the hill the tired animals pulled the carts, six of them, up to the unfinished mission house and stopped. Adolphe noticed that there were four nuns in their usual habits, thickly covered with dust. Behind that cart there appeared to be two different families. One of the men stepped down from the cart and approached Adolphe.

"*Bonjour, Monsieur*," Adolphe said stretching out his hand to the man. He was dark skinned and greying, appearing to be Métis, but he spoke French like a native Frenchman. "We are looking for Father Lacombe. Is this his mission?"

"*Oui, Monsieur*," Adolphe smiled in welcome and his eyes travelled across the dusty, weary party of men, women, and children. The women's bonnets, shading their faces and covering their hair from the sun, were covered with dust and grime. They had travelled many long miles. Father Paul and Father Grouard, who had been helping Adolphe in placing the split logs for the building, also came forward and greeted the man whose name was Pierre Berard. From the cart behind, another man came forward to greet them and introduced himself as Joseph Moreau.

"This is Father Lacombe's mission but he is away travelling in the south right now. I will take you to see Bishop Grandin," Adolphe offered. "It looks as though you have travelled far today."

"*Oui*," the man called Joseph Moreau replied. "We have travelled from the Red River Settlement in what is now the new province of Manitoba. Father Lacombe was with us in the Red River Colony. He was our priest. We have always been buffalo hunters of the plains and traded in hides, pemmican, and meat just like the Indian tribes down there."

"But there are hard times and much bad feeling. The Indians felt we did not belong–even though we had spent our lives there," Pierre Berard added with a look of defeat.

"We tired of fighting, and since Father Albert invited us to come west and join his mission, we came," Joseph said unhappily.

"Now we feel that we do not belong anywhere. We had to give up everything on the Red River, and now we face a new kind of life here in Ruperts Land," Pierre spread his hands hopelessly. "When we met up with the Grey Nuns who were looking for people to travel with them, we were happy to join them. We were so hoping to see Father Albert ....." Pierre Berard's voice trailed off.

"Come with me," Father Grouard bid them. "I will take you to Bishop Grandin. "I think you will travel no farther."

Adolphe stepped forward and extended his hand up to the nuns to help them down from the cart. "Mother Superior will be very happy to see you. They have been looking for the Sisters of Charity for many months."

"Sisters, I will take you to Mother Superior and get you settled in," Father Paul offered and bid them follow him. "Adolphe will see to your cart and boxes."

As the oxen began to move restlessly, Adolphe stepped forward to help the other carts' occupants down and bid them step forward into the shade while he and Brother Jonas unhitched the oxen to lead them away to the corral.

During the bustle of movement, Adolphe reached up to help a slight female figure down from Pierre's cart. Somehow, he was startled at the light soft touch on his hand and looked into a slim, fine-featured face with skin nearly as fair as his own. Her eyes, hazel with flecks of gold, smiled at him, and her dark hair fell away from its bonnet restraint as she bent forward ready to be guided down the wheel of the cart. Impulsively, Adolphe, feeling that this girl must be light as a feather, picked her up in his arms and deposited her on the ground beside him, his hand lingering for a moment at her back.

"*Merci*," the sweet little voice said with a happy lilt, and Adolphe paused in his busyness to look again into the smiling face.

"*Bienvenu*," Adolphe flashed straight white teeth in his attractive smile. "What is your name?"

"*Je suis* Julie! Julie Berard," she said, giving him a beautiful smile.

As he hurried away to help the others and look after the carts, luggage and oxen, he could not help but look back occasionally for another glimpse of the slight form of Julie Berard.

24

Lucy, Interpreter and Trader

It was a mutual exchange of language and culture between John Lenny and Lucy Gladu, with the men teaching her a little English. But they needed to know how to speak French and to understand some Cree. Lucy was eager to learn something of their culture, and they tried to give her some knowledge of money for trading purposes. Lucy learned quickly and was anxious to make them understand, and to make herself understood.

When the trio arrived back at the trading post Lucy was as happy and eager as a child. But when they entered the cabin she was shocked and astounded to meet the other two men. They had no way of preparing her for the meeting. Duncan and Murdock were just as astounded to see John and Alex enter with the young Métis girl. To them she was an Indian girl; they saw no difference.

"Whah hae ye goh here?" Duncan leaped up from the chair by the stove. "Air ye daft? Or in the habit o' pickin' up the natives along yer journey?"

"Ye were supposed tae bring back furs noh Indian lassies," Murdock gaped.

"This be noh a native lass," John explained with a hand on Lucy's shoulder. "This is Lucy Gladu, a Métis lass from the village of Lac Ste. Anne."

"Ach, I see," Duncan said, nodding his head knowingly. "Ye twa decided that the winter is tae long and lonely tae be spent wi'oot female companionship. Ye decided tae bring back soomethin' tae keep yer bed warm."

"At least ye could hae brought twa back–one fer each ae ye," Duncan teased as he looked at Lucy in an openly suggestive manner.

Lucy, gathering what was taking place in the conversation, slunk back behind John shyly, her head lowered.

"I suppose ye realize that fraternizing with the natives is frooned on by the Bay–even if it's ainly tae keep ye'r bed warm on a winter night. Ye canna bring her back to Yark Factorry wi' us–ye ken thah!" Murdock scowled at him. John and Alex were getting themselves into some kind of a mess.

"It's nairly spring and we'll be pickin' up the furs and headin' back doon the river soon," Duncan warned. "Whah air ye plannin' tae do wi' her then?"

"Nae, nae!" John shook his head with impatience. "It's noh lak thah at all."

"She's gae'n tae teach us the language–French and Cree. We need tae ken them in this area. She'll help us talk tae the Indians when they come in," Alex explained while Duncan and Murdock smirked and winked at each other knowingly.

"She had tae leave her village tae avoid gettin the smallpox. It hae started up again. The village was startin' to come doon wi' it," John said seriously. "We needed an interpreter, and she needed tae escape or die ae the disease."

Both Murdock and Duncan scowled. "Ye came back here frae a smallpox infested village and brought a lass thah was exposed tae it? Air ye daft?" Duncan demanded.

"White people air noh as vulnerable tae it as the native population," Alex tried to assure the two Scots who had stepped back a pace as though to avoid getting too close to these two who had been exposed.

"Dinna be fooled by thah notion," Murdock nodded knowingly. "I hear that the disease is runnin' rampant all over Fort Edmonton–white and Indian air dyin'. I thought we were safe oot here in the woods."

"There's nae need tae run frae it," John spoke reasonably. "I'm noh surprised that Fort Edmonton is doon wi' it frae all I hear ae the drinkin' and brawlin' and the whorin' goin' on. The way they live….."

"But dinna ye forget, John." Alex raised his eyebrows. "McGillivray said that the preacher McDougall's daughters died frae it."

The four Scots looked at each other in silence, the warning hanging between them, and their gaze again fell on Lucy who shrunk farther behind

John, unable to interpret what the conversation was all about, but knowing that it had to do with her and that it was not good.

"Regardless," John insisted, "We hae tae learn the language and this is the best way. If she is noh showin' signs ae the smallpox by now, I dinna think she'll get it."

"And how will ye be explainin' tae Campbell and Douglas aboot the livin' arrangement when we come doon this way in a few weeks?" Murdock asked.

"I guess ye'll hae tae let us worry aboot thah." John stood his ground.

Duncan and Murdock backed off then and no more was said. They ate what the two men cooked, the rabbit and the porridge, in silence. Lucy, feeling that she was somehow the cause of the trouble, took her portion of the food and sat cross-legged in the corner in the dark to eat with her fingers. She tried out the porridge gingerly, decided that it was all right, and cleaned her plate. Here was another part of the culture that she must learn to accept.

John gave her a robe to wrap up in and she spent the night in that corner while the two strangers still skirted her warily.

Early the next day they left, and Alex and John struggled with the problem of Lucy. They left to go hunting. Food was needed, but they also persisted in searching for the elusive fur-bearing animals.

"Noo look whah ye hae goh us intae!" Alex scolded his friend. "We've goh another mouth tae feed and barely enough food tae keep ourselves alive. And Duncan was right! Whah air we goin' tae do wi' her when we head back tae Yark Factory?"

"Ye ken thah there hae been many other men who hae taken in tae their quarters Indian women, whether they married them or noh." John pushed the bushes aside, checked out his empty snare and saw no tracks about. "Where do ye think all of the Métis came frae? And where do ye think they learned to speak the French language–these Métis people? And where air they noo, these French voyageurs?"

"Dead - most likely," Alex answered off-handedly as he set off looking around for tracks. "After they left behind their Indian woman to raise a child wi' a French or Scottish name," Alex added as he turned and threw his remark back over his shoulder at John.

"But some of them stayed. Didna ye notice that some of the factors where we stopped along the way hae Indian women–or wives," he added as an after-thought, "working fer them?"

"So ye hae goh plans fer this lass?" Alex turned abruptly to ask. "She's ainly a lass, ye know–noo more than aboot fifteen."

"Sixteen, McGillivray said. And nae, I dinna hae any plans fer her. It's just that I think she'll be valuable to us. We need tae ken the language and all aboot whah's gae'n on in this area. They ken aboot what is happenin', thae natives do, and she can help us find oot."

It was not until the two men got home that evening with nothing but a skinny partridge, that they realized the truth of John's remarks.

Smoke spiralled up from the chimney in their little cabin, and they opened the door to the smell of stew cooking in a pot on the stove and the two chairs around the little table with a plate of pemmican in its centre. Their mouths fell open. Where had she found enough materials for a stew and pemmican?

Lucy found some berries that still clung to branches outside their cabin, and she located some dried meat and some grain that they had stored away. Pounded together, mixed with water, and cooked on top of the stove, it produced a tasty pemmican that would last a few days.

The stew was made with the rest of yesterday's rabbit, a few scraps of potato that she found buried in the cellar, and roots that she dug up from under the snow. They praised Lucy profusely, trying to use the French words that she had taught them, and she glowed under their thanks. It had not occurred to her to accept praise for something that was her duty to perform, so it overwhelmed and embarrassed her. She wanted to prove that she could demonstrate her worth to them in some small way.

The next surprise in demonstrating her value to them came when the Indian boys, Gabriel and Paul Beaver, stopped at the trading post. At first, she stood in the shadows behind Alex and John as they struggled to understand the two men. Suddenly, she stepped forward and started to speak to them in Cree. At first the Indian men looked at her in astonishment. They obviously had not realized that she was there, and they were amazed that she could speak Cree.

At first, they refused to answer or look at her. They wanted to pretend that she was not there. It was not until much later that John understood that the Indian men looked down on the Métis. She was neither Indian nor white and unworthy of talking to them as she did, as an equal. To John and Alex, she looked Indian, but to the Cree boys she was nearly white, or masquerading as white. To the Indian she was obviously not native, but neither did she deserve the respect of being treated as white.

Lucy was not going to shrink back into the corner and behave as a 'squaw should;' she belonged here and it was her job to help John and Alex understand. She straightened her shoulders, stuck out her chin, and spoke up to the men in answer to their questions of John and Alex. She demanded that they lay down their barter on the counter before she got the things that they asked for.

Finally, when John and Alex continued to stare back at the Indians, they had to do as Lucy asked. They brought out their wolf pelt and laid it on the counter without looking at her. She felt it, turned it over, and commented to them on the fine way it had been dressed out while they stiffened proudly. Then she set about to gather up the purchases they requested. She rolled out the cloth from the bolt and clipped it off. Then she pulled out the Hudson Bay blanket from the pile on the counter.

In French, she asked John if that was enough to satisfy the value of the hide. With words and signs, she touched the bullets and the knife questioningly to ask if she should also give those articles to the Indians as they had requested. John, suddenly coming to life, realized that he had to live up to his job as a factor. He went through the charade of feeling and inspecting the wolf hide before holding back the bullets and shoving the knife forward on the counter.

Ah! This was the attitude that the men were looking for–a chance to bargain. They demonstrated how large the skin was. What soft and pliable, unmarred condition it was in. Lucy spoke a few more words to John indicating what it was that the men wanted.

After listening to Lucy's French and pretending to understand it all, John nodded and shoved the bullets forward as well. Then he took the pelt, carefully folded and tucked it under the counter.

Trying not to accept the deal too eagerly, Paul and Gabriel extended their hands and spoke the words in Cree that they had taught John and Alex. 'Friends!" They picked up their purchases, still ignoring Lucy's part in the deal, and walked out of the door proudly. They made themselves understood to these stupid white men, feeling as though they bested them in the bargain.

John beamed at Lucy, and before they left the storeroom to go into the next room, the living quarters, he had her explain to him what the French and the Cree words meant. Slowly they were learning.

The stack of furs under the counter was very meager, embarrassingly meager. They had little to show for a winter in their area, almost half of what they got the year before.

The weather warmed every day as winter slowly melted into spring, and the streams began to run down the banks of the river and beside the ice. It would not be long now until it was time to pack up their furs, make a list of supplies to bring back in the fall and wait for the York boats to come down the Saskatchewan to pick them up. Still, John did not know what he planned to do about Lucy. He obviously could not take her with them, but he could not leave her here alone either.

Lucy still curled up in a corner alone at night. Early in the morning she was up to make their breakfasts though the fare was dwindling to almost nothing. Only Lucy's ingenuity and knowledge of the roots and tubers in the woods saved them. They found no animals to provide meat and only an occasional bird. Their store of food was gone. Starvation was only a step away. The only thing left to do was to try the river for fish when the flooding went down.

Spring was slow in coming. Temperatures stayed cold, and snow fell occasionally, causing the floodwater to flow into the river and across the ice. Daily, they were visited by travelling Indians who came to trade for food except that they had nothing to trade with and neither did the two white Hudson's Bay men. The Indians left very disgruntled, and Lucy, who understood what they were saying, was disturbed. When John pressed for translations she averted her eyes, looked down, or shook her head refusing to explain.

Since the two men were learning to speak more and more French, she finally relented and told them what she had found out.

"The Indians and the Métis are becoming very angry. While travelling across the country they find no moose for their hides, no buffalo for meat. On the flat ground along the river the Indians used to find buffalo that waited to sacrifice many lives to the people for food before passing through. The white man, they say, has spoiled all of that. The buffalo come no more.

"The white man has stripped the country of all the furs, and now they even want what little food we have left. They have many blankets to keep us from the cold, but they will not give us any. They have bullets for the useless guns, but they hide them away.

"And now they tell us that all of this land that we have been given by the great spirit–the land that he allows us to use as we will–the white man says is his! He says it belongs to his Great White Father. The Cree think that it is the white man that should be driven from this land that he has tried to steal, and that he sets his wooden wigwams upon. They feel that I am also trying to be white as well, and that I am not to think of myself as Indian ever again.

"It is the white man's diseases that are taking our lives. We were never sick before they came, and now we die terrible deaths, dropping like flies across this land."

Lucy ended with her head down, trembling and feeling cold. She did not know how much they understood, but both John and Alex were able to piece things together very well. They knew that what the Indians said was true, but they were helpless to do anything about it.

They were silent through their meager meal of thin vegetable soup while their stomachs growled for meat. Recalling the early days as fur traders when they gorged on ten pounds of meat a day and threw the leftover animal to the bears or the wolverines, they were shamed. Rolling back into their bedrolls, they listened to the storm outside as another snow squall howled around the little cabin.

Lucy heard more in the voice of the storm than they did, and she trembled with fear over what the spirits were saying. Then she shook herself and told herself no! Father Remas would be angry with her at the way she was thinking. She took out her carefully re-strung beads and ran them through her fingers under the shelter of her blankets. "Holy Mary, Mother of God," she whispered under her breath. "Pray for us sinners now and in the hour of our death, Amen."

But she trembled in fear for the two white men that she came to care for–especially the one called John with the fiery red hair. But he made no move to take her into his narrow cot at night, so she kept herself aloof–for now. It seemed the other man, Alex, prevented any closeness between them—so be it. But she could hear the gentle red-haired John tossing about on his hard cot and she knew that he was also worried.

25

Fire and Farewell

The next morning John and Alex decided that if they hunted all day, they would come home with some meat. Lucy would search the woods for new growing shoots, but they had to bring home a bird or a small animal. Their stomachs growled without breakfast.

"So whah did ye decide tae do aboot wee Lucy?" Alex asked as they stopped in the woods looking about for tracks in the soft ground, still sporting a skiff of snow from last night.

"I canna tack her back to Lac Ste. Anne, Alex," John answered. His thoughts were also on Lucy. "If the smallpox is still ragin' she'll be walkin' right back intae it. I hae been wonderin' if we couldna take her up to Rocky Mt. Hoose and she could stay there fer the summer."

"And whah would happen tae her up there over the summer until we got back in the fall?" Alex shook his head, and both imagined the rough traders, hunters, and lumbermen that would grab her up and treat her as their personal possession or a private slave. They dropped the idea immediately.

"Maybe Campbell would consider tackin' her along as a camp cook—there would be room—she's a light wee thing…." John's voice faded out. He knew as he said it that Campbell would not allow it.

"Then, even if she could stand the trip," Alex scoffed, "Whah aboot when we goh tae Yark Factory? Whah would ye do wi' 'er then? And would ye bring her back again in the fall? Or would ye then marry her and leave her with yer parents tae look after while ye ran the rapids and falls all the way back?"

"Nae!" John groaned, "We canna do it. The ainly other possibility is fer me tae stay here." Even as he said it John rejected it. They were out of food

185

and nearly out of supplies. What would he do sitting here in the post with no trading goods and a hostile neighbourhood?

"And wait fer me tae break my back on the paddles tae bring back the supplies in the fall while ye sit on ye'r duff in the cabin playin' hoose wi' wee Lucy!" Alex ended in a huff. "Nae, the only thing tae do is t'tack her back tae her people and hope fer the best. We can pick her up again in the spring."

Just as they turned to make their way down to White Whale Creek, they smelled smoke. "There must be someone aroond here wi' a campfire," Alex speculated.

As they climbed a rise above the creek, they saw a curl of smoke spiralling above the trees in the direction of the river.

Worry began to steal into their minds, and they turned as one, wordlessly, and headed back in the direction they had come. The more smoke they smelled, the quicker they stepped until they topped the rise and looked down with a shock at the sight that met them. A soot-blackened sky threw a pall of gloom over the river and shoreline. Angry tongues of flame licked upward greedily. Their trading post, their cabin that they took such pride in building, was in flames. A warm wind rushed by them in a sudden furious gust as they ran down the hill towards the cabin knowing that it was useless to try to save their home.

Then suddenly Lucy appeared beside them, her eyes red and dry from the smoke.

"Whah happened?" Alex demanded. "Who did this?"

"Cree," Lucy answered simply and ominously.

John, his jaw muscles tightening, bent slightly as though from a blow to the stomach and growled through clenched teeth. "Why? Noo we hae lost everything! They hae burned our furs, our supplies, our bedrolls – everything we spent so long in makin' and gatherin' taegether."

"I do not believe the furs or anything were burned. They would have first searched and taken anything that could be used before they set the fire," Lucy said in French.

"We treated them well. We always gae them whah they asked fer their furs," Alex shouted angrily in his imperfect French.

"*Mais non!*" Lucy shook her head. "It is not just you! It is a message to your white fathers to leave this land. They do not want you here anymore."

"Setting fire tae our post is noh gae'n tae change anything!" Alex thundered beginning to pace back and forth while sparks scattered high into the air, descending onto their shoulders as grey ash.

Then there was spattering around them, hissing in the flames. Sleet was whipping at them, and the cold wind it travelled on pelted them with the pellets like tiny arrows of ice. The flames, while pushed by the wind, were beginning to shrink back as though conceding the fight.

"We canna stand here starin' at the fire," John shouted, jolted into reality. "We hae goh tae find shelter – soon. If this sleet turns tae rain we'll be soakin' wet."

"And nae beddin', or food tae eat," Alex reminded them.

"We canna travel in our boat upriver tae the next fort. We'll hae tae walk," John sighed deeply but turned and started towards the path that would lead them upriver.

"Wait!" Alex cautioned. "Whah if the Indians hae burned the fort upriver tae."

Stopping in his tracks, John turned towards the two following behind him. "Perhaps we should head downstream, towards Fort Edmonton. Thah fort is closer anyway. Let's hurry. It's gettin' late."

Plunging into the woods, they followed the path along the river and up the bank, slogging through mud and sleet to the top. Here they turned and looked back. The fire was beginning to burn itself out and the black skeleton that had been their home stood out starkly in the pall of smoke. Then they turned, ready to leave the warm spot in their lives and face the unfriendly forest.

Suddenly up ahead, there was movement in the bush and shadows approached. Alex and John reached for their guns slung across their backs, thankful that they had at least saved them. Grimly they stood their ground and waited as the two men approached.

"Ho there!" a voice hailed them in English, and they breathed easy again and lowered their guns.

"It's Ewen and Willie McRae," Alex shouted. "Air we glad tae see ye!" They walked quickly forward with outstretched hands. But the other two were not smiling.

"Where would ye be gae'n?" Willie asked. "If ye were comin' tae see us there's nothin' left. The damned Indians burned doon our post." Then he seemed to suddenly realize that Lucy was bringing up the rear, and he stopped and scowled. "Whah hae ye goh here? An Indian squaw! Whah did ye do that fer? Thah's likely why they're angry. Ye took one ae their women! Dae ye know that they burned doon our post because of ye!" Willie shouted the accusation while he shot ugly looks Lucy's way.

Lucy understood a little of what they said. While she was teaching them French and Cree they had taught her some English in exchange. She shrunk in behind Alex, confused and wondering why they were so angry with her.

"Nae, nae!" John put out a hand. "They air noh lookin' fer her. She's noh an Indian. She's Métis. Thah is noh why they air angry."

"They burned our post doon as well," Alex shouted. "We were oot huntin' and when we goh back it was in flames."

"How d'ye know that the lass did noh dae it?" Ewen demanded angrily.

"She was oot as we were, gatherin' food fer us. All of her things were burned as well," Alex blustered in Lucy's defense.

"Why is she wi' ye then?" Willie asked, a little less irate. "Whah wah' she doon livin' wi' ye anyway? Ye heard whah they said at Yark Factory. Nae consartin' wi' the natives. I suppose ye thought on tackin' her back like a trophy doon the river tae the Bay!" he accused.

"Nae! Nae!" John denied, but he still had no idea what he was going to do with her. "She's been helpin' us tae learn French and Cree. She had tae leave her village or she'd be sick and dyin' wi' the smallpox."

By this time, Ewen had topped the ridge and stared at the smouldering black skeleton that had been their trading post. "A lot o'good it did tae hae the Indian lass, they still burned ye oot."

"I told ye she's noh an Indian, she's a Métis," John insisted in irritation.

"Whah right hae they tae burn doon the post?" Ewen demanded. "They'll get nae supplies, and there'll be nae place tae trade their furs when they do get them."

"They've had plenty ae provocation," John tried to reason. "Lucy could understand what they were sayin' and she told us thah they are very angry wi' the white man. They think thah we brought the smallpox tae them. They never had it afore the white man came tae this country."

"And they blame the Hudson Bay Company because there's nae more animals tae hunt, and they hae very little left tae eat," Alex reasoned.

"And whah aboot us?" Willie demanded. "Dinna they understand thah we air also wi'oot anythin' tae eat? Whah good did it do tae burn the posts? That willna bring the animals back here. They hae just migrated further north nae doot."

"Never mind thah noo," Ewen turned while hoisting his pack to his back. "We hae got tae gae further upstream. Maybe the devils hae na burned Alistair and Cameron's post doon. We may hae tae walk all the way tae the main post at Rocky Moontain Hoose. I guarantee they didna burn that doon!"

The men started down the ridge on the path upriver single file. John fell in behind Alex until he looked back to see that Lucy was not following. "*Viens,*" John invited.

Lucy shook her head sadly. "I can not go with you."

"But ye can not–stay here. *C'est–rien ici–pour vous,*" he spoke in his halting mixture of French and English. "Ye hae just–*cest petit couverte–about votre épaule,* nothing –a manger," John argued.

Lucy smiled slightly. "I will be warm enough and I will find something to eat. It is springtime." Lucy replied in French.

"But it is cold at nights–and the ground is wet. You will die out here alone," he pleaded, struggling with his French. "You can not go back–to your village with the smallpox. Where will you go?"

"I have kin close to Fort Edmonton. I will go to them. It is closer to go there than it is to where you may have to go. I will be fine. Go now with your friends. It is better. We will meet again some day. God go with you, John Lenny."

The last that he saw of Lucy was a slight wave and her sad smile before she disappeared through the trees and was gone.

As he turned and hurried to catch up to his compatriots John thought, *'Of course she will be fine.' Lucy, though young, was very resourceful. How did he think that she would be better off with him? She could look after all of them in the wilds of the northwest better than they could look after themselves. They might not make it, but Lucy would.*

He saw the look on Lucy's face when Willie and Ewen verbally attacked her. She did not reveal to him how much she understood of the conversation about her. But she knew that she was not welcome to continue the journey with them. She could tell that the other two men were not happy about her being with John and Alex. They even suspected her of burning the post. She did not need to understand the language to get that message.

Alex was already starting back down the path to find John when they met. "Whah happened tae ye?" he demanded.

"Lucy is nae comin' wi' us," he told Alex, a lot more matter-of-factly than he felt.

"Thah's a relief," Alex sighed. "Noo ye will nae need tae figure oot whah tae dae wi' her. She'll be better off wi' her people." Alex turned and hurried to catch up to Ewen and Willie with John following behind.

It should not have been so hard sending her back to her own people. She would be a lot better off than with him. But why did he feel so unhappy?

26

Adolphe, a Dinner Guest

Edmonton was almost completely in quarantine from the smallpox epidemic. So many had died that others trying to avoid the scourge were leaving in droves. Though St Albert denied them access, they were still slipping in and the Sisters of the mission were called on daily to help the sick.

Adolphe, with the help of Pierre Berard and others in the village, had worked tirelessly on the bigger church until it was finished. They were so proud of the larger structure, eighty-four feet by thirty-two feet, built of split timbers and smoothly planed boards with its high vaulted ceilings, its high steeply-sloped roof and cross high on top. It was the tallest structure around. Built on the highest point of ground in the village it towered above everything else and could be seen for miles away.

The church could accommodate a hundred people, but it was still too small for their purposes. It should have been built to accommodate four hundred, Vital Grandin stated. Adolphe was proud of it, and had lovingly hewed, planed, and rounded the pews, the altar, and the windows, which would some day be filled with beautifully stained glass. Adolphe devoted himself to the building. No one else was quite so single minded in his purpose until Pierre Berard came to the Mission. His love and devotion for construction and architecture was nearly as intense as Adolphe's and the two became immediate friends.

Though there were many years between the two–Pierre was over fifty years old–the two got along very well. Adolphe was closer to Pierre than even Pierre's own sons. They did not, Pierre complained, have the patience to spend time with the fine work. They did not mind cutting down the logs, hauling them in, and sawing them into lumber, but the fine, fussy work made the men impatient. They were not artists; they were lumbermen, they laughed. They did not understand someone like Adolphe who treated each piece he worked on with tender loving care. But their father did.

Adolphe's other passion was the church and its teachings. Bishop Grandin relied on Adolphe more than any of his priests or lay brothers. Before Pierre and his family arrived, Bishop Grandin, through a ceremony in the old church, had officially pronounced Adolphe a 'Lay Brother.' He was unofficially in training to become one of Bishop Grandin's finest priests. This was something that he had looked forward to for so many years and could not believe that it was finally going to happen. *Father Baptiste would be so proud of him*, he thought, *and wondered if they would ever cross paths again.*

At the dedication of the new church, the ceremony honoured all those who were instrumental in the dream's completion. The Sisters sang, and both he and Pierre knelt before Bishop Grandin, felt his touch upon their heads and heard his warm words.

Julie came forward to congratulate her father, and extended her hand to Adolphe as well, as they milled about visiting and taking part in the lunch that the women set out. She was sixteen now, and Adolphe was struck today more than any other day by her beauty. Many times he saw her as she came to bring her father lunch or a drink. Her bonnet always half-hid her face or she looked down discreetly. But today she was dressed in a brightly coloured dress that hugged her small waist, and her dark hair, hanging in wavy curls, was drawn back with a bright ribbon.

As Julie passed the plate of sandwiches and cups of juice to those assembled, Adolphe's eyes followed her.

"I said that I think the epidemic is nearly over," Father Blanchet repeated to the distracted Adolphe.

"*Ah, excusez moi, Père Blanchet.* I did not hear you," Adolphe snapped back to attention. "What were you saying?"

Father Blanchet doctored the smallpox sufferers tirelessly for weeks–Métis, Indian and white. Luckily, none of the sisters or the priests came down with the disease, though they were exposed almost daily. Father Blanchet, because of his ability with medicinal herbs and treatments, was the most in demand and over-worked until Bishop Grandin said that he must rest. They could not afford to lose him to the disease, and they would if he did not look after his health and get some rest.

"I said, Brother Adolphe, that there have not been so many deaths lately and more people are surviving this epidemic due to all of our diligence. I was worried about Joseph Moreau but it ended up to be just a bad cold. I understand that he is related to Pierre Berard, is he not? They came together from Victoria, north on the North Saskatchewan River and before that from the Red River Colony, I believe."

"*Oui,* Father Blanchet," Adolphe finally forced his attention back to the good doctor, "because even if they survive the smallpox, they end up horribly scarred and pock marked. It would be a shame for pretty young faces to be so badly marked for the rest of their lives."

"Well, Joseph Moreau has not a pretty young face, but I am sure that his family would be glad that you are concerned. Unless your concern is for the family contacting the disease." Father Blanchet smiled slightly, an appearance that seldom graced his serious countenance.

Adolphe gave him a startled look and then flushed under his tanned skin as he turned away and changed the subject. "I hear that Bishop Grandin will be sending Father Paul out to a charge of his own soon, somewhere north of here–Father Grouard as well." Adolphe tried to keep his mind on the topic at hand and the present company.

Before they left the celebration, Pierre Berard, smiling and flushed from the praise he received for his work, invited Adolphe over for Sunday dinner. "Now that the ban is taken off meetings and get-togethers, it is time that you came over and met my family. We can then get to know you better, my friend," Pierre told him as he gathered his things together and began rounding up his family to leave.

"*Merci beaucoup*, I will," Adolphe replied, more grateful than Pierre Berard knew.

"Come in," Pierre bid his friend and fellow worker at the door of his small cabin just up from the bank of the Sturgeon River that wound its way through the village. Pierre built a cozy log home for them. It was built in the style of most of the Métis homes in St. Albert–simply, with very few furnishings, blankets set up for privacy between bedrooms and kitchen, but not enough to block out the heat from the one corner stove.

Pierre built it himself and needed to get very little from the traders in Fort Edmonton. Most necessities they had brought with them from Victoria, and before that, the Red River Settlement.

"I hope that I have not come too early," Adolphe apologized. He was eager to come since early in the morning but delayed until he felt it was a more appropriate time. A partridge roasted in an underground oven surrounded by root vegetables that the women searched out and dug up, and was steaming in its succulence on the narrow table extending out from the corner cupboard. They would sit on the floor mats to eat as Julie and her mother, Louise, passed the platter around. The other children, Julie's two younger brothers and one sister, sat shyly out of the way, waiting to be served.

Like her daughter, Louise was slight of build, swarthy skinned and with a heavy long braid liberally sprinkled with grey, that hung down her back.

Pierre's father, also Pierre, was white and came from Quebec. He was a fur trader—a voyageur, who plied the waters of the Great Lakes and portaged to the Red River. He decided to settle down in the Red River Settlement. He did well, having had not one Métis wife, but two, as was accepted in those days.

"What made you decide to travel west from your land and your settlement on the Red River?" Adolphe asked, licking his fingers after having finished a leg of partridge and a slice of barley bread. "It must have been hard to leave it all, your relatives and your land."

Pierre frowned as he soaked up the juice on the platter with his barley bread. "It was no longer our land. There was much fighting and bloodshed because we were allowed to claim that land as our own. When the new government divided the land of the new province of Manitoba they said that the land was not ours—we were only squatting on it. The priests interceded for us but it was no use. They told us to come out West and settle in this new land. We would be able to claim the new land in our names.

So we came to the Northwest Territories and stayed for two years at the Victoria Mission. The holy man there, whose name was Reverend McDougall, promised that we would have land for our own, to hunt, fish, and to tell other people the land was ours. But he had no authority to assign us any piece of property. After two years we were tired of waiting for his empty promises. We each claimed our land but soon discovered that it had never been ours, and it really belonged to the Hudson's Bay Company. At a council meeting there were many hot words, and we separated after the smallpox took many of the Métis."

Louise stepped into the conversation then. "Marie Louise, Philomene, Josephte and Sarah left with their husbands further north into the territories," she said sadly. "I do not know if we will ever see them again."

"But there was little to live on up there," Pierre interrupted. "Louis and Roger were but eighteen and nineteen years and were anxious to go in search of adventure. They said that if the buffalo were not coming into these territories, they would go north in search of the caribou. But, me," Pierre thumped his chest, "I'm too old now to go chasing caribou in the north. We came here when Pierre Savoyard, Marie Louise's husband, told us about Father Lacombe's mission. I no longer trusted the Victoria Mission to treat us right. Down here we would be close to Fort Edmonton to trade and to find 'Arsokitsiparpi' the man the Blackfoot called 'The Man with the Good Heart.'"

"Besides," Louise added, "We were afraid of the smallpox. But Francois, Philomene's husband, was going to stay at the Victoria Mission and so were Pierre Rocheblanc and our Sarah. He was not going to leave the land that they claimed. They would fish and trap–they would live. But we came here with Julie, Henry, Caroline and Marie Virginie. And we are very glad. Father Lacombe's mission has been good to us."

Adolphe looked around the room as he picked out twelve-year-old Henry, ten-year-old Caroline and four-year-old Marie Virginie who were born in the Red River Settlement. They sat quietly in the family circle on the floor looking at Adolphe with dark serious eyes.

Fifteen-year-old Julie sat down next to Adolphe as she reached to tear off a piece of the chicken and pick up a water chestnut from the platter that sat on the cloth sheet on the floor between them. Adolphe was acutely aware of the scent of her hair and the touch of her skin as her arm brushed his, but he tried to concentrate on his host and the discussion between the two of them.

"If it had not been for Louis Riel we would not have stood up against the new government that told us we could not move about on the land of the Red River." Pierre Berard began to warm up to his topic. Since Adolphe had shown some interest in why they had moved to the West, it opened it all up for him again. His dark eyes flashed and his black hair fell out of the thong he had tied around it and fell down to his shoulder making him look more Métis than before. "But then Riel escaped across the U.S. border, and we had no leader. They said that we had no title to the land we chose. They said that we could not move from one plot of land to another if we tired of it. We had to stay on one strip of land and not move about to another that suited us better."

"So we left," Louise stated abruptly. "We loaded all we had onto the squeaky old Red River carts, traded what we could for the oxen to pull them, and followed the priests to this new land. Now we have an even smaller patch of land that we can not live on."

"Some of our group decided to stop off in the district of Saskatchewan, but we decided to come to Father Lacombe's new church where the land was not the bone in the fight between the Canadian Government dogs and the Hudson Bay Company hounds." Pierre stuffed the partridge meat into his mouth and wiped his fingers on his leg.

"Soon you will be able to claim a piece of this land," Adolphe nodded knowingly. "Bishop Grandin said that you will be able to stake a claim on a piece of land by stepping it off and marking it. You just need to ask him how to go about it."

"But how big?" Louise demanded, her uniquely hazel eyes flashing. "Another strip of ground to argue about with your neighbours?"

"No," Adolphe assured her. "Out here the land is big, and it is yours for the promise to build on it and clear it. We can investigate tomorrow where a good spot would be."

"I do not want to build a cabin, and then have someone come along and tell me to get off, or tell me what I must or must not do with it," Pierre said warily.

Again Adolphe was distracted when Julie got up, brushing by him as she left to get him some tea. His eyes followed her about the room.

"And what about you?" Pierre asked as he began to notice how the young man's attention wandered. "Will you be claiming some of this new land for yourself? Some day you will want to settle down with a wife and family, and you will want to have a place. With your talents for building you could build your own house. We could get land nearby and help each other with the cutting down of the trees and planting the barley."

Adolphe's attention snapped back to what his friend was saying, and it suddenly brought him down to earth. "Oh, no! I am an associate brother, a novitiate, and pledged to train as a priest with Bishop Grandin as a guide. I am not allowed to own property, have a wife, or move away to land of my own. I will be living with a brotherhood in the rectory. We are now in the process of building it. Then I am pledged to serve the people of the mission, to live frugally, and to live the life that Christ ordained for me."

Shock reverberated around the small dwelling. Julie's eyes widened, and her brothers and sisters stopped eating while looking around warily. Louise lowered her plate and stared while Pierre raised his black bushy eyebrows, his eyes boring into Adolphe's.

Realizing what his words caused, Adolphe lowered his eyes and felt the silence suddenly close in around him like a smothering blanket. How long they sat in silence, he did not know, but he expelled his breath in a sudden rush when Pierre spoke.

"Well, uh, a man has got to do what he thinks is right I guess. I knew you were a brother in the church as well as being a very fine builder, but I did not know you were planning on .... When will you become a priest? I did not know you were in training–or have you been....?"

The atmosphere suddenly became strained and though Adolphe tried to make everyone feel relaxed around him again, he soon discovered that he was rattling on, filling the silence with words. "Bishop Grandin told me that if I served as lay brother and trained under him with daily lessons, which I have been doing ever since I arrived, that I could be installed as a man of the cloth by next spring.

"I would be a member of the 'Oblates of Mary Immaculate.' It is the order that I have been working with ever since I arrived in Montreal. They paid for my training as a carpenter and for my keep ever since I arrived as a boy. Since I followed my friend Father Baptiste to this new land, they have not turned their backs on me, and it is my way to give back some of what was given to me. Ever since I served the church under my good friend Father Baptiste, I lived my life in preparation for carrying on in Father Baptiste's footsteps–carrying on his work in the West as he would do. And even though I have not seen him since he left Montreal, I know he would be doing as Father Lacombe is–serving the people and serving the Lord."

No one was talking, and Adolphe was aware that he was monopolizing the conversation, sounding more like a sermon the longer he carried on. Finally, he stopped and again silence fell uncomfortably on the household. Then Louise broke it by scurrying in nervously to urge Adolphe to sample some more of the tender partridge and tasty roots.

Adolphe looked around to catch a glimpse of Julie, but she had slipped away and was nowhere about. Suddenly, there was a heavy sinking feeling in the pit of Adolphe's stomach, and he no longer was hungry. The warmth had gone from the room.

27

An Abrupt Meeting

For days, as Adolphe and his helpers hurried to get the barn and sheds finished to protect the animals and the grain and vegetables from the winter cold, he strained to catch sight of Julie but to no avail. She no longer came to bring her father his lunch and water for them to drink. Pierre seemed cool with him now and treated him with a new reserve and respect. He missed their previous warm friendship. It was not that he was no longer a friend–it was just different.

As he stepped inside Bishop Grandin's study, he felt a weight of weariness on his shoulders. "Come in, Brother Adolphe. Sit down. You have been working too hard lately, I think. If the snow catches us before the barn is finished and the crop is in, it will not be a calamity. You throw yourself into everything you do as though there were no tomorrow."

"The boards are not planed that must go up on the barn front tomorrow," Adolphe complained. "The snow will blow in upon the hay. I knew that the front of the barn should not face the west. What is the delay at the sawmill?"

"Brother Adolphe, forget the building now. How are your studies coming? I was hoping that we could hurry your installation as a new priest by the time that Father Lacombe arrives. Did I tell you that he is coming for a visit in a few short days?" Adolphe was startled to hear the news.

"Bishop Grouard is going along with Father Lacombe to his placement up north–as Father Lacombe did with Father Giroux. The sisters are already planning a welcome for Father Lacombe, home from his work with the Blackfoot in the south. It comes at a good time with the harvest all in."

"I suppose I would be sent to a placement up north like Father Giroux and Father Grouard," Adolphe commented with a lack of enthusiasm, that made the bishop raise his eyes to Adolphe with startled intensity.

"You do not sound enthusiastic about that possibility, Brother Adolphe. Not too long ago it was all you talked about. You looked forward to a charge of your own, to your people to guide and lead to the Lord. Has something changed?"

"It is just that I have made friends here." Adolphe forced a brightness into his voice that he did not feel. "I would prefer to serve under you, Bishop Grandin, and my work–there is so much to do. And now that the church is finished we've been talking that it is going to be too small. We talked about building the new large church, that will span the entire hilltop and which will be a beacon to all the faithful for miles around. I would not be around to see it to its conclusion."

"Of course it will be a little way in the future before you are ready to go out on your own so let us not hurry things along too fast. Right now, show me what you have written on the book of Exodus."

"I am sorry, Bishop Grandin–truly sorry. I have been working so long on the barn that I have been flopping into bed at night and up at the crack of dawn."

"My son!" Grandin said sternly. "Remember that your most important job is to serve the Lord, not to build a barn. I want you ready to be ordained when Father Lacombe arrives even if you have to leave the completion to Pierre Berard and his Métis crew. Now let's get started."

When Adolphe was working on his studies with Bishop Grandin, he lost all thought of everything else and soon became involved with the selfless journeys of St. Paul. Time flew, and he left Bishop Grandin two hours later on an excited high. He could not wait to meet the most famous giving and forgiving man the West had ever known, Father Lacombe.

He threw himself into his work, his studies, writing, and his lessons with the bishop.

Leaves drifted down around him in a glory of brown and gold until it became a carpet under his feet, crunching and blowing with the wind. As wisps of cloud sailed through a leaden sky, snow began to fall, dancing on the wind and drifting in to cover the leaves.

Adolphe stopped to watch and catch his breath at the beauty of the swirling, wind-driven clouds and the smoke spiralling up from the cooking fires in the chilling air. Happy cries of children playing in the mounds of golden leaves and catching snowflakes on their tongues drifted across to him from the other side of the narrow wooded riverbank. Families would soon be curling up inside their cozy cabins away from the winter storms.

Evening shadows began to drop a grey curtain upon the hillside as Adolphe walked down to the river below, the downy white flakes settling on his bare head of dark curly hair.

Across the river he could see the Métis women in their cotton dresses with blankets about their shoulders, coming down to the river for a bucket of water. Men made their way home from a trap line or with a furry-footed partridge slung over their shoulders. Or they trudged home from their jobs at the sawmill, hungry and eager to taste the meal their wives had prepared for them. Then, Adolphe speculated idly, they would fall asleep in each other's arms, man and woman, happy in their innocent comfort.

After staring for awhile at the golden leaves that floated like displaced stars on the dark water Adolphe turned away abruptly and nearly ran into the slight form of a woman. She appeared so suddenly as she ran home down the hillside path, that he put out his hands to catch her while she tried to regain her balance on the uneven slope. In the dim light in the shadow of the tall trees above them, he recognized her. It was Julie.

He did not take his hands from her shoulders where they held her to support her until she righted her balance.

"Where are you going in such a hurry?" He laughed. "You could fall in the dark running down the hill at this time of the evening. It is a lucky thing I was here to catch you."

Flustered and breathless, Julie became defensive. "If you had not suddenly popped out in front of me to bar my path, I would not have been in need of catching."

Stung by the sudden rejection and the angry tone, he took his hands from her shoulders. But he smiled as his eyes took in everything about her from the long dark hair streaming in wild abandon across the shawl that hung from her shoulders, to her bright cotton dress that circled a tiny waist. He even noticed the little moccasin-beaded slippers on her feet, peaking out from under the hem of her skirt.

To escape the intensity of his eyes, she turned away, but he had not seen her for such a long time that he was loath to let her go. He probed her face with his eyes as he barred her way on the path trying to find out what lay behind the silence.

"I have not seen you in a very long time," he began, "ever since the time I went to your place for dinner. You left without saying good-bye, and I think you have been avoiding me."

Her voice suddenly changed from an angry challenging tone to a polite unemotional one. "*Excusez moi*, Father, I should not have been so impolite. I did not know then to whom I was talking. You mislead me. I thought you just an ordinary carpenter and here you are masquerading without your black robe."

Her polite tone stung him more than the angry one. "I am not a priest as yet. I am still Brother Adolphe. I am sorry that I did not tell you about my intentions. Can we not still be friends?"

"*Oui*," she apologized, "I swallow my bad words." She stuck out her hand formally to clasp his. But instead of releasing it right away he held on to her slender hand, feeling an excitement in their closeness.

"Now tell me," he said with a hint of a priestly tone, "why were you hurrying so? Or were you frightened by the approaching night?"

"*Ma mère*," she suddenly pulled her hand away and turned to leave. "I went to fetch Sister Alphonse for my mother. She is very sick and can not get up from her bed. Sister Zoë sent Sister Marie Alphonse, and she is on her way. I must hurry and see what I can do to help. The neighbours always fear that it is the smallpox when someone gets sick. They do not want to come near." Julie hurried away leaving Adolphe staring after her. He handled this very badly. This was so unfortunate. He must talk to the Bishop about it. But he stopped as he headed up the hill towards the rectory and stared at the ground.

What would the bishop do about it? he asked himself. Adolphe could not explain to himself what he expected in this relationship.

28

Pow Wow for Father Lacombe

A great feast was planned for the arrival of Father Lacombe. The branches were long since stripped of their autumn brilliance, and the wind rattled the dry limbs in warning against the coming storms. Today the sun shone down with unseasonable warmth. The celebration would be held outside on the warm south slope below the church.

"It is too bad that the church is not large enough to hold all of the people who will be coming," Bishop Grandin remarked unhappily. The temporary construction of the platform at the bottom of the incline, just above the riverbank, was under way. It stood beside the three-hundred-foot wooden bridge that Father Lacombe directed and seen to completion. It was the first wooden bridge in the new territory and made the daily crossing of the often-perilous river a much simpler task. Everyone up the hillside would be able to hear Father Lacombe when he spoke to them.

The huge roast of venison turning on the spit with the help of four Métis boys wafted its mouth-watering smells all up and down the valley.

Bishop Grandin and Adolphe stood at the top of the incline watching as many of the Cree, wrapped in their colourful blankets, families began to assemble on the sunny slope to sit on the ground and await the appearance of the founder of their village. 'Arsokitsiparpi, (the man with the good heart) is coming today,' they murmured among themselves.

"When they heard that Father Lacombe was coming, Indian and Métis alike began arriving from miles away." Adolphe nodded as his eyes drifted overhead to a flock of geese that reluctantly began their ancient migration south. "Let us hope that the weather holds out, and that everyone can see and hear. The women are baking the bread in the outdoor ovens as we speak."

"And the Pow Wow will begin as soon as the talking is over. They look forward to that." Brother Jonas broke in, joining them. "The dancers are getting their costumes ready, and the fiddlers and drummers are warming up."

Their attention turned to the flat area up the riverbank, to the well-trodden area where the central fire was to be lit, and then a wider circle behind that, where several other fireplaces would burn. The eagle-feather staff would be placed in the centre when the time for the dancing was signalled.

"And of course, another reason for the excitement, other than the harvest celebration and the arrival of 'The Man With the Good Heart'," Bishop Grandin said with pride, "is the fact that Father Lacombe's sister, Christine, is with us on her way to the north country. She is a person of curiosity and has caused a stir wherever she has gone. Father Albert will be accompanying her to the north country where she will be helping to set up a mission."

"We must take these boards down to build the platform for the table," Brother Jonas told them as he and Brother Francis made their way down the slope with the cumbersome boards.

"You did not mention, Bishop Grandin, that one of the reasons Father Lacombe is stopping with us is to baptize the newly born and to bless the marriages that have taken place. Many have travelled from miles away to have Father Albert bless their unions," Adolphe added hesitantly, not wishing to insinuate that his superior was being forgetful.

"*Mais non*, Brother Adolphe! I would not forget that. There will be very many, and that will happen before anything else is begun–almost as soon as Father Albert arrives, so that there will be time for the festivities before everyone becomes too hungry. That is why I wanted to talk to you. I would like you to organize them so that they come to the platform in an orderly fashion. All the names must be recorded properly. This will be the only record that anyone will have of this important occasion. You will have the help of Father Blanchet. He is becoming skilled with the Cree language and will help you with those who can not speak French and do not understand what you are asking of them.

"By the way, Brother Adolphe, I must chastise you for your negligence with your lessons. I had been hoping that this celebration would also include your induction into the priesthood. Your lessons in the Cree language have also been neglected. Is there some reason that you have been so tardy?"

Adolphe looked away, reluctant to meet the Bishop's eyes. "I have been very busy with the building and...."

"*Oui*, I know all that!" the bishop waved the excuse away as an irritant. "For some reason you are putting off entering the priesthood. Why is that Brother Adolphe?"

"*Je ne sais pas*," Adolphe shrugged. "I – I guess I am just not ready. I do not feel prepared." Adolphe threw up his hands in frustration.

Bishop Grandin smoothed his long, black, buttoned-down-the-front coat that covered the black cassock. It was starting to become worn, and it did not fit as well as it had now that he had put on weight around his midsection. He did want to look his best before such a large crowd today and before the famous and much loved Father Lacombe and his sister. "If you no longer wish to become a priest, it is time that I know. You realize that it is imperative that you be completely committed."

"Ever since I was a boy I have always wanted to become a priest," Adolphe began his impassioned appeal. "Ever since I followed Father Baptiste over to the New World and then came West to follow in the footsteps of the revered, have I dreamed of becoming a priest with a parish of my own in the West. I have thought of nothing else for years. Being 'a Man of the Cloth' has been my life's ambition until ...."

Adolphe began to pace in agitation and Bishop Grandin raised his heavy black eyebrows, puzzled. "Until what? What has made you question the reason for devoting your life in the service of God? Have you become frightened that you could not stand the rigors – the deprivation – the weight of responsibility? What has made you doubt yourself or your chosen life's work?"

"No, it is not that." Adolphe was adamant. "I am not afraid of the rigors, the weight of responsibility – the challenges of a frontier priest. They need us. The Métis and the Indians are like children, a wandering flock in need of guidance, looking to us to teach them the way of the truth, the light."

"Then I shall expect you in my chambers tomorrow with your studies done and your dissertation written, for which I have been waiting." Bishop

Grandin dismissed the subject. He had much on his mind. There was so much to do before everyone arrived.

Adolphe became so busy with organizing the many people who lined up for their baptisms and the blessing of the marriage unions that nothing else had room in his mind.

Excitement mounted at the arrival of Father Lacombe. His sister came down from the convent on the hill accompanied by the Sister Superior, Emory Leblanc with the severe expression, the prim mouth and the frown hovering over a large nose. That expression never changed as she met Father Lacombe, the line of people who waited and chattered excitedly, or the children who danced around the famous priest and his sister with joyous abandon.

In contrast, Christine and her brother greeted each other with wide smiles and hugs. Father Lacombe had such a kindly pleasant face with an easy smile for all, and yet his eyes were a piercing brown that seemed to look into one's soul. He carried himself tall and straight with a wiry strength that belied the fact that he was not really a tall man but of only slight and average build.

Christine, very much like her brother, shorter and slighter of build, was not beautiful but had a quality about her that drew people to her.

Her brother was quite relaxed and at ease with the crush of people who crowded around him. His trace of Indian blood made him a part of them even though he spent much of his time with the Blackfoot in the South. He was still the man who established his school with the Cree, learned their language, and wrote a Cree dictionary. He shot, though not fatally, while trying to keep peace between the Cree and the Blackfoot. The man who preferred battle to inactivity fought for them–the Cree, the Blackfoot too, and, of course, the Metis. He was their champion against the white people who often dealt with the Natives of the land unfairly.

Adolphe always knew him as a missionary with a wild streak and a thirst for adventure–a missionary who faced every problem in the new frontier head on, and challenged anyone who mistreated or 'took' from his children–the Métis.

Brother Blanchet and Adolphe had their work cut out for them trying to organize the Métis into an orderly line before Father Lacombe. While Adolphe struggled with that, Father Blanchet set their names, times and places of birth down with the new entry–the time and place of baptism or blessing on the marriage. As far as Bishop Grandin was concerned, it was not a proper marriage until the official stamp was made on paper that he would sign. It would, he told them all, be in the book that would remain in the church for all to see. That fascinated the Indians, and they all planned to come up to see their names in the book with the official stamp of approval.

The blessings and baptisms continued most of the day. It was difficult trying to get the names right and pin down the line of family origin but Adolphe and Father Blanchet worked tirelessly until the last person came through and Father Lacombe addressed them in their language that Adolphe struggled to wrap his mind around.

"My people," he shouted through the valley, and his voice carried across the hushed throng who sat on the hillside. "You have given up your wandering ways to settle here in this your village. You have started to attend my school so that you can learn the new language, learn to read and write, and do things in the new way.

"You have come to the church to learn that the Great Spirit is also the God of the white man and of the Blackfoot and the Beaver. He wants us all to live together in peace, to forget the wars, and to work together to raise food on your own plot of land so that you never again will be hungry....."

The people looked at each other in amazement. *Surely Father Lacombe did not mean that each of them would claim a piece of land and live on his own, away from the village? Away from the community where they helped to bring in the moose for the women to tan? Away from the hunting parties, the fishing expeditions, the pow-wows, and the fire circles?*

This was a revolutionary proposal. Food and fur were hard enough to find out there. If it were not for the mission giving them meat from their tamed animals, the Métis would have to range farther and farther away from camp. But how much longer would their domestic animals last? The mission even saw to it that there was enough grain for bread.

Some of the Métis who came from the Red River Settlement and the Victoria Mission nodded in satisfaction. Maybe it would finally come about this time. They would get to own their own land. They wondered, however, if even the great Father Lacombe would make that happen.

After the address and after Father Lacombe broke the bread, blessed it, and blessed them all, everyone happily helped themselves to the communal roast and bread.

Evening shadows shrouded the valley below the hills, and patches of light and darkness played upon the land. The gentle touch of the autumn breeze soon sent people migrating towards the central area where a new fire crackled lustily.

The wider circle of fires was lit and the blazes danced upwards, the flames becoming streamers of light. They scattered their red glow throughout the dark spruce along the river. The Indian and Métis moved in closer where old logs were placed for seating. Half covered with moss and dead leaves they became a theatre for those who clustered around, well back from the central fire, and near the smaller fires. Some sat on the ground, some on the logs, while some stood behind, farther back from the heat and the swirl of sparks that rose into the air like fireflies in the night.

The excitement began to build as the drummers started a steady and throbbing beat. Voices as ancient as the great fallen trees on the forest floor began a chanting song and men began a steady thumping of sticks on the ground. For some, it reminded them of the days when spears thumped the ground as the war party prepared for battle.

The steady pulse of the drums and the drumming of the many sticks on the ground filled the arena of that primal valley. It tingled under the feet and travelled through their bodies until they felt their heels thrumming to the beat. At the point when the braves would leap into the circle gyrating and ululating their keening cry, a new and different sound was begun.

It was the song that they learned from the sisters and the priests. It combined the music of the drums, the chant of the liturgy and the verses of the rosary. The familiar melody soon was picked up by many voices.

After a pause, a new strain was picked up, the voice of the fiddle. Homemade strings from the back of the moose stretched across the thin wooden body of the instrument were tightened across a delicately carved wooden bridge of bone. Over this, the musician drew a bow made of horsehair and rosined with tree sap from the black spruce. The fiddler played to the beat of the drums while people clapped and stamped to the beat.

Then from out of the darkness another musical voice was added, the sound of a small button accordion playing a French tune, that took many back to the early days of the French voyageurs, and tentative voices began,

"En roulant ma boule roulant. En roulant ma boule," and then the boisterous *"Youpe! Youpe! Sur La Riviere."*

After a hush, it was obvious that something exciting was about to happen. The focus of everyone's attention turned to an elder who, in full regalia, marched into the circle of light proudly carrying the eagle staff, a pole decorated with eagle feathers, high above his head. This he placed in the ground extending high over the heads of all. He spread his arms wide encompassing everyone there as he loudly chanted in Cree.

Well behind the circle, Father Lacombe spoke quietly to Adolphe in explanation. "This is their most sacred ceremony. This is the prayer of the Cree for peace and prosperity."

On the other side of Adolphe, Bishop Grandin voiced a quiet opinion. "It is lucky that the government, through the urging of the missionaries, outlawed the 'Thirst Dance' or the 'Sun Dance'. I have seen ceremonies like this turn ugly when braves sacrificed themselves to the violence of self mutilation in these ceremonies."

"Oui," Father Lacombe agreed. "But when the missionaries began forcing their opinions on what was evil and ugly in the Indian culture, that was when the missionaries went too far. Hush, watch this!" and he turned their attention back to the fire circle.

The elder faced the four directions and intoned a brief prayer before the drums began again and everyone saw the crowd part to usher in a line of dancers. They danced slowly and sedately into the circle in prescribed order. Some of the dancers were women decked out in ornate costumes, long brightly coloured skirts with bustles fastened to the back. The men also wore a bustle of feathers ornately fashioned. Some wore skirts of grass with no bustle.

"The bustles," Father Lacombe spoke in a low voice to Adolphe, "represent the hunters, disguising themselves as they sneak up on their prey. The grass dancers wear no bustle. Their dance has special sacred roots. See how they stay apart from the others. This is a healing dance.

"Now those," Father Lacombe pointed out the men who did not dance sedately as the women did but bent, straightened, leaped, and threw their hands high into the air with great exuberance, proud, powerful and defiant. "Their dance, is a pantomime of stealth–stalking the enemy.

"Those are the fancy dancers. They represent the warriors of the past. They all wear two bustles, but they no longer paint their faces because the white man thought this to be a war party and refused to allow it. Instead the women paint their faces in their dance."

He pointed out to Adolphe the line of women entering the Fire Circle with beads and bells twined into their hair and hanging from their long skirts.

The men with the drums changed their chanting song and the women moved sedately, twisting their shawls about over their heads, low in front, to the sides and behind as they circled with them. The strength and dignity of the jingle-dress dance and the shawl dance suggested to Adolphe that this was also a sacred dance, and he watched the movements in wonder.

Suddenly, in the glow of the firelight, Adolphe recognized a familiar figure. He stared in fascination and his pulse quickened. It was Julie. From then on he saw no one but her. Every movement she made seemed seductive, beautiful. As the firelight played across her beaded hair, it gave her a crown of amber, and when she turned her face to the sky and leaned back, dipping her shawl behind her, the moonlight played across her features with an angelic glow. The sight stirred in him feelings that he never before experienced.

As she danced by, unmistakably their eyes met, and it was as though he was touched by warm rippling fire. Something passed between them at that moment that neither could fathom nor explain.

Julie's steps faltered and for a moment the noise around them vanished. The look in his eyes belied everything he said in weeks past. Then as one of the other dancers bumped into her, she was jolted back to reality and moved woodenly back to her position trying to remember at what point in the dance she was.

Adolphe was jolted out of his stupor, being thankful for the darkness that hid the high colour in his face and the burning in his eyes.

After the dance was over, the people milled around dancing to the new beat of the fiddle and the button accordion, Adolphe stayed for a time idly talking to the others, not really knowing what they were saying. Snatches of conversation came to him:

".. but to the Cree, spirits dwell within every living thing, a horse, a bear, a tree ...."

" ... thunder, wind and sun are among the mightiest spirit powers ...."

"Their traditional religion is a lot like ours. They identify their suffering in the Thirst Dance or the Sun Dance with that of Christ. That is why they are eager to switch to Christianity."

"That is why our job is so important. They need our help to guide them, for they crave help and pity from the Spirit World." Words suddenly jerked Adolphe back to reality. "Adolphe is nearly ready to take his vows in pledge to that end. Their Spirit World is the same as our Heaven. But we must see that they do not lose themselves along the way. What do you say, Brother Adolphe?"

It was Bishop Grandin directing his question to Adolphe. The confusion numbing his mind left Adolphe at a loss for words. He could only mumble some trite remark that did not answer the Bishop's question, but no one seemed to be looking for anything wise or divine from him anyway. At an opportune time he slipped away to his quarters. He needed time to think.

29

The Tryst

Adolphe had to see her again. He could talk to no one else but her about this thing that was happening to him. But the winter was hard upon them. He had much to do to finish the buildings before the storms burst in upon them. And the village was hard-pressed to find enough food, particularly the moose, for clothing, hides, as well as meat for pemmican, to last them the winter.

One cold day in December as Adolphe worked on the lean-to on the barn, he looked up before pulling the door into position on its leather hinges. Northern ridges of thick black cloud loomed dark and foreboding overhead, and a sudden shift of the wind sucked the door from his hands sending it crashing against the lean-to. Feeling the cold bite against his face, he realized that this would have to be the last of the outside work for awhile. He would have to work inside the building to make it as windproof and snug as he could.

With numb fingers he nailed the door to the leather hinges and the hinges to the wall, before pulling it shut, leaving the wind outside to shake the door. Turning around in the dimly lit bare dirt-floor interior, he sensed that someone was inside with him. As his eyes became accustomed to the dim light he saw her standing just a few feet away from him.

Eyes wide and luminous, she looked at him almost like a bird prepared for flight if he should step closer and yet in trembling determination to face what she must face.

"Oh, Julie! I did not see you there. When did you ...? Were you here before....?" Finally giving up trying to find out how she had slipped past him without his knowing, he swallowed and forced a casual friendly manner. "It is cold out here. This is where the cows will come to be milked. Do you want me to show you around? There is much to do in here. But the other part is finished. Did you see it?"

"No, I did not," she relaxed slightly as she looked around. "I know that you built this lean-to nearly all yourself since my father has been working on homes down in the village."

He showed her through the barn, pointing out the pen for the pigs, the storage for the grain, and the stalls for the horses and the oxen.

"We had to insulate the walls with sawdust and straw to make it warm enough in here. This area is for the chickens. Here are the roosts. If it is not warm enough and they don't feel secure and comfortable, they will not lay and the sisters would like eggs for winter."

He led the way to the stairs to the loft. "We were lucky enough to fill the barn with hay this year to feed the animals all winter. Would you like to see ….?" She was already heading up the ladder to the loft, and he followed her. "The front is open to the weather, and some of the hay at the front could get wet or have the snow blow in on it, but it is better than closing it in completely because hay, if it is wet, could heat and that could be dangerous."

Talking to her so casually made all of the tension of the past weeks melt away, and both enjoyed the new feelings between them. Adolphe was so pleased with her visit that he felt he was babbling on.

At the front of the barn opening, they stood in silence for a minute looking out over the pristine white hillside below, cloaked with last night's snowfall, and inhaled the bracing air. Then feeling the cold bite against his face, Adolphe turned to see Julie shivering.

"Come away from the edge. You are getting cold, are you not?" He shrugged off his coat and draped it around her shoulders as he guided her away from the open front.

"*Mais, non,*" Julie protested, starting to give the coat back to him, "You will be cold."

"*Non, non!*" Adolphe tucked the coat back onto her shoulders and guided her towards the back of the loft. "This is where the hay will be forked down to the mangers below. Be careful," he pulled her back from the edge where she peered over to see the stable below. "I have not as yet put in the hatch door and ladder with a guiding railing." Falling back with a little squeal on the hay behind her, Julie avoided the dizzy feeling of tottering on the brink. She laughed at her sudden fear of falling, a light musi-cal laugh that delighted him.

Sitting down on the hay beside her, he caught her hands. In the gather-ing gloom of late afternoon shadows, her hazel eyes were large luminous pools of dancing light, and Adolphe's heart jerked. Gazing into those eyes, Adolphe's soul burned within him as he pulled her up from where she had fallen back and gathered her towards him. Suddenly, he crushed her to him in an embrace too powerful to resist. His lips were on hers in a long tender kiss that left her gasping, her heart throbbing wildly in her breast.

Julie looked up as he pulled back, into eyes that burned with that new passion she had seen when he watched her dance. Breaking free, she felt her fear crowding in on her, the fear of an unspoiled confused heart. "I must go. It is getting late," she gasped. She scrambled up from the hay, edging towards the loft steps. Her voice trembled and she discovered that she was vibrating so violently that her teeth chattered, and yet under her coat and his, which she had pulled closely to her chin, her skin burned.

"But you have not told me why you came." Adolphe leaped up in an attempt to detain her. He followed her to the top of the steps while she descended to the bare stable below. Her obvious fear of him shamed him. He knew why she was escaping, but he did not want her to run from him like this.

At the bottom of the steps, she turned to face him. "I came to find out why, Brother Adolphe." She seemed to gather her resolve and forced her voice to a calm that belied the trembling inside. She spoke between teeth clenched to keep them from chattering.

"Why?" Adolphe asked as he faced her, the heat rising in his face.

Finding strength in the offensive, again Julie plunged on. "Your mouth says you do not want me as anything more than a friend, but your eyes when you look at me, your touch and your lips tell me a different story. I came today to find the truth, but I am no closer to understanding."

Adolphe could see that she was upset. Her lips trembled, and she rubbed at her thighs with nervous hands. "You are soon to become a man of the cloth. My mother says that I am a temptress to a man of God. If I am this, tell me, and I will no longer look into your face."

"*Mais, non, Julie!* Do not say that! It is my fault." He winced as he tried to explain what had happened. How could he explain that he was drawn to her by emotions beyond understanding? And even though drawn to her, he fought a tide of guilt that threatened to overwhelm him.

Time was spinning away from them; a gap widened between them as they faced each other, and still he could not find the right words that she waited to hear. With eyes that stung with threatening tears, she turned and ran from him.

His eyes burned and his throat felt dry as he stared after her retreating form disappearing down the hill, and he said nothing to stop her.

All that night he tossed and turned in his bed unable to sleep. He felt as though he was losing something very precious to him—felt it slipping away, and he was powerless to stop it. When he finally slipped into a dream, he felt himself drifting on a boat in a stream with no paddles. Someone was reaching out to him on the shore to keep him from being carried away. At first it seemed to be Father Baptiste. Adolphe was so glad to see him; he stretched out his hand but the boat drifted by and Father Baptiste waved goodbye, smiling sadly.

Then on the shore he saw Bishop Grandin and Father Lacombe. They reached out to catch his hand. "You are going to miss the group leaving for the North Country." Father Lacombe seemed to be shouting across the water as he drifted by. "You will be the one chosen to head the mission on the mighty Peace River. It will be named after you—the 'Perrault Mission.'" Then Bishop Grandin's face became Bishop Constantine and the river, turning swifter, became the St. Lawrence.

'*If I do not get rescued soon, I will drift out to sea*,' Adolphe agonized to himself. On shore was another group of people, among them Pierre and Julie Berard. While Pierre waved, Julie wrung her hands.

"I will swim to you," Adolphe called, in nothing but a whispered croak as he prepared to slip over the edge of the boat.

"*Non! Non*! You cannot! It is too late," they called out. But Adolphe slipped into the water that sucked him along with a mighty speed. Campfires along the wooded shore winked out like so many fireflies, and he gave in to the current that carried him away.

He woke in a sweat, his blankets tangled about his legs, and it was suddenly very clear to him what he had to do. It was not too late. It was NOT too late!

215

30

The Magic Circle

Bishop Grandin was in his office as Adolphe entered the church, closing the door firmly against the cold wind that whipped across the bare hilltop. He stood outside the study door, his heart thudding against his rib cage so loudly that he thought Bishop Grandin must surely hear it from the other side of the door.

He knocked lightly and entered the office that was always cold. The bishop was bundled up in a warm sweater and woollen gloves that allowed him to write with his quill pen, although with difficulty.

"Thank you for taking time from your busy day, Brother Adolphe," he said with a touch of sarcasm. Adolphe had made excuses not to come to his classes. The time was long past since he should have been ordained. Lately, when the Bishop sent for him, he made excuses not to appear before Bishop Grandin.

"It is a new year, 1871, and I must make a decision about sending a party to the fort at Pouce Coupé and to the mission on the Peace—the one named after Father Dunvegan. I have decided that you should be the one to go. Now I know what you are going to say." Bishop Grandin put up his hand to stop Adolphe from speaking, feeling the objection coming. "You are not ready. You are not ready to be ordained, and you feel you are not capable of filling that kind of position. You feel you have to finish the work you have begun here. It has been your project from the start, and you don't want to leave it unfinished. But, Brother Adolphe, this is a much bigger project, and you could make such a difference in the lives of the fur traders and the Indians. They need a man like you."

"Bishop Grandin," Adolphe began slowly and quietly, looking down at his hands braced against his knees. "I have been going to come into your office for weeks to talk to you, but I lacked the courage. Now this must be said. I can no longer continue in my training as a priest."

There! It was said! How many times had he come into this office to say those words and left without having said them after the Bishop had spoken of the exciting plans for the missions? Things that Adolphe would do as soon as he became ordained, he expounded on. What an asset Adolphe would be to their growing group of priests as missions were springing up in the North Country! Villages were named after these priests, and villagers flocked to the churches in growing numbers. What good things were being done in the name of God and the Oblate Mission! Soon Adolphe would be part of it all. Adolphe left then, guilt-ridden and frustrated. But now it was out!

"Nonsense!" the Bishop waved away the protestation. "Have you not always wanted to become a priest since you stowed away on board ship, following your childhood idol?"

Before the man could go on tearing away at Adolphe's resolve, Adolphe plunged on. Today it would be settled! He would not leave one more time, carrying his lonely burden of guilt. "Hear me out," he interrupted. "I have sinned in thought and in deed. I have lusted after a girl, a girl not yet fifteen. I have thought of nothing else these past months but possessing her. Every moment that I am separated from her, I suffer loneliness that I cannot bear. I cannot swear vows of celibacy, because she now means more to me than the church."

He stopped then. A stunned silence fell over the room as Bishop Grandin stared as if thunderstruck. Finally, he spoke icily: "Am I to understand that you have taken this girl to your bed?"

"No, I have not. I have not shamed her, and she respects my profession of faith. But I have…," He hesitated, then plunged on. "I have kissed her."

"Well," the Bishop relaxed slightly, his voice still tight and formal but conciliatory, "that is but a slight transgression that can be dealt with in Confession. It is not something to sacrifice your…."

"You are not hearing me," Adolphe raised his head with determination, and he straightened his back to meet Bishop Grandin's eyes in a determined lock. "I do not want to become a priest and forever lose something that has come to mean much more to me. This separation from her, that my vows to the church would make irrevocable, I can not bear to face."

There was silence between them while Bishop Grandin closed his eyes and lowered his head in a silent prayer over clasped hands on his desk. Finally, he raised his head and sighed. "It seems that you have made up your mind, and nothing can dissuade you from the course you have chosen to take."

Adolphe breathed out explosively. It was done! He was free. A weight fell from his shoulders that had grown too heavy a burden to carry anymore, and he stood, preparing to leave the office a free man.

"One moment," Bishop Grandin put up his hand to detain Adolphe as he stood, "I ask that you do nothing about this now. Say nothing to anyone~not to the girl or another of the brothers~nothing! Not until I have heard back from the Oblate Mission in Montreal."

Adolphe was so overjoyed to be freed from his vows that he readily and happily agreed. He did not realize how long it would take for the Bishop to get the message to Montreal and to hear back from them. All that mattered to him now was breathing his new freedom, freedom to think about Julie and plan his new future.

"Remember," Bishop caught him as he was about to go out the door, "not a word to the girl~you should be able to stay away from her a little longer, if only in gratitude for all that has been done for you. Do I have your solemn promise on this?"

"I promise not to say a word to anyone. It shall be as though there were no change in my circumstances. I will stay away from Julie until after I hear word from you." Adolphe hurried out the door and breathed deeply of the brisk January air. He looked down the slope below, across the wooded ravine at the smoke from the cook fires curling upward in the frozen air, and he smiled. One of those fires belonged to Julie and her family. She was there waiting for him.

He stopped suddenly. *Was she going to wait for him while he stayed away, pretending that he did not care?* The thought made him wince, but he shook it off fiercely. She was but fourteen years; it was too soon for other men to begin beating a path to her door. Yet, the thought nagged at him. How could they miss her beauty, that tiny form and face, those hazel eyes and long dark hair with the auburn lights, those soft slender hands and straight white teeth and the smile that lit up the world around her like a torch? He had to see her–if only from a distance.

Adolphe began visiting the Cree and Métis in their cabins and at their work. He helped with the skinning out of a moose–a lucky find, and the portioning of the meat. He watched and became engrossed in the work of the women, the tanning of the hide and the gathering of wood for their fires. He discovered that the heads and innards of the animal were their favourite foods as well as being important for other uses, the brains for tanning and in making head cheese. The innards were cleaned out by the women and stuffed with barley, meal, berries, tubers and fat to make sausages. So much depended on a depleting supply of wild game that the other domestic animals did not fill.

As well as learning, Adolphe was keeping an eye out for Julie. She studiously avoided him, and once when they came face to face she quickly apologized for blocking his way and moved resolutely on.

Just when he decided that she had no other suitors, he saw her down by the river with a young man of about her age. They were laughing and talking as the young man lifted the pail of water out of the hole where they drew their water. They both reached for the pail at the same time and bumped heads. The young man, whose name was Michel, carried her water pail up the hill to their cabin and stood talking to her for some time before leaving her to her work.

Adolphe was seized by such an attack of jealousy that it was all he could do to keep from charging over and dispensing with the young man while claiming the young lady for himself. He kept an eye on the young man for days after that and took it upon himself to see to it that he was sent out with a party that was cutting timber for the rectory extension.

Every day that went by and the Bishop had heard no word, Adolphe grew more frustrated and impatient. Finally, as spring approached, plans took shape for the departing priests who would be leaving for their new placements. A dance would be performed, and there would be a ceremony of the elders–women and men. The young men would dance in celebration of the end of the long winter. Some would be celebrating becoming men–one of them being Michel. The mission school children under the tutelage of the sisters would be singing prayers and dancing.

During the practices, the priests were busy with preparations and set-ting up. A wagonload from Fort Edmonton came in with two new priests from the East to coincide with the celebration and dedication. Adolphe was certain that they would be bringing news from the cardinal in Montreal about his release, and he threw himself into preparations to be busy. Others already asked him curiously, 'Was he not to be ordained this spring?' He sidestepped the questions, and so far had avoided any premature announce-ments.

But when the two priests arrived, they had no such message for Adolphe. Adolphe hurried into Bishop Grandin's study as soon as the visitors left his office to find their accommodations. Bishop Grandin was too busy to talk to Adolphe. There was too much to do. He would talk to him later.

Feeling ignored and pushed aside, Adolphe became angry. He had waited long enough. Just last night he watched the lithe young body that was Michel dancing about the fire, his young muscles rippling under the light shirt, his teeth gleaming white in the firelight as he smiled at the observant Julie. She was dressed in her soft new beaded, fringed buckskin dress that hugged her slight form with the budding bosom and narrow waist. He swore then, that he would tell her tomorrow when the wagon from the fort arrived.

Adolphe had waited long enough. He felt that Bishop Grandin thought this was just a passing fancy on his part, and the girl would move on to other prospects. Then Adolphe would return to the fold.

Hurrying down to the fires that night, he searched for Julie to no avail and he feared that it was too late. Had she left with the young man? He found her again talking to Michel. They were working out a partner dance. Adolphe had seen the dance and knew that it was usually performed by promised couples before the ceremony of marriage and in circling each other it became a dance of tacit seduction. He was eaten up inside with jealousy-his soul filled with the silent scream of outrage. Was it too late? Had he waited too long? This was an arena that he could not enter, could not compete.

"Julie," he called to her from the sideline. She turned and met his burn-ing gaze – not the usual friendly, vulnerable, gentle look that she caught in his eyes before, but this time a different message. They held a strained angry expression, with a reprimand. But what had she done? Her heart constricted.

"Sister Marie Susanne wishes to see you up at the church," he announced churlishly, his jaw muscles tightening.

Worry clutched her. Sister Marie Susanne had been instructing her and the other girls with their letters and with their needlework. What could she want of her this hour of the evening in the middle of their practice? Her eyes widened as she stood like a bird trembling in flight before dashing away.

Nervously entering the dark church, she stood for awhile until her eyes adjusted to the light and stared around the dark benches in the dim light from the windows. The altar and pulpit were empty and in darkness. No one was to be seen. Waiting a moment, she puzzled before turning slowly to leave.

As she turned to leave, the door opened and Adolphe entered, closing the door behind him. Staring at him in the dimness, the light from the moon spreading a silver path across the benches behind her, she was gripped with a tingling fear that stole in on icy fingers.

"There is no one here. Did Sister Marie Susanne really want to see me or did you tell me a lie, Brother Adolphe? I'm sorry! It must be Father by now." She tried to edge around him to the door. Her voice was supposed to be confident and challenging but it ended up being tremulous and weak. "Why did you want me to come up here?"

Before, when she met his intense look down by the fire, she felt herself a defiant woman. Now, she was a frightened little girl. She had no more brave words to throw up like a wall between them.

"It is not 'Father' and it never will be," Adolphe told her, still barring her way to the door. "After today it may not even be 'Brother.' I told Bishop Grandin that I no longer wish to become a priest."

She stared at him, trying to search his face in the dim light. "Why? Why did you do that?"

"Because to accept the church and its vows of celibacy, I would have to give you up, and I can't do that. I knew this a long time ago. I told Bishop Grandin, but he asked me not to tell anyone, not even you, until he heard back from the cardinal in Montreal. When someone renounces his vows it is a serious matter."

Julie felt the heat spread across her face, and her heartbeat quickened until she thought he would hear it pounding in her chest. "Then my mother was right. I am a temptress. You are giving up the life of a priest, the people who need you, and the life you chose to live. It is my fault."

"No Julie! It is not your fault. I made the decision. I want you in my life more than I want to live alone with my choices." He stretched out his arms and folded her against his chest. Tilting her head up to him, he gently kissed her lips and felt her welcoming response. He clutched her tightly, and she clung to him until her heart slowed to a normal beat.

Pushing back from her slightly, he looked down into her eyes, beseeching, pleading. "But we can say nothing about this to anyone yet. If word gets out before the Bishop announces it, this will cause a lot of trouble for us both. I could not bear seeing you becoming so close with Michel and doing that dance with him when I will soon be asking you to be promised to me."

"So that is why you told me about this so suddenly– tonight. You thought that I was going to be promised to Michel. Otherwise you would have gone on letting me suffer–thinking you did not like me at all," she said impishly.

"You know as well as I that at one time that dance was a pledge, instead of a display for entertainment. Michel would have the right to carry you off, and the contract would be fulfilled." Adolphe's voice was tight.

"That was a long time ago. Things have changed," Julie waved it away. "How do you even know about our customs?"

"The priesthood has been here in the Northwest many years before you were born and before your parents were born. A lot has changed because of the presence of the church."

"Well, it is not true." Julie put her hand in his shyly. "When we perform the dance, it will just be a show. And I will keep your secret. But," she pulled away and retreated to the door, "I had better get back to the dance rehearsal before they wonder where I have gone."

"Julie," Adolphe called after her, and she closed the door again. "Meet me when it is over. Meet me at the barn, in the loft. I will be waiting."

She nodded, the colour creeping into her cheeks, and she slipped out of the church.

Down in the deep green woods near the winding river, the campfires danced in a circle, throwing a kaleidoscope of colour across the glen and the brown faces of the blanket-wrapped Métis and Cree who sat waiting for the dance. Lined, toothless faces of the old men, strong, rugged faces of the youth and the round, serene faces of the older women waited in expectation for it to begin. They talked and laughed, their eyes red and dry from the wood smoke while the smell of burnt fat and roasting meat permeated the cool evening air. The fiddle and button accordion started playing, accompanied by the steady throb of the drums, and soon the dancers with a pulsating primal scream leaped out in their decorative costumes into the brightly lit arena. The fire played on their bodies as they leaped and twisted while muscles rippled and tightened.

Their hearts swelled with happiness and pride as the girls danced out into the lighted arena doing their sedate dance, stepping, tapping and circling. Michel followed with his dance miming his first kill, preparing him for adulthood, and leaving childhood behind.

Then Julie joined him in a demure, provocative pattern of movement while he circled her, a glitter of excitement in his brown eyes and a dimpled white-toothed smile. The two fifteen-year-olds drew a murmur of delight from the audience as they met face-to-face, their hands clasped high in the air before running off through an opening in the crowd. Nods and delight played across the watching faces, which imagined the ending for the pair.

Then one of the elders came forward and pronounced the 'magic circle' had brought the end of the winter and the arrival of spring. Bishop Grandin, followed by the troop of priests, entered the circle. While they knelt, he blessed their coming to the West, and the parishes that they would soon head up in the Northwest. With a wave to the church spire jutting up into the cloud-strewn sky, he announced that the solemn part of their vows would be recited tomorrow in more suitable surroundings. Now it was time to eat and celebrate. This feast was supplied by the priests.

Questioning glances darted about as they noticed that Adolphe was not among the black robed dignitaries, but they said nothing, and it was forgotten in the flurry of the feast. No one noticed Adolphe slip away in one direction and Julie melt into the shadows in another.

The shadows of cloud danced before the moon, splashing the dark earth with a patchwork of silver dappled light as Julie ran across the clearing in front of the barn. Panting, her heart racing, she crept inside, closed the door, and climbed the ladder to the loft.

Pausing at the top of the ladder, she glanced around the hay in sudden alarm. *What if he decided not to come? What if the Bishop convinced him that he must go through with his vows?* Poised for flight, wondering why she had taken this dangerous chance, she turned to face the ladder again.

"Over here!" Adolphe said in a husky whisper, and she saw him sitting in the hay at the front of the loft opening. Bathed in moonlight, they sank down into the nest he had formed so that they could look out at the blue-silver sight below. The clouds sifted by the full moon, and the stars, the sirens of desire, twinkled with excitement.

Leaning back against Adolphe's arm, she raised her face to the sky. The music from the fire circle below floated up to them distantly. The scent of the hay and the lodgepole pine mingled with her dusky perfume, as he crushed her slight form to him in a powerful embrace. His breath was warm upon her flesh, and the heat from their bodies mingled, igniting the blood in their veins. That night they found in one another's arms a perilous ecstasy.

31

Sacrifice or Fulfillment

Adolphe aimed determined steps to Bishop Grandin's door and opened it without knocking. The Bishop looked up from his writing in surprise and laid down his quill. With the Bishop, was none other than Father Lacombe!

"Brother Adolphe! What brings you to my door in such a stir?" Grandin demanded.

"I am so sorry," Adolphe blurted out, his voice intense and tight. "I did not know you had company. It is good to see you again, Father Lacombe. I thought that you had left with the last expedition to the North Country. I know that they planned to trek to Dunvegan with Father Grouard."

Father Lacombe stood, smiling, and holding out a welcoming hand to greet Adolphe. "Brother Adolphe, it is good to see you. I see your handiwork all over the Mission – you have done a good job. No, they did not need me to accompany them to Dunvegan. They had enough help. And besides, it is time that I travelled back south. This is home to me, but I am needed on the plains since the disappearance of the buffalo. The Blackfoot are forced to live on dog meat. There is starvation, and my people are dying."

"You see, Brother Adolphe," Bishop Grandin appealed, "how much help is needed all over the Northwest. Father Lacombe can not do it all himself. This, his own parish, rarely sees him anymore with the burden that he carries."

Father Lacombe chuckled, his dark kindly eyes, high cheekbones, and white hair reflected his eastern native heritage. Somehow, from the way everyone spoke of him, Adolphe expected to see a huge, imposing man. Instead he was slight in stature, shorter than Adolphe, careworn with deep forehead and facial creases. "My parish covers thousands of square miles, from the American border to the mighty Peace country. While any of my people are starving or in trouble, I must help."

"Adolphe," Grandin aimed his remark towards Father Lacombe, "has been hesitant to take his place beside the priests who form the army that will lighten your burden, Father Albert. He fears that his projects here will be neglected."

"No," Adolphe hurried in quickly. "The building I could leave, Bishop Grandin. That is not it. I discover that I am not prepared to take my sacred vows. I can not do that now in view of ..." He hesitated.

Grandin's voice was disappointed as he filled the void. "Adolphe has become enamoured with a young lady and is considering giving up his future in the priesthood because of her." He sighed heavily. "When there are so many things that must be done.

"Father Lacombe started the first school here and helped Father Scollen open the first school in Fort Edmonton. There are many more to come – *many more to build.*" Bishop Grandin added the last to impress Adolphe as to how he could fit into this grand scheme. "Father Lacombe, Adolphe, prefers battle for his native people to inactivity."

Ignoring the reference to his flagging spirits and action, Adolphe plunged on. "I am not considering this step, Bishop Grandin." Adolphe explained again, "I have *decided* not to become a priest."

A flicker of irritation appeared across Bishop Grandin's face. "You would sacrifice the people that you set out with such high courage to serve and save?" he accused. Adolphe flinched and lowered his gaze.

"Vital," Father Lacombe addressed his old friend familiarly, "we can not all follow the path that others set out for us. We have got to shape our own futures. Who, but God, knows what destiny has in store for us? Brother Adolphe must have thought about this a very long time and would not have gone into this lightly."

"It is over a girl, Albert, a Métis girl. If she left here, he would have forgotten about her in a matter of weeks. It would be sheer folly to sacrifice your career for a fifteen-year-old, giving up your vows of chastity ..."

"*Non*" Adolphe interrupted boldly, causing the Bishop to raise his heavy eyebrows in surprise. "I will not forget her, and it is too late for vows of chastity. I want to marry her." *There, it was said*! Bishop Grandin, stunned into silence, had nothing to say.

"Then, I think, Vital, that the decision has been made. There are some of us who are cut out to wander in search of adventure and fulfillment of duty to our calling, and others who are content to settle down and devote themselves to one special person and to the land. Of course, our Lord in his wisdom has ordained it, but we can hope that He will also be there to guide. This is in His hands." Father Lacombe leaned back and smiled gently nodding.

"It appears as though I have no choice but to agree since the decision has been taken away from me," the Bishop sighed again. "But who will go in Adolphe's place? It was all arranged ..."

"The Lord will send someone else. He has plans of His own for this servant." Father Lacombe stood up. "And now it is time for me to travel south to meet with Chief Crowfoot." The action precipitated a fit of coughing that wracked his body. "Fear not," he put up his hand to ward off solicitous advances. "It is my pleurisy acting up again. I will be fine."

"Farewell and God go with you!" Bishop Grandin took Lacombe's shoulders and touched his cheek to each of his friend's.

Watching him as he climbed on the waiting horse, bareback, as the natives travelled, Adolphe could see what a toll his service to the natives of the West had taken on this amazing man, and again Adolphe was glad of his decision not to follow in those moccasins.

The following month Julie and Adolphe were married by Bishop Grandin. That same year, the year that the first white settler staked his claim on land near Fort Edmonton, lots were portioned out to Métis along the river spreading up and downriver from the mission. It was a small lot, stretching out from the river the same way that the land was divided out of Montreal and in the Red River Settlement, long and narrow, but enough to plant grain, raise animals, a garden, and build homes of their own.

Adolphe and Julie were assigned Lot Sixteen where they happily began to build a farmhouse and raise a family. However, he would still serve the mission and continue with his work as carpenter. These were the happiest and most contented of Adolphe's twenty-five years.

32

New Directions

When John Lenny and the fur trading crew got back to York Factory, they found many changes. John's father, Andrew, died in a storm at sea and his mother died in great pain of an unknown ailment. His sister, Isabel, went away with a young fur trader heading for Fort Garry. The other voyageurs met with similar changes in their lives.

Since the fur trade had met with its, if not demise, serious curtailment, York Factory itself became a shadow of its former greatness and importance as an outpost. With the fur trade becoming only a trickle to the East, the York boats lost their transportation contract.

Supplies were still needed in Fort Edmonton and the North Country, however, and boats still paddled from Fort Garry to the West. So John and a few of his fellow voyageurs left York Factory for Fort Garry. Some went as far east as Montreal looking for new employment. But the fur trade, plying the waters of the Northern Rivers, was all they knew, and they would inevitably come back to the river trade.

Fort Garry was a bustling, humming, western frontier town when they arrived. The territory had become the newest province of Canada–Manitoba. The city was in the midst of a name change–Winnipeg. The ferry trade from the south across the American border brought in an influx of American adventurers. The supply boats and wagons brought their loads in from the East and transferred them onto boats heading north on Lake Winnipeg–the river route, or to wagons that rolled across the prairie.

Just crossing the streets of Fort Garry (Winnipeg) was a hair-raising adventure. Ox carts with supplies or settlers on the move west set up a screeching that terrified the horses so that they reared and wheeled, the whites of their eyes showing wildly. Frontier women in their bonnets and long dresses struggled to move parcels home on the uneven wooden sidewalks. Men in frontier buckskins, white bearded men in their high fashioned silk hats, entrepreneurs up from across the border, pushed and shoved along the crowded sidewalks. Métis in wagon or ox-cart with their blanket-clad women and children tried to find a new place for themselves after being elbowed off land that they had claimed as theirs. Such a cacophony of sound the men of the Northwest had never heard before.

It was late fall, and a cold north wind whipped through the Winnipeg streets chilling them into the realization that winter was not far away. They had to find somewhere to hole up for the winter before they could travel back west. They were more determined than ever to return to the new land.

Eventually, they found jobs unloading and delivering supplies from the supply wagons and Red River ferry until freeze-up. John and Alex ended up together, staying in a small cold attic room upstairs over a storehouse. The other men moved on farther east. John and Alex meant to ride out the winter until it was time to travel upriver to Fort Edmonton. They would be ready to sign on to the first supply boats heading west at break-up.

After unloading the supply boats at Walter's Landing in Fort Edmonton, Alex and John noticed a big change. A Scot named John Walter had come West on one of their York boats and put his mark on the North Saskatchewan flats where they unloaded and loaded supplies and furs. Both Walter and D.R. Fraser founded a company to receive logs that were formed into logbooms and floated down from upstream. They built York boats and scows to transport supplies upriver.

Hundreds of settlers heading upriver to build homesteads, villages, and settlements loaded these scows with all of their possessions and provisions. A tent city existed on the shores of the busy river. Grey canvas structures of various shapes and sizes huddled together while their owners busied themselves with daily living until arrangements were made for them to move. In the meantime, smoke spiralled up from each dwelling while articles of clothing flapped in the breeze from the tent rope fastened to a tree. Horses, cows, pigs, and chickens were tied or penned up until it was time for them to be moved downriver to prairie land farther east.

Amidst all of the shouting and flourish of activity, John and Alex unloaded supplies destined for Fraser and Company, and some would be shipped from there, farther north to the Athabasca.

"Hey!" Someone shouted at John in English. "That's flour–and that's grain," he pointed out another sack being passed to John. "Be careful it doesn't get wet. It comes to this scow over here." The man with his pencil and paper flourishing in the air was waving and pointing to a well-built four-sided scow tied up to the dock. Alex and John already knew that the shipment was flour and sacks of grain. It was well sealed with oilcloth and they were warned many times that this was a valuable and delicate commodity. All of the crew were hand picked at the start for their care and experience on the river.

Since John had left York Factory and moved to Fort Garry, he no longer slipped into Gaelic but spoke English without such a heavy accent. He was thankful for this because he planned to stay in Edmonton with the predominantly English speaking. He decided not to return to the East, but to get a job in the West. Both he and Alex determined that this was the land of opportunity, and since they heard about John Walter and how his fortune was skyrocketing since he arrived, this would be where their fortunes would begin.

The man taking such care in loading the scow was John McDougall, the son of the preacher. John Lenny had heard about him too. He was the earliest pioneer merchant in Fort Edmonton. This was one shipment of which John McDougall took great care. If it got wet, that would be a big financial as well as a personal loss for many.

When John and Alex were finished, and were paid by the crew master, they were free to wander about. Uppermost on their minds were two important things: finding a place to bed down for the night or for however long they would be here, and getting something to eat. After that, they planned to see John Walter about a job. Walter was in charge of building the scows and York boats that transported men and supplies downriver.

It had to be John Walter, Alex and John agreed, that would be the key to their future here. He, after all, was also a Scot, and from the Orkney Isles. This was the end of the line. The two men would not be returning with the York boats. This was the first day of their life in the West.

Alex marvelled at how many women they saw loading their possessions on the scows, leading small children down the riverbank, coming from the canvas tents, and preparing to travel north and east to set up their colonies. Since 1872, when the Dominion Lands Act was passed, settlers were beginning to push West. When last Alex and John had come to Fort Edmonton they saw mostly fur traders and Indians. But settlers sealed the fate of the last fur brigade from York Factory in 1871. The change was obvious.

"John, I think we should set up our tents among the others up the hill. Why noh just pick a spot until we find where we'll be," Alex said distractedly as he leaned against the wharf post, his packsack slung over his back, staring around at the stream of humanity that pushed by him.

"It's lucky we learned English for when ye gae lookin' for a job. I hear John Walter can speak English verra well," John commented to Alex.

"I'm thinkin' thah maybe we should gae talk tae John Walter right away. Ye never know when ye might be missin' an opportunity."

"Ah, but John," Alex moaned, "I'm hungry and we hae been on the paddles all day. Why noh start oot fresh in the mornin'?"

"But how many others will be lookin' for him in the mornin'?" John warned. "There's still some daylight left. Ye never know. He might be able to tell us aboot a place to live and find something to eat. I hae ainly got a bit of hardtack left in my pack."

John raised his head and sniffed the breeze as the smell of meat cooking on an open spit came to him on a mixture of wood smoke. "Maybe we'll see if we can find John Walter first."

They traced him down at a small wharf where several men were in a small backwash or bay, building rafts and scows. Walter was supervising a boom of logs that was floated downstream. It was gathered together to feed into the inlet and hoisted with what they called a log jammer onto a pile before being squared or split into boards and cut into the right length for scows or rafts.

The river transportation was needed immediately to ship supplies downriver to the Barr colonists. He was shouting instructions above the noise below him, while nimble-footed lumberjacks ran across the moving logs with their peavies and canthooks trying to avoid the logs riding over top of each other. This was dangerous and precarious work, John observed.

One slip and they could land between the logs and be crushed. Alex and John looked at each other, John in alarm, and Alex with an excited smile.

"Mr. Walter," John ventured tentatively after Walter received a piece of paper from a worker and stowed it away in a shirt pocket with a pocketful of papers that bulged out alarmingly. John Walter turned to face the two young men with a frown that said, 'Hurry it up, boys. I've got no time for chit-chat.'

Then John continued in Gaelic that made John Walter raise his heavy blonde eyebrows in surprise. But he did hesitate. He recognized and re-sponded to the language of his youth. "Alex and I are lookin' for jobs. We thought ye could help. We came up on the York boat and we want to stay in the West and work. Someone told us ye might have a job for us."

"And what might ye'r name be, friend of Alex's?" Walter boomed out in a hearty voice.

John flushed up to his red hairline. "Ach, I'm John Lenny, and this is my friend, Alex Macleod. And we need a place to sleep tonight and a meal to eat."

"And we're willin' to work right away to earn it," Alex added hurried-ly.

"Did ye see the sign up there?" Walter pointed to the sign on the little building up the bank that served as an office and living quarters. "That says, 'Only Irishmen need apply.' Are ye Irish?"

"Nae, we're Scots," John answered looking up at the sign for the first time in consternation.

"We thought ye were a Scot too," Alex spoke up with concern. "Someone said that ye were. That's why we ..."

"So ye thought ye'd touch me for a meal and a bed and then ye'd take off for some other likely spot where ye wouldna have tae work tae hard, did ye?"

"Nae," John hurried to assure the man. "We been workin' hard since we first picked up a paddle for the Hudson Bay Company at York Factory. We ain't affeerd ae hard work!"

Then John Walter threw back his head and laughed a big belly laugh that attracted attention for yards around. "Well, I believe ye John Lenny and Alex Macleod. Why did ye not tell me ye were frae York Factory wi' the Hudson's Bay? The reason the sign is askin' for Irishmen is that they are the only ones that can stand the loggin' work on the river. But if ye been wrestlin' them York Boats up that river with the fur trade since ye was b'ys, ye're as good as Irishmen. I need a crew to go up the river to cut timber, live in camp for the winter while ye get the logs tae the waher, and herd them down in the spring when the ice goes oot. We need logs to build with. People farther downriver are livin' on the prairie where there be nae building material. And I need the crew to ride horseback upriver wi' supplies for horses and men to last the winter. Are ye up for that, b'ys?"

"We are!" Alex broke in with enthusiasm. Alex had a reckless streak of which John was sometimes leery. They had never been timber men and walking across those logs as he saw the men do below them, made his straight red hair stand on end.

"We've been jockeying those big boats across rapids and up falls. We've even spent a winter or two up in the tradin' post in the woods, huntin' and trappin'. So this is one more river job to learn." Alex shrugged with a nonchalance that John knew he did not really feel.

John gulped but did his best to portray the confidence that Alex was displaying, although he did not add anything to the recitation of their history on the river.

"All right, b'ys," Walter spoke up agreeably. "Ye're hired! As soon as I heard ye were from York Factory … Ye *were* from the Orkney Islands, weren't ye? I knew ye could handle this job. Go over to the camp kitchen on the other side o' the river and get ye'r-selves a meal and a bunk and report tae me in the marnin'. But ye should know that I dinna own this operation. I know about building these things; *that's* why I'm here. This," he swept his hand out covering the flats along the river and across from the fort, "belongs to two men called Moore and McDowell. Ye answer to them. " Then Walter left them and took up shouting instructions again to the men on shore below them. "Pete, those logs have gotta go into a scow that goes downriver with the Barr colonists. Check with Kenneth over there with the mules."

Alex leading the way, the two men crossed on the ferry to the other side of the river in silence and made their way to the camp. As they got their ration of stew and were shown the bunkhouse where they would bed down for the night, John finally brought up what was bothering him. They had sat at the long table away from the others at the far end. Because the majority had already eaten, as they were among the last to the table, they had the privacy of a quiet discussion.

"Alex, why in the Laird's name did ye till him thah we could be timbermen and push those logs down the river in the spring? We've never done such a thing afore. We cut doon a few trees for our cabin up there – that was all! We only ken aboot paddling a bumboat up the river and gettin' it o'er the rapids. Did ye see those men runnin' across those wobbly rolling logs like as though they were hummocks on the moors?"

"Ach, how hard could thah be?" Alex waved it away. "If we could learn tae push those heavy monstrosities up the North Saskatchewan we should be able tae learn tae steer a few logs doon the river. Besides, we'll hae lots ae help. Maybe we willna need tae actually get oot and ride a log. Sometimes they'll need someone bringing up the rear in the boat or ridin' the horses."

"And thah's another thing," John said in exasperation. "Whah dae we ken aboot horses? We hae never ever had a thing tae dae wi' 'em afore."

"Ach! John! We could learn. It all sounds like a great adventure tae me. Besides, they're noh gae'n to put a couple ae *greenharns* out on those jobs right away. We'll hae a chance tae learn."

John wondered where Alex heard that expression. He was taking to this new adventure like a duck to water. There was nothing to do but go along and make the best of it. Alex was right about one thing. They had learned how to become voyageur/fur-trader/bumboat-paddlers so maybe they could learn to be river drivers and timbermen. But he had a sinking feeling that this was really going to test their mettle.

33

Fate of a Lumberjack

The next day, they assembled and were given their instructions. First they had to get their list of supplies, number one of which was caulked boots. Heavy winter clothing, a bedroll, and a waterproof sack where papers and materials could be stowed to keep dry were next. Each man got an advance on his pay to buy the things he needed at the company store, so Alex and John came out sporting heavy mackinaw, shirts, trousers, heavy wool socks, and sharp caulks screwed into the soles of their boots. They felt heavy and clumsy, and John wondered how the men moved so nimbly across the floating logs with these on their feet.

Then, as John feared, he and Alex were elected, among a few other recruits, to ride the horses upriver loaded with supplies–food, bedding, utensils, and materials for setting up camp for the winter. Others took the big York boats also loaded with supplies–stoves for kitchen and bunkhouses, axes, peavies, pikepoles, saws, chains, springs, block and tackle, nails, roofing and many other necessities.

Each would ride one horse and lead a packhorse or two. One cow was also led on a rope to supply milk, cream, and butter for the camp. John broke out into a sweat as he approached the horse that he was assigned. It had a halter on, and was tied to the hitching rail beside the barn. He was to bridle and harness the horse, and was to ride it with the harness on rather than a saddle, since it was harness that would be needed in the bush. Then the traces of the harness were buckled up to rings on the breaching across the horse's back, so that they would not dangle until they were ready to be hitched to the load in the bush.

He had no idea how harness the beast and was not sure that it would stand still long enough for him to practise the operation. The harness hung on the post, a tangle of leather straps, steel rings, buckles, and snaps. He decided, however, that he liked the smell of this leather. The heavy odour of oiled leather and horse began to grow on him with a comforting calm. He watched the man next to him.

"Ye look as though ye know what ye're doin'," he commented to the man's back. The man turned, and John found that he was an older man of about fifty. His face was weather beaten, and his sideburns were sprinkled with gray under a battered old felt hat that had seen better days. Lines around his eyes, a faded gray, were deepening. His age startled John as he compared him to the young robust drivers that milled around preparing to get into a boat or onto a horse.

"Are ye havin' trouble?" the man questioned in a deep rumble of a voice with an Irish accent.

"Aye," John admitted as he stood helplessly holding the tangle of leather. "I hae never had a thing tae dae wi' a horse afore. I was a river man."

The man whose name was Matthew, the camp cook, chuckled, and the sound rumbled in his barrel chest. He picked up the harness like so much string and threw it effortlessly over the horse's back as he showed John the proper way of harnessing a horse and putting on a bridle. John had a little trouble with that, as he tried to force the bit between the horse's teeth and pull the bridle up over her ears. Luckily for John it was fairly gentle and compliant, and with guidance from Matthew, and cooperation from the horse, he was rewarded with a successful bridling.

"Whah's her name?" John asked just before Matthew turned away to lead his horse up the trail by the river.

"Pick one," Matthew called back. "Sure'n if she had one before, oi don't know what it was. Ye're assigned, by the way, to ride behind the cow as I lead her and herd her along."

John's legs were long enough so that getting up on the horse's back was not such a big problem even if she was a big horse. She was strong but agreeable, and John thanked heaven for that as they fell in behind the string that headed up the bank and followed the well-worn trail to the West, behind the cow that Matthew led.

All the way along that day, he puzzled over what he would call this big black mount. He was thankful for one more thing. He had no reason to guide this horse with the reins. She followed the rest quite happily. He was glad that he was not one of the riders who had to lead a pack animal. It was a long trek. He had lots of time to learn how to ride, handle the reins, and think of a name.

Alex was not as fortunate. Before he could figure out how the harness fit onto the horse, the rest of the horses were leaving and his big gray animal wanted to be among them. The big grey thought he was being left behind and began to pull back on his rope that was tied to the hitching pole, and to move around restlessly and anxiously. This made it harder for Alex to do up the harness and to get the bridle on.

"Whoa! Whoa!" he commanded as he had heard others say, but the animal was in no mood to listen to him. As far as the horse was concerned, all of the others were going and leaving him behind with this fumbling idiot.

Finally, one of the other men, who had already started out, came back. "Havin' trooble there, are ye?" a man with an Irish accent asked. Without waiting for a reply he jumped down and took over. With the presence of the other horse, Alex's calmed somewhat. The Irishman, whose name was Mike, had the harness snapped together and the bridle on in a matter of moments.

"There ye are," he said briefly and turned to mount his horse, but not before Alex noticed that he had a decided limp. Then Alex had to struggle to get on his horse while the anxious animal began to try to follow the other horse.

"Whoa! Whoa, there!" Alex called out as he tried to catch a falling rein and scramble up the harness while running along beside. Mike returned and stopped Alex's horse while Alex managed to get up on top.

"Wait just a minute," a voice shouted. "You're leaving a pack animal behind." Mike returned for the horse with the large pack strapped to its back, threw the rope to Alex, and then hurried to catch up to his own packhorse that had wandered ahead, following the train of animals. This new man was really green! It was obvious that he'd never been on a horse before.

Alex not only had to learn to ride his anxious mount but had to lead another horse that either kept trying to pass his own, or to stop for a mouthful of grass or a drink of water along the way. Alex was exhausted by the time he got to their camp that night, but he discovered that he could not just walk away and flop down onto the grass. He had to look after the needs of his horses first—feeding, watering, and tying them so that they would not wander away, tangle in the rope, or fight with the other horses.

In contrast, John seemed quite exhilarated. After helping to set up the sleeping tent, he and Alex sat on a log and ate their beans and hard tack. "Ye certainly do geh a different view o' the country up here compared tae the river. The horses hae quite a climb up these hills and banks. I'm glad I'm riding and not walking. The horse just follows the others, and ye can look around and enjoy the ride. I decided tae call my horse Morag, after someone I remember back home, a good Gaelic name dinna ye think? Whah's ye'r horse's name?"

"They hae names? It never entered m'mind tae wonder. It's aisy fer ye tae concairn ye'reself aboot names. Ye dinna hae tae wrestle with contrary animals that do their best tae try ye'r nerves and mean tae do whate'er they please. Ye dinna even hae a pack animal tae pull behind ye. They tell me it's noh a horse at all—it's a donkey!"

"But it should still hae a name, should na'it?" John persisted. "Maybe that's the trouble. If ye could call it along when it went astray, it maught be more cooperative."

"Maught be that *ye* should hae the stubborn animal so that ye could find out whah it's like," Alex replied in irritation.

"Or maybe someone else should lead the pack animal – so thah ye could concentrate on learnin' tae ride." John got up and went directly to Matthew. Alex could see him as he talked, pointing his way and then at the horses.

Alex flamed with embarrassment. Now everyone would know that he could not handle the first job they gave him, after he spoke so knowledge-ably. But he did not know it was going to be so difficult. They would brand him a fool, a kid who could not handle the first simple task.

But the next day, when he was relieved of the packhorse, he gave a grudging thanks to John, especially when he got up in the morning nearly crippled from the day's ride and chafed from riding the uncomfortable har-ness. How he wished that he had been allowed to take the boat upriver!

Later on that night, John found a chance to talk to Mike. He was also an older man, as was Matthew. Still long and lean, he had the strength and stamina of many men his junior, but his limp had him hopping along to save his leg or wincing with pain and discomfort, often rubbing his leg absent-mindedly when he thought no one was watching. He was beginning to develop a stoop to his shoulders and a weariness that made him seem older than his forty-some years. He seemed to be in charge of all the horses and the cow, and he lost his patience only when one of the riders mistreated or neglected one of the animals. Naturally, he preferred to ride. That evening he rode about, inspecting the horses to see that they were bedded down properly. He milked and fed the cow, and he treated his own animal with tenderness, even when the animal behaved badly, an attitude that many men only saw in a father and young son.

John found an opportunity to sit next to him as they ate. "Hae ye been on many trail rides up tae the lumber camps?" He finally eased into the topic he wanted to discuss after the introductions and pleasantries were out of the way. He seemed to be a lot quieter and more reserved than the other wild Irishmen that John met back at the fort and in camp.

"Sure no!" Mike replied as he adjusted his position again to compensate for his leg. "Oi started out as a river driver – so oi did. We cut the logs in the winter and pulled them to the river. Then when the ice went out, the logs were carried down to the fort."

"If the river is doing all the work, why do the men hae tae gae along wi' them and 'drive 'em,' as they tell me thah they do?" John knew what the answer would be, but he needed Mike to tell him the whole story.

Mike chuckled. "Be damned if the logs don't saim t'know how t' get there in the best arder. They git hoong up on shaare or in the rapids or on the sandbars. A boonch o' thim pile up t'gither in a narrah part or on a sharp bend, and they ride up o'er top o' each other, shooting inta the air. A hape o'things kin happen. They kin get tangled up and cause a dam, so that no logs can get by, and the water canna flow properly aither. That's whin the log drivers have to move the logs along by runnin' out across the top o' thim with a peavie or pike-pole and steer thim in the right direction."

"It sounds like it could get dangerous!" John commented after noticing the frown flash across Mike's face. He waited through a period of silence and then decided to ask the question, the answer to which he wanted most to know. "Is that how ye got ye'r leg hurt– oot on the logs?"

There was a long pause as Mike looked down at his feet, and John began to wish that he had not been quite so brash.

But Mike told the story as he puffed his pipe and leaned against a tree, gazing off into the distance.

It was spring and the men cheered the break-up. They could not wait for the order to start the logs running. The boss needed the water high to move the logs along, and it was very high that spring. Excitement fairly crackled in the air as men grabbed their peavies and pike-poles and got ready for the ride of their lives as they knocked the blocks from underneath the decks up on the banks and started them rolling down the bank into the river. Mike was one of the first to run out across the logs with the current.

There are very few rapids in the North Saskatchewan, and when it was in flood, very few sandbars and islands. That's why it was a good river for a log drive, Mike told John. But it does have a lot of bends and turns.

All summer and fall they practised the log rolling in the river as far as the 'boom' that they set up for practice. Mike was the champion log roller. Everyone that got up on the log with him could not stay with him; he dumped them all.

The de-limbed trees crowded up beside him, but that was all right. He needed the logs to run out across if one of them was about to get hung up, or ride up over another. The danger only sharpened the wits.

He had turned his head and noticed his friend Paddy running across the logs just a little behind, pointing with his peavie as the logs began to pile up against a steep bank, riding up the face of the rock and falling back down on the logs below. He was going to clear the jam.

At the same time as Paddy, Mike noticed a rogue log that was jamming up the works, and he could see that Paddy meant to climb up that pile, across the buckling and upending logs, and grab the culprit with his peavie.

Mike saw Paddy climbing the logs against the wall, leaping higher from log to log like a kid would on a woodpile. But a rogue log from underneath pushed up and toppled over.

Paddy's pike-pole snapped like a toothpick, and the log crashed on top of him.

One of the rogue logs then rose up from underneath unexpectedly and came down on top of Mike's log. It knocked him down, and sideswiped his leg before he could jump to another log. The pain, a white-hot dagger, grabbed him, and he thought he was going to pass out. All he could do was cling to the log like a leech.

He gathered another log snug up against the one he rode, and anchored it with his peavie. Then he could get his leg across the logs to keep the other logs from hitting against it.

Other drivers caught up to them and took over, trying to steer the logs, including the ones Mike was riding, safely the rest of the way down the river to Fort Edmonton.

Through a fog of pain and shivering, he heard one of the drivers call out, "What's that ahead of that log?"

It was Paddy. Every bone in his body was broken and his face was beaten to a pulp.

"Oi woke in me bunk," Mike told John. "Me leg was shattered, but the doc set it the baist he could, while oi was knocked out with his aither cloth over me face.

"Oi knew oi'd niver ride the logs again, and oi still have a lot o' pain. The only thing that hilps is the whiskey." He took out his bottle and took a long swig. "Because of this," he held up the bottle, "Oi'll niver ride the logs again even if me leg does get back to narmal. It makes me numb from the pain and from the rage that aits at me soul. Oi ain't tillin' ye not to ruin ye'r life this way 'cause I know the lure of the log drive will suck ye in. Ye'll say, like they all do, 'It ain't gonna happen t'me. Oi'm good!'"

Their meal was over, and it was time to set up camp for the night. As John crawled into the tent with the others, leaving Mike to check out the horses, he thought for a long time while setting out his bedroll for the night. Even before he talked to Mike, he doubted that he would make much of a log driver. Now he was convinced. That was why John played the music while the others danced, he realized. He was not as nimble on his feet.

Alex, on the other hand, would be excited with the challenge. He would dive into anything and be sure he could best the rest at it. *Oh well, no use worrying about it now.* The drive would not be until the spring, and fall was nearly upon them.

Searching for small trees to use in making their buildings for camp, John rode Morag up a steep incline. Suddenly struck with the beauty of his surroundings, he felt as though he had been there before. When he reached the crest of the hill and looked down across the valley below and the blue ribbon of the North Saskatchewan meandering through it, around a river island that rose out in the middle, he knew what he was remembering.

Morag came to a halt as John gazed out across the river valley and the bumboats that travelled distantly below, heading upstream to survey the shoreline. John suddenly realized the similarity to the place where he said good-bye to Lucy. In his mind he seemed to see the little creek beside which they built, the little fur trading post, the one that the Indians burned to the ground. That was nearly three years before. He looked around, half expecting Lucy to be standing there waving good-bye. The trail was more well travelled, wider to accommodate wagons and teams as well as single file walkers, riders, and Indian Travois.

Alex was there and two other riders heading down the steep bank and across the creek. John held on, gave the horse her head, and let her make the descent on her own, angling downhill and away from the steep riverbank. But he could not help looking around for some sign that they had been there before. He tried to catch Alex's attention, but Alex was busy hanging on to keep from sliding off in the steep descent, and then the ascent up the other side. He seemed to be unaware that the terrain was familiar. But then, this was closer to the first of the trading posts – closest to Fort Edmonton.

They continued to angle away from the river to avoid the steep banks of the Saskatchewan and to circle around, heading back to camp. John kept a watchful eye for familiar landmarks or sign of life. Again his mind drifted back to that time and place. What had Lucy called it? Mewassin, that was it! He stopped Morag and stood looking across the wide valley where he was sure she said the buffalo used to come to shelter under the banks and near the trees. The grass used to grow as high as their bellies, she told him. Then one year the buffalo came no more. They were all gone.

The Indians used to watch for them and light the fire on the hilltop to signal the hunt. Their fires of celebration of a good hunt and of sacrifice to the Great Spirit, the Master of Life, were made from that hilltop. Up there by the fires with the wind blowing across the hills, they cut the bison in strips and dried them on pole racks. From there, also, the tribe watched the white man's big awkward boats as they moved slowly up and down the river, she said. And they signalled other bands up and down the shore that the white man was here.

'*I would go back some day*, John thought, *to 'the good land', that is what Mewassin meant*, he remembered Lucy explaining, '*The Good Land*'.

34

Logging Camp Accident

It was a hard winter in the foothills timber country. It was so cold at times that the trees seemed to crack like rifles firing in the night. When the loggers stepped out of the bunkhouses, the snow crunched noisily underfoot and their breath caused hoarfrost to coat the eyebrows and eyelashes. Hanging low to the south, the sun struggled to slant through the ice crystals that hung in the air like a white icy curtain.

With little enthusiasm, John left the bunkhouse and headed towards the outhouse to relieve himself. Leaving the warmth of his cot and going out into the cold to bare his behind to the cold, let alone sitting on the icy wooden seat, took steely resolve. But there was no avoiding it.

Alex beckoned him to where he was standing by the cookhouse door, but John signalled him to wait until he returned. Nothing could be that important, John decided, to postpone this morning visit.

"Whah is it?" John demanded as he rounded the corner after hunting down his friend who disappeared when he got back from the outhouse.

Alex washed his hands and face, and was smoothing out his wild dark blonde hair with a wet hand when John found him. The washstand was just outside the kitchen/dining longhouse. Matthew always insisted that all the men wash up before coming in from the outhouse to eat, and a bucket of hot water sat on the stand with a dipper for that purpose, while a stained ragged towel hung beside it. This morning the water in the basin was nearly covered with a skim of ice before John got to use it. Mathew always told them, though, that no one ate until they washed. All they needed, he said, was for someone to spread the diarrhea to the rest, and then blame it on his cooking. They did eat well, John had to admit.

Leaning on the doorjamb as John washed up, Alex talked. "I was think-ing," he began. They both spoke English all of the time now. English was the language the whole camp spoke.

"That's a good idea," John cut in and chuckled at Alex's expense. "Thinking is good."

Ignoring the jibe, Alex went on, "Maybe I could work with ye with ye'r horse, pullin' the logs to load from the skidway onto the sleigh. I could hook the loggin' chain around the log and help ye get it from the skidway onto the sleigh."

"Well, Alex, I dinna need any help gettin' the log to the skidway and there is Harry there, helpin' all the skidders to get their logs up the skidway onto the sleigh. Besides that, ye said ye didna want to work with the horses. Ye wanted to work on the end of a crosscut saw, ye said, cuttin' doon the trees, de-limbing them and sawin' them up into the right lengths. What made ye change ye'r mind?"

"Well," Alex started off slowly. "It's Clarence," he finally blurted out. "Him and I canna work together. He thinks I'm some kind o' a greenharn. And he will nae get off-a my back. Like yesterday, he sent me up to the camp to get a left-handed crosscut saw. He said that's the raison I was al-ways gettin' the saw stuck. Then when I got up there, Mike told me just to stand on the other side of the tree–that was all that was needed. While I was gone they had their break, so I didna get one. Then he had me cuttin' off the limbs with the axe, and Chester came along and told me it would be aisier if they got the big ones with the crosscut saw. He was doin' the smaller ones and givin' me the big ones. Then yesterday I heard him and Lester talking in whispers, and I heard my name.

"From the very first day that I started to work on the timber cuttin', and they sent me with the axe to chop notches in the trees, so that they could come behind with the crosscut saw, I knew they were out tae get me." Alex was getting heated with his agitation.

"How was that?" John asked as he hung up the towel.

"Well, remember? It had snowed the day before and I never realized that the spruce branches held up a load of snow. The first swipe that I made at the spruce tree, a load of snow came down on me, sliding down my neck and makin' me cold and wet. They were right there tae laugh as though it had been planned."

Entering the long room that served as kitchen and dining room, the two noticed that several heads came up and looked their way with smiles aimed at Alex. No more was said as both men sat down at the long wooden table, the bench of which was a half log on top of two blocks of wood. No nails were used where notches and naturally formed 'y' branches could cradle the split logs for the table.

"Top o' the marnin' Alex! John!" Chester called out and the others followed suit.

As they left, after putting their tin plates and cups into the basin by the door, Clarence bent over Alex's shoulder and said in a low confidential tone, "See ye out at the site."

After the others left, and John and Alex finished the rest of the sourdough hotcakes, Alex continued quietly. "So, if I took the job of haulin' the log tae the sleigh like ye dae, would ye help me learn?"

Getting up from the table John turned to look at Alex squarely, "They're really gettin' tae ye airn't they? Ae course I'll help ye. But ye'll have tae talk tae Ira. He's the headman ae this operation. There he is talkin' to Mike."

Alex hurried over, and John watched out of the corner of his eye while he got Morag out of the barn and harnessed her up. Then he watched as Alex walked slowly towards him, and he knew the result of the appeal.

"Ira said that there is noh another horse available, and I would hae tae arrange with one ae thae men on that detail tae exchange jobs wi' me," Alex related unemotionally. "Would ye change wi' me?" he finally asked John tentatively after a pause.

"There's nae time noo tae teach ye ye'r job, Alex. We're late noo." John was becoming a little irritated with Alex and the pressure that he was putting on him. "Try tae put up with it fer taeday. Maybe come morn the boss could arrange somethin'. Giddup now," John clucked to his horse and he left Alex standing by the barn.

It was a poor barn, little better than no shelter from the snow and wind. The cracks between the slabs and logs were wide enough to stick a hand through. It, like the other structures in the camp had been hurriedly put together. Small poplar trees were cut down, notched, and fitted together into cabins. The roofs were slanted slightly with branches crisscrossed over it and tied down. They were not meant to last. In the spring they would move the logs down the river and find a new site the next year. The location was chosen on crown land or Hudson Bay Company land, so that timber would be cheap. If the site had an abundance of heavy timber, they might return to it next year and move the buildings closer to the cutting. But the buildings were very temporary. They lived in tents for the rest of the summer and the fall while the camp was being set up.

While the building went on, firewood was cut – deadfall and dry wood brought in to last the winter. Bunks and tables were hewed, and the men took time to practise and train for the coming log-run in the spring. A backwash was roped off with a log boom, and the men had their contests to see how long they could stay up on a rolling log before getting dunked or before someone bested them, and knocked them into the water. They practised running across the logs, leaping from one to the other to perform feats of speed and strength, until they were like flies on a wall.

Alex so anxious to get started with his training that he plunged into the fray, lasting no longer than five minutes before being unceremoniously dumped into the water. The sight brought shouts of laughter and teasing from the adept Irishmen, who had found a new form of entertainment. Eventually, they helped him, and he began to stay on the log for longer and longer stints. However, before freeze-up when the water was too cold to venture into, he was not trained well enough to tackle a drive. That was John's observation.

Ira, the drive boss, was doubtful, but was willing to give him a chance to prove himself. The rest of the drivers were overwhelmingly in favour of letting him try a drive. He would learn as the drive went along, they said confidently. He was a natural, some said enthusiastically, but with wry smiles that did not encourage John.

John had done his share of training during that summer, but spent more time in the water than on top of the log. He admitted to Matthew that he was hopeless. "I dinna hae the balance, and I am nae verah nimble. To tell ye the truth, I am too clumsy to manage the log. I'll never be a driver in time for spring. I'll hae tae stay on dry land."

"Well, look at the bright side of it," Matthew sympathized, "Ye're getting' a good bath – often – and ye're getting' your clothes washed. I dare say they needed it after the work setting up camp, working with the horses, and cutting feed for the cow in the heat of the day. One thing I will say about ye'r friend, he's determined to be a log driver this spring–that he is. He's out to prove his'silf."

John nodded sadly as they watched Alex making headway with the leap from log to log and struggling to keep his balance.

"Atta boy, Alex!" the men shouted in encouragement while they held their stomachs in glee watching Alex's legs and arms flail the air in an ungainly manner. "Ye're gittin' better."

It became such sport to tease Alex over the summer and fall, that when the logging operation set in with the first snowfall, which came in October, the men still wanted to continue with the one-sided entertainment. John had not provided near the sport that Alex had. He just gave up on the water sport and continued to work hard at the jobs that needed to be done with the animals, chopping and stacking wood for the stoves this winter, and helping to build what was needed inside the structures in camp. He wondered how long it would be before the teasing and hi-jinks went too far, and Alex had enough.

Alex picked up his axe and small Swede-saw and stomped off to the cutting site where Clarence was set up with the saw at the tree that had been marked or notched for cutting.

"The divel takk a lazy man!" Clarence called out to him as Alex approached, axe over his shoulder, dragging the saw. "Ye're late this marnin'. The others are about three trees ahead o' us. Ye know they expect thirty trees out of us t'day. The horses will be around to pick up the logs before we git them limbed, and they'll be waitin' at the skidway."

Alex lost all patience and stalked on past Clarence, throwing a remark over his shoulder. "Do it ye'reself then. I'll cut down the trees with the axe and Swedesaw and trim the branches off in half the time it'll take ye to operate that crosscut saw. If ye're so smart," he turned slightly, "ye should be able tae dae the whole thing. But ye'd better sharpen up the teeth on that thing wi'out me tae help ye."

Clarence stared after him and then shrugged. Instead of crosscut sawing with no one on the other end, he searched out Chester who, with Sean O'Donnell, was chopping the limbs from yesterday's trees, sawing them into the right lengths, and notching them ready for the chain to half-hitch around it and haul it away.

"What air y'doin' over here?" Chester demanded, his hawk nose red with the cold and the frost rimming his lashes and brows.

"Alex took off on me. He told me to operate the crosscut by meself and he'd cut his own trees down with the Swedesaw and axe."

"The crazy fool!" Sean shook his blonde head. "It'll take him all day to cut one o'thaise trees with an axe. They're three and four fait across!" Sean was slight, fine featured, and agile, almost boyish. He practically danced across the logs in the bay. No one could stay on the other end of a log while facing him. He made it look too easy. Alex was determined to keep up with him but failed.

"Oi know," Clarence sighed and sat down. "But now oi'm without a man on the other end of the crosscut. Oi guess he lost his sense o' humour yesterday."

"So while he's gone away to pout o'er a bit ae taisin', we're all gonna pay the price when the boss comes around to see what the hold-up is all about," Chester growled. "Well, let him stew in his own pot. We'll show 'im he's as poor a logger as he is a log driver and horse rider. Here, Sean, ye saw the limbs off the rest of these and oi'll go help Clarence. Then oi'll come back and hilp y'saw these into the right lengths. Be damned if he thinks we're gonna chase 'im and plead for him t'come back, he's gonna wait a long time. We might work twice as hard, but it'll be worth it to show 'im the camp can do without his kind."

Clarence and Sean nodded in agreement, but without much enthusiasm. The fun had gone out of the camp. Now it was going to be just plain hard work.

Alex stalked off to the other side of the site, keeping the marked trees in sight. He wanted to be as far away from all of them as possible. He stopped and could not hear a sound – no saw, or axe ringing across the crisp cold morning. This was perfect. He would start here. He would pick a tree that was not too big, but yet was one the size that they needed. *This did not have a notch on it, but it should have*, he thought.

He swung the axe repeatedly, relishing the release that he got from his anger and irritation. Enjoying the bunching of his muscles and the jolt that his body experienced as the tree shuddered, and the blade bit deep into the wood, he swung over and over. Sometimes the blade would bind up in the wood, and he would pry it loose, but he liked to see the chips fly. He exulted in the strength he felt welling up inside travelling across his shoulders, and down his arms.

Finally, winded after his burst of energy, he stepped back to survey. He was really not making very much headway. He tried with the saw for awhile. The change in activity was as good as a rest, and he plunged into it. But the saw kept binding up on him and was really slowing him down. He remembered how Clarence yelled at him for not pulling steadily and making the crosscut saw bind up when they were deep into the tree. He remembered Clarence hollering, "Pull, damn it! Pull!" And he yelled back the same thing.

Now he had no one to yell at. When he was about halfway through, he thought it would be a good idea to notch the other side of the tree deeply and then put a wedge in on this side to help open up the space and make the sawing easier. The snow-covered ground was rough, studded with great boulders and outcroppings. The trunks of great dead trees lay everywhere. Looking around, he found some deadfall that he could chop into a wedge. He found chopping at this angle much easier, so he took a big swing with his foot propped against the log to keep it steady.

The deadfall was frozen, and his axe skidded off the mark. Instead, the blade glanced off the tree and plunged into his foot.

Pain exploded on him like a hot poker. He shuddered as it knifed through his foot and up his leg. In horror, he looked down to see the axe had cut through his leather boot, split his toes apart like a hot knife through butter, and buried into his arch. A scream that he hardly recognized escaped his lips and filled the quiet around him. He fell to his other knee with a screech of panic, and like a man possessed, he yanked the axe out of his foot.

Instead of relief as he somehow hoped, his pain increased tenfold. He was so desperate to get it out. The blood poured from the wound and oozed in a red widening circle onto the frozen ground. His only thought was to stop the bleeding. With numb and trembling fingers, his body vibrating like a leaf in the wind, using every ounce of strength and determination he possessed, he managed to untie his boot and pull it off.

Now, he thought he was going to faint. Then he broke into a fevered sweat, and he thought he was going to be sick. *'I've got to stop the bleeding,'* he panted, and he took off his jacket, tying it around the foot as tightly as he could.

'*Why did I do that?*' he thought in panic. '*I'll freeze without my coat.*' Using a dry stick as a crutch he tried to heave himself to a standing position, but the pain ran through his body like a firebrand and the bleeding increased. '*I'll freeze to death out here!*' He panicked as he felt the hot sticky blood flowing into the jacket and running out the edge. '*My God, what have I done?*'

"Help! Help!" he screamed and the echo came back to taunt him. '*I've got to get back to camp,*' he decided, suddenly so cold that his teeth chattered. Then came realization. '*I'm too far away to limp like this into camp. I'll bleed to death. But who will come looking for me?*' Awful realization twisted his heart, and he fell weakly to the ground, holding onto his mangled foot and repeating over and over as loudly as his weakened voice could manage, "Help! Help! Help!"

John came by to pick up one of the logs and glanced over to where Alex should have been sawing with Clarence. Walking over to the pair who stopped working as he approached, he asked, "Where's Alex?"

"Sure'n he decided that hai'd rather work on his own," Clarence answered off-handedly though he was now feeling guilty.

"Be damned if he didn't run off with his axe and hand saw – goofin' off, oi'd say!" Chester grumbled. "Oi think he just got tired o'bein' on the other end of the crosscut. "Hai'll be back whin he finds out it ain't so aisy on ye're oon." The two men set back to work with loud shouts of, "Pull! Pull! Pull!" so John backed away with a frown. This was not good.

He wrapped the logging chain around the end of the log and hooked it, so that when it tightened under Morag's force it could only slide up as far as the notch cut around the end, and he clucked to his horse to pull away.

As soon as John left, the two stopped cutting and their gazes met. "He's been gone a long time, and oi've heard nary a sound. How far did he go?" Clarence wondered earnestly.

"The divel takk 'im, he's likely sittin' a little ways away on a log hopin' we'll come and beg him to come back. Let's git at it." Chester grabbed the handle and the two began sawing again.

Sean put in an appearance next. "Hey! What's happening over here? Oi've finished all oi can wi' the de-limbing. Oi've been waitin' fer ye to come and hilp wi' the crosscut saw. Bert will be comin' back with the horse soon and oi won't have any logs fer 'im."

"Well, oi can't do two jobs!" Chester complained.

"Has Alex not come back yet?" Sean took out his pocket watch and looked at the time. "He's been gone a long time. It's nairly time to finish for the day."

"Aye!" Chester agreed with some sarcasm. "Sure'n he should be back braggin' about the hape o'trays he cut down without us" He laughed as he pulled back on the crosscut again. "Oi'll finish this tree and then come o'er and help ye, Sean. Then Clarence can chop these limbs."

Sean frowned, watched them awhile, peered through the trees as the sun's rays reflected dimly through an icy haze and made a decision. "That's enough o'this craziness. Sure'n it's startin' t'snow. Oi'm goin' t'look fer 'im." Without waiting to see what the other two would say about it, he strode off in the direction that Alex's tracks made.

After tramping and searching for Alex's tracks that were increasingly hard to follow in the deep woods and the steadily falling snow, Sean hesitated and marked his bearings. '*That's all I need*,' he reminded himself, '*to get meself lost out here. Then they'd be looking for the two of us.*'

He began calling out, "Alex! Where are ye?" Sean could see no sign of activity – no marking or chopping of the trees, no sounds of the axe or saw – this was very strange. "Alex! It's gaittin' dark. Toime t'quit." The shadows of evening started darkening the forest in the northern winter soon after four o'clock, and Sean guessed that it was after three-thirty already. He knew that Alex was angry with his work partners, but he was carrying this too far.

Sean had a loud piercing whistle and he started using that in long and short patterns of an S-O-S, long – short – short – long. Then he stopped to listen. No sound came in answer. Now he was getting worried. In a long listening pause he picked up the distant mournful howl of a wolf, then another. The thought of what could happen to a lone traveller in the forest, either to Alex or to him, sent a chill up his spine.

'*I think it's time for me to go back while I can still see my tracks, and get help,*' he finally decided, and turned. As he did he thought he heard something. He listened but heard nothing. Sean tried another long and piercing whistle that carried high and shrill across the spruce forest and listened again intently. '*Maybe I'm only attracting the wolves,*' he sighed with chagrin.

But then he thought he heard a weak call for help, and he listened again, aimed in the direction that he heard the sound. Calling, whistling, and listening he made his way in the direction that the answering calls for help were heard faintly until finally he pulled the snow-laden spruce boughs back, and there was a huddled form before him on the snow.

At the same time, he caught the flicker of bright eyes and a grey shadow that melted into the woods. They were out there, the wolves, waiting to move in. "Alex," Sean called out and ran forward, hoping it was not too late. Then he noticed the circle of red on the snow around him. "Air ye all right?" He knelt down beside the huddled form as Alex raised his head.

At the sight of Sean's boyish handsome face below his toque fringed with his yellow-gold hair Alex saw an angel come for him. He started to feel warm, and was sure he had just left the earth. Looking up at Sean through fever-glazed eyes he said, "Ye came fer me. Ye finally came."

35

Break-Up

"Oi'm here, Buddy." Sean surveyed the situation, saw the red saturated jacket wrapped around Alex's foot, the signs of frostbite, and the broken stick that Alex tried to use as a crutch. He looked a few yards away and saw the half-finished tree cutting, the bloody axe, the mangled boot and knew what had happened. "Can ye stand up? Oi'm goin' t'try to git ye to camp."

The cold halted the bleeding for the time being, but the toes were starting to freeze, and the jacket was in no shape to be worn again. Sean wrestled Alex to his shoulders, legs draped over one shoulder and arms and head over another. Sean was surprisingly strong for his size, but it would be an impossible task for him to carry Alex into camp while clambering over logs, through spruce branches and deep snow.

As movement began and after Sean draped his coat around Alex, the pain returned and the bleeding started again. Now Alex knew that this was no angelic visit; this was reality, painful reality.

As darkness slowly settled over them, they struggled through the woods until they heard another distant whistle. Sean stopped, leaned his load against a tree, and freed his hand to bring his fingers to his lips. He whistled another piercing shriek and waited. An answering whistle, this time closer rewarded him, and a few minutes later two more people emerged from the forest in front of them, one leading a horse. It was John and Clarence. The sight they beheld shook them.

The men fashioned a travois with saplings from the forest, attached it to the Morag's traces and strapped Alex to the travois. They wrapped Alex up in jackets to keep him warm and bound his foot, attempting to stop the renewed bleeding.

It was dark by the time they reached camp, and the others were already worried as to their whereabouts. "Oi'll git the sleigh ready, nail boards to the bunks so that he kin be taken t'Edmonton. He's lost a lot o' blood." Mike shouted orders. "John, ye git the team harnessed up. Ye and Clarence will take him. Sure and Ira knows the most about lookin' after accident victims. Lay 'im doon on a cot inside and get him raidy fer the trip. Get lots o' blankets from the bunkhouse. John, Clarence will drive. Ira will show ye how to look after his foot on the way."

Alex was in for more pain when Ira took away the socks and jacket from his foot and when he warmed the toes with his hands to bring back some circulation. Then as the blood flowed again, he bandaged the wound and showed John how to apply and release a tourniquet for the leg to keep Alex from bleeding to death before they reached Edmonton.

All the way to Fort Edmonton, fortified against the pain with only two or three swallows of whiskey, Alex alternately moaned, cried, babbled, shivered and cursed as he tossed feverishly under the blankets. Clarence pushed the team to go as fast as the rough terrain of the trail would allow them. All through the night they travelled, the sleigh lurching along over the rough frozen terrain. The next day they arrived at the fort, and John Walter led them to the doctor's small operating room behind his office.

"He'll be all right," Doc Miller assured a worried John Lenny. "Luckily, he didn't lose any toes and with your tourniquet you kept him from bleeding to death or losing his leg. But he won't be walking around on that for awhile. He'd better stay out of the bush and stay in the fort with his foot up for a time."

The three men looked at each other with the same question in their eyes. How would he do that? The logging camp was the only home he had. He knew nobody in Fort Edmonton, but John Walter, and Walter could not look after him. Alex could not work for his keep, and Walter had no place and no time to be nursemaid.

There was only one thing to do. They took him back to camp. That was his only family right now. If he could not get around on foot, John would look after him.

When Alex hobbled painfully on his walking stick to the bunkhouse after they got him back to camp, Chester shook his head, "Sure and he ain't gonna be doin' any log drivin' this spring."

255

A remarkable change took place in his former tormentors' attitudes for the rest of that winter. They could not do enough for him. They waited on him hand and foot. They brought him anything he wanted and went to see him whenever they got in from work. They even did their best to entertain him and inquired ceaselessly about his welfare while they were away in the bush. When he went to the outdoor toilet while they were away and hurt his foot, opening his wound and re-starting the bleeding, they agreed that he should have an indoor pot under the bed, and they would take turns emptying it.

One particularly stormy night when the temperature dropped to forty-two below and a wind howled around the shack bringing the men as close as they could to the heater at the centre, they decided on something special. They discovered that John played the bagpipes. While someone was searching through the bunkhouse trying to find a lost boot, they found the pipes poking out of John's satchel. When they inquired about it, he showed them his kilt and sporran as well. After urging, he played for them, and that was the beginning of an impromptu party.

Men fashioned drums, sticks to strike, homemade harps and whistles, even towels to do for kilts while others stamped, tapped, and hummed the tunes. Unable to keep quiet, Alex began to sing some of the old Gaelic tunes he remembered, and the Irishmen could remember them as being familiar. Out of that, grew other songs in English, and they all responded with their instruments. Alex on his crutch with Chester and Clarence on either side of him, their arms supporting him, swayed back and forth singing an old ribald song, almost forgotten from their youth.

John was overjoyed to see the new camaraderie between Alex and his former tormentors, but he knew the reason. Alex never revealed to anyone why he went off alone in the woods that day, or the way that they treated him that forced him into such a situation. Alex took all the blame upon himself. He did not tell Ira what drove him from camp that day – only that it was in a fit of temper. That endeared him to Clarence and Chester as nothing else could have.

But most remarkable was the new bond that was forged between Sean and Alex. Alex behaved as though Sean was a long lost friend, and he asked about him every day if he did not see him. He would try anything if Sean suggested it, and his eyes followed Sean about the room, almost with a look of awe.

"One thing I'm gae'n tae regret the most," Alex said one day, "is that I will nae get a chance tae drive the logs this spring and see Sean in action – maybe get some pynters from him." The others were very good at log driving, but Alex remembered only how good Sean was.

"Ye will get a chance to be a log driver next year, Alex," Sean smiled, amused, and delighted to be Alex's hero.

By springtime, the men were in a fever of excitement. The logs, all of uniform length, were lined up on the riverbank ready to be rolled from their decks into the river. The ice went out and the water was running high. The men waited only for word from Ira that the time was right.

Everything was loaded up on the horses or in the wagon. Nothing would be left in this camp except the bare bones of the buildings they had constructed. Next fall it would be another camp in another timber area. The men who would ride horses down to the fort were loading and searching for any signs of things that were left behind that might be salvaged.

"It's a mite sad, like laivin' hame," Alex had commented as he limped around, helping to harness the horses and tie on their packs. "I'm gae'n t'wait until the logs air rolled in, and the drivers take off from shore, like Mike."

"That might not be 'til t'morrow, and they'll travel faster than we will," John said, continuing to check out the packs. "I'm laivin' right away. Besides, I hae t'lead the cow. She'll make me travel slower." John had also grown fond of Ruag, the cow. He had named her, too. It was never too much trouble to give her all the time she needed to travel behind the wagon on her lead rope. Most of the care lately, in looking after Ruag, John had taken on. He milked and fed her, turned her in and out of the barn. And he helped build a corral so that she would not wander away or fall prey to animals.

"Ye're learnin' how to be a regular farmer. Sure and that y'are," Matthew commented, quite pleased that the care and milking did not fall on him anymore.

The journey back to Fort Edmonton was slow with the wagon and urging Ruag along. The wheels of the wagon bit deeply into the soft trail, and the horses had to pull their feet out of the mud each step they took. Alex and Mathew, who caught up with them down the trail, commented that the drive would be at the fort and built into bumboats and scows by the time they got there. At times it took them an hour to cross a creek with the wagon. At times they had to dig the wagon wheels out of a bog.

The strength of his big black horse was a marvel to John. More and more this animal felt like his own. He cared for her, worked with her, talked to her and depended on her all these months. When they got to John Walter's station at the fort he did not know what would happen to her. When the logs got to the fort their job was over unless Walter had other plans for them. It worried him.

Alex was right. The logs came down the North Saskatchewan waters before they arrived, with no trouble and were gathered in the log booms set up to catch them.

The men were to get their pay from Mr. Moore and his partner, Pat McDowell, and then they predictably hit the taverns of the fort in search of entertainment. Fort Edmonton was a rough town in the winter, with wild sled dogs roaming everywhere, their drunken masters in the taverns. There was no control on theft. Fights and murders occurred without punishment. In the spring when traders and log drivers hit town it was even wilder, noisier, and more lawless. It was the best place for a hard-working, danger-facing log driver to lose all of the pay he had earned all fall and winter in the forest.

As Alex and John lined up before the paymaster with the rest of the crew, each had different ideas about how he would spend his pay and what was next.

"I'm gae'n to stay here and wark for Walter and his partners buildin' the Yark boats. Maybe I'll gae doonriver to the colonies and deliver supplies," Alex told John. He had a lot of his confidence back since his foot was so much better.

"I hear Walter is tryin' to set up a sawmill that will operate all year round and produce planed lumber that will be used to build a city," Sean commented. "Oi'll likely stay workin' fer him over most of the summer and then go up to the timber camp again in the fall."

Others were going downriver with the boats to pick up a cheap piece of land. Mike said that there was land being claimed north of the fort on a lake called Big Lake.

"Maybe it's time I settled down on a pace o'land o' me own. There's a settlement there on Big Lake – lots o'good water – even fishing, open meadowland and the mission from St. Albert is goin' to set up a sawmill to supply lumber fer building. There's a Métis settlement near there, and the first settler staked out his land a couple o' years back. Maybe there'll be some left fer me. If I can't make it as a farmer, maybe I can git a job in the sawmill or loggin'." Mike seemed to be only musing, not really caring if anyone was listening. He had been thinking for a long time that it was time he gave up the bush camps. But John was listening intently. Big Lake sounded familiar to him.

Suddenly it came to him. When Lucy left them, she said that with the smallpox at Lac Ste. Anne, she did not dare to go back, but she had relatives around Big Lake; that is where she would go. He started thinking about her again, when they had come to the place where their cabin had been, and this had started him wondering again where she was – if she had gone to Big Lake and if she was still there.

"So whah hae ye goh tae say, John?" Alex said. "Shall we sign on wi' Walter buildin' the Yark boats or shall we operate a transportation line doonriver tae the colonies?"

"Or hang around the fort carousin' until the money's gone, and then go lookin' far a piece o'land?" Chester laughed. "The land'll always be there; it ain't goin' nowhere. And if ye worked for the Hudson's Bay they've still got miles o' land around the fort reserved – so they do."

"There's plenty o' land t'be had," Clarence added. "Sure and there's a hape o'open land t'the south and east of us, if that's what ye want."

By that time Alex was up to the counter and collected his pay with high spirits. He was afraid that they would refuse to pay him since so much of the winter he was laid up with his foot, even though he helped Matthew in the kitchen as flunky for the last part. He was thankful for whatever they gave him.

When John moved up, he held the rest of the line up while he asked them about the horse he was working with. "Who owned her? What was going to happen to her over the summer? How much would it cost to buy her?" And then came the question that stunned all of them. "Could I own the horse instead ae takkin' my pay?"

After a brief consultation with Moore, they agreed and gave him a certificate of ownership. Moore even threw in a saddle for the balance of the pay even though the big black was used to harness not a saddle.

"Whah air ye gae'n tae do wi' it noo?" Alex asked astounded. "Ye canna take it doonriver in a boat. There's nae timbers tae haul where we're gae'n!"

"Ye may be gae'n doonriver, Alex, but I will nae be there. I'm gae'n tae start oot north ae here tae a settlement up on Big Lake. Me and Morag air gae'n tae start life as settlers. I'll nae be comin' back tae be a log driver. I ken ye want tae be one, but I think it's time tae gae our ain ways, Alex. I think that it's time tae say good-bye, auld friend. This is where our roads lead in different directions."

With that, they shook hands and with heavy hearts they parted. John tied on his bedroll and backpack to his first valued possession. He waved good-bye to friends he came to enjoy over the past several weeks, and to the one friend that he had gone through many a river mile in the fur trade with, and who had been like a brother to him since they left York Factory. He rode away without looking back. If he did, he had a feeling that he might change his mind. He was on his own for the first time since he left York Factory. All except for his new friend, Morag. This was one friend from whom he did not want to be separated. He had to make a choice, and he knew this was the right one.

36

Lac Ste Anne Gathering

Lac Ste. Anne, in the summer of 1874, was a gathering place, as it was every summer for hunters and their families. Métis and Indian alike travelled for many miles to meet for festive activities and to dedicate themselves to the great hunt in the name of the Great Spirit as well as the white man's God. They had been coming to the lake for many years in hopes that the Father of all would bless them by giving them success in their hunting.

Elders gathered them all around a fireplace and heard their tales of hunting in the past and in the present. They danced to the beat of the drums and the sticks. In the absence of spears pounding on the ground, there were the heels of the warriors. This would invite the Great Spirit to their gathering, and the appeal would be made to his mercy and help.

This year it was more important than ever for all his people to gather. For the buffalo, north and south, were disappearing from the land. The chiefs would meet and let their people know what was to be done. The moose and the fur-clad animals were also hard to find. The chief of the white man at the mission on the sacred lake would also be there to appeal to his God and somehow they would have to convince the Great Spirit to bring back the buffalo to the land.

Then the oppressed, the hungry, and the sick would wade out into the water of the sacred lake and wait for the miracles that were surely to come. As those on shore sang, the greatest of the chiefs struck the water. The blessing of the fish that the Great Spirit always allowed them every year would surely come.

Lucy Gladu also came with her family who lived on the shore of the small lake that others had named Gladu Lake after them. They claimed it as their land. It was not far from Big Lake where many other Métis families claimed land and settled. Every year it was their custom to load food, tent, and supplies to last for several days on their backs and trek to the gathering place. This year it was more important than ever because the fish and the animals seemed to have left their special lake.

It had been a wonderful lake, Gladu Lake. All the water they needed was there for them, fish right out of their back door, and the deer and moose came down to drink so that they could have meat and material to make clothing and robes. Even the water roots were there for the harvesting, and this year they harvested barley in their small meadows. They had no need to wander in search of the things they needed.

Since Lucy had come to stay with her Uncle Louis, and his family, she was happy and well fed. She contacted her father and mother, who left Lac Ste. Anne with her brothers and sisters to live along Gladu Lake as well. They survived the smallpox epidemic except for Alexandre. But they all returned each year to Lac Ste. Anne for the sacred pow-wow along with many others from Big Lake.

It was five years since Lucy left the trading post with the white traders, John and Alex, but she wondered now and then where they were, and if they had ever come back to the Mewassin, as she had named it that day – the Good Land.

She was twenty years old now. Secretly, her Aunt Genevieve and her mother Marie Amable hoped that at this gathering of the clans she would find a husband. On the other hand, they were not anxious to let her go to make her home away from them. She, being the oldest girl, was so good to help at both homes with the skinning and tanning, making the clothes, salting away the fish, or looking after the children while her family went away on a hunt or visit. They could always depend on her, no matter how long they were away.

But she was getting too old to still be an unmarried woman. Genevieve and Marie tried to interest Lucy in other young men that they knew, but Lucy let them know in no uncertain terms that she was not interested.

The sacred lake was not a long trek for Lucy and her family – not as far as some clans came, from the south in Blackfoot area, Fort Edmonton, and from the north, the Peace River, to Athabasca Landing and the Victoria

Mission. Some people walked for many days and started out a long while ahead of the gathering.

There is a happy turmoil when they all arrive as old friends who have not seen each other for a year. Tents and cooking fires are set up and the large open grassy area soon fills up. And, of course, the big fire where they will all gather as the sun sets, spreading her beautiful rays of light across the placid surface of the lake, is designated and rocks are brought up to encircle the fire. After the children gather dry wood to burn, they run to the shallow lakeshore to meet and play.

Lucy's brothers, Henri, who was seventeen, Celestin, fourteen, and James at twelve were too old to run and play. They looked forward to the contests and games of strength and agility that would start as well as the team games. Henri was embarrassed to admit that he was two years past fifteen and he had not yet had his first kill to tell about, unless you counted the rabbits and partridges. Perhaps that would not even be brought up this year. They would have to count the prowess in the contests as bravery and skill.

The job fell to Lucy and to eleven-year-old Anne to watch out for the younger children, six-year-old Marguerite and four-year-old Adelaide. Their mother, who was pregnant, had her hands full looking after the setting up of the camp. She lost a baby last year or she would be carrying one on her back this year – either Lucy or her mother. The men, including Henri, set up the tent and then went hunting for meat, perhaps a partridge or a rabbit. They were not to fish until after the ceremony, and then they would set out the net all together.

People shouted as they hurried by, busily arranging for their tent site. "Lucy! *Bonjour! Comment allez vous*? Some would wave and shout out greetings in Cree but most who came to the mission or to the St Albert Mission School knew French. It was good to meet friends again.

Heading down the gradual slope towards the lake, Lucy saw a familiar form ahead. "Emelie!" she called out and hurried to catch up as she held her little sister Adelaide's hand and Marguerite hurried to catch up. "Emelie Belcourt!"

The young woman ahead turned her head and stopped. Waving and smiling, she waited for Lucy to reach her. "Not Belcourt any more," she informed Lucy when they reached her and exchanged hugs. "That was when we lived here at the mission five years ago, when we went together to Father's catechism class and we learned to speak and to write French."

"I remember well," Lucy laughed with her old friend who was also her cousin, her mother's sister's daughter.

"I am a married woman now, Emelie Dumont. This is my little girl, Louise." She indicated the little one who appeared from the other side of the tent that Lucy realized must belong to her friend. "She is three and is always disappearing, making me hunt for her. And this," Emelie indicated the basket in front of the tent, "is our baby, Pierre." A six-month-old baby squirmed and wriggled in the basket at the tent door, batting away the flies that insisted on landing on his face.

"I did not realize that you were married and had two beautiful children." Lucy dropped to her knees beside the basket and then reached out to stroke the little girl's hair.

"But who is this?" Emelie asked. "These are not your little ones, surely?" She looked Marguerite and Adelaide over with surprise.

"These are my two youngest sisters. Marguerite was only one when I left the mission, and Adelaide was not born."

"Then you have not married?" Emelie raised an eyebrow in surprise. "I thought that you left with ...." She stopped and bit her lip in embarrassment. "Well, that was the same time that I left the mission – the time of the smallpox epidemic. Uh – I thought that you ..." She ended in embarrassment and escaped to tending the baby, picking him up and parking him on her hip.

"No, I have been coming to the mission for the past three years, but I guess I have not seen you to let you know what happened to me." Lucy sidestepped the question on Emelie's lips. "Where have you been?"

"I left the mission after losing my parents to the smallpox," Emelie charged on. "I went to live with some cousins in the valley of the Chacutenah River. It was there that I met and married Daniel Dumont. There was so much fighting between the Blackfoot and the Cree that it was not safe. And besides that, the buffalo were no longer plentiful. There was not enough to eat. We were living on the edge of the prairies, and Daniel decided that we had to find a new way further north."

"But where are you living now?" Lucy wanted to know. "Did you travel all the way from the edge of the prairies?"

"No," Emelie gathered her little girl in to her lap as she sat down on the ground beside Lucy, and the little girls got acquainted. "We moved up to Big Lake, east of here. We heard that the Métis were allowed to claim land in the area north of the fort. It was time to learn to live beside the white man and make peace – especially since we are more closely related to them than the Blackfoot, Daniel says."

"Big Lake!" Lucy was delighted. "We live not far from Big Lake. It's called Gladu Lake because so many of our family have settled around there."

"Then you are living with your family again?" Emelie said in surprise. "And so close by! There is so much going on over by Big Lake. They are cutting much timber, the white man and Métis from the St. Albert Mission, and we will have logs to build our homes. Then with so much clearing of the land they are going to plant more fields of barley. Already they have built a dam across Priest's Creek and there will be a mill to make flour from the barley grain. We will soon have plenty of bread to eat. It has been good since we came to Big Lake."

"I would like to come down and see sometime soon," Lucy told her old friend. "Will you be down to the lake to the fish netting?"

"As soon as Daniel gets back. He has gone with our horse to look for game. If he gets a moose, I will have my work cut out for me. Will you come to help me? Not many in the village have horses so they are depending on him to chase the game down to the trap and to pull the game back here to camp on a travois. Some white men in the village connected to the mill and the lumbering have horses."

"I notice that there are some native tribes here as well as Métis," Lucy commented as she watched two Indian women heading towards the lake with their net.

"Eeeh! Abraham Salois will not be pleased. He wanted everyone to wait until after the ceremony," Emelie lowered her voice. "Those women want to get to the fish before we get them all."

"They say that Salois is the chief of the Métis on their hunts; it has nothing to do with them."

"Who is their chief? Maybe Abraham Salois should talk to him and combine the ceremony before tempers flare up. What should we do?" Lucy glanced around apprehensively.

"What can we do? They do not want to listen to what the white man tells them and they say the Métis are given much and they are given little. Adams, the manager of the Hudson Bay Company store, will not give them any more credit because they are not paying up. They do not have any furs to pay with, and Mr. Adams will not take the fish. He has too much, and the fish are not smoked or salt-cured because they say he will not give them the salt. The fish are spoiled when they bring them to him, and the tribes are over-fishing the lake. The people do not bring him moose because they need it themselves, they say."

"Maybe Father Dupin can talk to them," Lucy ventured.

"I do not think so," Emelie shook her head sadly. "He is just another white man, they say, who is trying to starve them. They no longer will go to the mission house. He does not speak to the Great Spirit. He talks to his Great white father in Heaven."

"That is not true," Lucy objected. "They are the same."

"I know that," Emelie retorted. "It is *they* who say that – not me!"

"Maybe they will come to the big fire by the lake tonight and listen to Chief Salois. I must go. I will see you later by the water. I will be one of those who wades out into the lake with the net." Lucy gathered her sisters together and hurried them down the hill with her bucket for water.

On a rise, his back to the lake, and the Métis sitting on the grassy bank before him, Abraham Salois raised his arm for silence. His swarthy features and long black braid proved to all his Cree background, but his French accented Cree, and his dark suit of clothes including his leather laced up boots advertised the white influence. His tall form, still straight as an arrow in spite of his sixty years, was an imposing sight, backed by the setting sun across the lake, its beams spreading arms of pink light across the sky.

"People of the forest!" he shouted out in his low but strong voice. "The Great Spirit has again given us two moose and three deer to feed and clothe our families." He raised his hands to the heavens, and all those before him thrilled to the benevolence of the Master of all. "Daniel Dumont is to be thanked for his assistance with his horse in the work."

"Henri Gladu, son of Marie and Joseph, and Albert Ducharme will dance about the fire tonight in celebration of their first kill. They are blessed this day and will be celebrated the newest men of the Métis nation." All beat their feet and sticks on the ground and hooted loudly in response.

From the back a voice hooted a little longer than the rest. "But they are not the newest warriors – are they?" the voice demanded in angry Cree. "They are nothing to the nation! To the whites, it means nothing. These new warriors are like dogs with no teeth."

Many Métis started shouting back angry replies until Salois with a booming rebuke brought them back to silence. "We have learned to live in peace with the white people. They are helping us to replace the animals in the forest with other things of value to sell–the fields of barley, the cattle and hogs, the trees that he needs to build his ...."

"Trees!" shouted one or two voices. "Can we take the trees to the Hudson's Bay Company store for knives, bullets for our guns, and salt for the fish?"

"All the white man gives us is his disease that kills and scars. They steal our land and cut down the trees so that the animals have no place to go." More voices shouted others down.

"Then they send us their 'Black Robes' to give us new names, a new language. They count us, and they say that only their way to join man and woman is right. They even name the babies. Then they want us to come to the mission to learn their ways."

"They want to steal our children," a woman shouted.

"It is wrong, they say, to do 'The Sun Dance.'"

"They claim land as theirs that has always been ours since the first sun rose over the lake. And you," someone else shouted in accusation, "you who are the daughters and sons of white fur traders are satisfied with a little strip of land that he gives back to you after taking all. You are no better than the dogs that eat the scraps left over from his table – the heads of the fish thrown over the wall. And you would like to tell us when we can take fish from the lake!"

This last insult started fighting at the back of the crowd. Screams and loud scuffling could be heard as more fights broke out. As darkness settled across the placid lake, bloody battling spread along the shore. The festive and religious activities that would have followed the good catch of fish, the hunt, and the Métis boys who had become men, were cancelled.

As the fire died, angry voices faded when men were dragged apart and people drifted or slunk back to their tents. Silence reigned and the loon could be heard calling its forlorn salute to the day.

Perhaps relations between the native tribes and the Métis would never be the same. Perhaps they would get even worse as hunger ate away at the bonds between them.

The next day, family by family they folded down their tents, took their share of the fish and the meat and sadly left for home. The Métis had come to feel their small piece of land was theirs, and they accepted the concept of 'home.' But to the native tribes all the land they roamed and hunted was theirs. Home was on their backs until they found a new place to set up their tipis. The concept of ownership – owning a piece of ground under their feet was so foreign to them.

It had not occurred to most of them, 'How was it that the Hudson's Bay Company should slice up the land all around the fort and for a days journey away from it? How was it that they claimed the land as their own and then divided it up into lots for the Métis people to stake out and call their own? If they were lucky enough to be there to get the slice, and have their mark on the paper with the squares. Then the priest from St Albert Mission had to come out and bless their land in their name. But it was very puzzling, because there were not enough slices for everyone. They were beginning to wonder if it would be better to have all of their people in a village to work together and have some hunters to roam the land bringing home the meat for all to share. This way they had to do the work themselves with no neighbours to come in and help. They wondered if the white man's way was working very well.

37

Big Lake Reunion

The trek to Big Lake from Gladu Lake was not long. Bishop Grandin would be there from St. Albert to baptize babies born around the settlement and officiate at weddings. Lucy was looking forward to seeing everyone together. It was a social time. And since it was fall, her father would be taking his barley to be ground at the new mill that was set up on Priests Creek. It was close to the settlement.

Close to that, was the settlement trading store. Lucy worked for months on a beaded buckskin dress that she wanted to trade for things she needed, and her mother Marie Amable needed things as well. Besides, it had been a long time since she had seen girls her own age. Maybe she would see Emelie; she had not seen her since the Lac Ste. Anne expedition.

It was quite an eye-opener for Lucy and her family when they discovered what was happening around Big Lake. Many big trees were chopped down and hauled to the St. Albert Mission sawmill where they were sliced into long boards and brought out to the little tributary that flowed into Priests Creek. The boards were used to build the mill that ground the barley into fine flour to make bread. Huge millstones were also brought from St Albert. These millstones were moved by a huge wheel that was turned by water. The water fell onto the paddles attached like scoops to the wheel and turned it as they fell to the next. The water moved the wheel and the wheel moved the millstones that crushed the grain. A fan blew off the husks and chaff leaving the seed, which was ground into meal.

Lucy remembered the hours that she spent pounding the barley in a smoothed-out wooden bowl with a wooden pestle to take the husks from the grain. Then she pounded it into a fine meal, a little at a time until she had enough for pemmican. How much faster this was and how very much it could do at once!

Joseph, her father, would sell his grain there, keeping out an amount for themselves over winter. A mark on the paper taken to the trading store would tell the factor how much they could get in trade.

Nearby, men were building a sawmill, which would cut the logs, slice them into long boards, and plane them smooth. This would avoid the need to take the logs all the way to St. Albert. White men were building on the structures that the men would be living in while they worked at the mill. A man leading a horse was pulling a small log that was to be used in one of those buildings.

As Lucy and her family passed near on their way to the settlement, they stopped to watch as they had observed the operation of the barley-grinding mill. Her brother, fifteen-year-old Celestin, openly admired the horse wishing that he had one like that to do the work at their lake.

Lucy was staring, not at the horse, but at the man walking beside and leading it. There was something familiar about him. He had red hair that stuck out from underneath an old felt hat and below that was a bright red beard. He was tall and thin and carried himself as proud and straight as if he were marching in a parade.

A shadow slipped into John's periphery, and he looked up to stare into a slender face and a pair of smiling brown eyes that he remembered very well. "Lucy!" he gasped, "*C'est vous?*"

In a voice sweeter than the wind, she replied. "I knew that you would return some day, John Lenny." And his heart swelled with happiness.

Halting his horse, he drank in the sight of this dear familiar face and memories flooded back. No longer was she a little girl but a woman. Even though she was slight of build and small in stature, she was a woman!

Standing unmoving, she returned his gaze, and he felt a warm closeness. She felt it; his heart called to her in a secret song, and she did not want to destroy the feeling.

"I wondered if I would ever see you again," he said in French. He had recently learned how to speak it all over again since he started working in this French speaking settlement.

"Lucy," she heard her mother Marie call back to her, "*Vite!*" and she hesitated, glancing back, and then at John like a bird pausing in flight. "I must go!"

"When will I see you again?" he asked suddenly afraid of losing track of her again. His horse moved around restlessly.

"Do you work here every day?" she asked.

"*Oui!*" John answered while trying to pull Morag around.

"Then I will find you," she told him with a smile that made his heart race. She turned and was gone, hurrying to catch up to her family.

John wandered into the settlement riding Morag that summer with not a penny in his pocket, no food – just his bedroll and his horse. He circled Fort Edmonton and stopped several people along the way asking the directions to Big Lake. No plan in mind did he have, not knowing if the things he heard about Big Lake were rumoured or true.

The lake was not far from the fort, north on clearly defined trails that led him right to the settlement. He asked for a Hudson's Bay Company trader and was directed to the post that was a store for trading whatever people had of value. It was a small hurriedly put up log building that stood on log skids in a sea of mud. After a recent rain, feet enclosed in moccasins or well-worn boots slithered and sucked in the cold muck. Wagons or carts pulled by oxen churned the one street of the little settlement into ruts of mud.

Haphazardly, native tents circled this log cabin while Métis waited to find out where their land would be located in relation to the Lake. All wanted to extend out from the lake. Magistrate Francoise Plante, appointed by the Hudson's Bay Company, indicated on his paper that he had rolled out onto the counter, where each strip of land was located.

After the few Métis grouped around the paper had dispersed, John moved forward and introduced himself.

"*Excusez-moi s'il vous plais,*" he started off in scarcely remembered French. "*Je suis Jean Lenny*, Hudson Bay Company employee *avec York Factory.*"

The man's head shot up, and so did his eyebrows. "What are you doing here?" Plante asked in French. "You are a long way from the fur trade."

"I have left the fur trade. It is no more," John cast around for the right words. "I heard that there was land to be had around Big Lake. Since I am

– was with the Hudson's Bay, and since I heard that they had reserved land for their trade for a number of acres around the Fort, I hoped that I would qualify."

"Open land is to the north and east of here. This is the placement for the Métis," Plante explained, "but if you are here to work with that big horse of yours," he glanced out the window to see Morag tied to the hitching rail, "I may just have a piece of land for you."

Encouraged, John relaxed a bit. "I am experienced with work in the timber, and I see you are building a saw mill. I would be willing to work at that if you have some land for me."

"You are the very man for whom I was looking." Plante smiled and beckoned John forward to look at the map. "The sawmill was not ready when they built the barley mill on Priests Creek. They had to haul lumber all the way from St. Albert Mission sawmill. With the help of more like you and that horse, we will build a big settlement right here, one to which the Métis can come from their land locations to trade. We will soon attract people from the fort to set up their places of business right here– blacksmiths, leather and harness shop, livery barn, carpenters, stock merchants, laundry, a post office – even a doctor, shoemaker, café operator, and a barber."

"Well," John apologized, "I can not do any of those things."

"You do what you can do. This is just the start of what will eventually come. With the sawmill built we will need a millwright, a sawyer, teamster, edger, bush foreman, and lumber grader. We need a steam-powered sawmill with a boiler man to operate a Dutch oven. And with all the land clearing that's happening we need a blacksmith to shape the plowshare, the scythe, and the wagon wheel. And above all else, we need someone to train the Métis how to do all of these things.

John looked out of the window. It did not even sport glass to fill the space – just a gauzy material to keep out the insects and to allow a filmy look at the surroundings. The area around the post was just a hole hacked out of the wilderness. Underbrush was scattered around, growing up between logs fallen haphazardly, waiting for an axe or handsaw to cut them into firewood lengths or de-limb them into fence poles or building material. Métis tents sat out between them, and some of the dry sticks were being used for the smoky fires that spiralled up in front of each tent. *Yes*, he thought, *it's going to take a lot of organization before this settlement is livable. Everything is happening at once.*

"I will take you over to meet the millwright and boss at the sawmill," Francois told him as he rolled up the map, "and he can put you on the payroll. He has got a small crew over there. What you bring him will keep the buzz saw busy but it will not put out enough for the demand for lumber. What he got up so far was enough to build the Barley Mill on Priests Creek and some was shipped to the Mission itself, but he needs to put up a lot more."

"But," he hesitated before going out the door, when he saw John standing unmoving, "I guess you are probably hungry. You have been travelling a long time."

John nodded, and let out an audible sigh. Francois chuckled. "Earl can see to that too. The cookhouse is small at the mill – just a few workers so far, but the food is tolerable – Métis cooking – barley bread and moose meat, but it fills a big hole in the stomach." John smiled and followed him out.

After John signed on and ate he sought out Francois again to find that stretch of ground he could call his own. Morag needed to be fed and watered, and they both needed shelter.

John's lot stretched west along a stream that flowed into Priests Creek. It was completely covered by forest, but John felt an exhilarating sense of ownership. He immediately went out and inspected each corner of the hilly property. The stream was a bonus – water right by his door. Up the shallow bank, on the other side of the stream, was land belonging to Shorty Wilson, the edger, at the mill. Shorty had put up a small log cabin on the other side of his lot and closer to the mill. But John liked the seclusion. With Morag, he always had a ride into the mill.

Little by little, every day after finishing hauling logs from the men who were cutting, he would work on his own shack and the lean-to that he built for Morag. He had to keep his end of the bargain that gave him ownership of the land. He had to put in his ten hours a day hauling logs for the mill or hauling the scrub trees from the mill, forest, or the clearing to Métis shelters, and sometimes he would drag an iron scoop that dug a hole or cleared the ground away for a building. His days were full, but he especially enjoyed seeing his own quarters take shape.

One day while talking to Shorty, he discovered that by cutting down timber that he was not using on his lot he could make extra money. He could cut the timber into cordwood and ship it or take it into Fort Edmonton. He always seemed to need extra money to buy lantern, candles, lard, tarpaper for his roof, nails, coal oil, stove, tools or buckets.

Then he became concerned that he had no time to get some hay for Morag. Under the trees on his lot, there was very little foraging. So he took off time to take his scythe that he borrowed from Shorty and cut a lot of hay down along the lake. He raked it in by hand and loaded it on a stoneboat, a platform build on log runners, and hooked up to a single-tree for Morag to pull. He had to make way for another building to house all the hay that Morag would need over winter. Morag needed to be housed out there also since he had to turn the lean-to into storage to keep his wood dry and various other things that he had no room for in the one–room little shack.

He worked from before sun-up to sundown just to keep up. At first he thought he would not bother to put windows in his shack since he left it in the dark and only came back to crawl dead tired into his bunk at night. But he finally cut in two small windows, covering them with hide as the Metis did so that you could not see through but light entered.

The day he met Lucy changed his life and his way of thinking considerably. Thoughts of her filled his mind. At night when he lay in his narrow, hard, straw-filled bunk he wondered if she really would come to see him again. He did not know where to find her, and he worried as the firelight from his little stove flickered on the walls, and sounds of the night closed in.

One day as he hauled a scrub log from the clearing that was gradually becoming ready for the business venture that Francois hoped would move in, she was there. John had calmed Morag down after she was sideswiped by falling underbrush that was chopped down for firewood. He shouted out a stern reprimand at the culprit who stepped back in alarm. He had not meant to injure anyone, let alone the big horse that the whole settlement admired.

"*Pardonez mois! Pardonez mois! Je repent!*" Marcel stammered as he backed away.

Ignoring the plea, John's concern was for Morag, and he checked her over carefully, feeling her back to her feet for injury after he finally quieted her down. His heart was still racing with fear for his animal friend when he heard the voice from behind.

"It was only a little brush, nothing but a tickle. Would it have been better for the tree to hit Marcel?"

He whirled around and caught a mischievous smile on Lucy's face. To cover his embarrassment, he scowled and turned back to his investigation of Morag's side. "I would rather it be me instead of Morag. Were it not for her this work would not be done for any of them," he growled, his voice tight.

In a gentler voice Lucy said, "Of course. You were afraid for him. Everyone could understand that."

Now it was John's turn to smile. "Morag is SHE. This is a female horse. She is the only friend I had for many weeks."

"Then I apologize for my thoughtless words. I would not want you to lose your best friend." Her long dark hair with that tinge of auburn blew about her like a cape, wild as the wind occasionally whipping across her face. The playful expression changed to tenderness, gentle as the wind's caress.

"Come and stroke her side and touch her nose and she can be your friend too," John invited.

"No, no!" Lucy backed away. "I have not been close to a horse ever before. I am afraid."

"Come," John suddenly took two steps over and pulled her close to Morag, placing her small brown hand on the black hide.

When Morag stood quietly through the stroking, Lucy relaxed. John moved her hand across Morag's shoulder to her mane and then to her head. When the horse turned her head towards them, John urged her to touch Morag's soft nose. She jerked it back nervously when the horse snorted, but John urged it to stroke the skin again, and this time Morag allowed her nose to be stroked from her eyes down to the nostrils.

"It is so soft! Like a baby's skin." Lucy squealed and John laughed. With Lucy so close, just under his arm and touching her hand, he felt the thrill of their closeness. It caught at his breath. When Morag moved her head suddenly, Lucy backed into the security of John's enveloping arm, and he dropped her hand and turned until he was looking down into her face. Then tilting her chin up to him he lightly kissed that sweet mouth that he dreamed about.

A look of wonder crept into her eyes, and she said in a soft voice, "Why have you stayed away so long, John Lenny? I thought you meant never to return."

"I have been all this time trying to get back to you."

She looked up into that angular face and lonely blue eyes, and she knew the wait was over. Leaning toward him as leaves toward the sun, her eyes, the windows of her soul, told him the answer to his heart's question.

"Stay with me now, Lucy, " he whispered against her ear. "Do not go away from me again."

People walked by and seeing them, turned their eyes away discreetly and kept going. Her heart beat furiously. All she could do was nod and step back to avoid the prying eyes.

"I will unload this log and quit for the day. Wait for me by the edge of the trees over there, and I will take you to my shack. We must talk."

Though it was a task to talk her into climbing up on Morag's back with him, she finally agreed with much nervous trembling. It was only his insistence and confidence that finally pushed her into accepting the ride for she was determined to walk and refused his offer many times.

Up on Morag's back, she began to settle down and to stop trembling. The rippling of the big horse's muscles and the feel of its strength beneath her as she looked around gave her a new sense of power. Straddling Morag she had, at John's urging, put her arms around his middle in a death grip. But as she relaxed a little, she loosened the hold on him. To her, he began to feel very comforting and protective.

Ducking and twisting, they dodged the branches of the trees as Morag pushed through them, and Lucy hid behind John's strong back so that he took most of the swats and scrapes. Morag descended the ravine, waded through the stream, and climbed the other side while Lucy clung onto John and tightened her legs until the harness hurt them.

Finally, the horse stopped, and John called out, "Here we are! This is where I live!" He raised his arm so that it encircled her, and she slid underneath his arm and down to the ground, while pulling her twisted skirt to rights. Then John slid off beside her.

Lucy looked around her. Under the trees by the edge of the ravine, stood the tiny log cabin. It was made of logs that stuck out at the corners so that each nestled into the slot he cut out for it. The roof was low, hardly a slant on it at all, built of small saplings and a ridgepole of a big log in the centre to raise it. Covering the saplings was sod slices and branches woven in for stability. The door was small; even she had to duck to enter. John bent over a lot farther. He had built in one window on each side and, as was the custom, instead of glass, hides were stretched across so that light would enter but you could not see in or out. Made of saplings with leather hinges, the door wobbled in a rickety fashion when he opened it for her. Against the wall, wood was piled while basins, pots, and tools hung on pegs.

When her eyes became accustomed to the dim light, she made out the little stove, homemade table piled with food materials–tin cup, plate covered over with a cloth, and a chair. A narrow straw-covered bunk with a couple of blankets was his bed. Otherwise, this simple structure was where he lived.

"It seems to be very cozy," she commented glancing around. "You can tell that it is meant for only one person."

John smiled, and a look of mischief twinkled in his blue eyes above that red beard that covered so much of his face that Lucy almost missed the smile. "It would be a bright day if someone were to come and share the cabin wi' me. Are ye offering?"

Lucy flamed with embarrassment that was not so evident under her dark skin, but she turned aside as though to survey the walls. "I have much work to do at home on Gladu Lake. Why would I ask for more? All that a man wants is for some woman to do his cooking, haul his water, and warm his bed. A woman would be crazy to ask for that kind of slave work."

"You did it for us before when you were just a young girl. But you did not warm the bed; I remember that you slept in the corner as far away as you could." John's eyes still twinkled, but he turned her until she faced him, his high cheek-boned thin face unsmiling. "My life since then has been as empty as that bucket." He indicated the empty water pail on the block by the door. "My mother and father are both dead; my sister is gone, and I've been wandering in search of something that I left behind. I never stopped looking until I saw you that day at the edge of the clearing." He stopped speaking and searched her face. She was so little that he had to tip her face up to look at him. "Since I came back to this country, I've been searching for you in every face I saw, around every corner."

With a sigh, no longer trying to deny her feelings to this man who had been on her mind since she saw him disappear from her life, forever, she closed her eyes squeezing back the tears. "I, too, John Lenny, have been looking for you. I looked for you in other faces that I met, but you were not there." She opened brown luminous eyes in that lovely tiny face mirroring her love.

Reaching down, he picked her up as though she were a feather, carried her to his narrow bunk, and gently laid her on his blankets. They would not need much room. Lips joined in a fevered kiss, then flesh, sudden ecstasy in oneness, and then peace.

38

In Debt and First Born

It had not missed Marie's attention when her daughter got home late that first night, and when Lucy made excuses to go to the settlement often after that. Marie suspected that it was a boy she had met, but Lucy did not tell her, so she said nothing. Secretly her heart rejoiced that Lucy finally found someone to share her life. When Lucy went about their little home humming and at times stopping in the middle of bean shelling or drying the venison over the smoky fire to gaze out across the placid lake, she wondered.

The gold and reds of autumn were flaming in the trees and the cool breezes warned that winter was on its way. All hands were busy preparing. The men hunted and prepared the hides so that the women could make warm clothing. They prayed to the Great Spirit to send a bear so that they could render much needed bear oil. The barley and the garden needed to be harvested.

Finally, one day Marie noticed something different about Lucy. Her clothes were not fitting her anymore. It was a long time, she thought, since her moon time. Alarm bells went off for Marie. She asked. "Lucy, you went to the settlement again last night, and you returned very late. You brought nothing home. Is there not something you wish to tell me?" Marie's small-pox scarred face puckered with concern.

Lucy, almost relieved that it was going to be out in the open, turned slowly to face her mother. "My Maman, I have wanted to tell you for a long time. I am with child. I have been seeing someone that I love very much." She noticed her mother suck in her breath and pale.

"Should not the man come forward and tell us what he intends to do about this? Does he not know that you are about to make him a father?"

"*Oui*, Maman! He is working every day after his job to make his cabin bigger so that I will be able to move in with him. Right now there is no room. There is more that I can do here to prepare than sitting down in the trees while he is making the cabin bigger. We are going to marry. We planned to see Father Dupin, but we heard that Father Dupin is being replaced at the mission and will be leaving before winter is out. We had no time to travel to see him, and now it is going to be winter soon. Perhaps we can travel there to see the new Father in the spring."

"Perhaps!?" Marie gasped. "And maybe by springtime this man may have changed his mind. Maybe he will decide that being a husband and father is too much trouble. He seems to have managed so far without having to take you into his home. Who is this Métis man without the backbone to come forward to talk to his future father-in-law about the way he has been treating his future bride? We should have been having the fire of promise – his pledge to ..."

"Stop Maman! You do not know him. He is trying very hard to hurry but there is so much to do and ...."

"But he has the time to take his intended bride to bed night after night. That took no thought or plan." Marie raised her voice in anger, and this surprised Lucy. Her mother was always quiet, never raised her voice, always calm in every situation. Now she was suddenly unreasonable.

"You never bothered to tell who this man is that you have given yourself to." Marie, hands on ample hips, faced her daughter with sparks of fire in her eyes.

"He works for the mill, pulls the logs with his big horse. Remember Maman? You saw him the day we all went to the settlement. He was tall and thin, red hair and beard; his name is John Lenny."

Marie felt a weight dropped in her lap. She sat down, sudden and hard, in the chair behind her, all the breath knocked out of her as though she was hit in the stomach. *A white man! Lucy had fallen for a white man!* Her memory flashed back to another time, another place. Marie's mother told her about a white man who made promises to her. He told her those sweet lies as he took her to his bed. He was from the fur trade.

All winter he laid with her while the storms of winter moaned about their shack. She brought him his food that he had not the resourcefulness to find for himself. She tanned the hides that clothed him against the cold, made snowshoes for him, found wood for his fire, and always kept it going, set the traps for the rabbit and the weasel, and nursed him back to health when he was so sick he thought he would die. When her baby was born after suffering alone and frightened in the shack with no one to help, all he gave her was his name. When springtime came he went down the river with the furs and left promises that he would return. They never saw him again.

Lucy was promising herself to another white man, another man with no honour, someone who used and used and never gave back. She put her head in her hands and wept.

"Maman! Maman, no! He is not like the rest. John is a good man. He loves me. You will see! He is one of the men I stayed with when I had to leave the village during the smallpox. He was an honourable man then, and he is one now. Please Maman! Do not cry! You will see! You will see." She fell on her knees beside her mother and held her in her arms, rocking her gently just as her mother rocked her hurt away so many times in the past. "Be happy for me Maman because today my soul sings."

On the clearing of the settlement the snow was carved by knives of wind into sharp edges, and the crust squeaked and groaned underfoot. John was concerned about Morag's legs being cut as she pulled the logs to the hungry mill. There were other horses now and more men hauled logs on sleds with steel runners. He could hear the whine of the saw as it bit into the log. Now there was steam power as the engine used the water from Big Lake.

There were so few daylight hours as the weak sun shone through the violet haze of frozen air and wood-smoke from the fires of the settlement. Morag's breath made puffs of steam, and eyebrows and lashes were coated with frost.

Thoughts of going home were all that kept him going in the bitter cold. He could not wait to get back to Lucy in the warmth of their cabin. She was with him all the time now. She no longer travelled back and forth to her parents. There was a fire inside his life now on the silent bitter, frozen nights. When they lay together in a nest of hides and blankets his world turned inwards.

It amazed him how resourceful she could be. When he thought that there was nothing to eat in the house, he came home to the smell of a rabbit roasting, and barley bread. Barley was freshly pounded and fried like a pancake on top of the stove, and a candle from the bear fat she saved, sputtered and glowed gathering them into its circle of light as they ate. The floor was covered with a bearskin, and the walls were draped with blankets to seal in the warmth. Along with the cabin, John made the bed bigger. The other cabin was turned into a storage house for frozen meat, a root cellar for their seeds, tubers and dried berries. An alcove was blanketed up the walls and circling the front, to enclose the bed. Inside this box bed, the hay-stuffed mattress was covered deep with fur robes where the two enjoyed another creature comfort.

Through the winter months Lucy grew bigger and bigger, and John became more concerned. He had promised her that they would go to the mission and be married in the spring. But what would they do if the baby should come along before that? He wanted to be married before the birth, but Lucy was already getting too big to travel – especially in the winter. And what would happen if the baby was about to be born and he was all she had to help? Or worse – no one was there to help! He knew that Lucy's mother did not approve of her living with him without the blessing of the priest and without the pledge before the rest of the settlement. But he just wanted to marry Lucy – not the whole community!

John's train of thought was broken by the sawyer, Grant Mackenzie. "It's about time you got here, Lenny! We've been waiting. When are you going to get a team and a sleigh? Now that you're hauling from so far away it takes you a long time to get here, one log at a time. Our stockpile has dwindled away to nothing. We've only got one other team and sleigh, and ten loggers out there cutting down trees. They can cut down a good hundred a day. How many can you haul a day with that one-log-at-a-time set-up?"

John was flustered. His 'set-up' was all right in summer when he was hauling building logs for the settlement and clearing the area for buildings. But now it was winter, and he was hauling just for the sawmill. "I know! I would like to have another horse and a sleigh but I do not know where to get them," John ended lamely.

"Well, I can help you with that." It was Augustine Calliot who was unhooking the log John brought in, ready to roll it down the ramp to the circular saw.

"Paul Beaudoin wants to sell his big sorrel. He had a team until one died. He was getting pretty old but Paul used to drive him, keeping after him to try to keep up with the younger one. The other day the roan died and rolled down the ravine. So now he has a sleigh for hauling logs and only one horse. He told me yesterday that he would like to work at the mill here and sell his other horse and sleigh – harness and all."

John tried not to sound too eager but his heart leaped at the thought. "Where is he? I would like to talk to him to see if I can make a deal."

"He is over there behind the bunkhouse. They are working on the steam engine. He likes those things – and he's good at it." Augustine pointed across the yard to a big dark-haired man with grizzled black beard, dressed in buckskins like most of the Métis he saw about the settlement.

With a big voice that matched his huge barrel-chested body, Paul greeted John with a hearty handshake that nearly rearranged the bones in his right hand. John smiled in spite of himself when he recalled stories that he heard the Irish loggers tell in camp about another Paul – Paul Bunyan. He could almost believe that they were talking about this logger, Paul Beaudoin.

"I hear you might like to sell your horse and sleigh," John said quite calmly, as though he really had the money to buy a horse and sleigh.

"I heard about you, John Lenny," Paul boomed from his imposing height. "I'm glad you came to see me. You need a horse and sleigh, and I'm willing to let mine go."

"I have nothing I can offer in payment," John apologized, saying what he had to say. "But I would very much like to have that big sorrel. He would be a good match for my black, and I do need your sleigh."

"They are yours!" Paul slapped John on the shoulder – a blow that nearly propelled him into the snow-bank. "We will make an arrangement later for a part of your wages."

"That would be a real fine deal!" John tried not to be too effusive, but he felt like whooping and pumping Paul's hand like a fool. "We will go and make an arrangement with the pay clerk at the office right now. I have a new wife – well, she soon will be – who is about to have a baby and I owe at the office now and at the store, so there might not be much left but I will start paying you right away."

"Do not worry about that. It would be good for the company to get another team and sleigh out there." They walked along congenially, Paul's hand on his shoulder as they moved toward the office. "I hope to be part of this company some day. So what is good for the company is good for me."

Others were in the little log building that served as an office when Paul and John walked in announcing their deal. "We will not take too much off his pay now," Paul told the clerk, leaning over, elbows on the counter. "John here has got a wife to look after."

"I did not know that!" Augustine raised his eyebrows in surprise. "I knew you had moved her in, but I did not know you married her."

"Well, not yet, but I plan to by spring – maybe before the baby is born." John turned his attention to signing the paper that the clerk pushed before him on the counter.

"She is Indian. I have seen her family at the store. They are from out by that little lake to the northwest of here." Ned Carmichael, the mill-wright, who was pinning a paper on the Bulletin Board turned his head to comment. "She is willing to live with you and look after your needs. Why bother marrying her? That can cost you a lot of money in the end. Why buy the cow when you can get the milk through the fence." He laughed loudly at his own joke, but only Augustine joined him half-heartedly.

"She is Métis," John informed the millwright facing him, flushing from his neck up to his forehead, his mouth a tight line.

"If I were you, I would not tell that joke around here again." Mackenzie scowled, an imposing figure facing Ned, his shoulders wide and enormous. "Many of us originated from the union of French-Canadian fur trader and an accommodating Indian girl who took him in and kept him from dying at no advantage to her. And she was left to make her way alone and abandoned."

Now it was Carmichael's turn to flush. He backed away retreating out the door with a mumbled, "*Mon Dieu*! It was only a joke!"

John could not wait to tell Lucy about the deal. He hesitated though. Would she understand that there would be no money to buy things at the store, especially now since there would be no more credit – just like the Lac Ste. Anne Mission store? Would she understand that he really needed the other horse and sleigh? But then, he thought, now he could take her in the sleigh behind the team. He just had to build a box for the sleigh bunks – if he could get some boards at the mill to build it, that is.

He put the team away in the shed that served as a barn and fed them some hay from the stack he had put up in the loft above the shed. It was not much hay to last two horses through the winter. He had not thought of that, and he had no area to turn them loose to paw for grass under the snow. He wished that he could give them some grain, but Lucy was using that to grind into flour for their bread or pemmican. He felt crowded into a corner.

It was dark in their little cabin when he pushed the door open, and there was no smell of their evening meal cooking. All was quiet, and his eyes had not adjusted to the dim light inside so he called out, "Lucy! Are you home?"

He heard a muffled sound from the bed, and with a stab of alarm rushed over to her. "Are you all right?" he asked in a worried voice.

She lay on the bed in a turmoil of blankets, her thick dark hair a tangled mass, beads of sweat standing out on her forehead. "Lucy, ye're in labour. I will ride over and fetch your mother."

He turned to rush away when she reached out to him saying with definite firmness, "Non! You – can – help. We can do this. I will tell you - what to do."

"I canna Lucy! I dinna ken how tae help!" he gasped in terror at the prospect, not realizing that he had slipped into Gaelic accented English.

"You can do this, John Lenny! Just do as I say." Then she was caught by a spasm of pain that doubled her over as she turned on her side. Panting, moaning, and grimacing, she writhed and clutched the side of the wooden bed-box while John stood helplessly rooted to the spot.

When it passed, she spoke again in between panting. "It is nearly time. This is the birthing sheet covered with the rags to catch the water when it breaks. Take my hand – help me to a squatting position; it is time for me to bear down."

"Shall I get a knife to cut the cord?" John asked, casting around helplessly for all that he could remember hearing about the birth of babies.

"No! Just hold – onto my hands." Eyes squeezed shut, teeth bared in a grimace of pain, Lucy squeezed his hands so hard that the pain he felt was nearly as bad as hers was as she squatted over the birthing sheet. With a gush the water broke, and the rest happened quickly.

She fell back on the blankets while John picked up the tiny slippery form in his two big hands and handed it to Lucy. Lucy found a cloth near her, wiped the little face and pulled something from its mouth with her finger as she turned the little body upside down and slapped it on its bottom. When the baby took an audible breath and set up a racket that shattered the silence, John reeled and fell to his knees beside the bed. His head was beginning to spin and he thought that he would faint. Clinging to the side of the bed-box, he watched as Lucy took a sharp knife that she had hidden under the side of the mattress and sliced through the cord. She tied the little knot before gathering the wriggling slithery form up in a sheet that had also been tucked beside the mattress. It was then that John realized that Lucy intended to do this all herself if he had not arrived home in time. She was completely prepared.

As his frozen body thawed and came back to life, he watched Lucy wrap the infant in the blanket and place the naked child against her skin. She wrapped them both in a blanket before she collapsed in exhaustion against the pillow and closed her eyes. Her coppery coloured face was placid and in peace, but wet hair clung to her skin.

Finally, John came to life and hurried to get a wet cloth to wipe her face and smooth the hair back. She opened her eyes and smiled wearily. "It is a girl! We have a baby girl. She will be called Annabelle." Then she drifted off to sleep while baby Annabelle lay across her tummy and also slept while making whimpering sounds. They had both passed the trial, and they needed rest and sleep.

For a long while John watched his daughter and her mother as they slept. He tucked the blankets around them, stoked up the fire, so that its dying embers came back to life and warmed the cabin, lit a candle, placing it in the centre of the table, and began to get some food ready. It was up to him to look after the two of them now – he would take it from here.

39

Dumont at the Lake

To the whole settlement's disappointment the barley-grinding mill on Priest's Creek was shut down. For three years in a row the water that kept the millwheel turning, diminished until it was but a trickle. It could not turn the millwheel and could not grind the barley so the Métis went back to the old long hard way of pounding it by hand.

A hot, dry summer day in 1877 John and Lucy made their way to Lac Ste. Anne in the wagon. Annabelle, almost two years old, sat between her parents on the wagon seat enjoying her first outing that she could remember in the wagon behind Morag and Jock. She was all eyes and ears, clucking at the team as she heard her father do, and calling out to the horses.

Lucy smiled at the little girl's excitement. It was the first that they went on a long trip since Annabelle was a couple of months old, and they had gone to Lac Ste. Anne to baptize the baby and to get married by the priest at the mission.

Lucy remembered that day well. They had to wait until the end of winter, and the muddy, mucky days of spring. Then, John built a wagon box from leftover lumber at the mill. They could not use the sleigh that he used all winter. Wagon wheels, built for him at the mill, were fitted onto the hubs along with the iron rims, with help from Paul.

Lucy did not know the new priest, Father Vegreville, and there were many others looking to him to perform marriages and baptisms. Each child who came to him to be baptized or who crowded around to observe, Father admonished the parents that he had not seen them in a long time at the mission.

Later, at the group blessing and service, he reminded them that St. Albert had a school to which he urged them to bring their children. An education, he warned them, is important if they are going to adjust to the new society. As well, their religious training was being neglected. "When you go away on long hunting expeditions," he told them, "you are able to leave the children at the residential school until you come back for them. When you are travelling to find a new settlement, this is hard for you and the children. You can leave the children at the convent, and they will be trained in the language, the catechism, and all the things they need to know in this new society. The Great Spirit needs his children to know him."

It happened so quickly, this marriage and the blessing of the child. There were more waiting in line behind. Lucy felt no different after she was married than before, and Annabelle had slept through it.

The important part of their being there was the big hunt. The night of their marriage, Métis and Cree alike had gathered around the huge fire as excited braves and Métis planned the buffalo hunt. Emelie and Daniel Dumont were there. Lucy was so excited to see her again and show her Annabelle and her new husband.

Daniel shouted to everyone around the fire that he was leading the expedition to Kisiskatchewan River where large herds of buffalo were sighted. Those who had horses would be able to make the trek down there.

Since John's Cree was poor, Lucy translated to John what was happening. John could not help but be fired up with enthusiasm at the prospect of being involved in the hunt. So it was agreed that he would take his wagon to transport some of the kill home. Other wagons were put into service, but those that were on foot would ride down on the wagons in hopes of being involved in the joyous occasion.

Emelie was proud of her husband, especially since he was the cousin of Gabriel Dumont, the famous buffalo hunter of the plains. He was a good friend to Louis Riel, who would soon head up a government in the West that would belong to the Métis and the natives. Gabriel went south into the United States to visit with Riel. He said that what could not happen on the Red River was going to happen here.

The hunt was successful, and the Métis and natives returned in fine moods with much to celebrate. They danced around the fires for hours.

The previous year, however, Lucy and John had not attended the celebrations and the dedication to the hunt, although she heard that it was attended in even bigger numbers. More horses and wagons made the trip down, and buffalo that escaped the pursuit of tribes on the plains fled to the hills and into their traps. Around the fires there was much bragging by braves about the mighty deeds accomplished.

This year Lucy did not nag her husband into going to the summer meet, but she brought up to him several times that Emelie told her this was to be a special meeting. Gabriel Dumont would be there, and he asked all of the Métis to come to hear him before they had the big hunt. "It is important," he said, "that all Métis unite and prepare the way for Riel to lead us in his new government.

John was not sure he should be there. He enjoyed the hunt, and he was given buffalo meat to last for most of the winter. He was happy to help others, but at the campfire meetings he felt out of place and awkward. His red hair shone like an unwelcome banner flopped in the face of a buffalo bull. But Lucy wanted to go.

The green slopes beside Lac Ste. Anne were nearly white with tents when they arrived, and the noise level of the squeaking wagon wheels, barking dogs and the squealing of children filled the air. More came than before–native tribes from the north, Métis from St. Albert, and from the east and southeast.

The fires danced high into the air, and men readied themselves for the travelling in the morning. Women set up household around the tents on the sunny slopes preparing food and setting up drying racks for the meat. Flies buzzed, and children scampered around the tents in their play.

Lucy began preparing the evening meal of pemmican and partridge that John killed on the way, quite accidentally when it flew out in front of them. They noticed the family in the tent next to them. He was obviously white, and had curly dark hair. The couple's youngest, Joseph, the same age as Annabelle, toddled over to meet them. The woman, slight, pretty and a little older than Lucy, had two other boys, one about five and the other a three-year-old. The oldest, Vital, was trying to look after the toddler, Joseph, so that he did not fall into the cooking fire or wander away.

The man stepped forward and introduced himself to John. "*Bonjour! Je suis Adolphe Perrault, et vous?*"

"My name is John Lenny," he replied, noticing the fine easy way Adolphe spoke. "This is my wife, Lucy and my little girl Annabelle."

After they got to know one another they talked freely across the cooking fires and told all about themselves and how they came to be there.

"My wife Julie has always wanted to come to the summer meet at Lac Ste. Anne," Adolphe said as he sat cross-legged on the ground ready to eat. "But this is the first that we have had a chance to come. This year, she heard that Louis Riel might be here, and she insisted on coming. Riel came from the same place in the Red River Settlement as she did. He fought for them – stood up against the government and armed them to fight for themselves. When Louis Riel fled from the police, however, the rest who fought with him left their homeland and came west to St. Albert. If it had not been for the Riel Rebellion, I never would have met Julie. I had to come and meet the man who impressed my wife so much." Adolphe ended his introduction, taking a drink of Oswego tea made from the flower of the purple Bergamot. He sipped from a tin mug and settled back on his elbows.

John then told Adolphe of his adventures in coming to the West while the women handed the food to the children and tended to the cleaning up.

After they ate, they all drifted closer to the fire as darkness settled over the lake and stole up the shoreline.

Drums began to call everyone close, telling them that something important was about to happen. On the rise near the fire, his back to the lake that mirrored the rays of the setting sun against the clouds, stood Daniel Dumont, his hands raised for attention. Immediately the drums stopped, and Daniel was joined by another man, his cousin Gabriel. Huskily built, broad shouldered, in buckskins with a red kerchief tied around his black hair that fell to his shoulders, he had an intense gaze that commanded attention. He wore white man's plaid shirt, a mackinaw, felt hat, and dungarees, leather boots and Indian leggings below his knees. As he spoke in Cree, Lucy translated quietly to John who caught a word here and there. They situated themselves well to the back and in the shadows so that John would not feel obvious.

"People of the Beaver Hills, the river valleys Kisiskatchewan and the North," he shouted in a voice deep but clear and commanding. "I fear the hunt this year will not be as successful as it was last year and the years before. The buffalo that had moved to the hills have gone except for a few scattered small herds. They are becoming less all the time. Without the buffalo, the Cree and the Métis will soon disappear as well." There was a murmur of dismay from the crowd. This was not a speech to stir the hearts of the people and build up courage for the hunt. This was not a blessing, an appeal to the Great Spirit for a good hunt! What was he telling them? Just when they thought that the buffalo were back again, he was dashing their hopes.

"After the hunt last year the white men had a new trick to trap us with," Gabriel went on while many asked themselves and whispered to others nearby, 'Where is Louis Riel?'

"At Fort Pitt, the chiefs abandoned our cause," Gabriel went on. "They signed what the white man called Treaty Number Six. The native tribes used to have the opportunity to hunt buffalo all over the prairie and up into the hills. But the white man took our land and now they offer us back a small piece they call 'a Reserve'. Any timber or part of this land could be traded back to them, they said, for some of their money. The burning stones that they call 'coal' could be sold to them from this piece of land." Gabriel stopped for a moment and looked around while silence reigned, before continuing.

"The chiefs got clothes for their backs that make them look silly and a medal to hang around the neck as well as a piece of cloth on a stick they call a flag. If they can make us forget about the buffalo hunts and stay on that piece of land, we can have their money instead of the buffalo."

Muttered words of angry indignation could be heard. "Money is supposed to take the place of buffalo meat to feed our families, or for hides, for robes and our tents? What good would be the ground and the trees if we sold them back for money? And who can sell the Great Spirit's ground?" Gabriel raised his voice from a rumble in his chest to a sharp demanding tone.

"They want us to accept that everyone should own a piece of this land and call it his 'private property.' No one else can step onto his property." Gabriel shouted everyone down.

"We need to hunt all across this land. The buffalo or the moose or the deer are not going to stay in one place and we are not going to either," someone shouted loudly.

"How they lie when they say the Indian can hunt all across the land for the buffalo if he has already driven the buffalo away for good," someone else shouted.

"Yes, my people! That is right!" Gabriel spoke above their mounting complaints. "That is why we are asking a representative to the government, our new leader of the new government in the West, Louis Riel, to come and change what is happening – to represent us."

"There," Julie whispered to Adolphe. "He is talking about Louis. Now we will hear if he is coming."

"The white men from the East have taken our women as their wives to work for them and make them white. He has taken away all the furs and the now the buffalo. They brought us their disease, the smallpox, and they outlawed our old beliefs in the Sun Dance and the Thirst Dance," another native voice demanded.

"We will not go to their reserves, to their missions and their schools," came shouts mostly from the native Crees. "We will follow the buffalo!"

And another voice shouted out the sentiment that they all echoed in their souls, "My heart runs with the buffalo; it will not graze with cattle."

Quietly, the three Lennys stole away into the darkness behind them and made their way back to their tent. Annabelle hung on her father's shoulder, asleep. In the dim light of their fire in front of the tent as John lay the sleepy little girl down in their blankets, Lucy could see that John was disturbed.

"I felt like a living corpse at my own funeral," he told Lucy in agitation. "Anyone near me looked at me strangely as though I was a spy. Am I to take the blame for all white men who have performed badly as far as the Métis and native people are concerned?"

"*Non*," Lucy assured him, "They are not blaming you. Only all of the other white people who have taken away the Métis and Indian's livelihood and have not tried to understand."

"We are packing up and leaving tomorrow while all of the excitement of getting ready for the hunt is happening. They will not notice us leaving. They will think we are going to the hunt as well," John announced in whispers as he undressed to get into his bedroll.

"What of the Perraults next to us? Will Adolphe not feel as you do? He is white as well – from across the big sea Julie said. And what of me, Jean? Who am I now, your wife, or a Métis like the others out there?"

"What a question to ask?" John sat back on his heels, leaning in from the edge on the tent. "You are my wife. If you believe as they do, that all white men are bad – loving nothing but their money and the land they can buy with it, go to them." He rolled into the blanket beside Annabelle and stared up at the sticks that met and crossed over at the point.

"But I am both," Lucy said softly as she took off her garments folded them and climbed in between Annabelle and John. "I love my family and my people. I am what they made me. But I love you even more, my husband. I will go wherever you decide. I know you are a good man, Jean Lenny, and soon you will show that to my people. My people accepted their land on Big Lake as their 'property' and soon they will have to accept the white man's way of life. But they will also keep some of their own and that will be good. Things change."

John took his very sensible and wise wife in his arms, the heat rising within. '*What an incredible woman he had chosen! A woman of strength, beauty, and great courage.* She whispered soft words against his cheek, the words she had spoken to him before, "In our hearts we share the same song, my Jean!"

As they drove home the next day, a rain drizzled down on them as they huddled under the expanse of their spread out tent that arched over their heads on the willow supports. Annabelle was not feeling well all the way home. Her head burned with a fever, and she refused to eat.

"She will be all right when we get home," Lucy assured John although the dry cough and the bleary eyes did not encourage the confidence in her own words.

She did not rally when she got home. For a week she lay in bed, tired and weak from coughing. When the sputum that she brought up was tinged with blood and Annabelle became short of breath, Lucy became alarmed. In the weeks that followed, the little girl became thin and emaciated. No treatment that Lucy administered did any good. Sometimes when she coughed, Lucy wondered if she would take another breath.

One morning Lucy awoke early before the sun was up. She could hear no raspy breathing, and she leaped up to attend Annabelle in her little bed next to the stove, for she seemed to be so cold all the time. She used to take her in bed with them, but her threshing about and coughing in their narrow bed made it impossible for them to sleep. So she put hot rocks in her cot to warm her and covered her well with blankets, checking on her frequently. Could it be, she wondered that the coughing sickness had finally left? Hurrying to her little cot, she found Annabelle's lifeless body.

Lucy's keening wail woke her husband. He tried to comfort his wife, but she rocked the lifeless form, cried and wept in mourning until he thought she could not be comforted.

John spent some time outside with his horses, not going to work and yet not going into the house. When hunger finally drove him in, he found Lucy had made breakfast and was going about the business of preparing the little body for burial. She knew just where she wanted the body to be buried – in the little graveyard at the mission.

Lucy soon accepted the death and prepared for the coming of her next child in a few months. When John mentioned the little girl, she told him, "There is no purpose in clinging to what was not meant to be. We had her for a little while, and now God has taken her with him. We must prepare to go to the mission today and see Father Vegreville. "The Life River flows on."

40

Big Lake Meeting

Rain, carts, and wagons had churned the roads into ruts of mud, and behind the wagons trooped the long lines of drenched humanity. Women were carrying children on their backs, and babies were slung at their breasts. Their feet slithered and sucked in the cold muck. Some were barefoot, the mire having swallowed up their moccasins. Their entry into St. Albert was quiet except for the fitful crying of hungry babies, the squeal of the carts, and the squeak of the leather harness.

The first wave of the starving Métis was streaming into the mission. This was the Soya Tapi, the Prairie People. The buffalo were gone and the Soya Tapi, over the past winter, tried to exist on a diet of gophers and mice. Many stayed on the prairies to fight for the right to hunt on the land they always freely roamed and hunted.

Some Cree and Métis at Father Lacombe's urging finally agreed to follow him to the St. Albert Mission where they would escape the starvation on the plains.

"But what can we do?" Bishop Grandin pleaded with the weary Albert Lacombe. "We can not possibly feed and care for all of these poor people!" The Bishop stood out in front of the mission church looking across the wide ravine at the stream of people in drenched and soiled clothes carrying sodden bundles down the hill. In shock and dismay, the bishop slumped against the hitching rail.

"They are desperate, Vital," Father Lacombe pointed out. "They would be happy with your stable, a dry tent behind your barn."

Bishop Grandin was a little upset with his friend Albert Lacombe. He realized that with the loss of the buffalo on the plains their situation was worsening, but surely they could find some way of feeding them on the

295

reserves that were being set up. They were driving in large herds of cattle from the United States.

"Vital," Father Albert explained patiently, "these people have to be fed NOW. They are dying on their feet. We passed by Fort Edmonton and were turned away. It is our responsibility to feed the flock."

"Of course," Vital Grandin swallowed, remembering the words he had often quoted from the Bible: "*Feed my flock.*" "We will find a way."

Adolphe emerged from the church basement he had been building on. "The church is too small to fit many into and the large new one, of course, is only at the basement stage, covered in, and has been turned into storage area, Bishop Grandin. But what about the school that we just finished, built onto the nuns quarters? You will probably need to turn the women and children over to the nuns anyway and the school is large with tables."

"Of course," Bishop Grandin agreed. "Bring in as many as you can, and I will get Brother Francis to order the killing of a calf immediately. And pemmican! Round up all we can. Get Mother Superior down here. She will know how much we can spare.

"We are at the end of a winter when our granaries are nearly empty." He turned again to Father Lacombe. "We have to save some for planting soon." Father Lacombe's buckskins were threadbare, worn and mud spattered. The lines had deepened around his eyes and in his forehead. His hair, now completely white, was thinning, but there was no mistaking the look of weary compassion in his eyes.

Everyone scurried around to make room for the dazed and weary travellers. The schoolroom was finally full. This would be the first step in the education process. First they would feed the body and then the mind.

The roasting calf smelled so good to the huddling mass that tried to dry out by the fireplace, and as soon as it stopped raining, they would build a big fire outside. The taste of beef, foreign to the refugees, was finally accepted. For bellies that longed for the taste of buffalo, it was bland but palatable. It was filling; they could not afford to be fussy.

When Adolphe got home that evening to Julie and his three children, he sank wearily into a chair by the kitchen table. "Father Lacombe has to stop bringing refugees from south of the Kisiskatchewan. We can not look after all of these people. Our own will soon suffer with disease and starvation." Under the light of a coal oil lamp in the middle of the oilcloth covered kitchen table, Adolphe spooned out a helping of stew and freshly baked barley bread, and passed the bowl to six-year-old Vital next to him.

"It is not their fault that they have to leave the plains and come to beg from their Northern cousins," Julie bristled. "The government men and the white traders are taking away their livelihood. The buffalo are gone because of them." Julie filled her plate and filled four-year-old John's plate. Then she gave a portion to three-year-old Joseph.

"Maman, I do not want stew – I will just have bread," John pleaded. "I am not hungry."

Julie turned to her middle son with a sigh. "You have to eat, John. How can you run and play if you do not eat?"

Soon after John came back from the Lac Ste. Anne Celebration he became sick, and instead of getting better as time went by, he worsened. He became thin and tired all of the time. A dry cough lingered.

"Look at Joseph," Adolphe pointed out their three-year-old. "He is going to be a big man some day. See how he eats! If only those children over at the Mission School had what we had to sit down to a meal to, they would be so happy! Here let me cut up your meat smaller."

"No, Papa," John protested quietly. "If I eat, I will be sick."

"Leave him alone, Adolphe. I got this meat from *mémère* two days ago. It was from the moose that Alfred shot – that he shared with the village. I made the rest into pemmican and it will last a long time until someone else brings in a kill. Perhaps the meat in the stew tasted old and dry."

"There is a hunting party going out tomorrow. Perhaps they will bring in some partridge, and the geese and ducks should soon be back. Now that it is spring, we will see more wild life returning. We have a lot more mouths to feed now." Adolphe scooped the stew from John's plate and transferred it to Joseph's.

Julie got up heavily from her chair at the table, her hand to her back. She was due to have her baby in June and was beginning to be uncomfortably large. Her dark hair hung down her back in a long thick braid, and she had taken to tying a band around her forehead to keep strands from hanging down over her forehead.

Adolphe insisted on building a table and chairs for them, even though she tried to tell him that their house was too small for a lot of furniture. Her family always sat on the floor to eat, and they slept on the floor as well, rolling up their mats and robes during the day. But now she admitted that she was getting used to chairs, even though she was forever bumping into them with her extended stomach. They were easier to get up and down from. The plates and forks and knives, though, made a lot more work. They used to just sop up the stew with the bread and fingers.

"What are they going to do with the new people in the village? Will they adopt them into the community? Will you build them homes?" Julie placed the cups of tea on the table and sat down again.

"Bishop Grandin and the nuns will instruct them how to live differently without the buffalo. They will teach the children how to read and write, and teach the women how to make foods as the white population does, and how to grow gardens and fields of barley."

"Hmmph!" Julie scoffed. "Of course the white man's way is the right way! Then when they do all this, the white man will chase them from the land as they did in the Red River Settlement. Did you know that Louis Riel, because he tried to help the Métis and the natives, tried to get them to treat us fairly, was declared an outlaw and had to run away across the border? Then when he came back they accepted him into the government, but that was a trick only to get him declared insane and put into an asylum. But he escaped and there is talk that he is coming out to the western territories where we are. Here he will make a new government for *us*!" she ended triumphantly.

"You must remember, my Julie, that you are married to a white man! You are partly white yourself." Adolphe said reasonably.

"But my heart is with Riel in his fight; just as Gabriel Dumont stands by his people, so do all the Métis." Julie's eyes flashed, proud and defiant, her tiny pointed features set in the dark complexion an obvious mixture of native and white.

"And where do I fit into your heart?" Adolphe asked gently. Those brilliantly blue eyes that had won her heart reached across the distance between them and drew her in. Her love leaped up inside her like an unquenchable fire, and her heart remembered. The look that passed between them, melting, rich with pride, spoke all that needed to be said.

"My loyalties are first to my husband and family and then to those who stood beside us and fought for us – who called us his people." She patted her abdomen. "But what can I do? My biggest job is coming up – a new life to concentrate on. If it is a boy, I am going to call him Louis after the man who will free these people to go back to the plains they love. Then Riel will chase all of those people from the land that want to fence and plow it up into dirt mounds. Then the buffalo will return and the people will be happy. The land will return to the people that it belongs to. Oh!" she laughed as she placed her hand on her belly, "he kicked me. I think he agrees with me. Yes, John, you can eat your bread on the floor. Adolphe, help Joseph down from his chair. This table does not fit him."

"*Oui*!" Adolphe attended to his boys. "I have to get up early to start building on the residential school. The parents will be living in their tents and moving about, hunting for food and finding a place to settle, but the children will stay at the school where they can be cared for."

"The parents will not like that – leaving their children behind," Julie shook her head as she washed the plates in the basin at the end of the cook-stove.

"It is for the best," Adolphe shrugged. "The children have to learn to handle a whole new way of life, and to speak French and learn new skills."

"Perhaps." Julie sighed and turned back to the stove.

Louis was born in June, 1878 in their little house near the mission at St. Albert with Julie's mother, Louise attending her. The three boys went to their grandparents' house until the birth was over. Adolphe carried the sleepy-eyed Joseph over his shoulder and with Vital on one side of John, and Adolphe catching his other hand, they stumbled out of the house into the darkness to walk the short distance where Pierre awaited their arrival.

"But, Papa, why do we have to go to Grandpapa's house now? Could we not wait until morning?" Vital complained sleepily.

"Because tomorrow we will have a surprise for you when you get home," Adolphe explained patiently.

"But why can we not wait there for the surprise? After I sleep, I can see it in the morning," Vital reasoned.

"*Mais, non*!" his father told him. "We need time to get the surprise ready."

Vital gave up and consented to being led through the night down the path to his grandfather's little house.

"The women these days," Pierre Berard complained, as he opened the door to the little troop and bedded them down on a blanket in the corner of the room. "In my day babies were born right in the same bed that the parents slept in, and when they woke up in the morning there was a new sister or brother. Or else she went into the cabin while the children stayed out to play, and when she came out again, there was a new baby, and she carried on with her work with the baby on one arm. What a lot of fuss just to keep the children from knowing!"

Pierre was talking in such a loud voice that Adolphe winced and glanced at the corner where the boys lay curled up on the blanket. His father-in-law's long black hair, beginning to thin, was drawn back with a buckskin lace, and he sat cross-legged on the floor in front of the low heater, which was propped up off the floor by stones.

In a quiet voice, Adolphe changed the subject. "I am thinking of adding onto our little house. It is too small already for the family we have now, let alone for the new baby. But then there is not much room on the little lot that we built on so I might move us out to the settlement at Big Lake. There we would have room for planting grain and a bigger garden."

Pierre was silent for a moment, staring at the heater and watching the flames that showed through the opening at the front around the door that let in the air. Finally he spoke. "Yes, I was thinking the same thing. Since they have been opening the lots on Big Lake to all the Métis in this area, it is a good opportunity to get one before they are all gone. When were you planning to go out there to look at them?"

"As soon as possible. I can see how big they are and where they are situated." Adolphe adjusted his position. He was not used to sitting cross-legged on the floor for very long.

"That is just what I was thinking!" Pierre spoke out in his loud voice again, causing the boys to stir on their mats. He had two voice volumes, loud and louder. "Maybe we could go tomorrow – if everything is all right with Julie, so that you can get away," he added with a question in his voice that made Adolphe smile to himself. *So*, he thought, *he is not so casual about this birth as he pretends.*

"Well, perhaps not tomorrow," Adolphe cautioned. "I have got to see if we have enough lumber to finish the work on the residential school, and if not, I should order some more at the sawmill while we're up there. And I have got to tell Bishop Grandin about the birth. He will want to register it and plan a baptism. I hope you and Louise will be available as godparents?" Adolphe rose, slowly unfolding his legs, and stretched. "Now I have got to go home and see if it is Louis that is born, or Louise." He chuckled briefly, and Pierre looked at him with a curious frown, uncomprehending. "Goodnight, I will talk to you tomorrow."

Little Louis was baptized by Bishop Grandin in the church on the hill above the settlement with Pierre and Louise attending as godparents. Two days later Adolphe and Pierre travelled with the wagon to Big Lake to pick up lumber for the school and to look for an allotment of land.

At first Adolphe was disappointed to find out that the allotments were for Métis, and he did not qualify, but Pierre did. Then it occurred to him that his wife was Métis, and his children, so it could be applied for in their names. When they heard that he was a carpenter and planned to build their houses, the magistrate, Francois Plante, was eager to have him join the settlement. Rules would be bent.

While at the Big Lake sawmill loading the lumber for the mission school residence, a man he recognized pulled in with a wagon ready to load on lumber that would be hauled to Fort Edmonton. The man was tall, lean and red-haired, but Adolphe could not place him. The man, however, recognized Adolphe.

"I recall meeting you at Lac Ste. Anne a year ago," he said with a smile. "You and your wife were set up next to us. I am John Lenny. I live here at Big Lake."

His face brightening, Adolphe put out his hand. "Of course! I remember you now. You had a wife with a toddler the same age as my Joseph. We went down to the celebration fires together before the last buffalo hunt."

John's face clouded, and he lost his smile.

"*Pardoné moi*!" Adolphe apologized, "It really was not much of a celebration, was it? It ended in shouting and fighting, and the hunt was a failure.

"*Oui*!" John agreed sadly, "but it was also when my little girl got sick and later died."

"Oh, that is bad! I did not know!"

John brightened again. "But we have another little girl born earlier this year. Her name is Mary Jane. She's a strong, healthy little girl. I have this new summer job delivering lumber to Fort Edmonton. And in the winter I haul logs to the mill."

"I am very glad for you, John Lenny. Do you live here in the settlement?"

"No, not part of the settlement. We have a little lot down the ravine. It is part of the land belonging to the sawmill company. There's not much land – not enough to grow grass to feed my horses, but then with my job in the lumber camp and hauling lumber I would not have time to plant and put up hay. But we did not pay anything for it. My wife has room for a garden."

"We plan to move over here to the settlement soon from St Albert," Adolphe shouted back as he climbed on top of the lumber beside Pierre. "I hope I meet you again." And they pulled away.

41

Sun Dance

Life was much different at the Big Lake Settlement. The lots were much larger. The Métis lived farther apart, and they were learning to be farmers. It was a disappointing venture for some. To people who loved hunting, trapping, fishing, and moving freely from place to place with the seasons farming seemed a ridiculous enterprise. They tried to continue the way of life they always lived.

They travelled North to find the fur bearing animals and the moose in the winter, to the lake at Ste. Anne to fish and meet for their celebration in the summer, before heading out in the fall to look for the buffalo, or failing that, the deer. In the spring when the ground was soggy, they came back to plant as the magistrate suggested, and to see how the animals, that had been left with those staying in camp, were faring.

The magistrate seemed irritated with them as he told them that farm animals must be tended all the time. They liked the milk from the cows did they not? They nodded, but they saw no reason to stay every day just to wait on the cows to give them milk. They always moved toward the foothills in the winter and the plains in the summer, except for those who were becoming domesticated like the animals they kept.

"The children should be attending school, and they should be here learning how to farm and to prepare new foods. What will happen when you can no longer find the fish and the moose – when they are gone like the buffalo?"

They shrugged. That never happened before. There had always been fish and waterfowl. If they stayed on their farms would not those animals soon disappear as well? And the tastelessness of their cattle was hard to become accustomed to.

"Adolphe!" It was Julie calling him as she hurried around the corner of the house he was building. Two-year-old Louis toddled after her falling on the rough ground and picking himself back up again without complaint. "Bishop Grandin is here to see you all the way from the mission."

This was the first time that Bishop Grandin came to the settlement on Big Lake, and Julie could not have been more amazed if she had seen the Great Spirit himself step down from a cloud. She had never seen him out of his robes and walking through the mud.

Adolphe dropped the board he was nailing around the doorjamb. "It must be important if he comes all the way out here to Big Lake. Where is he? In our house?" Adolphe had nearly finished their house before being called away to work on houses for other residents in the settlement. His carpentry talents were in big demand. Julie never complained that she wanted him to finish their house before he moved onto others. She just stepped over and moved around lumber that sat waiting for Adolphe to find the time.

"Vital! What a nice surprise!" he greeted the bishop who was sitting on the front step of his unfinished front porch. "What brings you to Big Lake?"

"I come in search of the best carpenter that the St. Albert Mission ever had, and to find out when he will be returning to work on the unfinished residence school and the church that still sits with the covered up basement," Bishop Grandin came to the point succinctly. He rose from the step and came forward as Adolphe, from old habit, bowed in reverence before him.

"I am so sorry, Your Grace," Adolphe apologized as he indicated the seat on the step again. He did not know if he would have a seat to offer inside the house in the midst of the turmoil. "I have been so busy! Everyone wants the houses built, and I have not even had time to finish my own – even though it has been over a year since we moved here. A year since we started to build and clear! Now that it is summer it's the best time. I need to get some help."

"Of course!" the Bishop agreed. "But the residence school is in the most need right now. I know you started work before you left, but we have many more children coming to live at the residence now." Vital finished with unmistakable pride glowing in his face.

"*Qu'est que c'est?*" Adolphe asked curiously. "So many? So soon? I am surprised that so many families have agreed to leave the children with you. The natives and the Métis have always insisted on taking the children with them on hunting and trapping parties. They always felt that the children learned best from their fathers and mothers. What has changed?"

"They finally agreed that the children are missing their religious instruction, and now that they are having to travel much farther for the animals, it did not make sense to drag the children along. The women now are staying as well – especially in the winter. They are coming to the mission for Sunday service and are able to get food if they are hard pressed. Most of the women now stay to tend the planting and harvesting because the men do not make out as well with furs as they did before."

"I know! They suffer from the drought. The crops were worth nothing last year and then the early frost," Adolphe added.

"*Oui!*" Vital agreed. "They are happy that the children, at least, are being fed and well-cared-for. They were warm and comfortable after the hard winter in the woods and in inadequate housing. So, more each year we get children, and more nuns have had to be brought in to teach the French, as well as the skills necessary to the new society. That is why you need to teach some men the carpentry trade, and the girls are being taught skills like cooking, knitting, and sewing along with their other school studies."

"I am sure they are all very grateful for the residence school but you are going to have to find more help. Not only have I committed myself to finishing these houses, but I have a new project in the planning." Adolphe straightened his shoulders proudly.

"Tell me," the Bishop said without much enthusiasm "what could be so important that someone else could not take over?"

"Well," Adolphe in his excitement started pacing back and forth as he explained, "The last time that I went to Fort Edmonton for supplies I spoke with a man who started a spark of an idea burning inside of me. I told him that there was not enough good stone and no stone masons for chimney and fireplace building and that mud fireplaces were not safe or adequate. I told him that back East we had bricks that were cheaper and easier."

As Adolphe talked enthusiastically, Bishop Grandin's attention was wandering back to the important topic that Adolphe was straying from, and he frowned, waiting for Adolphe to finish so that he could bring him back to the topic at hand.

"So we decided to start a brick factory in Fort Edmonton, and I am trained in brick making with the basics in steam engineering from my training in Montreal. He would provide the materials, and I would ...."

"Adolphe," the Bishop interrupted finally, "let us get back to the need at the mission school. I am expecting several more children this fall since another drought seems to be causing poverty and starvation as well as the hunters returning with little to show for their travels ...."

"But Vital!" Adolphe objected, "That is also what I am talking about. We could produce bricks to build not only chimneys but also houses. The new church and the rest of the residence could be built of bricks as well as lumber from the sawmill. The big places could be built of brick and the smaller houses of logs and boards. I could train some of your Métis to become brick makers and employ them in my factory. We already have the land, and we are in the process of gathering together the necessary equipment to start manufacturing." Adolphe waited in front of the bishop in breathless excitement.

For a few minutes Bishop Grandin stared at Adolphe while the information soaked in. Standing slowly, his expression changed to thoughtful study as he lowered his hand from supporting his chin. "You are right, Adolphe. It is a good idea. What are you doing here? Get down there and get started."

"I am waiting for my partner to get some money from the people who will invest in this. I do not have the money. I am going tomorrow to see how he managed. We may need workers very soon."

"Good Luck, Adolphe!" Vital Grandin touched Adolphe's cheek with his. "I will be waiting for great things from you.

John, high atop the load of lumber, urged the horses down the rutted dirt road to the Mission at Lac Ste. Anne. Sharing his perch behind him on the load of lumber bound for the mission was Lucy and her whole family. Her mother, Marie Amable, her father, Joseph, and Lucy's younger sisters found places to ride. Henri, Celestin, and James were now married with families of their own. They found their own way to the meeting place at Lac Ste. Anne. Lucy's youngest sister Isabelle was now six so she felt very independent. Lucy and John's daughter, Mary Jane, was nearly three years old and now their baby, Caroline, was going on two, and Lucy had to hang onto her or she might crawl away along the lumber. Now that she could walk, she was not happy about being held.

It was a beautiful July day, and they had the opportunity to ride to the meeting place rather than having to walk. It was always such an exciting trip to Lac Ste. Anne every year. And this year there would be people from farther away than ever before.

Lucy was concerned about her mother's breathing. It was worse this year. It seemed any exertion and she could barely get her breath. Lucy looked sadly at her mother from her smallpox-scarred face, to her bulky size, to her wheezing heaving of her chest, and felt that there must be something more that she could do for her. Father Grandin said that it was her asthma, and at this time of year, with all of the grass and flowers, it would be worse.

Under the direction of Henri Grandin, Bishop Grandin's nephew, a new rectory was being built at the mission. But he would have plenty of time to welcome the travellers and receive them as members in the church. That was where the lumber was bound – a special order from Bishop Grandin.

Lucy's sisters were of the age that Father Henri would be urging them to attend school. Those Métis and natives who lived near the mission were already attending catechism classes, with reading, writing and calculating taught by Christine Lacombe, Father Lacombe's sister. Only Marguerite, thirteen, Adelaide who was ten, and Isabelle, six, would be urged to attend. Anne was already married and travelling with her new family. It was too late for her.

A horseback rider moved up beside the wagon and hailed the Gladu Family. It was Daniel Dumont. "*Bon jour* to you and your family, *Monsieur Lenny*," he hailed. "You are bringing lumber to the gathering? What is it that you plan to build?"

"*Mais non! Monsieur Dumont.*" John laughed. "This is to build a new rectory at the mission. When it is unloaded we will be coming to the gathering."

"Many will be attending prayers at the mission, but afterwards we have our own special prayers, singing and dancing at the gathering." Daniel seemed to be impressing on them that the main reason for coming to

Lac Ste. Anne was not attendance at the mission, but the Métis-Native Celebration away from the Mission.

"We will be there!" Lucy waved at him as he rode away.

"Perhaps Daniel thinks that because you married a white man you do not want to attend the native celebrations," John commented.

"He is afraid that people are turning away from the old ways and doing only white man celebrations," Lucy answered quietly as she pulled Caroline back onto her lap. "Daniel still does not believe that our Great Spirit Manito is the same as the God the white man worships, though the priests have assured us this for many, many celebrations."

"I suppose it is because the celebrations in the mission church are so much different from the Métis and native celebrations," John observed idly. "Git up!" he shouted at the horses as they struggled to pull the heavy wagonload through a soft area in the trail, and the wheels bit deeply into the low spot.

Coming over the hill, they looked down on the sea of grey-white tents bristling with the support poles criss-crossed at the top. Beside some there were wagons with horses tied to them. Beyond that, were the placid blue waters of Lac Ste. Anne.

But it seemed to Lucy that there was a difference this year. The tipis were dilapidated, patched, and old, and the people walking about, mostly the children, were in rags. It seemed odd to Lucy that they did not run and shout, but seemed tired and listless.

Daniel seemed to read her mind. As he rode beside her, he commented. "There is much starvation. Many of those are the Cree from the south – the Plains Cree. They look to us up in the north to help them find food – to protect them as the feathers of a bird protect it from the frosts of winter."

"But," Lucy argued, "they have little in the way of shelter or clothes on their backs. We still see many moose and deer up in the north. Can they not find enough moose hide to replace the tattered buffalo tipi hide?"

"Nothing replaces the buffalo hide for robes or tipi. Deer or moose will make fine buckskin for clothing but it can not replace the buffalo hide for the tent." Daniel spoke sadly as they made their way down the road beside the tents toward the mission. "We will talk later around the fires tonight." Daniel veered off towards the tipis near the shore.

He left Lucy deep in thought, running her fingers through Caroline's hair to take out the tangles while the little girl winced and pulled away. Until now she had not realized just how dependent the people of the plains were on the buffalo.

It was nearly dark by the time Lucy and John got down to the celebration fires. They had to unload the lumber, talk to Father Henri, and have him see how much Caroline had grown since he baptized her. Then they set up the tents, both Lucy's parents' and theirs, and ate their hurried meal of pemmican and jerky.

Many gathered in a wide subdued circle around the fires that blazed high into the air as the drums set up their throbbing beat. Cross-legged, people sat, the familiar Hudson's Bay Blanket, though worn and dirty, wrapped around their shoulders, even though it was a warm July evening.

This was always an exciting time for Lucy. But this year there were so many new people - so many whom she did not recognize.

Father Henri told them that he would be down later to greet everyone and give his blessing so she was watching for him to arrive.

There was a stir of excitement to their right, and John and Lucy watched as a rider came through the crowd. He swung his leg down from his buckskin pony and climbed onto the natural stage slightly elevated, a flat-topped hill above the lake. Beside him, his hand loosely supported his high powered rifle, his buffalo gun.

His face was partly covered with a beard and moustache, which signalled that he was Métis and not native. With just a look from flashing black eyes under dark brooding brows, he hushed the throng. The deep voice seemed to rivet the crowd's attention. They knew him. He had come to speak to them before, to the tribes of the south as well as at Lac Ste. Anne.

"My people, I am Gabriel Dumont. I come from Batoche, the Métis town on the edge of the plains by the mighty Kisiskatchewan. I have chased the buffalo from the Red River to the hills at the feet of the mighty mountains. I am the general for the leader of all Métis in the territories, Louis Riel. He is the man who speaks for us at the Council of all of the leaders in this big land far to the east.

"It was he who spoke to Crowfoot on the Plains to the south and convinced him to join with all of the Métis in the Northwest in sending the white man from our land. Their broken promises are many. He will set up our own government here in the Northwest and they will have to answer to us before they take from our land. Maybe then the buffalo will return to us. He alone can stand against the white government men in the East. He has spoken to Big Bear, Poundmaker, Ermineskin, Samson, and the rest. They will join with us to take back our land. We need the buffalo. I urge you to pray to the Great Spirit Manito for Louis Riel and for the strength of the Métis Nation."

Then the drums started an insistent throb that matched their own heartbeats. It stirred them inside like no other sound before. Its thunder touched their souls and shook their hearts. As one, a group of young men before them stood and moved around the fire. Their bodies, naked from the waist up except for a headband, were burnished copper, shining with sweat and moving with sinewy effortless grace as they circled the fire in a meaningful dance.

The people sitting on the grass felt the ground beneath them vibrate, and their hearts swelled with feeling – rich with pride. These were the warriors – the pride of their nation. They fasted for three days and now they were appealing on behalf of all people, the Métis people, appealing for pity.

From the throats of all around the sacred fire welled the chant of prayers for mercy and strength from the mighty one. Then as the dancers moved in a slow circle of sinewy power, crouching, stretching, reaching, twisting, doubling, and quickly unfolding, the people watched in fascination. The movement told a story of the plight of the hungry, the cold, and the weary hunters who faced a grim future of starvation and emptiness.

Over and over, their prayers moaned and cried, swelling to throbbing fullness. Tears of emotion coursed down the faces, and they swayed to the drum rhythms.

Suddenly, one of the dancers leaped upon the knoll nearby where a tree stood. Unnoticed before, it was hung with prayer ribbons, each twisted onto a branch in an appeal to the Great Spirit, the One God. At the top of the tree was a large nest made of sticks, the nest of the thunderbird. Beside the tree at the dancer's feet lay a white cloth and on it a bleached white buffalo skull to prove the brave's trust in Manito's care. One of these braves was going to offer himself in sacrifice to gain the pity of Manito. A sudden hush fell over the assembly as the young man prepared himself mentally for the ordeal.

He raised his face to the sky as two rawhide lines were swung forward with skewers on the ends. A combined sucking in of breath could be heard because all knew what was about to happen. Then the chant started again with a new prayer, and voices were raised to a higher pitch.

Two other dancers stepped forward and pushed the skewers through the skin and muscle of the dancer's breast. The skewered brave then fell back against the lines swinging out and away, circling the pole. His scream was not one of pain even though all knew it was excruciating torture, but the ultimate prayer for pity from the spirit world. If the skewers tore through, he would have won his appeal and promise of mercy was assured.

Circling the tree swinging out on the rawhide thongs, he shouted out his prayer while the people around sang, repeating the words over and over: *"We your people, Great Manito, suffer and cry out to you. Look on us today. Come near us and see our pain. Release us, Oh Great Manito, and we will follow in your way. Let this sufferer see your face and feel the release from the torment that only you can take away."*

In the back circle of watchers, John and Lucy sat in stunned disbelief. Neither had ever seen such a thing before. This was a Blackfoot tradition and had rarely been done in the land of the Cree. When it had, years ago, it was during the first smallpox epidemic when so many lives were lost. Since the coming of the missionaries, it had not been performed in the Northwest.

"Is that the Sun Dance?" John asked in a husky voice at Lucy's ear while he hid Mary Jane's eyes from the sight that made his stomach lurch and his body grow weak.

Above all the noise of weeping and chanting no one else heard, and Lucy had to turn and aim her reply into his ear. Caroline was asleep in the sling at her mother's breast and was unaware of the drama before them.

"*Oui, Jean*, but we must continue to sing the prayer, or Manito will turn away from us." And she set up the wailing prayer that was heard all around them.

When the dancer dropped to the ground, the drums and the wailing stopped abruptly. Silence seemed to be accompanied by a breeze that wafted across them from the lake. It was a good omen. The Great Manito had replied. They were forgiven.

Drums took up a new rhythm, a rhythm of joy, and a great ululating cry issued forth from the dancers who hurried forward to pick the wounded and bloody, fallen brave from the ground and take him away. A lump in her throat, Lucy stared at the young man, blood streaming down from the torn muscles, his head hanging as though in death and his body limply supported by his helpers. Tears stung her eyes as she, along with the others, took up the cry as ancient as the old trees, of thanks to the Great Spirit.

The dancing continued around the fire, and happier songs were begun. A straight whistle pipe took up a birdlike song. The wounded man was taken to his tent to be treated by the healers and hailed as a hero. But John, visibly shaken by what he had witnessed, felt numb as they returned to their tent. He looked at Lucy walking ahead of him carrying Caroline, the long shiny blue-black braid of her thick hair swinging behind her in the dim light of twilight, and he suddenly trembled for their future.

42

Louis Riel

They were all aware of it – the excitement in the air. As each wave of refugees from the starvation in the south came through with Father Lacombe, or that were sent by Father Lacombe, the excite-ment grew. The priests in St. Albert were aware of it, but they did not understand it.

"They are starving. Why do they act as though there is a savior coming to lay a table for them?" Father Henri Grandin shook his head in wonder. Father Henri recently left the Ste. Anne Mission and was preparing for a placement. He was always an organizer of some note and was bound to move up. His Uncle Vital had commented many times on the changes at the Ste. Anne Mission.

"Perhaps if you are here with us for awhile you will find out, Henri," Vital chuckled. "We can thank you for the building that has gone on over there in the past three years since you have been there. The rectory you had built, the Stations of the Cross, and still you have had time to minister to the natives. They have been coming to that mission from the South in droves, and you have given so much time to them."

"Well, we do not have the residence school there as you do here, but those who come in to have me marry them, or baptize, or pray for them in times of sickness and sorrow, I do what I can to help. The mission acts as a school, hospital, refuge or a church when it can. But they do not stay long. They will be there for a season, and then they are gone to follow their instincts. Some stay year round, and I try to get them to settle into one place."

"It is the same here," Bishop Grandin admitted. "They are always mov-ing on and their children's education suffers. They do like to hear the sto-ries about God and about Jesus, and once you have prayed with them they

313

are happy to wander again. That is probably what will happen with these new groups that have come in with Father Lacombe. They are poor, starved waifs, but they are happy with whatever we give them, and they are away to the north or the west when the food runs out. Now, though, you see a lot more with horses and wagons than on foot. That is encouraging. Maybe they will be encouraged to accept the new ways."

"I hope so," Father Henri sighed. "I will admit that I was worried soon after I arrived out there. Remember? I was telling you about their reverting back to pagan ways with the Sun Dance ceremony? That has got to be officially condemned. It is no use in us telling them. It has got to come from the Northwest Mounted Police. That was a frightening time. I hesitated to get involved at the time, but I condemned it every chance I got. That young fellow nearly died when infection set in. But I dared not intervene at the time. How many children have you got coming to the residence school now, Uncle Vital? This is such wonderful work you are doing for the Lord in helping his children. But I can imagine that sometimes it is a thankless job."

"*Oui*, nephew, but some day they will realize that we have been helping them to face a changing West and they are learning about our God and learning to give up their pagan beliefs. It will bring us all closer together, and any sacrifice I can make toward that end will be worth it."

"Well, I must let you go to open your unfinished church and feed and bless your new refugees."

In their little house at Big Lake, Julie could not contain her excitement at what she was hearing all around the settlement. When she came back from the market place by the lake where the fishing nets were brought in from Big Lake, she could not wait for Adolphe to get home to tell him about what she heard.

Adolphe listened solemnly. He heard a lot as well, down at the brickmaking plant. There, however, the feelings were not of excitement for the coming summer but one of worry and foreboding.

"The newcomers have brought news with them that is spreading like the spirit wind everywhere that they go," Julie beamed. "Louis Riel is here in the territories and will be setting up his headquarters in Batoche, the Métis town on the edge of the prairies. Not only that, but he will be coming up to a prayer gathering this summer or late fall to Ste. Anne's sacred gathering place.

"In the settlement here at Big Lake all is in readiness to travel to the sacred lake to meet him and share in the celebration of his coming to form a new government and territory. The Territory of the Métis Nation will finally be organized into action." Julie's colour was high, and her eyes shone as Adolphe had not seen them before. He was again struck by her dark beauty. Her hair was still thick and long as it hung down her back in a long braid with a few wisps that escaped the thong clinging to her face. She had put on weight around her middle since he married her, but she was still small in stature.

"I have heard it said," Julie told her husband triumphantly, "that Louis is almost on equal terms with Manito – at least a spirit helper. The church and rectory in Batoche is the spiritual headquarters for him."

Julie set about the making of moccasins and leggings of deerskin for the boys for winter. Her father brought her the hide after he returned from his trip to the north last winter and she was finally finding the time to make the clothing.

"You know," Adolphe reminded her gently, "now that I am a brick maker and brick layer, I can afford to buy boots and clothing at Fort Edmonton. You do not have to make deer hide moccasins."

"I know." Julie tilted her chin up stubbornly. "But I like the boys to have warm feet this winter and those boots are not warm and soft like these. That is why I told Père to bring me the deer hide. And besides, it is how I find out what is going on. I took the moss and the long roots that I gathered. The women need the roots for threading the baskets together, and I traded for the fish. The women always need the moss to lace up inside the babies' buntings and for scrubbing the floors. It is always so necessary. But you could bring more Hudson Bay blankets back from the fort. They always like to trade food for those."

"And by the way," Adolphe interrupted in his quiet gentle way, "I am wondering if it is a good idea for you to travel to Ste. Anne for the gathering with Daniel so young – he is not yet a year old. And Louis is just five. John is ten, but you know how he coughs and suffers after any exertion. He is still so thin, and everything he eats seems to give him a stomachache or make his eyes and nose run. And they will be having such a crowd there ...."

"Vital will be there to help his brother. He always knows how to help him. And Joseph is nearly nine and such a big strong boy! John is no better with staying here sitting by the fireplace, and we will not be walking to the gathering so it should be no difference."

Turning her head away, Julie heard nothing that would talk her out of attending the gathering this year. She looked forward to it all winter. And spring was so dreary and cold. Everyone prayed for rain all last summer and more snow this winter. Neither happened, so they needed to pray at the sacred lake to end the drought and bring back the animals. And besides, this was her chance to again see Louis Riel. She had not seen him since they left the Red River Settlement. And she wanted to introduce him to his namesake, her little Louis. It was such an exciting time!

"Adolphe, will you check on the fish? It is in the baking hole under the hot coals in the yard. It should be done, and there are roots baking with it that I dug up. You and the children must be hungry." She side-stepped the discussion again.

Vital, their oldest came in at that moment. "*Maman*," he complained rubbing his stomach, "*Je suis affame! La poisson – la bon odeur!*"

Vital was going to grow into a big man. Already, at twelve he was taller than she was, and with dark curly hair like his father, square jaw, and wide white-toothed smile, he was already a striking young man.

Julie put down her sewing with a laugh. "You are always hungry! Call the others in. I will set the table." Julie finally accepted her husband's way of sitting at the table and using utensils and plates. But she still did not like all of the extra work it made with cleaning up – and so unnecessary, she thought. But after all, she was part white so this concession she could at least make.

Everything was loaded into the wagon. It was time to leave for the Lac Ste. Anne gathering. "I was supposed to start on the brick work at the St. Albert mission today," Adolphe reminded the excited Julie as she scurried back and forth loading up the food, blankets, iron kettle, axe, and other necessities while giving instructions to her boys.

"Joseph, the tent poles are to be set up in the wagon so that we have shelter in case it rains. Adolphe, could you help Vital put them up and the canvas over them. Louis, look out for Daniel! He will try to crawl out if you do not hang onto him. Oh, why did I have to have all boys with no girls to help share the woman's work?" She threw up her hands in mock exasperation. Secretly, she was proud of all of her boys and would not have traded them for the world.

Although eager to get underway, she sat on the seat with Daniel on her lap, calmly and placidly waiting for Adolphe to finish checking the horses' traces and climb up the spokes of the wheel to the seat. They even had a spring-filled seat with the big buffalo hide thrown across it. What luxury! Their chickens and cows were left in the charge of the elderly man and woman who lived nearby and were too old to make the journey this year. Most families did not own chickens, pigs, or cows. They still felt that keeping those animals was a nuisance. But those people were right there whenever they butchered the hog in the fall. Julie used the fat to make soap, which she used to trade at the market.

She glanced behind them at the children sitting on the floor of the wagon, sprawled over the blankets and robes under the tent tarp. Huddled forlornly in the corner sat John, his beloved little brown face looking tired and pinched. Her heart lurched in her chest. He had not wanted to come, but they could not leave him behind, and he had crawled out of his bed in the corner and allowed himself to be herded onto the wagon, his little back hunched, and the occasional cough wracking his slight form.

His breathing was ragged and uneven, and how it hurt inside to see him like this! Sometimes she would shake his shoulder in the morning to waken him, and her heart would race until she realized that he really was alive. The other boys walked to the school at the mission, but John could not even find the energy to listen while his brother Vital read to him and tried to teach him the words that he learned. She even went to the medicine woman who gave her boy the drink she brewed from the wood flower. Bishop Grandin came to pray with him, but there was no change.

Tears stung her eyes as she turned back to gaze at the well-travelled trail ahead. The early morning sun behind them flooded the wilted foliage on the trail with heat. Dust billowed up from the road, swirling behind them from the wagon wheels. It would feel so good to have rain now. She knew just where she could pick some edible mushrooms if it would rain.

They crossed a dry creek, and the shrill of mosquitoes swarmed out from the willows and thick grass. Turning again, she saw Vital swatting at them with a branch from in front of John who was too tired even to brush them away. Perhaps this was a bad idea bringing John with them on this trip. Like Adolphe said – it is too much for him. She admitted it to herself, a sob catching in her throat.

But they drove on, jolting in their slow progress that shook and jostled John's slender suffering body.

Adolphe could not believe the number of people who turned out – more than ever before. There were feather and fringe bedecked buckskin Cree from the plains, cotton-clothed Blackfoot in their long thick braids hanging down from a wide array of hats, Hudson Bay blanketed Iroquois tribe members from the mountains, Stony, Assiniboine, and Métis in their trading post clothes. The Frog Lake People, The Hobbema Tribe, The Beaver Hills People and the Rocky Mountain People who had always been sworn enemies of the Blackfoot. Now they all came together with a common purpose. Their gaunt faces and hollowed eyes said that they were hungry. The tipis that they had set up were ragged, patched, and shabby, a picture of the pitiful plight they found themselves in since the disappearance of the buffalo and the advance of the white settlements with their whiskey traders.

Adolphe and the boys set their tent up among those around them. A stir of excitement directed their attention to the arrival of a group of horsemen who threaded its way through the tipis toward the lake and the platform that had been built at the water's edge since last they were there.

"It is Louis Riel," Julie said in an excited whisper to Adolphe as they stared down the hillside at the man who swung down from the big black horse and mounted the platform. Immediately, the drums started up to call everyone in. More drums added their thrum until the insistent thunder could be heard for miles across the placid water.

Then the voices began, repeating over and over, "Oh, Great Manito, your servant, our spirit helper, Riel, is here to call on you to come close to us. He will speak for us. Do not turn your face from us. Come close and hear your people's need."

"Let us go down so that we can get close enough to hear," Julie urged as she gathered the children together and gave them blankets to wrap about themselves to sit on the ground by the lake.

"John can not go down. He is too sick to walk, Julie. I will stay here with him while you go with the boys," Adolphe suggested.

"No, No, Adolphe!" Julie insisted. "You must carry John down by the sacred lake. We will bundle him up. Louis must meet him."

"But, Julie." Adolphe was becoming alarmed. Not only was he a white man, mistrusted for what his kind was doing to the natives and Métis, but his wife seemed to think that this man was some kind of a god – some kind of miracle worker. A word from him or a touch was not going to change what was happening to his son.

"All right, my wife, I will carry him down there and bundle him up between you and the boys, but then I will go over to see the factor at the trading post and see the new priest, Father Chevrier. The feeling around us in the crowd, the things that are being said … I am frightened – for them and for … us!" But Julie did not seem to be listening to him. She was wrapping another Hudson Bay blanket around John who hung like a sack over Adolphe's shoulder. He seemed barely alive.

Panic rose inside Adolphe as they were swept along with the crowd that pressed towards the lake. *What were they doing here?*

As they got closer to the platform, pushing in with the smothering crowd, Adolphe looked up at the man on the platform. He was tall and straight with powerful broad shoulders, dressed in buckskin but with a pinstriped jacket over the shirt. His hair was thick and dark brown, blown about wildly into wavy turmoil, and he had a small black moustache and a full pointed beard, which distinguished him as Métis.

But most distinctive about the man were his eyes. They were black and flashed fire in the light of the blazing fireplace below him, and they danced and glistened as he spoke in his passionate manner. They were hypnotic and compelling, commanding attention and reverence. Instead of feeling fear, however, Adolphe calmed immediately because Louis was holding high a symbol he recognized, the symbol of Christianity and the church. It was a crucifix. Now he had no reservation in leaving his family sitting in the throng at the man's feet.

"I am going up to the mission and the trading post now," he told his wife quietly as he curled John into the curve of his mother's arm, still wrapped tightly in his blanket, his eyes barely open and a flush of fever on his cheeks. A stab of pity tore at Adolphe as he turned away, a lump in his throat. Then he melted away into the crowd.

The chanting and drumming came to an abrupt halt as Gabriel Dumont climbed onto the platform and held up his hand. In contrast to Riel, well educated, articulate, devout, charming and intellectual with his background and his history in the study of philosophy, literature, religion, languages and his years of leadership in politics on the Red River Settlement, Gabriel was hard-living, risk-taking, courageous and reckless. He had a big head and a high forehead, massive shoulders, and barrel chest. A black felt hat covered his black curly hair, and he had a full moustache and black beard sprinkled with grey. The soft well-worn buckskin raggedly fringed jacket and scraggly beard resembled the buffalo he hunted and proclaimed him as truly the 'Prince of the Plains' as he had been dubbed.

Gabriel could, it was said, call the buffalo on the plains, and he spoke French and five different native tongues, neither of them English. He was in awe of the revered Louis Riel whose name was on the lips of every Métis, Indian and white man in the country.

"People of the Northern Territories, of the bush land and of the Sacred Lake. I have brought to you from the plains of the Saskatchewan and from the Red River where he fought for your cause with the Canadian Government, this man who has come to unite the Métis and the Indian tribes. Hear him and learn. This is Louis Riel – the Prophet of the New World!" The deep and resonant voice of Gabriel Dumont rang out fervently across the men and women below who, hushed to silence, hung on every word.

Riel stepped forward; his eyes swept the crowd below, making them feel that he was speaking only to them. How awesome was this revolutionary who spoke so calmly! "You of the Cree, the Assiniboine, the Chippewa and the Métis, you are the 'Chosen People' of the Northwest! Do not forget that. I have no antagonism toward the settlers, but the trickle that started toward the West has become a *flood!*

"I do not suggest violence – I abhor violence! The Hudson's Bay Company and the Government are at fault. We have asked for nothing more than for the government to live up to its treaty promises. We ask only for the deeds to the land we have lived on for years! The Government has done nothing to bring this about. Just recently the Prince Albert

Colonization Society got Métis land from a government sale. Your rights have been ignored. They said that those living on the land were not living up to the Homestead Act.

"Chief Poundmaker told me that he tries to adapt to reserve life but he says the white authority promise everything but only deliver disease and poverty. That is why, since the Canadian Government has faulted on its functions, we must get control of our own country in the West. We must establish a provisional government. Our Bill of Rights and our grievances have been sent to the Government in the east but have been ignored. On top of that, they have sent only force to gain control. I am asking you to join this movement not only with body but with heart and soul."

A murmur that was almost a shudder rippled across the audience. Was he talking about war? They lived peacefully here and they did not want to have soldiers tramping into their lives.

One tremulous voice from in front voiced the question, and another voice another concern to all of them. "What does Father Chevrier say about this?" Their clergy always advised them on things like this. They no more wanted to go against the teachings of the clergy than a child would against a loving parent.

"No," Louis raised his voice in a passionate plea. "We do not want to fight with those in power. We only want to have them look at what they have been too blind to see – that we are a separate people – a nation unto ourselves. We have no voice. A governor needs to be appointed.

"As for the priests. Most of them are not about religion! They are about obedience to the Catholic hierarchy first, and to the government second – only obedience!"

Many young men in the back cheered loudly, but many in the front looked at each other. This was defiance! Rebellion! Blasphemy!

Looking at their faces, Riel read the doubt and the fear of challenge. "I tell you again," he insisted. "I am not saying violence. There will be no bloodshed. The East must be convinced that though the Métis are a meek nation with a humble heart and all the principles of goodness, we deserve to be heard. If the clergy will not stand up for us against the powerful white majority in the East, we must petition them ourselves. We shall not be pushed aside.

"Look at you!" Riel's voice became filled with compassion. "The buffalo are lost to you! The fur trade is all but gone. You are nearly ready to go begging at their door for food. Your tipis without the buffalo hides are in tatters, but when you try to turn to farming they say the land is not there to use as you wish. And if you leave your farming to travel the nomadic life in search of food and fur as you once did, the missionaries berate you. You become thin and weak with lack of food, proper shelter, and the diseases brought from the East."

As Louis looked down at the people in front of him his gaze paused at Julie, and a flicker of recognition crossed his face. Immediately he stepped down from the platform as the drums started up again and a chant was begun – one that one of the priests had taught them – one that was a celebration of the sacred lake – the Lake of Ste. Anne. They responded to the music with the slow movement around the fire that, after being replenished, shot into the air, throwing sparks and splashing its flickers of light over the dancers. Heels pounded the ground in time to the beat as Métis and native alike responded as they always had, since time immemorial. Those with children in their laps responded where they sat on the ground.

"Julie Berard, is it not?" Louis asked as he knelt beside Julie who cradled John in her lap while Joseph held the year-old Daniel, and young Louis crowded at her side. "You are the daughter of Pierre Berard from the Red River Settlement?"

Julie nodded, too awestruck to reply when he recognized her and came down to speak to her. When she finally found her tongue she pointed out her children. "Here is my oldest, Vital," she raised her hand to show the boy who stood behind her watching this great man kneeling before his mother. "And this is Joseph, my third, and Daniel, the baby, and Louis – he is named after you, Louis Riel. And here is my second, John," she finally finished, pulling back the blanket to reveal the ten-year-old who lay so thin and unresponsive in her lap."

"What is the matter? Is he ill?" Louis asked with concern. "His cheeks are flushed with a fever."

"For a very long time he has been sick and getting worse day by day," Julie choked out the words as she looked down at her son. "It has been a very long time. I thought that taking him to the sacred lake would help and I wanted him to meet you Louis. My husband, Adolphe, has gone to see the priest, but I do not think it will do any good. We have already taken him to three and to Bishop Grandin. He gets worse."

With determined purpose in his eyes, Louis Riel took the slight form from her, the blanket dropping behind in her lap, and he stepped up onto the platform still cradling the pitifully thin form in his powerful arms.

A hush suddenly fell over the dancers, and the movement came to a halt with the cessation of the drum beat and the chanting. In a voice vibrant with emotion Riel began to speak as though to the trees behind them or to the hills beyond. "In the Métis community of Batoche, a relative of mine has a wife called Rosalie. She was struck down by a debilitating disease that took control of her legs so that she could no longer walk. But friends brought a bottle of water from the sacred River Lourdes. During a ceremony of healing they rubbed the water into her legs, and she was made well. As a witness to this miracle, I can tell you that she is now walking. This boy now needs your help and the help of the healing waters of the sacred lake."

As if mesmerized, they stared at the limp form of the ten-year-old hanging like a rag doll in Louis Riel's arms. One after the other, they joined Riel in a repetitive chant for healing as he appealed to all of the saints. He called on his memory as a boy in the school of the Grey Nuns, on his short training in the priesthood, and at his mother's knee in the Red River Settlement. The fervent prayer grew in an appeal for the intervention of the spirits with their unpredictable mystical forces and God who sustained him throughout his life of persecution, surrounded by love-hate, rejection and idolization.

While the chant grew in intensity and the drums increased in volume, Riel stepped down from the platform and headed towards the lake before them.

In shock and fear, but with an irresistible trust, Lucy's mother and father, Marie and Joseph Gladu, watched from the back of the crowd. They recognized the child of the Perraults, her daughter's friends and their eyes filled with tears. The child was dying.

43

The Miracle

Adolphe entered the Hudson Bay Company trading post and found the factor alone. He was a different man from the one whom he met when he was in the trading post before.

"*Bonjour!*" Adolphe greeted as he held out his hand. "*Je suis Adolphe Perrault.*"

"I will warn you now that I do not speak French very well so if you speak any English, I prefer it." The man responded in halting flawed French dialect, "I am David McRae."

Since starting with the brick making at Fort Edmonton Adolphe realized the need to learn English. Most of the fort was English speaking so he was plunged into the learning of a new language.

"I was born and raised in France and have spoken no other language until very recently. I am just learning to speak English. How do you do –uh- manage speaking English in a land – uh- area – location - where they all speak French?"

"That's why I got the job in the first place," McRae went on in English, "I'm Irish, but because I could speak a little French they put me out here. If I can find people who can speak English, I usually ask them to switch because I'm not good at French. Besides, it's good for them to learn. English is soon going to be the main language spoken in the territories. So to do any dealings at trading posts and so on, you have to get used to it. It's only within the church that they continue to speak French."

"I see," Adolphe raised an eyebrow when he realized McRae's narrow-minded viewpoint.

At that moment the sound of the drums stopped abruptly. "Thank the Lord for mercies; that damned racket finally stopped! What's going on over there? There seems to be a lot of people trooping into the area. There are more tents set up than I've ever seen and a lot more excitement."

"They have special guest – who have come –uh – came – to talk de la prairies," Adolphe stumbled haltingly. "He is Louis Riel."

"Oh, sure! I've heard of him. He's some kind of revolutionary that's trying to stir up trouble with the Métis, trying to say that they're some kind of a separate nation, and he wants to start up a new government here in the West. He wants some kind of special concession for the Indians and half-breeds, and says that the land is all theirs. He runs around waving his crucifix in the air trying to scare away evil spirits or something. They say he's insane."

Adolphe coloured at the prejudice and intolerance of the man. However, he did not have enough English words at his disposal to refute the statement so he simply stared back at the man.

"Oh, I'm sorry; are you one-a them? I thought you was white – you look white," McRae made an attempt at an apology.

At that moment the drums started up again and continuous chanting that grew louder and more insistent.

"There they go again with that ki-yip-ing and howling – and the drums – oh, sorry – but it gets monotonous. Can't they find another song."

"It is not singing, Monsieur McRae," Adolphe said stiffly. "It is praying. Their prayers are chanted. In other cultures they would use an organ. The Métis and natives have the drum."

"Oh, to be sure!" McRae nodded knowingly. "They got that from the Catholic Church – all that chanting. I know, I used to hear that when I was a boy in the church."

"Actually," Adolphe measured his words carefully, "The natives were chanting their prayers long before the missionaries came west. They found that was one thing they had in common. It is the same as singing."

"Well, it gets bloody monotonous." McRae grumbled.

"Now I go to the church to see Father Chevrier," Adolphe informed the man as he turned towards the door.

"Yes, I don't think he'll be too happy with that nutty revolutionist talking to his flock. He better get right over there," McRae called out to Adolphe's back as he closed the door between them.

At the residence behind the church, Adolphe knocked on the door. The short pudgy form of Father Chevrier appeared in the dim light of the afternoon sun streaming in the window from the west. Father Chevrier was balding, and he had a slight wheeze. His short grey hair fringed out around the bald spot, and his mouth wreathed in a smile as he recognized Adolphe.

"Come in, my friend. How is that boy of yours? The one who was so ill? And the baby, what was his name? When you were last here you had had him baptized, you said, by Bishop Grandin. I hope that he thrives."

"*Merci*, Father Chevrier! *Oui*, the family is fine except that John is as yet no better. If anything, he is worse. He is up at the lakeshore with his mother, Julie. I am so afraid that we are losing him, Father. I wanted to bring him over to you, but Julie wanted to take him to see Louis Riel. You know that she remembers him fondly from the Red River Settlement. He is a hero to her – a saviour!"

As Adolphe turned to sit at the kitchen table where Father Chevrier indicated, he glanced up to see the look of shock on Father Chevrier's face.

"*Monsieur Perrault*," he addressed Adolphe formally. "That is blasphemy! There is but one saviour. Monsieur Riel is not a saint nor a member of the clergy!"

"*Pardonnez-moi, Père* Chevrier!" Adolphe apologized profusely. "I did not mean that literally. It is just that he did so much for the Métis Nation down in Manitoba during the struggle to bring about justice for his people. Many still proclaim him as the greatest patriot and statesman that the Red River Settlement ever produced. He fought for them as no man has ever fought for a nation."

"As a politician, he was much to be admired before he went too far and had to run away before he was arrested," Father Chevrier replied stiffly. "He treads very close to heresy in his zeal."

"I am truly sorry, Father," Adolphe apologized again. "Of course, I am only saying what I heard, since I was not there. He has made a great impression on all of those who came from the Red River Settlement."

"Those are my people. I have married many of them, baptized their children, and comforted them at funerals of family members. They are faithful members of the church. Riel is but a passing malcontent." Father Chevrier set down a cup of tea before Adolphe, and though he spoke nonchalantly, there was a twitch in Father Chevrier's pudgy cheek, and his hand shook a little as he lowered the cup.

"You do not feel that you should go up to listen in and find out what he is saying to the people?" Adolphe asked the priest. "Factor McRae calls him a revolutionist."

"If he is insane as I have heard," Father Chevrier said as he paced back and forth, "then it would be dangerous to face off with him and ask him to stop fomenting discontent with a contented people in the northwest." The priest wandered distractedly between the stove and the simple wooden table with its rough wooden chairs, his hands fluttering effeminately on the sleeves of his loose cotton shirt, and Adolphe recognized a nervous panic in his voice and actions.

"But they are not content, are they Father?" Adolphe pursued. "Every day they become more worried about their situation. With the disappearance of the buffalo, the fur trade, and the treaties that force the natives to the reserves and leave the Métis worried about the land they claimed, they become more discontented."

"Why is he here? That is the question." The priest became more agitated. "I will not be a part of his bid to have my people involved in his revolution to satisfy his grand design."

"A devout man who carries a crucifix before him and speaks with a quiet intellect, and a passionate caring for the Métis cannot be mistaken for a bloodthirsty revolutionist who ..." Father Chevrier cut him off abruptly as he sat across from Adolphe and leaned in.

"He would like to lull us into a false sense of security by masquerading as a man of God. The man is insane!"

"He wants the European, the British, the French, the American, as well as the Cree and the Métis to divide up the vast empty land of the Northwest in a rational, equitable manner," Adolphe said reasonably. "Excuse me for asking in all simplicity but what is so insane about that?" Adolphe knew that he overstepped, but the words burst from his mouth.

Father Chevrier stood quickly, nearly knocking over the teacups, his face reddening in irritation. "This man has the effrontery to charge in here without coming to ask first if this was agreeable with me! Then I want nothing to do with him."

"*Pardonnez moi, mon Père!* I did not mean to be insulting. I – I will go now. I should not have spoken so forwardly to you. Forgive me. There is much I do not know." Adolphe rose quickly and edged to the door.

As he took his leave, he realized that Father Chevrier would not go to meet Riel, as any priest should do, because he was afraid. Father Lacombe would have gone to greet Louis Riel and would have asked questions.

Now that he thought of it, Adolphe recalled that the priest paled when he opened the door, and then greeted him effusively but almost anxiously. When he heard the chanting or the drums stop or start, he grew more nervous and glanced out of the window or started when he heard an unusual sound that he could not place.

Adolphe was not trying to be forward or argumentative. He really did want to know more about how the clergy felt about Riel. He only knew what he had heard from Julie and Pierre.

Adolphe left his family there with a man who held a crucifix before him, and he accepted and trusted him. What was he doing here talking to Father Chevrier and the factor? Why was he not back there with his family? Both of them were new. It was not as though they were old friends. And who really was this man Riel? A sudden urgency to get back to Julie and the children seized him, and he fairly ran along the lakeshore towards the insistent throb of the drums and chanting that was almost shouting and crying.

Breathlessly, Adolphe arrived at a spot along the shore where the statue of Ste. Anne was erected, as one of the priests had commissioned before he had moved on. Suddenly he realized that a large group of people was assembled just across from him on the other side of the statue. They were still chanting, and their attention was on the lake.

Turning slightly, he saw that a man had waded out into the water towards the setting sun. A heavy bank of clouds billowed up from the horizon and lightning played across the blackness with bright fingers of light. As the sun disappeared behind the clouds, streaks of sunlight stretched upward in a brightly coloured fan from the dark base. The cloud resembled a head and the lining a golden crown.

Adolphe's first thought was, "A storm! Maybe this will be the end of this drought." His next thought was more anxious. "*What was that man doing out in the lake with an impending thunderstorm looming ominously.*"

Then he looked closer. The man was Louis Riel. The height with the powerful shoulders, the dark head of hair – what was he doing? He held something in his arms – no someone – a child. He was immersing the child in the lake – or was he drowning him?

Then with sudden dawning of realization, he knew that it was his John. Adolphe ran into the cool water with his clothes and shoes on, his throat too closed to call out, in the grip of panic. When he finally could speak, he croaked his son's name stretching out his arms. What was it that Father Blanchet had said? *The man is insane!* The water dragged at his legs slowing him down. *Let me reach the boy before it is too late.*

Riel met him and held the dripping wet boy out to him. His clothes, the light shirt, short pants and moccasins were soaking wet. "Behold your son!" Riel said simply as Adolphe snatched him and crushed the boy to his chest.

As he turned to head back to shore he noticed a difference in the boy. He did not hang limply as he had when Adolphe carried him to the shoreline in front of the platform and handed him to his wife. He wrapped his thin arms around his father's neck and shivered with a chill.

John squirmed to an upright position so that he could see over his father's shoulder the man who had held him under the water except for his face and had prayed a long prayer into his ear and then to the sky. He could not remember how he got there.

Julie met him at the shore, her face streaming tears and sobs racking her body. She reached for her son and stripped off the wet clothes, wrapping him in a warm blanket and rubbing him dry.

John shivered for awhile as his father carried him up towards their tent until he finally threw his blanket back and said, "I can walk by myself Papa. You do not need to carry me."

In shock, he set the boy down. John wound the blanket around his nakedness and walked by his father's side the last part of the way, chattering as they walked. "That felt fine, Papa. The water was warm, but the air was cold. Who was the man who took me out into the water?"

As though waking from a trance, Adolphe swung around towards the lake. The sun had disappeared behind the clouds along with the halo, crown of light, but the lightning still played across the thunderhead's surface.

"Riel," he said slowly to himself. "Riel did this, and I did not even acknowledge it." He looked around for Julie and saw her struggling to carry the baby who was crying in the push and shove of Métis humanity. Louis and Joseph hung onto her skirts and Vital was trying to pack the paraphernalia that they left behind. The thunderstorm was moving up fast, and a strong wind was snatching up anything that was loose and flinging it into the air.

People hurried to anchor their tipis as the wind tore them loose. Adolphe had to do the same. "I will carry these things into the tent Papa while you fix that corner that tore loose." John told him. Soon he was joined by Vital and Joseph who did the same thing, as normally as if there had been no recent miracle.

Hanging onto Daniel on one arm and holding Louis' hand with the other, all Julie could do was stand and stare as John moved around, laughing in the wind as though this were the most normal thing in the world.

They managed to hold the tent together and crowd inside with all of their possessions before the thunderstorm broke overhead and the deluge washed down the sides of the buffalo hide to the crash of thunder and the steady flashing of lightning.

The family curled up in their blankets and tried to keep out of the way of leaks or seeps underneath. The boys curled up inside the blankets giggling and squirming with delight in the summer's entertainment. They were warm and dry and revelling in family togetherness.

As the storm rolled away with just a steady light rain in its wake, John sat up in between his brothers and said, "I am hungry!"

His parents looked at each other and smiled, and Julie went rummaging for the pemmican she had tucked away.

44

Death of a Dream

The Land Commission was beginning to survey all of the land in the Northwest Territories. It had already started in the south and one of the things that Riel warned them about was not to expect to keep their land as they claimed it. Many of the Métis who came from the Red River Settlement stepped their lots out as they had before, stretching out from the river or waterway in long narrow lots. That was the way that made the most sense to them. Why should one person get the full use of the waterway for transportation or water usage and another family have to walk for their water?

The white Government men wanted to mark out the whole Northwest into large squares of land, even if the square fell in the middle of the lake. It made no sense to the Métis. Like the Métis at Frog Lake and along the Saskatchewan they were afraid they would lose the lots that they were granted.

Lucy and John did not go to the Spirit Revival Meeting at Lac Ste. Anne that year. Rose had been born not long before that, and she was too small to travel. Daniel was only two and was a handful for six-year-old Mary Jane and five-year-old Caroline to look after. A few days later Lucy's mother, Marie, came in the wagon to the trading post in the settlement and stopped in to visit with her daughter.

"You should have been there, Lucy. The Great Spirit was with us on the lakeshore that evening." Her mother wheezed into their one-roomed cabin in the woods near the creek. Lucy was more and more concerned about her mother's health. Marie Amable found it so hard to breathe that she gasped and puffed nearly every step she took. Her size did not help. She had put on a lot of weight over the years. Lucy did not get her size from her mother, it would seem. It must have been from her father who was thin, short, and wiry.

Marie sat by the stove on the cushion that Lucy offered and caught her breath after a coughing spell; her eyes reddened and watering. They had no room for chairs in their limited space, so they usually sat on the floor on blankets. Marie was also used to this arrangement, but she was finding it hard to get up when she got down onto the cushion.

"*Maman*," Lucy pleaded, "why do you not go to the medicine woman in the Big Lake Settlement. She could give you something for your cough. Sometime you might not get your breath back. It gets worse."

"I did go to her," Marie gasped and finally took a swallow of the Oswego tea that her daughter made for her. Lucy made it from the flowers of the purple bergamot found growing along the woods next to the trails. She added a touch of Hyssop for her mother's bronchial difficulty. Almost immediately her mother quieted and relaxed by the warmth of the fire as she sipped. "You make me feel better than she does. She is not the medicine woman that her mother was."

"*Mémère*," Mary Jane whispered as she curled up beside her grandmother on the blanket, "the leaves are falling down from the trees. Caroline and I bury inside a pile, and Maman can not find us."

"Mary Jane, you and Caroline must go now and gather moss. I need more for a liner to soak inside Rose's bunting, and I could find none to scrub the floor with this morning. I also need wood for the fire and water enough to fill the iron kettle by the fire."

"*Oui, Maman*." The girls left to dutifully perform their jobs though they would rather sit in their grandmother's lap and listen to grown-up talk.

"And Daniel is waking from his nap in the nook under our cot. Take him as well," Lucy called out.

"But Maman," Caroline complained, "he picks everything instead of the right moss – sticks and all, he fills the baskets with, and he drags behind trying to chase after the rabbits."

"That is your job to teach him the right way. How is he going to know if you do not teach him?" Lucy explained patiently as she turned away with a smile. The girls would have to be able to take over a lot more duties now that she was again pregnant. But they were bright and resourceful.

Mary Jane was six and Caroline was five. They were even learning to cook and to sew. She realized that she expected a lot from them, but they never complained.

After the children went out, Marie stretched out a leg and rubbed it. It had become painful to sit on the floor in a traditional cross-legged manner as well.

"I have a salve that I can rub on your leg, Maman. It will make it feel better. I make it from the balsam tree and from poplar buds. I will rub it on for you."

"I wish that I had you around all of the time, my daughter. But your small home can not hold any more. Your husband has built on a lean-to, but it is still not big enough for your family."

"*Oui*, sometime, Maman," Lucy waved it away. "Tell me more about the spirit meeting on the sacred lake. Tell me what happened that had you so excited."

"Oh, you should have been there, Lucy. Louis Riel picked up the son of Adolphe and Julie Perrault. He carried him into the lake as though he were a bent reed. On the shore, we all prayed for him not to die, but if the Great Spirit took him they would sing him to the land beyond the setting sun, where the spirit of the buffalo lived in the deep green valleys, and there is no more pain or starvation.

"Then we watched as Riel carried in a boy with the sickness washed away, shivering but smiling and hanging on to the strong wide shoulder of his big spirit helper."

Lucy's eyes widened, dumbfounded at the tale. "And others," Marie went on, "who waded out into the water to meet him and guide them in through the rocks and deep holes said that they felt a strange tingle in the water and a strength that seemed to flow up through their bodies. Father Chevrier could hardly believe it at first when we told him.

"But then later, in the mission church, he said that it must have been the water of the sacred lake and that they should build a shrine to Ste. Anne at the spot where they entered the water.

"Then there was further proof when Madame Lamoureaux, who waded out into the water to meet them, also felt the tingle right after she had fallen to her knees. When she got up she also felt a new strength, and since then she said she has not had the constant pain that she always experienced in her legs. The pain was gone – it never returned."

A chill rippled up Lucy's body and then an eager hope. "Maman, perhaps you should go to the meeting next year. Perhaps you could be cured of your breathing trouble when you think you might not ever take another breath and you struggle and wheeze."

Marie Amable paused for a long time before she spoke. "But this is very different from a weakness in the limbs. And besides, Louis Riel has gone back to Batoche."

But the hope hung between them like a bright light that shone just out of reach. "Perhaps he will be back, this Louis Riel. Maybe there could be one more miracle," Lucy murmured.

It was March, and winter still clung to the north country. After a long season of confinement to the cabin, Lucy longed to get out. Since William was born during the coldest of the months it kept her close to the fire, stoking it, keeping the cabin warm, only going out to attend chores that Mary Jane and Caroline could not do, and they stayed inside to look after the little ones. She could not wait until the warmth of summer came, and it would be time to travel to the sacred lake for the summer gathering again. This time she would not miss. William would be old enough. And this year would be especially exciting because they would take her mother. When they waded out into the lake, she would at last be cured of her lung trouble and asthma. It would happen because Louis Riel promised to again come for their prayers.

Of course, she heard of all the trouble down at Frog Lake and Batoche, but by then Louis and Gabriel Dumont would have won the provisional government. The Métis in the West would be declared a special people, a nation unto themselves, with special rights before the law. Louis Riel knew the law. In Upper Canada far away he had been part of the Government. He would see to it.

Lucy heard a sound outside. Knowing it was John home from work, she dropped the leggings she was working on and hurried to the door. The cold wind whipped inside as she watched John lead the horses to the low-roofed barn. The hay that he put up was nearly gone, and she knew that he was worried. It would be a long time before the new grass would be up.

And there was no grain for them. 'They can not work hard without grain to give them strength,' John had told her with concern.

A shuddering swishing sound could be heard, the sky drummers. She looked up into the dark blue overhead to see the ghost dancers of the aurora. The spirits were restless tonight. It was not a good omen; there would be more storms before the soft winds of spring blew. Perhaps she would not tell him that. It made him so unhappy when he wanted the grass to hurry and grow and they had no money to buy grain for the horses. What good did it do to worry about it? If it was to be, it would be. He could not fight it.

She pulled her blanket more tightly around her shoulders to keep out the cold as she walked to meet him at the barn. She watched from the door as he hung the harness on the wall hooks and threw down some of the remaining hay. His precious cow had to have some as well. Now that he had her bred – he took her miles to a farmer with a bull – he had to feed her. The calf would be expected in a month or so. He would have to buy some feed.

After helping him portion out the hay to the team and the cow they walked in silence back to the cabin. She noticed a troubled slump to his shoulders and a deepening in the creases on his broad forehead.

"It is time to make a change in our lives," John finally said as he finished his plate of stew and picked up his mug of tea. He said these very same words to her many times, but it seemed they were stuck in limbo, unable to move out of the inertia that they were living in.

"*Oui, mon mari*," Lucy agreed absently as she got up from her blanket on the floor to put his plate onto the cupboard. They had to dispense with a table and chairs to accommodate a bed along the wall for the three girls, Mary Jane, Caroline and Rose, so that Daniel and William could have their little spot beside their parents' bed. She could then reach out to William to comfort him in the night and bring him into her bed to nurse him. They still had the narrow bunk, just a bit above the floor, which made an ideal storage for much foodstuff underneath that could not be frozen, such as vegetables and canned goods. Even grain and meal was stored in sacks under there.

Lucy had a little rocking cradle-board for William, but he was old enough now to sleep beside his three-year-old brother Daniel. William was too big to be confined to the cradle-board anyway. She was able to reach out in the night and rock him as she had the others, but William could get warmth and comfort in the night from Daniel.

Lucy tucked the children in for the night, and she washed the plate and cleared away the stew pot, using the moss to clean it without the use of water.

The flickering light from the fire in the stove drew John's attention as it splashed its amber glow on the rolled-up blanketed forms of the children nearby. "*Non, ma petit femme.*" He spoke with such an odd tone that Lucy stopped her cleaning chores to turn towards him. "Things have changed for us. Sit down, I must tell you something very important."

Lucy squatted on the floor next to him, cocking her head to the side and frowning questioningly.

"Today I heard some news that you will find very disturbing." He paused, glanced at his wife, and plunged on. "It is all over the settlement about Louis Riel. In Batoche he has been preaching rebellion and was the leader in the fight against the takeover by Canada. They sent the N.W.M.P. and their troops to put down the rebellion. Riel told them that the Northwest was the property of the Indian and half-breed and that they could not take it over without negotiation with his new provisional government. But they did not listen. They fired their guns. People were killed. Riel surrendered and they took him away charging 'high treason.' There is anger and looting of Hudson Bay Company stores all over, at Ste. Anne and Hobbema. There is racial hatred everywhere between the whites and the natives."

"But Louis wanted nothing more than for the government to live up to the treaties they signed, or hand over the deeds to the land that the people have lived on for years!" Lucy was incredulous. "Did the priests not stop this from happening? They know how devout and good Louis is. He denied his own needs to help the Métis so desperately in need. He had supernatural powers with a mission to fulfill. He hated violence! He was a healer."

Lucy leaped to her feet, eyes blazing, her body vibrating with righteous wrath.

Rising slowly, John spoke with derision. "Priests are not religion! Only obedience to the Catholic clergy and to the government! They will not risk losing what they already have been conceded by the government. All the

Métis who believe everything that they are told by the clergy will soon understand that." John was just as righteously angry, but Lucy shook her head in denial against any suggestion that the priesthood would have anything to do with siding with the government against their people.

"*Non, non*, John! Father himself knows what a good man Riel is – how he brought about the first miracle of the lake. Now what will we do?" She suddenly stopped still at a new concern. "*Maman* was going to enter the lake this summer when Louis Riel was to come up for the celebration, and be cured of her asthma! *Mais non*! She was looking forward to this so much."

Upset, Lucy turned away with tears in her eyes while John approached to put a hand on her shoulder in consolation. "But that is not all of the bad news, Lucy," he apologized. "There is more. Something worse!"

"More about Riel?" Lucy swung to face him in alarm.

"*Non*! It is something else. It has to do with us." John dropped his hands to his sides with a sigh.

"What is it? What can be worse than this?" Lucy demanded as she braced for more bad news.

"I will soon no longer have a job. The sawmill will be taken down and moved into another location. The trees around here are depleted, and there are not enough to support the sawmill. For a long time I have been travelling farther and farther for the trees and the sawmill was shut down and waited for us to bring the trees in."

"So then you will find a job somewhere else – at another sawmill or maybe another job," Lucy shrugged.

"I do not know where that would be or how far I would have to have us travel to get there? And then where would we live?" John insisted on worrying.

"You would find a place the same way that you found this one," Lucy told him in all simplicity. "We would look for some land that had a nice stream, a river, or a lake for water. And you would look for some open meadows so that there would be room for your horses to graze and make hay for the cow – one with not too many trees but enough trees to cut some down to build a house for us. And when those trees are all eaten up by the white man's hungry sawmill we would find another piece of land when the big mill moves on again looking for more trees."

John broke into a rueful laugh. "*Oh, ma petite* Lucille! If only it were all that simple!"

"And it is not?" Lucy looked at him questioningly.

"For one thing," John explained, "You cannot park just wherever you wish to live. That land may belong to someone else. The Hudson's Bay Company owns a lot of land up here, and men have bought timber rights on some. Farther south, settlers bought their farmland, but up this way not much of the land has been mapped out yet; still, when you claim land you have to register it, or someone else could come along and say that we are 'Squatters' on their land."

"Squatters? What is Squatters?" Lucy wanted to know.

"That is when someone comes along and tells you that they legally own the land that you are living on – it does not matter that you got there first. We could stake it out, clear a lot of trees, and build a cabin only to have someone else say that we are sitting on their land. They were there first, and we have to get off."

"But **we** were here first – before the white fur trader," Lucy insisted. "The Métis and the native born were given the land by the Great Manito – by God! We could hunt and fish and even cut down some trees to build homes, but no one but God owns the land! The land is God's; no one can sell it!"

"Things are different now, Lucy," John reasoned. "We can not roam around after our meat and our furs and follow the buffalo herd. We have to stay on a piece of land and raise our own animals and grain and hay."

Lucy whirled around; standing straight, she faced her husband, and her eyes shone with intensity. "My grandfather once said, 'The earth belongs to the mystic Mother. Shall I plow the ground? Then I would be taking a knife to tear my mother's bosom. Then when I die, she will not take me to her bosom to rest.'

"Dig for stone the white man said. Shall I dig under her skin for her bones? Then when I die, I can not enter her body to be born again.'

"Cut grass and make hay the white man told me and be rich. How can I cut off my Mother's hair?'"

All that John could do was look back at her in sad understanding. He had seen it happening. The white man robbed Lucy's grandfather and her father and many others of their age-old skills. They weakened them with alcohol and the smallpox disease and they destroyed his self-respect trying to change him. John could do nothing but stare back helplessly at his wife who glared at him, straight and proud.

"This is our land, my grandfather said," Lucy went on fiercely. "It is not just a piece of pemmican to be cut in pieces and be given back to us."

"I know! I know!" John got up and came to her. Putting his hands on her shoulders, he looked into her flashing defiant eyes. "We can not turn back the river, and we can not turn back the flow of the white man into this country. We have to learn to live together, to share, and to learn from each other. If we try to accept the new ways, they can help us. Let us try to find where the land is available to us and try to become farmers like the government men have said."

Tears filled Lucy's eyes, and her shoulders sagged. "Let it be so, *mon cher*. Tomorrow I will go into the settlement. The government agent will be there to explain to the Métis and the many travellers who came from the south along the Saskatchewan, what they can do now that the 'Rebellion', as he called it, is over. We will see if they have changed their minds now that they have won, and we have all slunk away like dogs after the whipping."

Ignoring his wife's bitterness, John plunged on. "And I shall try to find out if the sawmill will be moved to a location where we can find a place to live. Maybe at the mission in St. Albert I can find news."

45

Scrip

St Albert had changed since the last time John Lenny saw it. As his horse picked her way up the incline, he looked down the slope and along the river at the many tipis and small cabins that climbed haphazardly up the hillside. Here the Métis came to find comfort and care when food was in short supply, and they were displaced. On top of the hill, though, was the biggest change of all. Construction was going on at a phenomenal pace. The biggest and most imposing was the new residential school for the Métis that they called the Convent. It was an impressive red brick – that new building material that was being made in Fort Edmonton.

The man supervising the assembly of the bricks for the Convent looked familiar to John, and he rode forward to investigate. When the man turned as John approached, he recognized the curly dark hair and wide smile of Adolphe Perrault.

"John Lenny, you are a sight to behold," Adolphe haled in his perfectly accented French as he stuck out his hand in greeting.

"I am so very pleased to meet you up here," John responded. "You are just the man I needed to see."

"Come and sit over here in the shade, and I will share a cup of tea with you." Adolph led John to a bench under a tree beside the mission church and haled a young Métis boy whose job it was to help in any way he could.

"I do not know if you realize, but the sawmill has shut down in the settlement up by Big Lake," John began, and when Adolphe nodded, hurried on. "It has put me without a job and without a place to live."

"*Ah, mais oui!*" Adolphe answered and added. "The new settlement is being surveyed and changed, I hear. Many Métis will be losing the land that they felt was their own because of the new divisions. The old method of long strips of land to the lake is no more. The large squares called acres will be measured out. All will have to move back from the lake."

"But how can they do that?" John wanted to know. "I remember when the Métis land agent told them which land they could claim in narrow strips from the lake back."

"But they could not make a living on that little strip of land. Now, they tell me, the new land arrangement would open it up for farming and they can start looking after themselves," Adolphe explained.

It sounded to John as though Adolphe agreed with the new arrangement, and he stared back at him aghast. "And do you know about the sawmill? Where will it be set up again? Where will you get your lumber for your buildings?"

"I do not know about the lumber. I know several sawmills that they will start to build on the creeks and rivers where the timber is thick, and the water will carry the trees down to the mills closer to the fort and to the mission. As you see, I have now gone into the business of building bricks. I am the only bricklayer on this job building the Convent so that Métis children can go to school and be taught the catechism. Some who are homeless will even be able to live here. Perhaps you could come and learn to be a bricklayer or carpenter," Adolphe ended.

"Where would you suggest that I live around here?" John asked quietly. "There is a claim on all of the land around here, and where there is no claim they will want money – I have none." He spread his hands in a gesture of futility.

"Maybe I could find a place for you and your family here in the village," Adolphe offered. "And the children would be close enough to attend the new convent."

"And what would I do with my horses and my cow? And how do I find the hay and grow the grain to feed them?" John asked, and when Adolphe hesitated, he went on. "No, I have to find land – a farm for my children to grow up on and for me to grow my own food so that someone else does not have to feed me."

"Then you must be prepared to travel away from the fort and the mission. You must strike out on your own. This is a big country with a lot of land that has not been spoken for or that does not have a timber lease attached." Adolphe stood up as an indication that it was time for him to get back to work, and John did as well. "By the way, how many children do you have now?"

"I have three girls aged seven, six, and one year, and two boys, aged three and the last one, William, the baby." John smiled proudly. "I hear that your son, John, is no longer as ill as when we last saw him," John added.

It was now Adolphe's turn to smile widely and proudly. "It was a miracle – the miracle of the sacred lake. He is growing strong and healthy. Just when I thought that he was going to breathe his last, he was snatched back from the very threshold of death after he was carried out into the waters of the Lake of Ste. Anne. There was no other explanation. It was a miracle!"

"I hear that it was Louis Riel who carried him out into the waters, weak and as limp as a wet reed. And Riel brought him back with new life and energy." The story fascinated John.

Adolphe sighed and glanced over at the unfinished job with the bricks piled up by the partly finished wall. He had this discussion so many times with his wife and then with Bishop Grandin. They each had a different idea about how it happened. And though he watched from the shore, he was now not sure how it happened.

Bishop Grandin and the priests at the mission said that it was Ste. Anne and the sacred lake that brought about the miracle. They said that it was not possible for Louis Riel to perform a miracle.

Julie insisted that without Louis it would not have happened. If it was not for the prayers of the people and that devout and forceful man, the water would have been as powerless as the waters of Big Lake. "What about Madame Lamoureaux?" she insisted as she paced about the little cabin in an agitated manner. "How many times did she wade out into that water in so much constant pain that she could barely walk anymore? And after coming in that evening with Riel and little John she has been completely free of pain. She walks like a young girl."

Adolphe was torn between believing Bishop Grandin and his wife. He had become tired of the whole discussion. Then when they took Louis Riel away a prisoner, his wife cried for days. Riel's life, it seemed was exchanged for her son John's, and even the priests had not done more to defend this amazing man. 'It was because he was Métis,' she decided. This was the end of the Métis 'Dream'. He was the last of the Dreamers. They were all at the mercy of the white traders and merchants. The fight was lost – there was no one to fight for them anymore.

"*Maintenant*!" Adolphe stated with finality, "I must get back to work" and he turned towards the partly finished brick wall. "Let me know if you need help finding a job here in St. Albert. Oh, and I forgot to mention," he added returning toward John. "A new flour mill is planned by a man called Gillespie here in St. Albert. You could work in the mill when it is set up. People are crying for flour to be ground right here in the territories, and farmers farther south are starting to get fields ready to grow grain. If you had land you could sell your grain to the flour mill."

"That's a pretty big 'if'," John mused and looked out across the trees and rolling hills to the west, "a very big 'if'."

They shook hands again as they parted, and John sprang aboard his horse, barebacked but bridled.

Lucy was already home when John rode up to the barn. She left the little ones in charge of seven-year-old Mary Jane and did not want to stay away too long. The baby, William, she took with her, slung on her back. If he were hungry, he would need to nurse. And Caroline, at six, was a big help. They knew how to get Rose and Daniel something to eat, if need be. They each had their jobs to do.

John was depressed. He had nothing to tell Lucy that was encouraging. They had to leave this place and all they had put into it and move soon, and he had no idea where. The creek gurgled at the bottom of the slope. It was still fairly high this spring but over the summer it would be almost non-existent. He speculated last fall about hauling water home from the lake. There had not been much snow during the winter to melt. *It was time they moved on*, he told himself.

Opening the door, he stepped in to the smell of pemmican frying on top of the stove and tea brewing. When there was nothing in the house to eat, Lucy always put a meal before them.

"I have news," she said as he closed the door behind him.

"I have nothing," John replied morosely.

The children sat cross-legged by the stove, sucking and biting on the hard pemmican piece they each held onto, the fat smearing their faces and fingers but savoured and licked off the fingertips.

"I was at the meeting in the settlement and the government agent was there to talk to us," Lucy told him as she handed him a plate with his supper and sat down near the children. "Now that the Rebellion has been put down, he said, the Métis are willing to take up farming. The buffalo and fur trade is gone and the Métis and natives are no longer waiting for Riel to bring them back and get control of the country so that we are all special and protected for the rest of our lives."

Lucy wrinkled her nose when she told him that. "Actually it was not Riel who was trying to **make** us a special people. We **are** a chosen people, a meek and humble people. The white man could not have existed in this land without us. They came to our land on the moving road, the Saskatchewan, to trade with us.

"We knew the wilderness. We were the best boatmen, the best guides, the best hunters, best trappers, and traders. That is what made us the chosen people.

"But now they forget all of that. They take our land and offer to give it back to us in small pieces if we will accept their way of life – to stay in one place and be farmers. But we did not remind him of that. He offered us what he called 'Scrip. It is a paper that says if we give up our claims to the land here, the land that does not reach the lake, we will be able to claim a bigger piece of land near a lake called Long Lake. And they will help to make us all farmers so that we can raise our own animals and be able to feed them."

"But that is wonderful, Lucy," John nearly shouted in his exuberance causing the children to stop their eating and stare at him. "I wanted to be a farmer, and have land of my own."

"It is given only to Métis," Lucy informed him. "But as my husband," she smiled, "you will be able to share in it." She reached into her pocket and took out the folded paper. The writing on it looked very official, signed and a seal at the bottom, but Lucy could not read it so she handed it to John whose eyes scanned it, and he nodded. "We must leave in three days with the others to stake out our land."

46

Under Attack

Long Lake had become a settlement much like Big Lake. Here they were able to stake out their long narrow lots right up to the shoreline so that they could use the water, use their canoes, and to fish. The only trouble was that the lake was very shallow, and they had to walk out on the sandy bottom for many yards before the water got deep enough to use their canoes. The fish were not very plentiful either, which alarmed them.

It was remote, however, and there were deer and moose, birds, and small animals in abundance. Most of all, they felt as though they were on their own, to arrange their lives as they pleased. They were back hunting, and the life they loved.

John alone, it seemed, noticed immediately that this was an arrangement to get them all out of the way – out of Big Lake area. They were supposed to clear land for planting because they were going to be farmers. A plow was sent with them. The government agent, Fielding, having come along with them and pointed out their lots, brought the plow and harrows on his wagon as well as sacks of grain for planting. They were apparently supposed to take turns with the machinery after they cleared the land of trees for the planting. In the meantime, the agent pointed out, since the water receded, it left an abundance of standing hay that could be cut along the lake for the horses and other animals to eat. Then he left for St. Albert again as soon as the families began to cut the trees for their cabins. In the meantime, they put up the tipis and built the communal fire down by the lakeshore at nights.

Many things bothered John. First it was the fact that the 'scrip' entitled them to one hundred and sixty acres each. This narrow strip was not one hundred and sixty acres. When were they going to get the one hundred and sixty acres that they were entitled to?

Looking out across the beautiful calm lake that mirrored the trees on the other side, it looked so pristine and untouched, and at the happy faces of the women who finally came through the long trek, it was hard to think of hard times to come.

He watched his wife and the other women dressed in their dull dark dresses that protected them from the mosquitoes, heading down to the lake with the laundry to wash. The girls in their bright calico giggled and teased as they ran barefoot into the water, pulling their skirts up to avoid the wetting, celebrating this new adventure.

How soon they forgot the ordeal they had all come through. The heavy Red River carts and loaded wagons sank into the sodden black muskegs and bogs and the men and horses waded up to their knees and bellies trying to pull them through.

Gales drove rain in torrents through the camp at nights, and left it waterlogged by morning. One particularly memorable occurrence came back to John. It was just before the thunderstorm, and they were hurrying to get to a better location for the night before it hit.

It was a blistering hot day, and every step was exhausting to the sweat-drenched troop. Every step they took through the deep grass along the nearly overgrown trail through the woods disturbed countless thousands of mosquitoes that attacked every inch of exposed flesh.

The dim trail took them by an algae-covered pond in the centre of a nearly weed-choked swamp that was open and free of trees. Suddenly a high-pitched whine, a high, unbroken, terrifying hum could be heard in the sky, and at that moment a cloud covered the afternoon sun. It was not the thunderhead; that was farther down on the horizon behind the trees. It was a phenomenon that many of their number who had come from the Red River Settlement had observed. It often preceded a thunderstorm. It was a huge swarm of mosquitoes, thick and dark enough to nearly block out the sun.

Frantically, the men tried to move their wagons into the bush, away from the open and attack.

"It is too late," someone shouted out over the screaming of the horses that sensed what was coming and tried to break free. "Unhitch the horses and let them find cover. *Get under cover!*"

While men hurriedly unhitched and turned the horses loose, the wind-born swarm bore down on the wagon brigade so fast that horses, dogs, cattle, and people were overwhelmed in seconds. Horses pitched, half un-hitched under the attack of the savage insects, and dogs writhed in agony on the ground.

John covered his cow with a blanket and tried to cover his team, but they pitched and snorted in terror and pulled away. He was covered with black stinging insects like a coat of fur in seconds and screamed out in pain.

"Leave them! Let them run!" Lucy called out over the deathly hum. "Come under the wagon. *Now!*"

Lucy took the children under the wagon and bundled them under their only buffalo robe. John, screaming with pain, ran and rolled through the grass and weeds until he reached the robe. He burrowed underneath a heavy blanket still dragging the horde with him, crushing and smothering them along the way.

It was stifling hot outside and even hotter and more smothering under the tightly rolled up robe and blankets.

"Maman," Mary Jane cried. "I can not breathe. I need to get my head out."

The other children cried with similar complaint, but Lucy warned them, "Keep covered up!" as she pulled the robe and blankets even tighter and struggled to kill the insects that worked their way inside and were un-mercifully attacking Daniel and the baby. "If you put your head out, it will feel like it is cut with a knife. It will not be long. Do not move the blankets. They will get in!"

The hum was deafening and terrifying as they could still hear the screams of people and animals around them. But after a sharp word from their mother, the children lay still even though there was a terrible urge in each of them to thresh about, tear at their skin, and fight for air. They listened to her soothing voice repeating a prayer she often recited to them at their sick bed, or when she rocked them to sleep at nights.

Then another sound took over. Thunder grumbled, then growled, and then roared its warning. It crashed overhead like an avalanche of rock falling upon them. The little troop under the robe relaxed and ventured to peep out. The mosquitoes were gone, and the rain pelted the wagon over their heads. The buffalo robe with its fur side in was keeping the water out.

The storm's violence did not last long, and soon the blankets and robes were peeled back, and the family crawled out from under the wagon. The first sight that they saw was their father's welted face, swollen so that he could hardly see, and hands bitten painfully.

Upon exploration they found a pitiful sight. Two dogs that had been attacked by insects six inches thick were lying bloody and dead. Two other men, before getting their animals and family covered, had been attacked so badly that their arms and hands streamed blood and their faces were unrecognizable.

Lucy went into action giving everyone soothing burdock leaves from the water's edge to put on the bites as a poultice.

John looked around in alarm and could not find his horses. His cow survived though her legs streamed blood, and he wiped her down with the burdock leaves.

Whimpering and crying could be heard from children suffering with painful bites, and searches were made for lost and escaped animals or youth.

An hour later, happy news arrived. Three of the older youth arrived driving the horses ahead of them. The boys successfully outran the mosquito horde by leaping on the horses and racing away ahead of the horde. When the thunderstorm passed, they rounded up the animals, some of them tangled in their harness and the trees and brought them back to camp.

Grateful beyond words and with a lump in his throat, John led his horses away, after gripping one of the young men by the shoulder and giving it a squeeze to say thank you.

It was like that with these people. They could have just run to save themselves or their own animals, but they searched until they found everyone's. It would have taken John days! They were that way about everything. When the Métis and Indian agent days later, brought in the cattle there was supposed to be enough for each man, but there was not. That was all right; several men said they would share theirs. Not only did they share, but they owned them and looked after them communally, making one big corral and taking turns herding them out on the grass by the lake. If someone did not have horses, the others shared theirs.

John was the exception. He did not want to share his horses and was embarrassed to have to refuse. But he let them know as gently and in as friendly a manner that he could, that this team was his own – the first thing that he bought with his money that he earned – the same with the cow. He marked her conspicuously so that all would know that this was his. They looked at him strangely, but they said nothing, and did not touch John's cow. John felt badly, but this was important to him.

There was only one other white man in the settlement who married a Métis woman, Danny Gunn, an ex-Hudson Bay Company man like himself. He owned very little so he was willing to share with the camp what he had in the way of tools or skills.

Danny was a lot like the Métis in temperament, easy going, not too ambitious or energetic, and they were fond of him. He was tall, lean, and sandy-haired with a prominent nose and blue-grey eyes, an easy smile and a love for the lake and fishing. Like many of the Métis men he loved to gamble. In their games of chance and skill he was a very willing participant and was quite talented and athletic, especially in the wrestling.

The other white man was the government agent, Thomas Fielding. He was a dark-haired, dark-bearded Englishman with an obvious accent, and had trouble speaking French but managed to make himself understood. He wore a black felt hat and had a powerful build. With their slight lean bodies, the Métis were obviously in awe of this man. He had a high forehead, straight nose, and intense blue eyes.

John felt an instant dislike for the man. He seemed to be talking 'down' to the Métis as though he was trying to explain something to a group of children. Fielding stayed with them only long enough to point out where their land extended and that the grain should be kept in a cool dry place until they were ready to plant. He pointed out that they should divide up their land equally as they saw fit and start to clear it as soon as possible and build homes.

When the mosquitoes attacked, Fielding panicked until one of the women forced him to wrap up in his blankets, but not before he was badly bitten and screamed for help like one possessed.

When Fielding brought the cattle on the second visit, he had not asked about the welfare of the people, how they were doing, or taken time to answer any questions. The only one he paid any attention to, or asked what had been done since he was last there, was John, and John felt that the man knew nothing so answering reasonable questions was useless. His departure was not noted, and his presence was not needed.

Every time John thought about him, it made him angry. He felt that some day the same thing was going to happen as had happened in Big Lake. They laid their lots out as they always had, but some day the land authority would survey it according to their regulations, and there would be upset and confusion.

47

Organization and a Métis Wedding

Every day at Long Lake seemed to be constant bedlam, and John resisted the urge to press for the land division to be completed, so that he could get started on his cabin. Summer was not going to last forever.

He felt close to one man called Janvier Majeau and his young wife Louise. Janvier was also anxious to get his cabin set up and his lot located. His wife was soon expecting her baby and he wanted her to be close to John and Lucy. Lucy began to make a name for herself as a medicine woman, and had already come to help Louise when she was sick.

Janvier knew that it was not something to be rushed. He said that first they have to organize a camp government to make decisions. That made sense to John.

Around a huge campfire, one night after they all feasted on a delicious venison stew from a young deer that the youth brought down, they met. John now discovered that the three young men, aged fourteen, fifteen, and sixteen were Michel, Gerard and Henri. He would not forget them for bringing back his horses, and now they were supplying the camp with meat.

The women and children retired to their circle of tents, leaving the men to their special meeting. Janvier explained to John as they sat cross-legged around the fire towards the back of the circle. "The supreme commander, or chief needs to be selected now that Fielding, the agent is gone. After the last few days of testing, talking, and observing, we need to select the best one to fit the job. Just the same way as they used to do in the buffalo hunts."

A Métis man, whom John remembered was Pierre, stood up to address the others. His muscled brown shoulders and arms that bulged from the sleeveless shirt glistened with lean strength. John noticed and admired the Indian and Métis men as fine people, well proportioned, tall and straight, slightly formed, but strong. These people were extremely active and enduring. Many times John contrasted them in his observations to the broad-waisted, short-necked Englishmen or the flat- chested, long-necked Scots.

"I have known Joseph L'Hirondelle for many years. He is a great hunter and chooses wisely in all things. He led many hunting parties as captain and spoke for us all when we needed to approach the Métis agent. Joseph is brave and wise. In stories around our campfires, he told of his adventures and his daring. I propose that he should be our commander in chief." Pierre sat down to enthusiastic pounding of heels on the ground and slapping of thighs.

Another name was not proposed, and John realized that they made this decision long before bringing it before the council. It was not a spur of the moment nomination.

Joseph stood up. An older man, with straight grey sprinkled long hair, hanging down from a battered felt hat, his brown face beamed his pleasure. Though not a powerful man, he was tall, straight, and strong, very likely the oldest one in the group.

Though obviously pleased with the proposal, he spoke seriously, his deep voice booming with authority. "I proudly accept this nomination and will do my best to lead the settlement of Long Lake to the best of my ability. I, in turn, would like to suggest that as captain we select the man who has led buffalo hunts on the prairies, hunting expeditions for furs, and has been the most successful of all in the hunting of the moose. Pierre Gauthier deserves to be captain of our Long Lake camp."

Again there was thunderous response to the suggestion, and, it seemed, all present agreed with the new chief's selection. This was a new kind of democracy but John marvelled at how well it worked.

There was the selection of guides next. John noted that this selection of leadership seemed to pertain to living in a hunting and gathering society, not to a community that was learning how to become farmers. What about the land and lot divisions and the building construction? Were they all on their own in selecting a site and cutting the trees? Who was responsible for school, community centre in the form of church or meeting place? They could not always meet out here on the ground. And most important, what about a trading post? Would there be one? They needed to trade with the white people for things they did not produce. It could be the trees that they take off their farmland – trees that were not used for their own buildings. There were so many unanswered questions.

John already investigated. There was a creek running into the lake that could transport logs down to a mill, but they had no way of transporting lumber or logs from there south to Fort Edmonton. The land was quite rough with muskeg extending back from the lake and hills beyond that – not very suitable for farming, but the trees could be harvested.

John noticed the discreet way the Métis had of avoiding his eyes and the eyes of Danny Gunn when the selection was made for guides and leaders. When their eyes did meet, it was apologetic as though to say, 'Although you are white men and bring to the settlement much information about the white world, for this job we need Métis. We need people who understand the inside workings of a Métis organization.' And that was all right with John. He just wanted to make a place for himself and his family in this new territory and among these people.

As time went by, and the trees were cut and used in the building of the cabins, he turned his attention on the several 'chains' wide, 'two-mile-long' lot that was assigned to him. He had to try to bring this piece of land into some kind of production. Pierre, the captain, had them working in groups of four, helping each other on their homes. On his, John specified how it was to be built, and though the others complained that this was much bigger than the other homes, he insisted on the design. With Janvier's help, he won out, and they worked together on their own designs long after they helped building other homes in their group.

None too soon were the bare bones of the cabins up when the chill in the air in the evenings indicated that the season was about to change. One evening as John and Janvier were working on lacing the bark pieces to the roof for shingles and adding pitch from the trees along joints to seal out the rain, Joseph called the men of the settlement together.

"It is soon the 'moon of migration,'" he announced after the usual chant to bless the gathering and to call all together. "The people that Pierre selects will leave the rest of the building to others and will trap and catch the geese for the women to prepare for the winter. A small party will travel to St. Albert to get what is necessary for preparing for the cold season–salt, bullets, and so on. Another party will gather grain heads and cut down and gather in hay along the lakeshore for the animals. The women will bring in bulbs and roots to store."

John and Janvier volunteered to stay with the building. He chafed to complete his own without having to spend any time on the other homes, and any chance he got, he slipped away to work on his own. Some were already moving into their unfinished homes, and John was trying to work around them. *As long as he had the stoves into place they could finish their own*, he thought. Others tried not to criticize, but they felt, that had he not been putting so much into his home, he would have more time to put to others.

Lucy was a godsend to him. She saw to it that a store of grain and seed was gathered in and stored in the structure that he hurriedly put up. The girls and even Daniel and Rose helped to bring in hay by the armful as well as digging up tuberous roots and the vegetables that their mother planted when they arrived. They would see to it that the horses and cow would have enough for the long winter – especially the cow; the horses could paw for their fodder if need be.

Before they knew it, the freezing-up moon was upon them. The evening sky and the trees around them were aflame, pulsing with the brilliant colours of red and yellows. The bugle chorus of wild geese filled the sky, and the lake throbbed with colour and sound. There was so much to be crowded into so little time before the long night. Winter, the relentless ruler of the land, would soon be upon them. A thin scum of ice bordered the long shoreline and began to creep out across the water.

As John predicted there was not nearly enough pasture for the cattle, especially once the hay was gathered in. The cattle tried to stray away from their community pasture, and the children were enlisted to herd them in areas that was cleared of trees, and other areas up the creek.

Grumbling started to filter down to John from those who thought that the cows were a nuisance. Someone always had to be there to look after them, and as soon as the hunt was on for the moose and deer, who needed them? Only two produced milk for babies whose mothers did not have enough milk, and the rest did nothing but cause problems. They wandered away, got stuck in the muskegs or in the boggy end of the lake, or trampled on the hay that had been gathered, or needed to be gathered, and they depleted the pastures needed for the horses. Oh well, the Métis men thought, if we have nothing else to eat we could always kill one.

John carefully saved his sack of grain to plant in the spring, but others used up the grain storage now with no intention of planting in the spring. While John worked hard grubbing out stumps behind his house and on the neighbours' land so that ground could be prepared for planting the wheat and garden seed carefully saved, others felt that they had land cleared for their homes; that was enough. They were not thinking like farmers!

John did admit with chagrin that there really was not enough land here that could be planted. Behind his cabin on his two-mile stretch to the west, there was a mile and a half of muskeg. Between him and the lake there was only room for garden, community purpose, and pasture. The muskeg was valuable to the women as they foraged every day for cranberries and moss, which was used for many purposes from scrubbing tool, or Oswego tea, to baby-bunting-soaker. They could also dig easily and deeply into the muskeg for cool storage. But to a farmer the muskeg was a waste of land and useless except for the birch wood or tamarack for posts that he might find on it.

Before winter arrived, and after most of the autumn work was done, a wedding was celebrated. She was a young fifteen-year-old marriageable Métis girl, and he was a handsome nineteen-year-old youth with dark straight hair and black eyes that danced and glistened with life and energy. Marie and Paul knew each other since they were little. He waited only until Marie was fifteen as her father demanded, and then he would marry her.

As a special wedding present, her father and his relatives would build their first home. The couple moved in right after the wedding and finished the home together. When it had a floor, a roof, and a stove built, it would be declared ready to live in.

Each hut was sometimes home to two or three families if it was large enough. For the wedding, though, it was decided that John and Lucy's house, being the biggest, would host the wedding. John shrugged, saying that it would be a good time for a house-warming.

The Métis loved a party, any excuse for a party, but a wedding was the happiest time of all. For weeks ahead, the relatives and friends prepared. Three big geese were killed to feed the guests and were roasted in a covered pit outside with a fire and hot rocks over the dirt covering to bake them through. On another outside grill over hot rocks, dough cakes were fried and potato galettes sizzled with wild onion and chunks of fat. Berry pies and puddings baked in an outdoor oven made mouths water.

A fermented drink made from the muskeg cranberry that was used as a ceremonial wine was poured out freely after the ceremony. Before the activity moved inside, John hauled out a surprise. He had come across it when they moved and again, when they unpacked to move into the new house. This would be perfect to celebrate a wedding.

As soon as the ceremony was over, John stepped out of the house dressed in his kilt, sash, and sporran. He blew up the bag of his pipes, and it emitted a sound like they had never heard before. All stepped back in shock and surprise, but the bride and groom rose to the occasion and marched down the aisle as though it had always been part of the wedding ritual - the lilting groan of a Highland tune. Soon everyone was following in a procession, in, out, round about, under arms, laughing and hooting until they ended at John's door and the music stopped. By this time the party was about to begin.

All furniture that John made, except for his stove, was moved outside to the shed to make room for everyone inside. As John put away the bagpipes, out came the fiddles expertly played by Pierre and Janvier. Soon the thud of moccasined feet thumping out 'The Reel o' Cats' and 'Pair o' Fours' could be heard all up and down Long Lake. Then there was 'The Red River Jig' which brought out all the men and women whose light foot and staying power might win them the title of 'Jig Champion!'

Hopefuls like Michel, Gerard, and Henri and many others crowded the floor, stomping, tapping, legs flying, leaping, and twisting to enthusiastic applause and shouts of encouragement.

Just as the song came to an end and the winner was proclaimed a shout of "Ho Ho!" was heard. A scuffle erupted in the corner and rolled out across the middle of the dance area against everyone's legs.

The groom chased after the culprit who stole the bride's shoe. The bride, as custom dictated, was given a pair of ornate shoes, hand made with white fringed buckskin, heels and laces that wound around her ankles, and ended in a bow over her instep. They were beautiful, a work of art. All evening she guarded those shoes lest someone should steal one of them, and then earn the right to ask for a ransom from the groom. In the meantime, while she and her new husband warily watched the precious shoes, she was expected to dance with all those who asked, but only if they presented a small gift for the privilege.

When one young man reached for her shoe as she sat on the ledge beside the stove, which was not as yet lit, he grabbed for the shoe and nearly managed the escape rolling under other legs. But Paul snatched it away just in time while the culprit, as expected, was ejected from the party. The frivolity continued, and also, as expected, the culprit crept back in but was not allowed to try for another snatch.

This time, however, the grab was successful and John saw young Jules Fourmond leap up behind the other dancers, having evaded the bridegroom, proudly waving the lovely shoe in the air. While the entire assembly clapped and slapped their legs, they called out for the ransom to get back the bride's shoe. Paul, joining in gamely, his black eyes sparkling with good spirit, hauled out his new carving knife, exchanged it for the shoe and put it back on the slim little foot, lacing it up so that it would not happen again. While he pulled back the bride's skirt so that the laces could be tied up as far as the knee the clapping and cheering, tittering and teasing swelled.

Then the music started up again, and the groom and bride led off a slow sentimental dance while the couple edged towards the door to make their escape. Other dancers kept heading them off and pushing them back into the middle of the floor until, after a quick break-for-it, they made their escape – as planned – as expected. And the party went on until all hours.

Revellers finally exhausted, one by one, two by two, faded into the night as the first flush of dawn was seen across the lake to the east. Drummers packed up worn and finger-marked drums; fiddlers squeaked out one last dying note; children who had gone to sleep in the corners were thrown over parents' shoulders and trundled home. Another couple was launched into marriage.

48

Miracle Birth

It was two years since they took Riel away, convicted him, and hung him, but Julie had not forgiven the white people, the government, and even the clergy that allowed this to happen. This Joshua, this prophet, this saint had been murdered, and no one had lifted a finger to defend him. Along with his life went the rights of all the Métis people. Her family moved from the Red River Settlement to the West and had not won their rights and freedoms.

Riel lost his life because he wanted to get the government of their land to live up to the treaties they signed. The native bands hated reserve life, but they signed the treaties looking for a better life.

For two years Julie refused to go back to the summer meeting at the sacred lake. Though Bishop Grandin called all the faithful to the mission, inviting them to the mission school and church, she would not go with Adolphe. Even though her husband was very proud of all he had accomplished in the building of the convent, she refused to attend.

"God has given us back our son; his life was spared. It was God who accomplished this," Adolphe pleaded. "It was not a priest or a lake or even Louis Riel. It was your Great Manito – God!"

Julie looked at her tall, strong, and healthy son John with the wide and beautiful smile, and her heart leaped again with gratitude. He was now thirteen, and his shoulders were broadening. For three years, she jumped up every morning to look at him rolled up in his tangled blankets beside Vital, Joseph, and Louis. When four-year-old Daniel declared himself no longer a baby and able to sleep with his brothers rather than the foot of his parents' bed, she found him curled up beside his favourite brother, John.

Daniel, with the dark curly hair like his father, the cherub face with the dimples, and the round saucer-like brown eyes, always brought out the urge to smother him with motherly kisses. Now he was no longer the baby. He was replaced in the cradle by Samuel. Samuel was a sweet baby, but he did not have that look of the angel cherub as did Daniel.

"Bishop Grandin still asks why you do not come to the mission school," Adolphe still pressed on. "The boys come to get their lessons, and they are so smart. The nuns said so. They know their numbers and their letters and recite their prayers every morning. Next year, Vital will be old enough to learn to be a brick-layer at my side.

"This is all you want for your sons?" Julie finally demanded. "Other people own the land, but you are satisfied only to work for the priests putting up their buildings and making bricks for them but not for yourself?"

Adolphe was shocked. Momentarily he had nothing to say. "Is this then what you would have for your boys? They should have no trade, but be a farmer and own land?"

"They should have skills, but they should be able to apply them to their own land. That is what the white men do. They seem to hurry to have their land marked out and state that it is theirs." Julie placed her hands on her hips and stuck out her little chin stubbornly.

"Do not forget, my Julie, that I am also a white man. If I sign on to one of the new land parcels on the other side of the river and up the hill where the men have surveyed, will you promise to come back to the mission? Will you then bring Samuel to be baptized and apologize to Bishop Grandin for being absent from Mass for so long?" Adolphe bargained with his wife with a twinkle in his eye.

"*Oui*," Julie agreed with a sigh. "Now bring me that bucket of water from the river. I have four big boys and their father waiting for their meal and I am always out of water!"

The farm was a good idea. With four big strapping boys and another two coming up in their footsteps, it grew in leaps and bounds. Adolphe took time off from building on the mission's needs to teach his sons the trades of carpenter, brick maker, and farmer. The boys loved the farm. They loved taking down the trees and readying them for use in their house and farm buildings. Adolphe loved to see the brown muscles bulge and the glow of health in those cheeks. They were all close enough to the mission to continue their education and Adolphe his service there.

It was at the mission the day that Julie brought Samuel to be baptized that she recognized someone she remembered from Lac Ste. Anne on the day that Louis Riel came to serve in the cure of her boy John. "Madame Gladu," she called out as Marie Amable and her husband Joseph were getting into the wagon to drive off. Marie was breathing audibly and laboriously with the exertion. "You are still having a very hard time with your breathing, I see," Julie commented as she approached the wagon. "I remember that you were at the lake when Riel brought about the saving of our son, John. I hoped that you would have been next to try for the miracle."

"As did I," Marie wheezed and puffed in a half whisper. "I came here - today - because I heard - of a man who has - performed miracles. I - asked - around the mission — but no one - has heard - of him."

"What is his name?" Julie pursued. "The priests here would surely know of him. They were saying only this morning when Father Lizée came to talk to Bishop Grandin that there are no more gatherings at the sacred lake since the rebellion. There is no more need for the ceremony in the dedication of the great hunt. They are all so disillusioned and disappointed that no one comes. There are no festive activities, no Métis and natives coming from many miles away."

Joseph interrupted the conversation derisively. "Of course they do not come! At first they were frightened for fear that they would be arrested as a Riel supporter. And then there was no reason to return. As a nation we are shattered beyond repair. We have no one like Riel to hold us together." Joseph, once a man strong and proud of his heritage, now was bent and tiring. He was now fifty-six, but starting to look prematurely to his last days.

"They need a reason to return," Julie announced. "If the sacred lake is what brought about the healing of my son, we need to take those in need of healing to the lake. We need another Riel to lead us to the lake again. Maybe we can find it in this man of whom you speak. What was his name?"

"Albert Calliot!" And the Gladus drove away leaving Julie with a new fire in her heart. She told Adolphe about it in hopes that he may have heard something. Adolphe shook his head, thought about it awhile, and then dismissed it. But Julie, through the winter that followed, pursued the idea like a dog with a bone.

When there was a meeting in the St. Albert Settlement in early November about a moose hunting party northwest of town, Julie decided to attend. Bundled up in her leggings and moccasins with the long laces that wound around the leg to the thigh and her blanket capote and mittens, she dressed the children and set off. It was so cold that the sled runners shrieked on the wind buffed snow surface. With frost trimmed eyes Daniel and Samuel peeked out of the blankets they were wrapped in. Around the bonfire the people, their breath spurting in a frosty mist, stamped their feet and gossiped while waiting for everyone to assemble.

"I hear," Julie started her rumours, "that there is a healer down from the cold north of the Peace River who will be coming to the gathering at the sacred lake next summer."

"I did not know that there was to be a gathering," said Madame Belcourt in surprise. She always knew gossip before anyone else.

"It is a new plan. Madame Gladu will be one of the first to wade into the healing waters to rid her of her asthma."

"What is the name of this healer?"

"I will try to find out." Julie moved on to talk to someone else. "Tell everyone you know about the gathering."

When Julie heard that Father Lizée would be coming to the mission to speak at Mass and to see the children in the residential school that he had baptized in Lac Ste. Anne, Julie again insisted on the whole family attending in the cutter. Again she spread the word to anyone that she knew that may have attended the gathering at Lac Ste. Anne before.

"I did not hear that the gatherings had started up again," said Marie Laderoute. "There has not been one for three years. What did you say that the healer's name is?"

"I am not sure – Alfred or Albert or something. But I for one am not going to miss it. You remember when Louis Riel brought about the healing of my son John. It was a miracle, and I would not miss another one."

The word spread from meeting to meeting until the mysterious healer was a fact - until the gathering was a definite happening. Excitement was beginning to build and Julie was beginning to panic. No one had ever heard of this healer by the name of Alfred or Albert. But people longed for the gathering as it used to be. It left a void in their lives these last three years since drought and starvation killed the practice. A terrible need was awakened in the hearts of many, and Julie was feeling the sharp stab of guilt. Fear wound around her heart at the thought of someone demanding that she admit it was all a lie.

In the early spring, the banks of snow started to shrink and rivulets everywhere sprang to life forming pools of slushy water. The Perrault farm was turned into a sea of mud. Adolphe had but three cows, a few pigs, chickens, and two horses, but they stirred the corralled space into soup with the sudden warm spell.

As yet they had very little land cleared, and as summer loomed ahead, they knew they had to make fields to plow and plant grain, as well as for hay. They needed to open the land into meadows for pasture. The animals would soon need to graze. That land needed to be fenced so that the animals would not wander away into the wilderness. Much to be done! So far they concentrated on their buildings, corrals, and clearing the small area around the buildings. That meant grubbing out the stumps, and putting up wood to be used in building corrals, or for firewood.

"Where is Louis?" Vital burst into the house to ask his mother. Already Vital was muscled, brown and wide in the shoulder. Though he was but sixteen, he was as tall as his father.

"And I should know this?" Julie remarked over her shoulder. She was busy making soap. On such a nice day she could cook the mess of lye, rancid fat, and wood ashes outside over an open fire. She had enough trouble keeping Samuel out of harm's way. Daniel would have to see to that. Ten-year-old Louis would have to be responsible and look after himself.

"The horses broke down the corral, and Petit-Rouge got out and wandered away," Vital told her in an annoyed tone of voice. "The horses are now in and the other two cows, but I sent Louis after Petit-Rouge. Joseph and John left the tree cutting to help me fix up the corral again. We cut new rails and strapped them together, since we have no more nails. Louis had one thing to do – bring in one cow. He is following the streams to the river more than likely, and forgetting his task. He wanted to take the gun out yesterday to shoot rabbits, but Père said that he was too young yet to shoot. He did not take the gun, did he?"

By this time, Julie forgot the soap making and started to worry. Louis was adventuresome. He loved to work with his hands, and if something was broken, he kept at it until he fixed it. The gun was his most recent fascination.

"But Louis knows enough not to forget about Petit-Rouge. He would stay with her until he brought her home." Suddenly another thought struck Julie. "Vital, Petit Rouge is going to calve soon. This is her first calf. Maybe that is why she wandered away; she was looking for a place to have her calf."

"The barn was right there," Vital argued. "And there was a stall with straw in it. Why would she go out into the snow, slush, and mud?"

"Who knows why animals do what they do!" Julie became impatient with her oldest. "You leave what you are doing and go look for Louis right now! If he found her, he would not leave her – you know that!" She pushed him out of the door, and then followed him out, standing in the middle of the yard littered with wood, the clothes line poles, the soap-making fire and materials. She twisted her hands inside her apron as she bit her lip. Watching Vital start out for the bush, she called out. "Vital, take John and Joseph with you. You may need help."

The sun was dipping below the horizon, and a thin pale crescent moon hung in the darkening eastern sky. Louis knelt beside the heifer and stroked her belly.

"Try little one. Do not give up. Your baby is trying to be born. See the little feet are sticking out. I will try to pull them. You should not have come out to this cold place."

Louis pulled with all his might until sweat stood out on his forehead, but the calf would not budge. The cow found a place in the shelter of a spruce tree that had fallen over, pulling up ground with it, and forming a hollow where there was no snow or water. With the sun's descent, cold crept in where during the day it had been warm.

The boy tried to get the heifer to walk home to have her calf, but there was no use. He could not bring himself to leave her here on the cold ground. At first, she struggled to birth the calf, but now she lay still and struggled no more, giving in to her fate.

Louis was not even sure he knew the way home now, and he shivered in his shirtsleeves and looked down woefully at his little jacket that he had thrown over Petit-Rouge. A terrible and unexplained sadness opened within him. Then a distant howl let him know that other animals sensed death and would soon move in if he left the defenseless heifer.

Finally, in frustration, not wanting to stay and not wanting to leave the suffering animal that he identified with, suffering the same agony, he threw himself down beside Petit-Rouge and began to cry. Great heaving sobs tore from his throat and he cried out to anyone who might hear him: "Help! Help me!"

Suddenly there was a light touch on his shoulder. He looked up, startled and frightened, to see standing over him a brown face with long black braids streaked with white hanging down from a battered felt hat. The man was dressed in buckskin and a blanket was thrown around his shoulders. But his eyes held Louis' like a magnet, soft brown, gentle, and sad. Crinkles of age lined his face and spread out from his eyes.

"What is it, little one?" the old man asked in Cree in a soft tired voice. Louis knew a smattering of Cree from his mother and understood.

He caught the man by the arm and begged. "Please help her. She will not try anymore, and her sides do not heave as they did. They are barely moving. If we do not help, she and the baby calf will die."

Looking down and circling the cow, the old man saw the little feet extending from the cow where the head should have been protruding, and he knew that the heifer could not do this; she was prepared to die. She had struggled for as long as she could - for most of the day and had given up. It would not be long for her.

Looking across the heifer at Louis, his little face puckered with sorrow and streaked with tears, the man's heart lurched. "I will do what I can, young one.'

He knelt beside the heifer and lay his hands on her extended belly. Then he lay his head against her side and Louis heard him moan. He heard a prayer in Cree, an ancient one that he could not understand. Between the moans and the increased intensity of the prayer in volume and emotion, Louis sat back and shuddered with cold fear and anxiety.

The man's hands on the belly of the cow vibrated and pressed; his shoulders bulged with the strength that flowed through his arms. Then a great cry tore from the man's lips, and he threw back his head, agony in his face, before collapsing on the belly of the small heifer.

At that moment there was a change in the animal. Her sides heaved, and a great surge of strength seemed to envelop her. Louis watched in joyous fascination as the heifer began to push the legs through. Steadily the calf began to emerge, and the old man moved to the end to pull on the legs, until the calf lay struggling on the ground in its delicate skin sac.

The man stepped back, and the heifer got to her feet, turned her attention to her calf, and began to lick him clean and dry. The new baby stood, with his mother's urging, on wobbly legs, and Louis cried with joy and relief as he began to move forward to help the calf, and to dry him with his jacket against the increasing cold of the evening.

Petit-Rouge would have none of it, however. She got in between the calf and Louis in a warning to stay away from her baby while Louis laughed through tears.

"Now you had better take these two home." The man spoke up and Louis turned to him, his eyes wide with surprise and gratefulness. Then he noticed that the man was dripping sweat, and his face looked older and more lined than he observed before. His shoulders slumped and he looked as though he might fall over with weakness. Louis moved towards him because it looked as though the man might stagger and fall.

"Lean on me, *Monsieur*," Louis pleaded. "Are you all right? You saved her. I thought that she was going to die, but you saved her." The words tumbled out as he reached out to the man in support. The hand that he placed on Louis' shoulder was so hot with fever that it burned Louis, but he did not flinch or pull away.

"Come home with us. I do not think I can find the way, but we could help each other," Louis suggested.

"The heifer will find the way. You only need to follow her and the calf," he replied in a voice so tired, so exhausted, that it was almost inaudible. "I will stay here and rest." Then he sat on a log and held his head in his hands.

The heifer started out towards home with her calf following on wobbly stilted legs, and Louis started to follow but returned in consternation for his new friend.

"But you must come with us. I can not leave you behind. Please come. You can sleep at our house for I see you are very tired." Louis spoke in French, but he was able to understand the Cree that was spoken to him.

When the man saw that Louis was not going to follow the cow and calf without him, he rose unsteadily to his feet and walked slowly and painfully beside them. The cow and calf were just as slow so it took a long time to make any progress. Strangely enough, Louis had no concern that he did not know where he was, or in what direction they were heading. The man said that the heifer would lead them home, and he trusted implicitly.

At one point when they stopped to rest, and Louis offered his shoulder for his friend to lean on, he asked, "My name is Louis Perrault; what is your name?"

"Albert Calliot," he replied.

49

The Hunting Moon

As John feared, no grain got planted that spring or the next. It seemed as though there was no room for fields, and there had not been enough trees cleared. Besides, the grain had been ground and used to feed themselves as well as animals they had taken along. What field area they did have, had to be for pasture or hay to feed the horses and cattle.

Then the cattle began to dwindle. The people began to use them as feed to carry them through the winter instead of building their herds. To be fair, it had to be remembered that no bull came with the herd, and they would have to travel many miles to have the cows bred. John's cow was bred before they left St. Albert, and his calf was the only new one in the herd.

The dwindling cattle herd did not bother the band. They planned their usual fall/winter hunting trip to the north and carried on much the same as before. The women, children and old men in camp managed as the days got shorter and colder. They fished from the lake and brought in ducks and geese.

John tried to plow up what land he could use to plant vegetables and a small field of barley, but the soil was poor and early frosts were a problem.

Without Lucy, John would not have made it through as long as they did. Along with a knowledge of herbs, she saved seeds to plant the following spring, salted and smoked meat to store away, dried berries and other fruits to use over winter, and made warm clothing out of the animals that he brought in. She saved and 'made do', using every scrap of material that she had, for buckskin moccasins, trousers, shirts and leggings for the family. As the weather got colder, she made their little cabin as warm as she could make it.

When it was time to leave with the hunting-trapping party, John at first refused, saying that there was much to do in camp. Corrals and sheds needed to be constructed. Those in camp needed to be looked after, and there was still much to do with the houses to make them warm enough to keep out the cold. Then he was informed that they would need his horses to help bring back the meat. The sleigh runners that he built under his wagon box would be necessary to skid all of their equipment in and out. Travois were not nearly adequate.

John was shocked. They intended to take his horses and sleigh without his permission or his being there. He was the only one who owned a sleigh, and it was necessary for the greater good of all. *Well*, he decided, *if his horses were going up north, he was going too.*

Lucy took it in stride when he told her that she would be on her own for several weeks. It was expected that he would go. Why did he worry about her? She, as well as the rest of the women in camp, would be fine.

The night before their departure, they had the huge bonfire. It was a cold night, and men huddled around in their worn buffalo coats and blanket capotes, otter hats, and woollen hoods. There was no priest for the ceremony but Elder Joseph performed admirably. He spoke at length in his expressive Cree, which was used for the blessing of the hunt. John always marvelled that he found it easy to learn the language, far easier than English, with which he was still struggling. Cree was expressive, rhythmic, and rich in vowels, with few harsh sounds. Whole sentences in English could be put into one Cree word. And it was more dramatic. The service was almost like a dance.

The speech was long, and the men and women echoed back combinations of Cree and French as they learned from the Church. They sang the phrases they learned from the priests and incorporated them with the age-old ceremony to bless the hunting expedition.

Stamping their feet and swatting their mittened hands to their sides against the cold that rolled across the nearly frozen lake, they struggled to stay warm. The wind flung the snow into their faces, stinging like little needles.

"It is past, the 'moon of the flying young ducks', the 'migration moon,' and now it is the 'moon of freezing up' – the 'hunting moon'," Joseph intoned in his rich deep voice. It was the signal for the hunters to do their dance around the fire. This was the ceremony for the Chepuyak, the 'ghost dancers of the sky.' Their bodies moved in time with the pulse of the universe, the aurora, the drummers' soft thrum becoming part of the pulse, and they were one – one people – one purpose.

The wind, homeless and heartless, screamed in from the north, and the first blizzard of the hunting moon laid claim to Long Lake Settlement.

The blizzard blew in the start of a long, cold winter. Lucy, alone with the children in her cozy cabin, listened to the night outside as she worked with the buckskin in her lap. This she could do sitting cross-legged in the dark with the light of the fire in the corner stove flickering warmly over the wooden board floor.

Caroline raised her head from the bunk bed that she shared with little Rose. Her long dark hair hung thick and tangled around her little oval face as she opened sleepy saucer eyes in alarm.

"Maman, someone is calling you. Someone is running through the snow to come for you."

Lucy stopped what she was doing and listened, cocking her head on one side. She got up from the floor and went to the window. They were lucky enough to have glass in one small window, glass that John had protected and carried from Big Lake. They were the only ones to have a glass window. The other cabins had hide-covered windows that let in some light, but could not be seen through.

Lucy could see nothing but the snow lying in bluish drifts against the trees beside her garden. She could hear nothing, but she knew her second oldest daughter's uncanny ability to know of something before it happened. Or perhaps her hearing was more acute than any of the others.

She threw a blanket around her shoulders, pulled on a pair of moccasins by the door, and stepped outside closing the door behind her. Two feet of snow had fallen since the hunters left for the north. The moon cast eerie shadows under the trees as Lucy searched them for a sign of life. Just as she was about to turn and come back inside the cabin, something caught her eye under a tree. A figure moved. Someone, a woman – a girl, was on her knees, leaning against the tree beside the garden.

Lucy hurried forward and dropped down on the snow beside the figure. Then she discovered it was Mary-Jane; she was holding her leg in pain.

"Mary-Jane, what are you doing here? What has happened?"

"Maman, I fell over Daniel's wagon that he built."

"Is your leg broken? Let me see. Can you move it?" Lucy moved and touched her daughter's leg with practiced fingers while Mary-Jane winced and sucked in the cold air between her teeth.

"*Non,* I do not think so. It is bleeding. I feel the blood running down my legging," Mary-Jane whined between gasps as her mother moved her leg.

"Come into the house so that I can see to tend it. Can you stand?"

"Non, non, Maman! You have no time. You must go quickly to *Madamme Majeau.* She needs you; it is the baby. That is why I am here. *Allez! Allez!*"

Mary-Jane was staying with Louise while she waited for the baby. When Janvier left with the hunting party, he wanted to be sure that she was not left alone in the house with the baby's time so close.

Lucy got up but paused like a bird in flight bending over her daughter. "But I cannot leave you like this – your leg – I must see to it."

"*Non, Non! Maman*! I will be all right. *Allez!* I can make it into the house from here. You can fix my leg when you get home or else I can bandage it myself."

As Lucy hurried the short distance to the Majeaus', she realized that at nine years old Mary-Jane was quite grown up and self-sufficient. Being her oldest, the girl cooked, sewed, tended to her younger siblings, including seeing to their scrapes, burns, and tummy aches as well as weeding the garden and picking berries in the muskeg. She was very likely quite capable of looking after her own difficulties as long as the leg was not broken. She worried about that until she stepped into Louise's kitchen. There was no time to think about anything but the coming baby and the mother's needs.

Louise was on her hands and knees by the cupboard. Lucy realized that Louise was trying to use the cupboard to strain against but she pulled the boards down with the straining. It would not take the weight.

"This baby is not coming easy," Louise ground out between clenched teeth. "I had to wake Mary-Jane – I have been at this for a long time, and the baby is being very stubborn."

"You should have sent for me sooner, Louise," Lucy scolded. "I could have helped make it easier." Lucy scurried around finding what she needed. She lay Louise's birthing hide on the floor below a selected rafter. Then she tied two rawhide ropes to the rafter dangling down above the birthing blanket. Between the ropes she tied a sturdy poplar pole, notched at each end to keep the ropes from slipping through. Then she wrapped moose-hide pieces tightly around the pole for handholds. They would not be slippery or tend to slide when Louise's hands became sweaty on their surface.

When she knelt, the crossbar came to Louise's chest and moss was positioned at her knees and at a joint in the board floor for her to dig in her heels. The stove in the corner was stoked with wood to warm up the cabin that had become cold. Blankets were hung and piled beside her to keep in the body heat.

The wind that started up outside whipped the taut skins covering the two small windows. Snow pattered against them as Louise strained against the pole and groaned with the pain. Lucy wiped the sweat from her friend's forehead and checked to see the progress of the infant.

"Wait, rest now, until it is time to push," she urged as she moved into a position to help. From behind, she caught Louise around the waist while her hands felt her distended abdomen to discover when it was time. "Now, push!" she commanded as she squeezed and lifted at Louise's waist, while pushing downward with her arms and hands.

It was happening. The baby slid out onto the birthing hide. Quickly Lucy moved around to pick the infant up and clear the mouth and nose with her hand. A quick slap to the infant's bottom brought a lusty cry. "It is a boy, Louise," Lucy told the exhausted woman who collapsed onto the pile of blankets. "And what a big baby he is! Look at all of that thick black hair! And listen to that set of lungs!"

"Give him to me," Louise gasped weakly, stretching out her hand.

"Just wait until I clean him off and wrap him up," Lucy said smiling proudly as though she was the one to birth the little boy. She took warm ashes from the ash-box under the stove and wiped him clean with moss and pulverized rotten wood that had been kept for use beside the wood-box. All the while, the baby screamed at the indignity as he waved and kicked about ineffectually, flinging his limbs about in the cool air.

When she lay the squirming baby in the mother's arms against her na-ked breast, he stopped his lusty crying and turned to find his comfort.

"Now let me get you into your warm bunk." Lucy busied herself fixing blankets and warming them by the fire before helping her friend into them. "I will come back to see you in a little while, but right now I have to get to my house and tend a girl with a bloody leg."

Louise did not seem to notice what Lucy had said. She was already drifting off to sleep, her new son making little sucking sounds with his mouth against a breast that had not yet started to produce the milk he would soon crave. In the meantime his mother popped a chunk of hard-ened fat that Lucy handed to her, into the baby's mouth. It would have to do the baby until his mother could produce the milk on her second day.

In the north woods, John and the rest of the hunting party fought the weather. The stringent air burnt their nostrils and throat and their breath spurted a frosty mist. In such temperature they learned to suck the air in slowly through their teeth because if they gulped in full mouthfuls it could be like knife thrusts to the chest. It could freeze their lungs in minutes.

The horses, frost covered from the bursts of mist from their nostrils, were in as much danger. John worried about them and made sure that they did not work too hard. The steel bits were not used because their tongues would stick to it. Instead, rope bits were used.

The sled runners beneath the wagon box shrieked on the wind-buffed snow under the sleigh that was filled with frozen moose meat and hides. Furs of fox, bear, wolf, coyote, wolverine and cougar were also gathered, reminding John of his years with the Hudson Bay Company.

John wondered as they struggled to get through the trees, muskeg, and swamp whether there would be anything left of his sleigh and horses by the end of this hunt. Sleeping in their hide-covered tent lined with bearskins, with the fire in the centre throwing its light across the bedrolls, was an endurance test. The smoky interior of the tent, the trips outside to make a toilet in the bush, the mind-numbing cold that never let up, and eating hand-to-mouth meat sliced off the outside of a haunch over an open fire, was difficult. Living in the same clothes day after day, night after night, sweated in and smoked up, however, was a torture test that could not come to an end soon enough. He could not wait to get home to Lucy.

Amazingly to John, many of the others seemed to enjoy this excursion. It was a life they knew. They were proving themselves the warriors of the forest.

It was not until Pierre announced around the campfire inside the smoky tent one night, that they were going to have to head back home the next morning that John breathed a sigh of relief. But when he heard the reason for the early departure he became more worried.

"Brothers," Pierre spoke seriously, "we have little or no ammunition left. When we get back to camp a party is going to have to go to Fort Edmonton to trade some of these furs and hides for supplies."

With what they would need, John thought, *how much of our material will have to be traded away? Once we get to camp there will be another long list of necessities.*

"Perhaps we could get another wagon and sleigh, a horse or two, a bull, laying hens, farming supplies, tools like forks, shovels, hoes, saws, ...," John listed.

They stared at him in silence.

"The women are going to need jars for canning, salt and sugar, flour, more seed for planting in the spring. Will there be enough furs and hides to cover all we will need? And then there should be educational supplies for the children and ..."

Pierre cleared his throat, and others looked away in embarrassment, avoiding looking at John. "The time will come for all of those things. Do not be impatient. You will agree, brother, that the guns are useless without bullets. Are they not?"

"But we can still trap; we do not need guns for that," the eager voice of Michel broke in. This was his first big hunt and he had yet to claim his first animal. Others nodded in agreement.

"We have only two teams up here and two pack horses," John reminded them casually. "My wagon is quite loaded down with all that my horses can pull. The trail up here was not meant for wagons; travois could barely get through. Now to get this load home it will be a difficult pull" He was gently reminding them that his animals and wagon were carrying the biggest load, and he was not about to kill them on a whim.

Danny Gunn then raised a voice of reason. "Why do we not we send John's wagon home with half the group to help, while the rest stay to trap since we need all of the trading power we can get?"

Pierre frowned momentarily at this impromptu suggestion from a novice in the band, but raised his hand to silence the babble that put forth their suggestions, or agreed or disagreed.

"I accept the suggestion from Danny Gunn. I will decide who will stay and who will return with the load. As he says, it will be a hard pull so a lot of help will be needed. Axes will be needed to clear a road and someone who knows the country to plan the route. When the settlement is reached Elder Joseph must plan the trading party, but no one will leave until we get there with the rest of the furs for trade. He will decide what will be on the list."

John was beginning to become irritated with the 'all-for-one-and-one-for-all' attitude in the camp and in the settlement. He moved to Long Lake with his wife and her scrip looking for a place of his own – land of his own – the ability to make his own decisions, his own plans, his own mistakes, if need be. Now nothing seemed to be his own to do as he wished, and getting ahead was looking more impossible every day.

Oh well, he thought, *he would get used to this communal way of living sooner or later. They were good ideas. He must not buck the system. Being on your own was not easy either.* He sighed and prepared for the long hard trip back to the settlement.

50

The Healer

Julie did her best to spread the word about Albert Calliot. It was hard to convince people to return to the meeting place at the lake. What was the reason? Why were they going? No longer were there hunting parties to be organized from there. No longer would there be joyful gatherings for prayer and song to dedicate to the hunt and the festive activities that went along with it. For baptisms or marriages they could go to St. Albert. Why wait until the summer meeting?

And most of all, there were the biggest reasons for staying away for the past four years. Since Riel was taken away and killed, it ended all chances of the Métis being an independent nation. Since the priests did nothing to save it, or save Riel, they drew away from their priests. They felt as though the priests did not care. Further confirmation of that line of thinking came when the government agents began to speak of a law that would prohibit the hunting of partridge and duck in the spring season and the fishing in the sacred lake. This was the time that it was necessary. They were no longer to fish with nets but one fish at a time with a pole and a hook was allowed. The priests did nothing to speak for them then either. They had nothing to say.

When Albert Calliot and her son, Louis, wandered into the farm that day, Julie could not believe it. After all of this time of searching and asking, he had come to her doorstep. When Louis said, 'Maman this is Albert Calliot. He helped our calf to be born or it would surely have died. Can he stay with us? It is cold out there and he walked all the way from Spirit River.' She was in shock.

Julie was so worried about Louis, and in he walked with this dirty ragged old man. She paled, felt faint, and then flushed. But she rallied quickly and pulled the man inside after hugging her young son and scolding him gently about worrying her.

After feeding Albert with the family, Julie insisted that he stay with them for awhile. It was only right, she told him, after he helped Louis and the cow find their way home, and of course, after saving their calf.

Adolphe liked him immediately and listened avidly to the stories Albert told. He spoke an ancient Cree in a voice soft and apologetic. Much of it Julie had trouble translating for Adolphe. This man, they discovered, was thoroughly incorruptible with a wealth of patience and knowledge of the past. Stories of happier days were recounted. Then he began to show that here was also a prophet as Julie had suspected.

"When the Dogrib People see the Chepuyak, the ghost dancers, they say, 'Look at my grandmother dancing up there.'"

"When one washes themselves with May snow it is medicine. You bless yourself with this snow ...."

"The world is coming to an end. At one time the earth was destroyed by water. The next time it will be by fire..."

"There is only one God – this I know. The Great Spirit loves us all. We are all part of the land. No man, be he red man, or white, can be separated. We are brothers." They hung on to every word and pondered about them later.

Gradually, Julie turned the discussion to what had happened to the gatherings at Lac Ste. Anne.

"Ah!" he nodded knowingly. "The Métis inherited the ancient culture, but also the problems. They need one another. The sacred wind that blows across the lake of the wanderers of the wilderness is a part of the pulse of the universe. They must return to the sacred lake."

Julie had her opening. "We are going to try to revive the sacred journey to the lake this summer. Will you come? Will you promise to be there to bring the blessings of the Spirit River People? Will you help to bring the magic back to the people? You know the ancient stories - the stories when the Cree and the Chipewyan and the others first met the French. Will you come and teach the young how to dream again?"

For a long moment Albert looked off into the distance behind Julie's head, the distance only he could see. It was then that Adolphe jumped in with an apology for his impulsive wife.

"*Ma chere Julie*! The time for the gathering is weeks away. Perhaps Albert has other places he needs to be. And are you certain that there will be a gathering? There has been no word; no runners have come."

"It could start small, but they will come. They will all come back. It may take years, but they will come." Julie spoke confidently, but she held her breath waiting for Albert's reply.

"I will come," he said simply.

It was surprising how many people responded to the call to come to the gathering place at Lac Ste. Anne. It was later than the usual time. This was not the spring hunt for the buffalo, or the time to bring in the partridge, ducks and geese. But perhaps it was still time for the net fishing. And, of course, they did miss the festivities and meeting people they had not seen for a long time. Even for the party, it was worth going. They were all curious as well. Amazing things were hinted at.

When Julie, Adolphe, and family drove in, there were many tents set up. The children were running and playing. Sporting events were happening, and their boys, Vital, John, Joseph, Louis and even five-year-old Daniel, were anxious to become a part of them.

"I told you we were late," Vital chastised his parents. He could not wait to help set up the tent before dashing off. He was now sixteen and anxious to show off his games' skills. John as well, had become lithe and strong, although not as tall and broad shouldered as his older brother, or even as tall and lithe and quick as his younger brother Joseph. Louis and Daniel had a lot of growing up to do and concentrated on the little boy games.

"I see the gambling games have started already," Adolphe remarked to Julie as he cast his eyes toward the men who stretched out on the grass by their tents.

"That is all right," Julie remarked nonchalantly. "Just wait until the gathering time around the fire. They will soon leave that when Albert Calliot arrives." She began busily setting out their bedrolls and the cooking area.

"Are you certain that he is coming, mon Julie. I have not heard of, or seen him since he left our place to wander off who knows where. And he left so suddenly without saying good-bye. He was just gone one morning!" Adolphe staked down the tent corners before coming to help his wife.

"He will be here," Julie commented confidently.

"I am going over to the mission to pay a visit to Father Lizée and see if he is surprised at the arrival of all of these people." Adolphe struck off towards the mission church.

When they met the first night around the campfire, there was some dancing, singing, and playing music but no arrival of Albert Calliot. No one looked around anxiously except Julie. Most people had forgotten the name, or had forgotten that he was coming.

Father Lizée arrived with Adolphe and welcomed everyone back warmly. Lizée, short and round, had a pudgy face, round glasses, and a cherubic choir boy appearance. He even blessed the gathering, and people smiled and nodded at each other. The priests were no longer angry with them.

Then Father delivered a surprise announcement. "Next year and every year at this same time, we will begin a new gathering. It will be called a Pilgrimage – the Pilgrimage to the sacred lake of Ste. Anne to bring homage to our God – the Great Manito! And every year we will have games and competing teams. We will have registration and celebration of marriages, and baptisms and the start will be the building of a new mission church."

The Métis gathered there cheered heartily. This was not only a time of religious dedication of a hunt but also a chance to meet new people and grow as a group. Father Lizée left the dais feeling a great sense of accomplishment. The rift between the Métis and the church was healing. He discussed this at length with Bishop Grandin. This group was a wonderful opportunity to launch the new idea of a Pilgrimage. Runners would be sent out to all areas where Métis lived and to white settlers who were known to be Catholic.

Father Lizée did not know that there was another reason for them being there - this year - at this particular time. Adolphe mentioned that Julie was hoping to see a special person who told her that he would attend, but Father brushed that aside as unimportant. He was just glad that, if only a few, they were beginning to return to the mission. He left for the church quarters feeling quite satisfied with himself, especially when several people followed him to ask him to take this opportunity to bless their marriage, or their newborn, or to hear their confessions. These were his children, his flock, and he would again minister to them.

Marie Amable was there with her husband Joseph. She struggled into the gathering wheezing, coughing, stopping, and resting every twenty steps, but determined not to let her asthma keep her from attending. Julie insisted that she come. Now as Father Lizée left, she did not move from her place on the blanket in front of the dais by the fire, even though her puffy legs ached and it was no longer easy to sit this way for long periods. Her bulk had increased with less activity, and her round lined brown face showed signs of strain. Her eyes watered, and she mopped them continually. Ordinarily she would have gone to Father Lizée and asked him to pray for her delivery from this condition, but she waited. She had endured her affliction this long; she could wait as long as she needed. If Lucy were here, she would find it easier.

Some drifted away, while some stayed to sing and sway by the fire, and some passed around a ceremonial homemade concoction. The drink ceased to be just ceremonial and now was used by anyone who enjoyed the taste. Some stood at the back and talked quietly, but all waited patiently – not sure for what they waited.

Suddenly, there he was beside the fire with them, refusing the drink they offered him. There was an aura about the old man that made the people around the fire feel drawn to him by emotions beyond their understanding. Adolphe recognized him from across the fire where he stood behind Julie and his sons.

"It is Albert," he whispered to Julie, and she passed it on to those near her, rather than approach the man herself.

Finally, Joseph Gladu moved to the front across from Albert. "You are Albert Calliot," he stated rather than asked.

"I am," the man replied simply.

"We welcome you," Joseph nodded in almost a bow. "We have been waiting for you."

The people gathered in more closely. All singing and action stopped.

"Why is it that you have this gathering and you have no Thunderbird Spirit Pole standing?" the old man asked calmly.

Joseph volunteered the answer in an accusatory tone with a caustic edge. "The clergy or the white government, or both, has told us that we can no longer have the thirst dance. Many things will be denied to us if we do."

"There is more that happens around the Thunderbird Spirit Pole than the thirst dance. That is what you are being denied," Albert stated calmly.

By this time, there was a crush of people moving in, trying to hear and see what was going on. So those nearby urged Calliot to move up to the platform.

"Our nation is like a great river," Albert spoke easily, calmly from the platform, and yet everyone could hear without his having to raise his voice. "It has been flowing before any of us can remember. We take our strength, wisdom, and our ways from the flow and direction established for us by ancestors we never knew. Their wisdom flows through us to our children, and grandchildren, to generations we will never know. It is up to you to see that the river never dries, never stops flowing. You come to this sacred lake and yet you do not know why it is sacred. You have never seen the vision. You have never seen the grandmother of us all. Where is your Thunderbird Spirit Pole? Do you no longer possess one?"

One of the young men from the back shouted out. "It is here." And he ran with another young man to the bushes beside the water and returned carrying the long pole with what looked like a very deteriorated nest hanging on one end. Embarrassed at its condition after long disuse, they set it down by the platform and backed off.

Slowly, Albert went down on his knees and soon the whole following fell to their knees. They watched as he took the bundle from his back and carefully opened it. Out of it, he took his medicine token wrapped in cloths and lastly a hide. The combined congregation sucked in their collective breaths as he unwrapped a pipe stem. It was about two feet long with no bowl, but was decorated with fur, feathers, quills, and beads. A braid of black hair attached to it was likely from a deceased relative, a fearless and brave warrior, 'a questor'.

In fascination, they watched as Albert approached the fire with short tapping steps, humming, then chanting a prayer. Others took up the chant, and the drums soon joined in. "Oh, grandmother, your people need you now. We are lost and no longer know our way."

He tipped the pipe stem up over the fire and sprinkled a substance over the flames, which danced in a sparkling blue above the fire and smelled sweet and pungent at the same time. Then he again ascended the platform to the sound of the renewed chant that joined him and the drum.

On his knees, he faced the pole lying on the ground. As the chanting, singing, and drumming filled the evening air Albert bent over until his forehead touched the platform, spreading his arms out towards the tree.

Tension built as the minutes went by, and people stared at the pole on the ground. Then, imperceptibly at first, as Albert's hands rose from the platform, so also did the pole rise, until several long minutes later, the pole was standing upright. Even the disreputable nest at the top seemed to be a crowning touch, and the pole seemed straighter and newly peeled.

With his hands stretched high into the air, the sweat streamed from Albert's forehead and his hands vibrated as with a chill. Past the pole, looking straight to the west across the lake, the people on their knees beheld an unnerving sight. At first it seemed to be a luminous cloud. Then it transformed into the image of a woman, face lined with age, and a scarf over her hair to her shoulders.

"You see before you the grandmother of us all!" Albert Calliot called out in a voice that clearly was on the verge of exhaustion and distress. Then he crumpled to the boards below him, stretched out as though dead.

Women rushed to him to bathe his heated wet-with-sweat face, listening to his chest, trying to assess whether he was alive.

In seconds, it seemed the darkness moved in, the image was gone from the lake and the pole was again on the ground. Onlookers were amazed. They had all seen it. They knew that it happened. They even felt the sacred wind that wafted over them from across the lake. They all became 'dreamers' again. They all witnessed a miracle.

The people moved back to their tents in the darkness, shaken, trembling, and yet invigorated and renewed. Joseph and other men took care of Albert, taking him back to a small tent and reviving him.

Adolphe was visibly shaken as he rounded up his family and walked them back to their tent. "What did you see?" he asked Julie after the boys were settled down to sleep.

"I saw what we all saw," Julie replied, surprised at the question. "The grandmother of us all."

Adolphe nodded but did not comment. He saw a woman; he was certain of that. But it was not a grandmother; it was the Mother Mary. Plain as could be, he saw the Virgin Mary. He must tell Bishop Grandin about this. Nothing else in his life had so affected him.

He would never sleep this night, he decided; he was too excited. After this year there would be no difficulty getting people to come back to Lac Ste. Anne.

Adolphe told Father Lizée that he saw the vision of the Virgin along with those around the fire, with the help of Albert Calliot. Father was, of course, very excited and wanted to see Albert. "The spot must be commemorated with the statue of the Virgin," he told Adolphe excitedly. "Bring him to me."

Adolphe was unable to find Albert until evening around the campfire when all turned out waiting expectantly for Albert to raise the Thunderbird Tree again. They would hang their cloths tied about the tree as an appeal to Manito to grant them healing from their many afflictions or tribulations.

This time, though, at Albert's instructions, the boys cut down and brought in a straight pole, free from all of its branches except for the newly built eagle's nest at the top. They dug a hole and raised the pole. Tamping the dirt solidly around the base, they raised their eyes and scanned its straight tall length with the bits of cloth tied around it by the petitioning Métis women. It was a spirit pole to be proud of.

The evening was damp and heavy with the smells of rotting earth, water plants, waterfowl, and algae. In her excitement and with all of the extra movement of tying her cloth to the pole, Marie Amable collapsed, grabbing at her chest and struggling to breathe. They had her lie down on the ground, but her face was turning blue with lack of air.

Standing back, the people allowed Albert in. "Please help her," Julie appealed. "You are a healer – the best that the Northwest has ever found. I know you can make her breathe again. This time she may suffocate if she is not helped."

Albert had the unique gift of seeing people's energy around them. He could move this energy and manipulate it. He knelt down beside the big woman and placed his hands on her chest. Pressing and breathing hard, his body vibrated and shook as though he was a leaf in the wind. That energy or pain he was able to move to himself – her pain coming into his body. He moaned and panted as though in agony, body wrenched with torture, his sweat damp shirt clinging to his back.

Finally, he fell back in a swoon, breathing heavily, and exhausted, his head hanging on his chest, completely wrung out from the experience.

He would have fallen over had not Julie and two other women come forward to guide him down to a supine position. For a long time both Marie Amable and Albert lay there as though dead while the others stood by, wringing their hands in anxiety.

Then one of the women started a tentative chant, a song of encouragement, and they circled the two on the ground swaying and chanting, the sound increasing in fervent prayer. Miraculously, it seemed, Marie Amable opened her eyes and sat up looking around as though puzzled.

Then she got heavily to her feet. There was not a sign of wheezing or heavy breathing. "What happened to Albert?" she asked as she looked down in concern. The rest stared at her as she again went down on her knees beside the man, with no effort it seemed.

All eyes turned to Albert who breathed shallowly but who still had a pulse, according to Julie, and whose chest still rose and fell. On their knees in a circle about him, they chanted in prayer until his eyes flickered, and he was back with them. They helped him to his feet, but his body swayed and leaned limply against them.

"Take him to his tent," Julie told Adolphe and her boys. "I will get him food and drink." Adolphe thought that he should wait until tomorrow after he was rested to tell Albert about Father Lizée's request to see him. Now it was even more important that Father see Albert. He was a healer – no doubt about it. Adolphe saw with amazement Marie Amable walk away with quick steps, chattering excitedly without a sign of breathing problems.

One more thing that Adolphe knew because he had observed, was that every time Albert performed a miracle, even the one Louis told him about the calf; it took more out of him. Perhaps next time he would not come back. He was so weak that they nearly had to carry him to his tent, and his breathing was so shallow that Adolphe wondered if he would take another breath. Maybe the next time that he gave of himself for his people, he would not return.

Before Adolphe left his side, when he lay the man down on his bedroll, Albert opened tired brown eyes that seemed to burn into Adolphe's soul. The seamed weather-glazed skin of his face seemed to try to wrinkle into a half smile, but he closed his eyes and slept.

"We have to protect him, Julie," Adolphe said. "He can not take too much more. It wrenches his whole body. That is why he is alone, wandering the North, I am sure. I know you feel happy to have found him, but we have to let him leave us again. We are all too needy. We will end up killing him. I am going to give him what he needs to escape, and maybe he will find a people who will not use him to save themselves."

Julie hung her head but said nothing. She knew that what her husband said was true.

51

Leaving Long Lake

It was 1892 and not much had changed in the way things had progressed at Long Lake Settlement. Life went on much the same as it had the year before and the year before that. The only thing that seemed to change was the fact that the Métis received less and less for their goods at the trading posts and stores in the fort. Traders did not seem to want the furs anymore, and the people got very little for them.

When John suggested that they sell the trees it had not worked out. There was no river near to ship them down to a big centre like Fort Edmonton. They would have to set up a sawmill of their own, and then they would have to haul the lumber on the frozen winter roads many miles to the city or towns.

Trading farm produce, cattle, pigs, and grain was a lost cause. They did not have the land in their long finger shaped valley between the high ridges and muskeg. John stopped pressing the Métis to be farmers. He had but one horse left anyway, Jock, and he was sway-backed and worn out. His other horse, the one he had purchased with his money from the lumber mill, Morag, had died. She had been used up on the work of Long Lake Settlement, part of the best working team they had.

The cow that he arrived with, went dry and the village eventually butchered it to tide them over a hard winter when the hunting was not as good as it should have been. They seemed to live hand-to-mouth, living on what they could gather from their land and muskeg. Thankfully, his wife was very good at that and they had not starved.

John still had his calf that had grown into a nice heifer. A long time ago he gave up on getting her bred somewhere. She would only go towards feeding the community anyway.

The rest of the community seemed to be quite happy with their easy-going life. Every winter, they made the trip to the north to hunt and trap, and if they had not enough ammunition, there were other ways of killing a moose or a bear.

There were still a lot of fish in the lake and the ducks and geese in the fall. They gambled and lost a hide of an animal that they had killed and cured, but that did not bother them. Next time they would win it back.

The women did things much the same as they had when they were young. Another baby came along and it was provided for. If you did not have enough in your household, someone else could help supply it. The Lennys always had enough, and they could share.

John finally accepted that he struggled seven years to become a farmer, and then ended up quitting when he realized he was fighting a losing battle. At first, he tried to stash away extra vegetables from the garden that he helped to produce. The seeds were carefully saved away so that they had a bigger garden than anyone in the settlement, but when the long hard winter came and knocks came at the door from starving neighbours, his wife handed over the extra food, leaving them starving like their neighbours.

John George was born in the winter of 1887. He was born too soon and died soon after he struggled to come into the world. It was while John was away up north, and Lucy did not know the reason for the premature birth. "Some babies come at the wrong time," she had shrugged. "Some live and some are not strong enough." She shed her tears, but then it was time to carry on and look after the family that was here with them.

John was sure that he knew what happened. There was a scarcity of food in the settlement. By January, they had eaten all of the food that was stored for the winter, and they were scrounging for enough to feed their families. Knowing his wife, John could imagine what happened. She made sure that her family had enough to eat and forgot to look after herself.

She was so thin. Her face, still a beloved russet brown smoothness, held those saucer-like eyes and a sweet turned-up-at-the-corner mouth. She could see no one suffer if she could do something to prevent it. He always marvelled at how strong and capable was this wife of his! But after this, he determined that he would not go north on any more hunting expeditions. If she would not look after herself, he would have to stay to look after her and his family.

In the summer of 1889 Albert was born. A happy healthy baby, he was satisfied with whatever his big family did for him. His sisters hauled him around on their backs when they picked berries and he crawled through the garden eating his share of dirt along with the potatoes dug out by his brothers Daniel and William.

Now, here in 1892, Lucy was expecting another baby, and John finally accepted the fact that things were not going to change from the way they had always been in the settlement. He may as well live with them.

John began to be concerned about his daughters, however. Mary Jane was fourteen, and Caroline was thirteen. They would soon be of marriageable age, and it was time that they met other boys. The ones in the village were either too young, or they felt as though they were brothers. Perhaps, he thought, they should go to the gathering at Lac Ste. Anne this year – the one they now called 'The Pilgrimage' according to the rumour they heard from the runner that came up from Fishing Lake.

The odd fishing or duck hunting party came through occasionally, but there were few people who came to stay long and let them know what was going on in other places. *Soon*, John thought, *I am going to have to look into the possibility of attending the Pilgrimage.* The more he thought of it and the more he talked about it to Lucy, the more he wondered why he had not gone back with his family sooner for a visit. It was very far, of course, but the trail to St. Albert was a lot better now than it had been when they came seven years ago.

It was the end of February, and they had come through another hard winter. With his one horse, John was able to do all of the pulling and carrying. The wagon/sleigh was now gone. It broke down on the trail home from the north with the hunters, and they left it there, packing what little meat they managed to kill on horseback and their backs. John was irritated that they had not tried to salvage the parts on the sleigh that could have been restored to build a new wagon. *He should have been there,* he fumed. But as far as he was concerned it was no longer *his* anyway! The settlement considered it public property.

However, for their trip to the Pilgrimage he had no wagon and only one tired horse. Even the tools that he arrived with seven years ago either disappeared or were in bad shape after being borrowed.

One morning, as was usual for him, he started out with a bow and arrow on an independent hunting excursion. A long time ago he started learning how to use the bow and arrow since bullets were in short supply, and he did not want to go to Joseph with an appeal for ammunition, even though he intended to share what he bagged with whomever was in need.

No hay was put up last fall so the grass stood tall around the edge of the lake. The lake was frozen solid, and he scanned it to the other side for any sight of animals that might come down looking for water at its edge after the brief warm spell when the water ran to the shore from the warmed bank. The grass now only fed the grazing horses since the last cow was killed for food last December. There were no animals in his corral or shed – nothing but his sway-backed horse.

He still had his snowshoes, and he trod the crust of snow that lay deep on the lakeshore. The sky was a pale cold blue; not a breath of a breeze disturbed the gray tangled branches standing naked and twisted in their bare winter sleep. The eastern horizon above the gray spiked trees wore morning's first blush. He aimed his steps to the opposite shore from the settlement intending to explore new territory after he checked out his traps.

Suddenly, before his eyes on the trampled snow as though it were a flag waving a warning, were strange footprints. They were boot prints, and the men in camp wore moccasins in the winter. There were very few boots worn every day in camp. He traced their origin, the direction from which they came, and where they headed. Then he saw three men standing on the edge of the small stream leading into the lake. One was Joseph, their headman, and the other two were strangers. Joseph was gesturing as though pointing directions and borders, and one man was drawing lines on a paper nailed to a board that he held. Warning bells went off in John's head, and he walked casually in their direction, hailing them as he approached.

The two men showed signs of surprise as this red headed, red bearded man walked up to them, blue eyes under bushy fair brows eyeing them suspiciously.

"These men speak to me in English," Joseph informed him curtly. "You speak the language. Perhaps you can understand what they are saying."

It was a long time since John spoke English, and he was not very accomplished, but he said he would try. He turned back to the English-speaking pair.

"What are you doing here in Métis territory?" John asked of the men.

The two men laughed and replied, "We could ask you the same question. What is a Scotsman speaking French in a Métis settlement doing here?"

"I live here with my wife and family up there on my land," John replied, waving his hand in that direction.

From that point on, they ignored the headman and spoke only to John while Joseph stood by frowning and trying to make out what they were saying.

"Then I have news for you," one of the men called Glenn Fisher, a tall, thin, young fair-haired surveyor informed him. "You are on property that does not belong to you. I am sorry but you have been misinformed. All of this area has just been surveyed and it does not show any settlement on our map. Besides that, you can own land close to the lake but no one can own the water. You don't own this lake," he finally addressed Joseph

John was thunderstruck. He had difficulty translating that information in his head but he knew he made out the gist of it. "No, you must be wrong," he finally found the words to reply. "I have – my wife has – we all have in our hands a paper – a – a 'scrip' that says we were given this land."

"Your land was not given to you. You have to buy land! Who told you it was given to you?" The other man called Harvey Banks interrupted in an imperious tone.

"I will go up and get my paper for you – my scrip." John, convinced that it was a mistake, prepared to hurry away but stopped to quickly inform Joseph. Joseph instead, stopped him, telling him to stay and explain. He, Joseph, would go to get his paper with the proof. He was closer. He lived just up from the stream.

John explained the circumstances surrounding the claim here on Long Lake. "The Métis always knew that this was all of their land. The agent was Thomas Fielding; he was the one to bring us here to this land. It was the new arrivals to the land that insisted on ownership; the Métis never did believe that pieces of land could be owned. Since then, they have needed to know what part of the land, then, was theirs. The Métis agent said to arrange the division of the land ourselves. We divided it in strips up from the lake as we have always done. From that tree, across the lake, our land extends up to …."

But the man with the board, Banks, cut him short. "We don't know any Thomas Fielding. That kind of land division went out of use a long time ago. We have been hired to survey all of this area, and we were not informed of a prior claim in this area. You are all squatting on land that does not belong to you. My advice would be to go to Fort Edmonton and talk to the land management officer. If you want this particular quarter section, you should go down there and file on it. Your friends should do the same thing with the quarter section next to it. Do the Métis think that they own all of the land? Do they feel that we have to come to them to ask permission to buy a piece of it?"

Their eyes turned to Joseph who joined them, handing them the tattered piece of paper triumphantly. He had been gone a long time and had probably reprimanded his wife many times for losing the suddenly important paper.

The man called Fisher glanced at it and handed it back unimpressed. "What you have is not a certificate of ownership but a lease of sorts on the land. It does not even specify how big an area or where it extends, how many acres, and how much of that each of you claims." As he tossed the inconsequential document aside, John realized how they had all been mislead, and he felt a cold anger welling up inside.

"You may want to stay for the time being until you find a place you can actually file on. Anything farther north than this, I have to warn you though, has not been surveyed as yet so you will still only be squatting until you file on an official section."

The men picked up their survey equipment and turned on their heels towards the south. It occurred to John as he watched the men depart, '*Yes, you feel quite self satisfied, but do you realize that you are taking advantage of the trails and paths in this north country that the Métis and Indian have trampled and planned. Otherwise you would have to hack your way through the bush and not find your way home.*'

After explaining it all to Joseph and seeing the look of stony disbelief he turned for home, his day's plans forgotten. They had wasted seven years of their lives, living a lie. John had some thinking to do.

Some of the Métis decided to stay there in Long Lake. Some decided to go down to Onion Lake or Fishing Creek to relatives there or to find other settlements to join. There, some discovered that the same thing happened. The 'scrip' was honoured, one-hundred-and-sixty acres of land valued scrip, but the Métis involved sold the land for a pitifully small price. Other Métis decided to stay right where they were because they had nowhere else to go, or they stubbornly refused to believe that they had been lied to. The Indians, they said, could not travel off their reservations, *but at least*, they said, *we can leave any time we want.* But where would they go?

John told Lucy as they gathered up all of their possessions that he was no longer going to follow the Métis way. Since doing so, he had lost all that he started out with. They would join the white world and depend on themselves. Maybe they would join the white population and fight for a place in the world next to them. On a travois behind his tired horse, they piled on all of the things that they could take, but, he declared, they would take nothing that was not their own.

Soon, they discovered what a pitifully small pile they could take. It was narrowed to essentials. Anything that they could make or pick up later would be left behind; large items could not be accommodated.

Their clothing, iron kettle, utensils for cooking and food, axe, gun, blankets were carefully packed and tied on.

"No, Daniel, not the little wagon," his mother told him.

"Maman," Mary Jane cried. "Madame Majeau gave me this rocking chair that Monsieur Janvier carved for her. I made this little cushion for it, and now Papa says that I can not bring them."

"I am so sorry, but you have to leave it behind." Lucy patted her oldest girl's hand, but firmly stuck to the plan.

"I will carry it on my back, Maman," Mary Jane pleaded. Her heavy dark hair framing the oval face was escaping from the rawhide thong and clinging wetly to the damp skin. She worked so hard helping to pack, and taking things they would no longer need to neighbours. Lucy hated to deny her, but she must.

"Mary Jane, you will need your back free to carry other important things such as blankets or cooking pots." Her daughter sighed and placed the rocking chair that she had so many times rocked Albert to sleep in, aside.

Then Lucy pulled the bagpipes and John's kilt and sporran down from the rafters. For a long time, they stared at them, saying nothing. Then, wordlessly, Lucy bundled them back up in the buckskin covering, tied the rawhide around the bundle, and stowed it in another corner of the travois. John, his eyes watering, could not say a word. He turned and went back to placing the pieces of their life onto their only horse, Jock's back bundle. The love he felt for his little wife at this moment overwhelmed him too much to speak.

Caroline turned and briefly looked back at the log house that had been their home for seven years. Then she faced the trail ahead with an unshakable confidence in the future that young people her age often possess. Her back, straight and resolute, she carried the load of clothing and footwear that would be needed by the family in the days and years ahead.

Even seven-year-old William would carry a pack, Rose and Daniel, too. Three-year-old Albert would ride up on top of the bundles and hides, but even he would have to walk a little. All would take turns at riding on Jock's back on the long journey back down the trail to St. Albert.

When they first decided to take the trip this year, the destination was to be Lac Ste. Anne. But plans changed. It was too soon for the Pilgrimage and their need was great for a home. St. Albert was like a welcome beacon for them. When the weary, worn, and desperate little family dragged into town, they were unable to put one foot in front of the other any more.

Both Rose and William were riding on Jock's back with Albert, and their heads hung as low as the old horse's. Many times Jock halted and hesitated, too tired to face any more trail. Lucy finally agreed to get on the travois and ride when she admitted to John that she had pains in her lower abdomen, and the baby had dropped lower into birthing position.

It was too soon and John feared that they would lose this one just like John George. And how would they cope with a baby being born on the open trail? Panic was rising in him like the swells of an ocean. The only young one who was not a weight on Jock was Daniel, and the ten-year-old was slipping further and further behind as he trudged along. Caroline had to keep returning to help him and urging him on. To save their feet, they walked in their moccasins lined with layers of moose-hide, but their feet were gradually wearing through the footwear. Daniel had to throw one of his ragged moccasins away and was now walking with one bare foot, wincing with each step he took.

Long ago, they stopped asking, 'How much further?' Mary Jane was just putting one foot ahead of the other. Bent over with her heavy pack, she seemed to be oblivious to everything around her but the hot sun in the day and the cool night wind.

Like an oasis in the desert, they welcomed the sight of the little town with its tall mission church spire on top of the hill. Just a little farther, they told themselves in weary agony, as they dragged their feet up one more hill to the mission. At this point, it was the only possible place for them to fall into.

The nuns helped them into the kitchen, saw to it that they were fed, bathed, bandaged and put into bed in the newly built dormitory. "*Mon dieu! C'est pitié le poile petit enfant,*" they marvelled when they discovered that little William had walked nearly the whole distance from Long Lake carrying a pack on his back.

Days later, when their bodies had healed, the Lenny family was ready to leave the mission. First, though, John had to find a place to take them.

As he stepped out of the mission into the bright summer sunlight one day, he met an old friend nearly head on. "Adolphe! I should have known that you would still be working here."

The two men shook hands warmly. "I am not here all of the time," Adolphe admitted. "I have a farm to care for. But when something needs to be built, like this new dormitory, they send for me. It should have been done by now, for I have hay to put up and a crop to cut and stook. But my boys are home looking after that in my absence. Perhaps Vital will not be there much longer. He is twenty and will soon be getting a farm of his own. He is going out nearly every night to visit a certain young lady. I may also have to help Joseph find a place of his own, since he is starting to talk fondly about a girl that he has been seeing.

"At present, they are all at home to do the work, leaving me to work late on this dormitory construction. So what, old friend, has been happening with you?" Adolphe ended and sat down on the bench patting the seat beside him.

John told him everything that happened since they left the Big Lake Settlement until they arrived at the mission. "Now I need to find work, and I need to find a home for my family. All I have to my name is a swaybacked old horse, a few household possessions, my kids and my wife, who is about to have a baby soon."

Adolphe listened thoughtfully and sensitively, and at the end his face brightened. "The best thing for you to do is have your family stay right here while you go out and find a job. There is no way that you could manage to get a farm. You need to build up a lot of necessities and a purse of money, to put down on buying a farm. In the meantime there are a lot of jobs for someone who is able to go where there is a need."

"You mean leave my family behind here at the mission and find a job somewhere else?" John swore that he would never abandon his family. The thought of leaving Lucy sent a chill to his heart.

"It would only be for a short while," Adolphe assured him. "While you are away getting a job and a home established, the children would be looked after safely. In the meantime, your wife would be in a safe place to have her baby."

It sounded very reasonable to John. The more he thought of it, the more he believed it to be a perfect answer to his problems. He grinned and commented wryly, "I was hoping you were going to say that I could come and work for you – to take off your crop and your hay while you are here working at the mission."

Adolphe laughed shortly. "No, no! My boys will be able to look after the work there just fine this year. And even if Vital and Joseph get married and move away tomorrow, I still have Louis and John. They are big capable boys, ages fifteen and eleven. And Daniel is nine and Samuel is seven. They are a big help doing the chores."

"I also have a boy Daniel, and he is ten," John added with a laugh. You certainly have a fine bunch of boys, so I see you do not need help."

"Yes, I am proud of my strong husky boys," Adolphe added. "But you need a job and I know just where you can find one."

"I will take anything as long as I can start right away and as long as it pays money," John leaned forward excitedly.

"It is in Fort Edmonton at the Acme brick-making factory. I used to own a part of it, but not any more. I was just there to pick up a load of bricks for the dormitory front, and they needed someone then. They had a young Indian working there, but he left on the spur of the moment. They really need someone who can learn the job quickly and do a good job. They are behind in orders.

"As far as a place to stay, there is a livery stable across the way and it would be a place for your horse as well as you. If you do not mind sleeping in the hay, you could stay there and earn extra money looking after the horses in the stable," Adolphe told him as he stood up pulling his pocket watch out and squinting at its numbered face.

"It is perfect! It could not be a better solution for me! I will go there immediately – as soon as I tell Lucy where I am going."

John shook Adolphe's hand enthusiastically. "You will never know how much you helped me today! How much you helped us all!"

They parted, and John felt as though a load had been lifted from his heart. His steps were lighter, and his smile returned. This was the first day of the rest of his life!

52

Separation

Lucy found the mission dormitory comfortable enough. It felt strange, though, sleeping on the narrow cot while her children slept in other areas of the dormitory away from her. She was thankful for the nuns who helped deliver baby Andrew. He slept quietly beside her on the crook of her arm.

William, Daniel, and Albert slept in the same bed in the dormitory and were happy as long as they were fed and had each other for comfort. Caroline and Mary Jane also shared a bed in the dormitory. The building was big, draughty, and empty since it was still being built and was not officially open yet. As long as they were fed, however, and did not have to walk anywhere for awhile they were satisfied. They wondered, though, what was going to become of them. They had not seen their father in many days, but they knew where their mother was and went down to see her and the new baby.

As long as the two boys could go out to the animals in the barns and play in the hay, they were happy. The two older girls enjoyed sneaking down the long hallways and many rooms. The dark nooks, the church sanctuary, exploring and imagining the uses of the materials they found, occupied and entertained them.

Rose did not adjust. She was terrified of the dark robed nuns and priests. Nighttime sounds like the eerie chanting of the nuns at their prayers, the bells, footsteps coming and going down the long dark hallways frightened her beyond words. Most of all she could not understand why they had taken her mother away in the darkness. She searched for her after hearing her calling out loudly one night. Huddled in the dark corners, she imagined someone coming to get her.

When her brothers and sisters came back to the large dormitory room lined with cots to say that they had seen their new baby brother, she was afraid to go for fear that it was a trick to grab her. Instead, she searched the long dark hallways on her own, hearing sounds that were not there, and imagining intentions of the nuns that had no basis.

At nights, she cried alone into her pillow, shivering and aching with loneliness and fear. Then one night, Caroline heard her crying and came to her cot.

"Why are you crying, Rose? Are you lonesome? Papa will be back soon when he gets a place for us to live and he will take us away," Caroline soothed and patted her little sister's back.

"Where is Maman? Can you take me to her?" Rose sobbed.

"She is up in the nursery with the new baby. Have you not been there yet?" Caroline suddenly realized that they had been keeping Rose in the dark. "Come with me. We will find her."

Holding Rose's hand, Caroline led her down the hallway, quietly unobserved by the chapel door where the nuns were at prayer and turned the corner down another dark hallway. Caroline learned from her clandestine explorations very well. Up a little set of stairs, they tiptoed quietly while Rose clung to her sister's hand, and her heart thumped so that it nearly smothered her.

Then, softly and cautiously, Caroline pushed open a door and there was her mother lying on a cot with the baby curled up on her arm. "Maman," Rose cried out and flung herself on her knees, while her arms encircled her mother's knees.

"Rose, there you are!" Lucy cried out. "Where have you been?" Then she cautioned her girl when she moved up to the baby. "Take care! Take care! I have to keep Andrew close to me because he was born too early, and he is too weak to suck. I must lie still for a few days yet as well. I could not come to find you." She patted her little girl's arm while Rose's huge tears overflowed and ran down her cheeks.

"Maman, I do not want to stay here in this place. I want to go home." Rose cried with her face buried in her mother's Hudson Bay Company blanket covering.

Lucy cried along with her daughter, her long dark hair wet and tangled on the pillow. "We can not go, *ma cherie*. We have no home now. Your father will come for us soon, but the nuns will look after us until then."

"*Non, non, non,*" Rose cried. "I want to go home now! Please Maman!"

Realizing that her sister was causing noise and upset, Caroline tried to urge her to come away with her now that she had seen her mother. "Come Rose! We must go back now. We are not allowed to be in here. Come!" Caroline tugged at Rose's arm, who pulled away and slid under the cot to the far side near the wall.

At that moment, one of the nuns came in. Her face under the white band with the black habit above was pulled up into tight annoyance. Her mouth was set severely into one small line. "What are you doing here?" she demanded of Caroline. "Your mother needs to be left alone so that she can get well enough to nurse that tiny baby and teach him how to eat. You must not get too close to him yet, until she builds up his strength and her own. Go! *Allez!* Back to the dormitory, and do not do this again!"

As the nun left, she took the lamp and closed the door.

"Rose," Lucy called gently, "come up in the bed. You can sleep here tonight at the foot. There is no room up here with the baby. If they come in here in the night, just curl up small and keep your head under the covers. You can go back to your bed in the dormitory in the morning."

When John came back to the mission, it was with good news that he happily shared with his wife. He was surprised and pleased to find out that the tiny baby arrived. Although struggling to catch up, he was going to make it.

"At the Acme Brick Factory, they tell me that after it starts to get cold in the fall, the hayloft will not be the best place to be, but I have already been looking for another place. There is a rooming house not too far away. The lady has only one room, but it would do for you and I and the baby, if the children can stay here at the mission for a while longer until I can find some place bigger."

"I do not like to leave them behind, Jean," Lucy complained sadly. "It is either be without you, or be without my family. What am I going to do?" Lucy wept into her hands.

"It will not be for long, my wife," John soothed and patted her shoulder. "There is no room for them there, but I can keep looking."

After John left, Mother Superior came for a talk with Lucy. Lucy sat in the rocking chair with the baby, humming quietly while Rose scrambled under the bed when she heard the footsteps in the hallway. She had grown good at sneaking up undetected and reappearing on her own bed. To their surprise there was the illusive little girl. Making excuses, her sisters told the nuns that Rose was out in the stables with her brothers or that she was emptying the chamber pot or gone to the kitchen.

Mother Superior, Catherine Leblanc, was the most severe of all of the nuns. She had a long face and a larger than normal nose. It always appeared as though she had a permanent frown with eyebrows that hovered low over small gray eyes and a small down-turned mouth. She stood ramrod straight for all of her fifty some years and spoke in her low precise French.

"Madame Lenny, it has come to my attention that your children have had no schooling and no religious training. They have had no training in the catechism and do not even know the Lord's Prayer. The girls do not knit or sew nor do they have any basic homemaker skills."

"I know. I am sorry. They have not been near a church or a school, and they had no materials to learn any skills for sewing or knitting. But they can cook some and have learned to work the buckskin," Lucy ended lamely.

"I hear that your husband plans to take them away to crowded conditions again with still no plan to give them the schooling that they need. Your girls are thirteen and fourteen years of age and can not read nor write. They are not prepared to face the world when they are on their own away from your household," Mother Superior continued.

"Perhaps we can get the girls into a schooling program now that we are closer to the big centres." Lucy bit her lip.

"I do have a proposal for you, Madame," Mother Superior paused until Lucy bid her to go on.

"When your husband comes for you and the baby, we keep the children at the Convent and give them the education that they lack. They can live right here and take classes that will be starting very soon - not only in the three R's but also in the skills that they will need to go out into the world on their own. The boys will get animal husbandry, mechanics, farming skills, and many more, skills. The girls will learn the skills they will need. The three-year-old, however, is a little young for this instruction, being nearly a baby himself."

Lucy grabbed onto the offer like a drowning woman clings to a life raft. "Oh, yes, Albert will come with us. That will work out very well because my husband is staying in a hayloft across from where he works. He can get a room for us though. It will not, of course, be big enough for the whole family, but as soon as he makes enough money, we can ..."

"Fine then." Mother Superior rose from the chair in which she sat stiff and tall with hardly a rustle of her gown. "We will start their classes immediately."

Lucy thought about the boys and how they would love the chance to work with the animals. William was seven, and he had begun to show an interest in numbers and letters when he saw them. The girls needed to learn those skills before they decided to marry. She wondered, though, as she hesitated, a clamp closing down in her throat, how long it would be that the children would have to be here. To leave without them .... She did not know how she could do that. Her children–leaving them behind. But, she told herself severely, *it is for the best – it has to be this way. But why must it be so hard – losing them all at once?*

She buried her face in the baby's blanket while the tears overflowed. Then she felt a hand on her arm.

"I will not stay here, Maman!" She had forgotten about Rose hearing all that was said from under the cot. "The rest can stay, but I will go with you and Papa and Albert. I can go right now and stay in the hay with Papa. I would like that – truly Maman. And I can be there always to help you with baby Andrew. But I will not stay here with these people in black. Promise me, Maman, that you will not leave me with them. Promise me! I will run away! I will not stay."

Feeling the little girl's arms around her neck and her tears against her face, weakened Lucy, and before she knew what she was saying, she promised.

Then came the day that John returned for his wife and baby, preparing to bring them home on horseback with their pathetic bundle of belongings. He planned to return later for the rest of their household materials that were left with the older girls. To his surprise, he found Rose waiting out beside the hitching post.

She carried her bundle of personal belongings and stood stubbornly waiting. "What are you doing out here, Rose?" her father asked. Behind her, he saw his wife approaching from the front door with the baby wrapped in a soft blanket given to him by the nuns, and Albert hanging onto her long skirt.

One of the nuns, Sister Florence, accompanied mother and baby outside. As John helped his wife to Jock's back and Albert behind her, Sister Florence put a restraining arm around Rose to pull her back against her apron. Rose fought and kicked, screaming and crying.

"*Non! Non*! I will not stay. Help me, Papa! I do not want to stay here. If you do not take me on the horse, I will run behind. I walked all the way from Long Lake; I can walk to the big fort. Papa, please let me go with you!" she wailed.

Sister Florence let the little wildcat go, nursing a bruise on her shin and a scratch on her arm.

"Let her come, Jean," Lucy said barely above a whisper while the tears ran down her face onto the baby's blanket. "We will manage somehow." She had said goodbye to the other children, but Rose was nowhere in sight then. She thought that her eight-year-old had run away to pout. She did not dream that it would be like this.

John walked beside Jock, leading her, preparing to walk the distance to the rooming house. But first he turned to say farewell and thank Sister Florence. The sister, still nursing her scratches and bruises, however, was frowning and silent, flushed and angry. So they turned and walked away.

Caroline and Mary Jane were good students but they had so much to learn – so much to catch up and make up for. The nuns were strict taskmasters and would stand for nothing but perfection. The girls' days were filled with learning to read and write, memorizing scriptures and verses of catechism, but they also had to perform their chores around the mission. Everything had to be clean, and if they did not do it right, they had to do the job over again.

The boys adjusted to the strict regimen with lessons and chores, but they did enjoy the chance to work with the animals. Nights were the worst. They missed their parents and often cried themselves to sleep. During the days, however, they could see their sisters. The girls became their protectors and surrogate mothers. They all wondered what had happened to Rose. Why was she singled out to be the one who went with their parents? Sometimes they harboured a small seed of resentment.

When more children began to arrive at the residential school, they found more friends to make the days easier to bare and not so lonesome.

The nuns and priests, however, were not good substitutes for their parents. They were strict, unbending rule enforcers. The children were to do the task as they were told to do it, be little 'men and women' and not snivel or complain. Something was missing in their lives, though they did not realize what it was. It was the love in the family unit that had been there before, and was now gone – perhaps gone forever.

They adjusted to their new life, and the boys even enjoyed becoming altar boys. Daniel maintained that he wanted to grow up to become a priest.

When their parents came to visit, the children enjoyed seeing them and asked about where they were living, but they soon stopped asking when they were going to be allowed to come to live with their parents.

The two older girls, on the other hand, looked forward to leaving the Convent when they reached fifteen and were able to get a job in Fort Edmonton. They heard about it from other girls who also lived at the Convent and stayed in their dormitory. Caroline and Mary Jane were anxious to leave and take up life in the real world.

Lucy was glad that she was able to keep Rose with her. She was such a big help with the baby and Albert. The lady downstairs at the Dobson rooming house commented on what a pretty little girl she was, the long wavy brown hair, the sweet little mouth, and the big brown eyes with the perfectly shaped brows.

Her brother, Mrs. Dobson said, was a photographer and when he next came to visit her, she would get him to take a family photo. Lucy shyly complained that they had no decent clothes in which to get their pictures taken. It was very hard to make herself understood, since Valerie Dobson, like most people that they came in contact with in Fort Edmonton, spoke English and could not understand French. Lucy felt very self conscious about being unable to make herself understood so she avoided people whenever she could. Rose, on the other hand, seemed to catch on quickly.

With her father's help she seemed determined to learn to speak English. She became her mother's interpreter and Mrs. Dobson's interpreter as well with understanding the French.

"That is no problem," Mrs. Dobson assured her with Rose's help. "I have some clothes that would fit you, and my husband has something for John. As a matter of fact, I have a box of hand-me-down clothes that my girls have grown out of and you and Rose can have them. There is something there for the little boy as well."

Mrs. Dobson was quite pleased to have Lucy at the rooming house. She had a boarding-house kitchen downstairs, and rooms upstairs. Lucy worked out wonderfully, at first just cleaning and washing clothes, but later with cooking. Lucy was such a diligent, hard-working woman, only wanting to be out of the way and not be seen by the roomers or the patrons in the dining-room.

Mr. Dobson was so pleased that he began building more rooms onto the rooming house and enlarging the dining area. So that her mother could work longer in the kitchen and on the washing and cleaning, Rose did most of the 'looking-after' Andrew and Albert. Rose was even given a tiny room in behind the kitchen so that the baby would be closer when his mother could slip in to nurse him, or get him to stop crying when Rose could not. That way there was no necessity for Rose to sleep in her parent's room on the third floor any more. She slept in the tiny room with Albert. It had no window and had been used for storage, but Rose was happy to have a corner of her own. Albert was company at night when the baby went upstairs with his mother.

For this work from Lucy, Mrs. Dobson gave them the room for nothing and all of their meals. *It worked out well all the way around*, Lucy thought; *there was no room to cook food in their little room anyway. They even had a regular bathroom, though they had to share it with the other tenants on that floor.*

Lucy felt very self-conscious about using the bathroom. If anyone had to wait for them she felt she had to hurry. Perhaps she should not be in there when the customers needed to get in. She always urged Rose and Albert to hurry. "Do not be long," she whispered.

The baby, she would bath in a tub in their bedroom and the baby's clothes as well, carrying the water from the hot water tap. It was such an amazing luxury to have warm water to wash in without having to heat it up on the stove.

The photo was taken in front of the lacy curtains in the parlor next to the fireplace. It was the parlor that the other rooming tenants were able to use before going through the archway into the café or up the stairs to the rooms. Lucy would never allow Albert to go in there for fear that he would mess it up.

John had just got home from work and at first resisted the idea of dressing up in the dark suit and white shirt with the bow tie. But the photographer was there, waiting impatiently with his tripod and camera set up.

"My beard has not been trimmed in a long time," John objected. "Why do we need a picture of ourselves? I will just be putting on the suit jacket and shirt and taking it right off again."

"That is all right Papa. That will not hurt," Rose placated him in her excitement over the new project.

"Hurry," Val Dobson urged. "There are others waiting. While you and Rose look after the customers in the dining-room my husband and I will get our photo taken."

When Rose translated to her mother, Lucy began to get very nervous and shook her head in agitation. "I can not talk to the customers. I can only cook in the kitchen."

"That is all right, Maman. I can do that. Let us get posed for the photo." Rose was so worried that they would fuss around too long, and she would not be able to be part of the picture.

"*Attendez! Attendez!* Wait! Wait!" Lucy jumped up from the wicker chair she had been seated in for the pose. "*Mon enfant!* Andrew! And Albert, *mon petit garcon!*"

When the photographer realized why she was about to run away, he explained. "I recommend that you do not have the baby in the picture. Babies can not stay perfectly still for as long as we need. They cry and they wave their hands about. Another time you can take the photo with the baby. Let us finish this now."

John explained all to Lucy, and she sat down again reluctantly. Then they had a hard time trying to make Albert sit still for the photo. He was wary of the contraption so they let him go back with Andrew and look after him until they got there.

John stood behind the chair, Rose placing her hand on her mother's shoulder. Several seconds elapsed while the photographer raised his light, put his head under the cover, and his eye to the lens. The flash startled Lucy, but she sat perfectly still without a twitch or a smile as cautioned.

Just in time, a cry was heard from the back room behind the kitchen. Andrew was awake, and Albert ran to tell his mother. Lucy hurried away to take off the borrowed finery and attend to her baby.

In their room that evening, Lucy again bemoaned the fact that the rest of their children could not be with them. The family picture was taken without all of the family being there. Even Albert had to be missed from the picture.

"We do not even get the chance to visit the children," she mourned. "It is so hard to talk to these people that I can not understand. It will be so much better when we can finally be on our own again – when we can leave this city and have that farm of our own as you told me we would."

"Soon, Lucy! Soon! It helps that you have been able to work here, and we do not have to pay for food and a place to live. All of my wage at Acme Brick Making can be saved, and we will find that farm." John sat wearily in the small wooden chair, head hanging down. He had been working long and hard to make extra money. No one wanted that farm more than he did.

Lucy got up from the narrow, lumpy four-poster and went to him. She rubbed his neck and shoulders and down his tired back. As she did, she looked around them thinking, *'We have pitifully little to take to a place of our own – pitifully little.'*

53

Release

When John rode up to the St Albert Mission in June 1894 in his new wagon behind a new team of horses, he felt that this was the beginning of a new era. He was coming to get his family.

"*Bonjour*, Jean Lenny!" a voice sang down to him from overhead.

Looking up, John spotted Adolphe up on the roof of the dormitory. "What are you doing up there?" John demanded.

"I am coming right down. I was replacing some shingles that came off in the last storm. The roof began to leak."

When he was down and standing beside John, he took off his work gloves and threw them on the bench. "You just get finished putting these buildings together, and they start coming apart. It's good to see you, old friend." Adolphe stuck out his hand to shake John's proffered one.

"We are going to miss those girls of yours here as well as those two industrious little boys. Daniel has been learning how to be a carpenter, but William likes working with the animals better."

"I am glad that Daniel has been getting good at building houses because when we get out to the farm there's a lot of building needed." John, Adolphe observed, was a lot more confident and relaxed than when he saw him the last time.

"Then you have some property now?" Adolphe questioned happily. "Where did you buy it? Is the land far away? Has it got buildings on it?"

"It's the land that I first discovered when I came here with the fur trade. My wife called it Mewassin because it means 'The Good Land.' We are both overjoyed at returning. It's raw land as far as I know. The survey has not been completed, but I have already paid my money to the land agent in Fort Edmonton. I did not have to put up very much money yet – just enough to reserve one hundred and sixty acres in my name. Maybe this time I will actually get to own it and fence it off."

"That is wonderful, Jean!" Adolphe congratulated him, mopping his face where the sweat had run down in rivulets from under his straw hat. "It is time that I stop this climbing up on top of buildings and leave it to the younger people. Now that I am officially on the school board and fifty years old, it is time for these boys that I have been training to take over."

"What about your own boys? Have they been trained like their father in carpentry?" John asked as he sat down on the bench beside Adolphe.

"Vital was always going to get a farm of his own. He married last year and decided that he needed more money than a farm could bring him. With his new buggy, he is set up for mail delivery. He has the big 'mail carrier' sign on the side. He meets the train in Fort Edmonton, picks up the mailbags with incoming mail from the express car and delivers them out here to our post office. He has a yearly contract for one hundred twenty-five dollars a month and lives here in St. Albert. They have a new baby, and he does not need anything else to make him happy. He will come out to the farm in the spring and fall, though, to help with the crops.

"Joseph, my carpenter, married last year as well, but he is not so happy as his brother. Betsy wants him to move to Fort Edmonton where her father is a rich man. He was instrumental in bringing in the railroad and wants his son-in-law to be involved in the railroad construction business. Just when I get him trained in carpentry at the mission, and talked into getting a farm nearby, she changes her mind. It will be a miracle if the marriage lasts – but not the way they are fighting about their future!

"Thank the dear Lord," Adolphe crossed himself, "for Louis and Jean. They keep the farm going. And Daniel, Samuel, and Hervé though they are but eleven, nine and seven, can do anything on the farm that they are called upon to do."

"You have all boys? No girls?" John wondered.

"*Ah, Oui!*" Adolphe laughed. "Twin girls were born to Julie. They are five years old. And Eliza is nearly three. Last year Jean Baptiste was born. So Julie has been busy. That is why I need to quit my duties here at the mission. I need to build onto the farmhouse – even though the two older boys have moved out. Then I had to take on more duties! The school board! The residential school, since your family moved in, has been bursting at the seams and, of course a lot of students come walking in from farms miles away and from right here in the village."

"I must go to talk to Sister Superior," John said as he rose from the bench. "The children will live for awhile at the rooming house until I get the place staked out. Then I will move my family out. It is a long way so they may not be coming back to the residential school. But then Mary Jane and Caroline are through their school training, and as long as Daniel and William can read and write, that is all they will need, along with other training they got here."

Adolphe did not smile, but looked at John a long time without saying anything. Finally, as John turned to go, he called after him "I hope it all turns out as you desire. Children have a habit of changing your plans. God go with you."

John hurried away, anxious to get his children loaded into the new wagon of which he was so proud.

It had not turned out quite as John planned, far from it. Everyone was chattering merrily on the way home, anxious to see their mother, sister, and brother. In his eagerness, John edged into the conversation.

"You did not notice the new wagon and the team," their father flicked the reins against the flanks of the spirited young bays. "Remember?" John urged when they hesitated, taking in that which their father pointed out. "When we came back from Long Lake, we had one old horse. Jock died, but I bought this new team and this fine sturdy wagon."

"It is very nice, Papa," Mary Jane patted the new comfortable spring seat that sat well above the box.

"And the horses, too," William commented. "Riding is better than walking."

His sisters laughed, but all remembered that year when they walked back from Long Lake. *This was a good time,* John thought, *to tell them about the rest of his good news.*

"Since I have been working at Acme and we have been living at the rooming house, I have been able to save up. Now we are finally going to be able to have that farm. It is all arranged. We are moving out there this summer. I have got a lot more besides a horse and wagon." He went on enthusiastically. "It may take a two or three trips to move it all out there, but I have bought all we will need to start building a farm: tools, a plow, a disc, nails, glass for the windows, shingles for the roof ..."

The children looked at him oddly and quietly, as though he was talking in a language they did not understand. Finally, Caroline, his bold one, started their father's education.

"Papa, it sounds to me as though you expect us all to go out to the wilderness with you. That would be like going back to Long Lake and starting all over again."

"*Non, non*!" John was astonished. "We have always wanted a place of our own – one hundred and sixty acres to build and grow on. Wait until you see it! Your mother called it Mewassin - 'The Good Land'. It is not far from the North Saskatchewan River and right on the old trail that leads to Fort Edmonton. We will be happy there."

This conversation was going all wrong, John thought with an edge of irritation. *I should not have brought it up this way.*

"Would this mean that we would not be going back to the school in St. Albert anymore?" Daniel wanted to know.

Daniel had not always liked the residential school. Many nights, he remembered feeling lost and homesick in the lineup of simple cots with a lot of boys he did not know. It was cold and draughty; there were never enough blankets to keep warm. However, no matter how he felt, he still had to go to the schoolroom and practise his numbers and letters. Then in the afternoons he had to practise his catechism and recite his prayers. The nuns scolded him for being a baby if he cried, and they rapped his knuckles at the table if he reached for something before he was offered some food.

Then he found a friend in Monsieur Perrault, and he discovered a fascination with carpentry. It made him feel very good to saw a board so that it fit and to hammer it into place. It was like a big jigsaw puzzle that gave one a huge sense of accomplishment when it fit together. And he enjoyed the praise people gave him for his work.

As well as Monsieur Perrault, there was Father Portier who took him under his wing and said that he was one of the best choirboys the mission ever had. He felt very needed and wanted, and - important. Now his father wanted to take him back into the forest away from all that he had grown to feel good about.

Nine-year-old William asked tentatively, not quite sure how he felt about this new turn of events, "Papa, what will you have on the farm? Will you have animals? Will you build a barn?"

"*Ah, mais oui!*" John was enthusiastic again. "I forgot to mention that I will be taking with us a sow that will produce little piglets, and a cow and calf – even some chickens. But we can not come to get them until we have built the barn and have cleared an area. Daniel will help to build the barn and the house, since he has learned how to build from the master, *Monsieur* Perrault." He ended triumphantly, giving Daniel a little pat on his shoulder.

"But, Papa I do not know how to build a barn. *Monsieur* Perrault did not tell me how to do that yet," Daniel replied in a worried voice.

"Oh, that is all right," his father assured him with confidence. "We will learn how together. If it falls down the first time we can start again and do it right. There is a whole forest of trees to practise with." John chuckled at his son's worried tone, not realizing that Daniel became even more worried at the flippant remark. He worked with boards with *Monsieur* Perrault – not with logs! Sawing a board was hard – what about a log?

"What would we do on the farm, Papa? Caroline and I?" Mary Jane asked in her timid voice.

"Well," her father straightened his back and propped up one leather-booted foot on the wagon board front as he began to imagine his family around him on the farm, doing all the little jobs that he saw the women doing at Long Lake. "You would learn to be a housewife, help to make clothes and soap, and you would look for berries in the woods and cook the fish that William would bring up from the White Whale Creek."

"And who would we meet to become the housewives of, Papa?" Caroline sat silent until now. Her question, low and casually stated, surprised her father. He was stalled for a minute, without an answer.

"It will not always be a wilderness. More people will move in. You will see. But we will be the first and pick the best land. And it will produce good grain – not like the stony, soggy land at Long Lake. This will be – 'The Good Land!'" He ended triumphantly.

William continued to ask questions and was growing fascinated, but the others were silent, caught up in their own turmoil of thoughts.

Caroline could not believe that her father intended to move them all out to a little house in the woods. It had not been a happy time for either her or Mary Jane over these last two years at the mission residence. After their parents left them there, Caroline wavered back and forth between resentment, hope that their parents would come for them the next day, determination to run away, and resignation.

The resignation won out. At first, they were glad of any place to stop the wandering in search of a home. Then the bitter realization overwhelmed her. She would be here under the care of the nuns for a long time to come. The regimentation was almost the hardest to take—up at six in the morning to attend prayers in the chapel after toilet and cleanup, then a hurried breakfast of porridge or bread and honey in the long dining room. They were then assigned their duties consisting of washing dishes, emptying slop water and toilet commodes, washing clothes, and ironing.

After the chores, they had to attend school in the big draughty room that smelled of chalk dust, oiled or varnished wood in the desks and floors, and old books. Then it was noon, and they trooped again to the dining room for a sparse lunch of bread and sometimes cheese

Sitting at the long rough tables and benches, they eyed their classmates, Indian children from the reserves or from parents who had abandoned the reserve and had gone to the woods, travelling or hunting, leaving the children behind with the nuns for care and instruction. The parents could no longer support them or care for them. The children came with nothing, their eyes wary, pain-filled, unhappy, and unresponsive.

In the afternoons, they went back to the classrooms for religious instruction, memorizing verses of the Bible that matched the beads in their hands that passed between their fingers. The rosary beads and the verses eventually became a comfort. Holding onto the string of beads each night at bedtime was the one thing that they had left to cling to.

After the religious instruction, the girls were taught how to knit, sew, and embroider. The boys worked outside with wood, gardening, feeding, and caring for animals, or learning fieldwork.

At first, Caroline became irritated with the tedious chores, especially when the nun in charge would scold her and slap her hands when her work was untidy or careless. She would rip the knitting all back and have her start again. The braids for the rag rug were sticking out all over and had not been tucked in neatly. So it had to be taken apart and she had to start all over again. Eventually Caroline began to take pride in her own work and revelled in a job well done. She was as strict with herself as the nuns were with her. She placed the rug on the floor, even though it would never touch her bare feet, and smile with pride at how flat it lay with the dyed colors of the rags for braiding matching, and tucked into the braid so carefully.

Before the evening meal, the children again had their chores, the girls inside, the boys outside. Each task again had to be done perfectly. The forks and knives had to be placed on the table just right, and the dishes had to be polished and placed away neatly. The floor had to sparkle, as much as a board floor could. Their own rooms had to shine. After a while Caroline realized that it was in her nature to want it that way. She would nag at her sister or the other children.

"Sister Marie Victorine is not going to like that! You pushed those pots in there without cleaning the cupboard, and you shoved the dirt under the braided rug that we just finished. You should shake it out."

Many times she helped her sister Mary Jane or capably did the task for her when Mary Jane dissolved into tears over it. Mary Jane would be so terrified that the nuns would scold her and slap her hands, that her hands shook and she could not get it right. So Caroline unobtrusively did the job for her.

What she could not forgive the nuns for was not for slapping her sister's hands, not for rapping her little brother on the knuckles with a ruler, not for churlishly scolding her brothers and sister until they cried, but for something which the others did not seem to notice.

It was for their attitude, and the way they spoke to the children. She caught little snatches of conversation between the nuns that she mulled over in her head later.

"... they are indolent and thoughtless, of course. We can not fight that. And they are clannish ..."

"... the parents are restless; they can not stay in one spot too long and so they are improvident. They can not look after their children ..."

"...drinking and gambling is a passion for them, of course. It is part of their natures. I suppose we can not change that! ..."

"... it is because they are unrestrained in their desires that they have so many children and nothing to their names."

Who was the 'they' that the others spoke about? Are they talking about us, the Métis people? Or are they talking about the native Indians? The tone in their voices was making her feel as though the colour in their skin was something that should be cleaned off if you rubbed it hard enough. It was the first time that Caroline ever had that feeling.

She felt like shouting, 'Look at me. I am not one of those dirty, ragged little brown waifs who cringes in behind the desk in the schoolroom. I do not need the Indian agent's permission to travel off the reserve. I believe as you do, in one God and our prayers to him. To be poor is not a bad thing. It is an honourable thing! Here I am! Do not look past me or through me. I am Métis! I inherited the Indian culture from my mother, and we have inherited its troubles. We made a place for you in the West, and now you are telling us how to fit into it?

There was always that feeling of being beneath a better and more powerful someone. No matter what the nuns' mouths said about how well you were doing, what a good job; there was always that feeling that you must lower your head. Caroline could not do that. She always kept trying to prove herself, to do it right. Mary Jane, she felt, would always wait for someone to tell her what she must do. Though Caroline was the younger she felt she must guide Mary Jane, or they would keep her down.

When they got to the rooming house, their mother broke into tears and kissed them one by one. Rose could not resist showing them how she had learned English and how to serve in the dining-room.

Their father assured them up in their room later, that this would be temporary for they would be leaving soon for Mewassin. The landlady gave them another room to sleep in, and she put them to work immediately in the kitchen and dining-room. Five-year-old Albert danced around his two older brothers whom he hardly remembered, eagerly trying to get their attention. And two-year-old Andrew clung to Rose in fear of these new people who swooped in on him.

Eventually, the time came when they began to pack up, ready to leave the fort and the rooming house to make their way into the wilderness. Caroline could keep silent no longer.

"Maman, Papa!" she began as they gathered in their parents' room the evening before, to talk about arrangements, "Mary Jane and I will not be going with you to the woods."

Mary Jane hurried to explain, afraid that her father would become angry with them. "Because we are old enough now to get jobs, Papa."

Lucy sucked in her breath in almost a sob, and John scowled without replying.

"The nuns at the convent told us we could get jobs doing housework for families and living in their homes, but Mary Jane and I could stay right here and get jobs in the rooming house." Caroline forged on without looking her father in the eye, sure that he would put up some opposition.

John Lenny was a lot older than when he first arrived in the West. His eyebrows were bushy, and his reddish blonde hair was sprinkled with grey. His grey-blue eyes, squinted when he tried to read, and his stature was not as straight and tall as it used to be. When he saw his beautiful young daughters step out of the convent, their hair long, dark and shiny, and their bodies blossoming into womanhood, he knew that it was time to let them go. How could he take them out into the woods away from civilization? Mary Jane was already two years older than most Métis girls in Long Lake and Big Lake settlements that were already married.

"I think you are right, Caroline and Mary Jane. You are well trained and ready to take a job." He hung his head and his shoulders slumped. He was just getting his daughters back, and now he was losing them again.

Just as the girls straightened and smiled their thank you, another voice was heard coming from behind them and pushing past to a place right in front of their father.

"I, too, do not want to go with you to the wilderness. I want to go back to the convent to train with Monsieur Perrault as a carpenter and work with the Church."

John's head snapped up. He had not expected this. "Daniel, you must come with your family. We need you to help build our home."

"You left me there for two years," was Daniel's quick reply. "I am only twelve. I cannot build a house yet. But I am learning how. I have much to learn, Papa. I can not learn it out in the wilderness, and I want to learn. Father Portier said that I was smart, and he wished that I could be around for a few years to learn to be everything that I could be."

Daniel was out of breath from his impassioned speech. He was not sure that he could do it, and if it had not been for his father's easy acceptance of Mary Jane and Caroline's pleas he may not have ever said it, and would have gone to Mewassin without saying the most important words of his young life.

"Maybe you are right, Daniel. This is probably a better thing for you to do than to come with us. Some day when you have learned all you need to learn, we will come back to see a rich man and a smart man. Or maybe you will come to see us first."

Daniel, tears in his eyes, torn between a need to be with his family and a need to start in the direction of his future, flew into the arms of his mother and father. John, with his Scottish reserve, even had tears in his eyes as he hugged his son, and Lucy hung onto him a little longer than she should have because she knew that it would be the last time. It would be a new life for all of them.

54

The Stopping House

As soon as John neared the familiar area in the old native trail his heart quickened. Coming up to the top of the hill he could see the North Saskatchewan winding in its good-natured manner between the familiar banks. He felt as though it was a welcoming wave. Looking to the wagon seat beside him, his eyes met Lucy's and she smiled quietly, knowingly. "Mewassin," she whispered. They had finally come back full circle, to the 'Good Land.' Up there was the spot at the crest of the hill where they said goodbye, thinking that they would never see each other again. She went one way, back to her roots, and he went the other to meet a new adventure, reaching for his dreams. They were right back here where they started.

"Whoa," he called out to his team of horses as he pulled up on the reins.

"Why are we stopping here, Papa?" William asked, popping up from the robe at their feet to look over the wagon box at the trees that marched up the ridge and the well-travelled winding trail ahead of them. "Is this where we are going to stop for the night?"

It was the spring of 1895, and the Lenny family had pushed through overgrown, deadfall-strewn forest trails from Fort Edmonton west to what would soon be called Mewassin by everyone who settled there. The trails were thick with mud at times, and sometimes they had taken a wrong turn off the main trail and had to backtrack because they ended up at a dead end. Mosquitoes plagued them and the nights were chilly with the odd snow flurry blowing in, but it was not enough to dampen their enthusiasm.

The wagon was piled high with all of the things that they would need to start their new life, and a huge tarpaulin that doubled as a tent, billowed overhead to protect them and all of their boxes and bundles from sun and rain. On the back of the wagon was a crate with chickens and another with a sow that would be having piglets in a few weeks.

Behind the wagon they led two cows on ropes. John would have liked to bring more along, but they hardly had room enough for themselves. Rose sat between them on the seat, her back straight and proud to be considered the big sister. Three-year-old Andrew and six-year-old Albert were her charges, and she guarded them like a hen with her baby chicks. As yet, she did not know that her Maman carried another baby inside that would be born in this new land, a baby they would soon call Adolphus or Dolph. It would not be easy birthing a baby in this new raw land. John determined that he would take his wife to Fort Edmonton since there would not be another woman to help her. He would take no chances. After all, Lucy was forty-two and nearing the end of her child-bearing years. This would not be as easy for her as earlier births had been.

"See where the trail turns north on the hillside up ahead?" their father asked the children who popped up one at a time from under the wagon seat, where they slept curled up together like little puppies. "That is where we will build our house. We will build a big house that will be a stopping house for all who travel the trail from the lakes and from the northwest to Fort Edmonton. They will stop overnight before they go on their journey."

They all looked up at him in surprise and awe. Even Lucy turned to him wide-eyed. It was the first that she heard of this plan. "I thought that it was a farm that we were building," she wondered aloud.

"It will be that as well. But first of all, it will be a stopping house. I always wanted to do that. Ever since I travelled down the trail from White Whale on snowshoes to the trading post down there on the river; I thought it would be just the thing to have. This trail will always lead people to the fort, and they need a place to stop. They would pay to stop and to eat," he ended triumphantly. It was another unfulfilled dream from the past that had not reawakened until this moment, but now he could see its realization in a flash of insight, and it thrilled him with its brilliance.

"On the sign out front it will say: "The Mewassin Stopping House – proprietor John Lenny. Giddup!" he shouted to the team, and they put their strength into the pull. They were nearly there.

As they started to set up camp at the chosen spot overlooking the valley, John was spurred on with excitement. Looking down the rolling hills that tumbled underneath the forested cover towards the river, he knew that the stream was there on the other side of the forested hills, though he could not see it. He remembered it as though he had ridden its brown waters yesterday.

Only one thing would have made the triumph complete. A twinge of disappointment nagged at him now and then, that his two older girls and Daniel had not come with them to share in the wonder of this moment. As he watched his boys scrambling over the wagon, disassembling it and searching for their treasures, he remembered the events of the past few months.

They took Daniel back to the mission and left him in Bishop Grandin's charge–unofficially with Adolphe Perrault. He trusted Adolphe to look out for him and to teach Daniel all that he knew.

At the Convent, Mother Superior advised Lucy to take the two older girls into Fort Edmonton. She gave her the names of two respected French-speaking women who would get them employment. For girls their age, the nun advised, the best job would be housekeeping. That way they could live right with the family and not have to pay for lodging somewhere. That sounded like a wonderful idea to Lucy.

Mary Jane got employment with a nurse who worked at the hospital while Mary Jane looked after her children and did the cooking and cleaning. The woman could speak French as well as English. It was then that John got the idea to bring Lucy into Fort Edmonton to have her baby. Mrs. Graham was a nurse and would be able to help when the baby was ready to be born.

Caroline was employed by a family by the name of Robertson. He was in politics and his wife, Amelia, was also involved. It was a big house, and Caroline would be expected to clean, cook meals, and prepare for the entertainment of many political associates of Amelia's husband. As well, Caroline would look after the children and help them with their studies, particularly learning French. Their first language was English, and the Robertsons would help with Caroline's English as Caroline helped the children with their French. What a grand opportunity for Caroline, John and Lucy thought, quite in awe!

Even though the family missed the two older girls, they were pleased that such a great future opened up for them.

"Papa," William called out from the back of the wagon, "What do we do first?"

"Well, William," his father shouted back, suddenly spurred into action, "we cut down trees, of course. We clear the area back about one hundred feet, then we square the logs, notch them, and start building the barn."

"The barn!" seven-year-old Albert complained. "How about the house first?"

"No, Albert," his father explained, "we can live in the tent all summer, but the sow needs a place to have her baby pigs, and the chickens need a place to lay eggs or they will fly away. The cows need to be sheltered so we can milk them, and a corral needs to be built beside the barn so they will not wander away. But first, before I do anything else and before someone else does, I have to stake out our land from this trail back to what might be one-hundred-and-sixty acres. When they finally come to survey the land they might move my stakes, but I will have been here first, and I shall claim my land. This has always been and will always be my land. These hills are my hills – my Mewassin!"

55

End of a Prophet – Beginning of a Prophecy

With baby Dolph on her back, Lucy and thirteen-year-old Rose climbed the hill to the clearing on top of the hill. This was where the berries grew the best. The chokecherries and saskatoons liked the sunshine, away from the tall trees in the heavier forested areas. Lucy always liked this windy hilltop on the southern-most corner of their land that overlooked the great Saskatchewan. At least this was the hill they claimed as their own, though no official survey had been made and no lines drawn.

"Here Maman!" Rose ran to the clearing just below the crest. "I told you they were ripe. Mmmm, strawberries are my favourite. Look down here."

"If you eat the berries, then there will be none left with which to make pemmican, Rose," Lucy chided gently as she caught up to her daughter, basket in hand. She readjusted the weight of Dolph's sling on her back as she emerged from the bushes. "Dolph," she said to him over her shoulder, "You are becoming too heavy to carry now that you are almost two years old."

It was then that they both noticed they were not alone. A man was sitting on the ground at the top of the hill. His hair, in a long braid that hung down his back, was snow white and he was dressed in ragged buckskins with a faded blanket slung across his shoulders.

Too stunned to speak, both Lucy and Rose stared at the man. They had not expected to see anyone up here on their special path and on their favourite hilltop lookout. They did see people frequently at the stopping house on their way down the Lac Ste. Anne Trail, heading to Fort Edmonton, or to Lac Ste. Anne Mission. Lucy depended on eight-year-old Albert or five-year-old Andrew to let her know if they had company for a meal – it was too soon for anyone to want to stay overnight.

The man turned to gaze at them, his wrinkled face a record of many years. "You are Lucy Gladu, are you not?" he asked in Cree of a startled Lucy.

They approached the man who remained seated, undisturbed by their arrival.

"I used to be," Lucy replied. "Now I am Lucy Lenny."

Rose, who had forgotten all of the Cree that she learned in earlier years, was not able to understand, and continued to stare. She thought him the oldest Indian that she had ever seen and wondered what he was doing here.

"I know you," Lucy said quietly in Cree. "I heard about you. You are Albert Calliot – the man who healed my mother Marie Amable of her asthma, are you not? It was at the sacred lake at the time of the 'gathering' – the first since Louis Riel's death, and the government 'scrip' that took us all away from Big Lake."

"Sit down Lucy. Take the little one from your shoulders and let him stretch his legs," Albert said. "Your mother – she is well?"

Lucy took the harness from Dolph and asked Rose to watch him and play with him for awhile. She watched as her sturdy boy ran off, with his sister following closely behind. Then she turned back to Albert.

"My mother is quite well. Since that day she has had no asthma. She would very much like to be here to thank you for her healing." Lucy sat down beside Albert and they both looked across the treetops, down the slope towards the river.

"It was not I who healed your mother, but the Great Spirit," Albert said calmly. "The Great Spirit heals through me. You know that this is a sacred hill?"

Lucy looked at Albert quickly – his profile strong and enduring in the sunlight. "I know that many tribes came here to light their fires while the buffalo came to the bend in the river under the cliff. I know that it was here where the ancestors and before them, and before them, lit the fires of sacrifice to the Great Spirit, the Master of Life. It was here, my father said, where the fires of celebration were lit for a good hunt. And it was here where the strips of meat dried in the wind that blew across the top of this hill as it does today. It was here, also, where they watched the white man's heavy boats come up the river, and they signalled to all up and down the river that the white man was now here."

"This is why you return to the hilltop time after time," Albert stated without asking the question, and Lucy looked at him, startled.

"I feel it is my hilltop; it is our land," Lucy replied simply.

"This is not your hilltop – this land does not belong to you," Albert announced quietly. "You can not own holy ground, Lucy. You know that! Your grandfather has told you that. This is the head and shoulder of the Mystic Mother of all and it is now in your charge for safe keeping."

He stopped talking for a long while as he gazed out across the south-sloping hillside below. Then he spoke again and Lucy listened carefully.

"This is what you must do. Gather the stones and build a monument on this spot. Neither you nor your family must move or destroy it. The tree that grows here you must protect and nurture, even though those who come to this land in the future may claim it as their own."

"I promise," Lucy pledged softly.

Albert seemed to slump as though suddenly very weary. Then he began to speak again. "Very soon more people will be coming to claim their share of the land. They will arrive with wagon, horse and oxen and they will build a landing down near the river. Boats will come up the river to the landing as the fur trade boats came.

"Your husband and your sons as they grow to be big and strong men will cut down many trees. They will haul them to the landing, and they will send them sailing down the river to the big sawmill in the city where your husband will be paid money for them. The neighbours will do the same.

"When much of the land is cleared of timber, more settlers will come. They will mark off the hills and meadows with posts and wire, and will dig up the fields with the plough. They will plant the grain, large fields of it waving in the wind. The white man will come to this land and change it – first in a trickle, as the rain starts a stream to flow. Then the stream will grow into a river of mankind – a flood!

"On the other hilltop to the west there will soon stand the white man's holy building they call a church. And on that hillside to the north and west, where the trees climb up the hill and seem to touch the sky, the white man will very soon have a building they will call their school. It will be the place where all of their children will go to learn. It will be called the name you gave this place – the name your husband gave to his stopping house – Mewassin School."

"Can the white people not be stopped? Who can stop this flood?" Lucy asked beginning to fear for the future.

"Who can stop the rain from falling?" Albert asked. "Your blood is slower than your husband's. He looks forward to these changes as much as you fear them. Soon you will change your mind, as your children grow into this new world. All I ask of you, Lucy Gladu, is that you keep this one spot holy, and as your sons grow strong and tall they know why you do this."

"I promise!" Lucy replied reverently

Then Dolph came running to his mother in tears from a fall with Rose right behind him still chattering at him.

When the tears were soothed, five-year-old Andrew emerged from the bushes with the announcement that a party from Edmonton had come to the stopping house and Lucy sighed as she picked up her things preparing to leave for home. As she turned to bid farewell to Albert he was gone.

Swinging the water bucket by her side, Rose picked her way down to the creek. The Loyer family who ate the evening meal with them, planned to stay overnight. Rose had been sent for a bucket of water from the creek for washing the dishes and for washing in the morning.

Rose loved the creek. The clear, sweet, water trickled over the rocks and the sun shone warmly on the grassy banks. The scent of spruce, loam, and dead vegetation pungently filled the air as she threaded her way through the trees on the well-worn path. They were lucky to have the shallow creek to supplement the water from the well and to provide for their farm animals.

Her little bare feet dug into the moss as she descended and dipped the bucket in while sweeping away the leaves and sticks with her hand. She always lingered here awhile washing and cooling her feet while she watched intently as an ant struggled to carry an egg home, or at a sparrow who edged closer to the bank for a drink.

Today she sat on her favourite log, that was rotting and comfortable, and extended out across the creek. Here she could become one with nature again. Suddenly she sensed someone's presence. The woods had grown silent.

He watched the girl in her faded cotton dress, hair cascading over her shoulders in a wavy brown mass, little bare feet idly stirring the water, and he stopped as a look of wonder crept into his eyes.

Like a frightened fawn she leaped to her feet and swung to face him. "*Qu'est-ce que c'est!*" she exclaimed feeling the urge to run.

Realizing that he had been staring, he flushed to his hairline and stammered. "I am sorry. I did not mean to disturb you. I just came down here for a walk."

He was tall for seventeen with a thick head of dark straight hair that stood up in places like antennae and fell across his eyes. But his straight, white-toothed smile was disarming.

"My name is Victor Loyer. I am with my family staying at the stopping house. We are travelling north towards Lake Isle looking for a homestead." He looked at her, entranced by the dark eyes and the fair skin, the wealth of wavy brown hair, and the sun dappled aura about her. Rose was developing into a woman.

She had not gone in to see the guests. She was busy in the kitchen so he had not met her. "I am Rose Lenny. My parents own the stopping house. I have come down for a pail of water." Entranced, she stared back at the young man with the intense blue gaze and her heart began to race.

"Let me help you carry that pail," he offered, reaching down for the bucket sitting on the rocks. In silence they walked side by side back to the stopping house while each was acutely aware of the other. Stealing a look at his profile, Rose observed the strong wide shoulders, the lean angular face and straight nose and experienced new excited sensations rising inside that made her turn quickly away with flushed cheeks as he became aware of her gaze.

When she reached for the pail their hands touched with an electric response and she jumped back.

"I'm sorry," he apologized. "I will carry this inside for you if you like. It is heavy for one so slight and small."

Feeling unaccustomed to the concern, Rose flushed again. She was strong and quite used to the weight of the water pail, but she was beginning to revel in the pampered sensation inspired by this handsome young man and allowed him to carry the pail into the kitchen.

Lucy, startled by their entrance, stared in surprise but said nothing. As Rose followed him out into the back porch and step she thanked him but was unwilling to go back inside and end this all too brief meeting.

For a long moment they looked into each others' eyes, trying to read the thoughts, the past, the intentions, afraid to say goodbye for fear that it would be final but not knowing what else to say.

The next morning at breakfast Rose was there helping her mother. Unspoken thoughts hung between her and the young man as their eyes met across the room. Victor caught a glitter of excitement before she turned away with a shy flush to her cheeks and a lowering of her gaze. She passed the platter of hotcakes along and disappeared into the kitchen.

They climbed aboard the wagon, his parents and younger siblings. But Victor hesitantly approached her. Leaning on the veranda railing she intended to watch them drive away and wave goodbye. Nervous but determined he asked quietly, "May I come back to see you again, Rose?"

Her breath almost exploding as though she had been holding it, she sighed, "I would be very happy to have you return, Victor. I hope you will not be living too far away."

"It will not *ever* be too far away," He smiled and walked away with a new spring in his step.

Blackbirds swooped low overhead loosing their high-pitched trilling calls as they rode the air currents up from the trees. Rose watched as the wagonload disappeared over the horizon and was suddenly lonely. She could not remember being lonely before; she always loved her solitude. It was a new feeling this loneliness.

True to her promise, with Rose and her boys' help, except for William who now went to work every day with his father cutting down the trees, they gathered stones. When Andrew and young Albert asked what they were building, Lucy told them that some day she would tell them when they had it built. She said only that it was to be very special. Some of the stones were so big that they had to painstakingly dig them out of the ground and pry them onto a tarp to drag them to the site. The boys worked tirelessly without question.

Then one day when Lucy climbed the hill, leading in single file her three children and Dolph, she saw Albert Calliot slumped against the pile of stones. In great excitement, saying to her children, "Now you will know the reason for the stones," she hurried up to greet the old man.

He appeared to be asleep and she touched his shoulder. To her surprise and shock he slid down to a lying position and she knew that Albert was dead. His face was grey and his body was cold and stiff.

John came with her as they all returned to the hilltop. Silently, he dug the grave where Lucy indicated so that the stones that they had collected acted as a headstone for Albert. With the children gathered around the grave, Lucy explained the story as Albert told her.

The children, unable to maintain a reverent attitude very long, soon drifted away to their play and exploration. And Rose, explaining that Victor might be coming by to see her, hurried away as her parents shared a knowing smile.

Lucy and John remained on the hilltop.

"Tell me Albert's story again about what is to come," John urged his wife.

When she told him exactly what Albert said, John looked out across the river below, his brow furrowed, the wind lifting his battered hat that he had jammed low over his forehead and frowned.

"He was a true Mystic – a prophet, and a healer." Then after a pause he said: "And over there is to be a kirk, he said? And up that hill a school? Will anyone believe us if we tell them? They will have to wait as we will. But I believe it will happen."

Then he caught Lucy's work-worn hand in his and led her away to the stopping house.

ISBN 142510091-0

9 781425 100919